River of Judgement

River of Judgement

DAVID SARTOF

*'What a man really
has, is what is in him. What is
outside of him should be a matter
of no importance.'*

*Oscar Wilde,
The Soul of Man Under
Socialism'*

Demeter Publishing

Demeter Publishing

First published in Great Britain in 2009
by Demeter Publishing,
a division of AM (Northern) Ltd.
This paperback edition published in 2010
by Demeter Publishing

ISBN 978-0-9564152-0-2

Typeset in Garamond by
Demeter Management Services,
a division of AM (Northern) Ltd.

Demeter Publishing,
a division of AM (Northern) Ltd.
Registered in England No. 05080874
Registered office of the company:
17 Central Buildings,
Market Place,
THIRSK,
YO7 1HD

www.demeter-ms.com

IN MEMORY

OF

MARGARET AND DAVID

ONE

Canada, Autumn 2006

SCOTT LINDON'S FEELINGS were impervious to all but the late-October cold. He did not like it; he did not like himself for it – this lack of feeling. Oh! There had been times, like this, when he wished his life had not been saved, but, after nearly twenty years, he'd become resigned to it all. He just needed to sort this frigging mess out.

As dawn broke over the small experimental oil extraction project, Scott calmly took in the scene before him. In his thirty-three year career, he'd witnessed many site accidents. Oil could be a dangerous, messy business indeed.

The front nearside wheel of the Ford Ranger pick-up lay half over the motionless, face-down form of Shufang Su. A bright graduate, at thirty-three she'd already made operations director for Tiger Oil plc, a small start-up company, head-quartered in London. *Another FRIGGING mess*, he thought. This time there would be repercussions – he could see that.

Scott checked the area. He could see no visible sign of anything out of the ordinary; it seemed to have been a tragic accident. He ran through the possible scenario in his mind: Shufang must have left the Ranger parked above the well pad. She'd gone down the slight incline to inspect the solvent injection system at the head of the single, horizontal well-pair.

1

She had most likely failed to engage the hand brake properly and, unbeknown to her, the heavy vehicle had rolled forward. It would have picked up sufficient momentum to take it silently down onto her. With the fur-edged hood of her Parka pulled up over her head against the wind, Shufang would have had no warning.

Scott, a squat, heavy-set man of fifty – all solid muscle – stood, shivering. He knew the local First Nation people, the Woodland Cree, simply marked October as the month of the great migration south. The month of the *real* freeze came next. He also knew that, despite a December of festivals, there would be a month of exploding trees, with ice tearing into the landscape, before February's great hope: spring.

Christ! he thought, *I'll be glad to get out of this open-air fridge.* For now though, the wind of October's closing days played around him, a maliciously meandering ice-serpent – a harbinger of the greater cold to come.

The area in which he stood lay some forty kilometres from the still sleeping town of Peace River, in Canada's North-Eastern Alberta. It formed part of the Boreal forest – a bountiful expanse of aspen-laden parkland, where the Woodland Cree lived out their hunter-gatherer existence, where fur-bearing animals thrived, where great multitudes of wild birds thronged, and where, beneath it all, lay huge deposits of oil. But, relentlessly, the development of the Peace River oil-sands ate away at the Cree's hunting, trapping and fishing grounds. It harmed the water they drank and the air they breathed. Still, according to a legend of the Beaver, another First Nation people, *if you drank the waters of Peace River, you would return.* And Shufang had returned to Peace River, for the last time.

Scott began to retrace his steps, up the incline. His car – a rental – stood some way down the roughly-made part-road, part-track access to the site. He glanced up. His gaze swept the horizon, registering the still half-light of the breaking day.

Reaching the top of the incline, Scott crouched down out of the wind – the tall aspen gave little protection in the clearing of the well pad. He pulled his hood further round his ears. This cold early morning would not see full light for an hour or so, and the biting wind made the five-degree-below-zero temperature feel even colder. Again, involuntarily, Scott shivered. He removed a glove and reached inside his jacket for his phone. With a last glance down to where Shufang lay, he flipped open his cell and called the emergency services.

Within minutes, along Highway 986, on the road out from the Peace River Township, blue and red lights flashed through the swaths of aspen parkland. They sped eerily through the belly of the nearby Shell Oil facility, and out in the direction of the Tiger Oil site, eight kilometres from the Woodland Cree Reserve number 226.

TWO

England, August 2007

FRIED GHERKIN. It was a curious, even ironic thought, but, in the muggy summer heat of the overcast Wednesday afternoon, to Finn Jackson, forty-six, Chief Executive of Tiger Oil, it seemed appropriate. He glanced at his watch trying, but failing, to notice the progress of the minute-hand towards its two-thirty destination. Nearly ten minutes to go.

Finn stood by the fourteenth-floor window of the boardroom, the only room used in the small office-suite in London's Citypoint tower on Ropemaker Street. The designation *boardroom* gave it an air of executive spaciousness it did not deserve. As he stood, a sublime, fleeting vision of his falling from an opened window flashed before his mind's eye. An involuntary spasm raked a chill through his spine. He shook his head, trying to clear thoughts of his rapidly descending body, flailing its way to a grizzly impact. He reached his mind out, to think of other, less macabre things. He recalled Ben Bernanke, in the last month's papers. *Focus on someone else's problems,* he told himself. The chairman of the Federal Reserve gave an appalling estimate of the cost of America's sub-prime lending crisis. It could end up costing the US up to one hundred billion dollars. Yes, *someone else's problems.*

The dampening of the credit conditions would certainly take the froth out of the careering excess of the financial markets. Finn could see, on this hot, sticky afternoon, those conditions now made things more difficult for Tiger Oil – difficult, but not impossible. Certainly no reason to consider jumping from a fourteenth floor window. The small door at his feet, the one that opened onto the enchanted garden of his childhood, stood now, in his maturity, transformed. The door to a city of riches. It was there, ajar. It tempted him. If he could just squeeze through it.

Home wasn't a happy place – he had grown detached. Aisling turned to her horses and to their daughters. He turned to the business. He'd forgotten who started to turn first. It no longer seemed to matter. But he did *miss* the closeness of their early relationship. He did love them all. *No!* He shook his head. *It did matter, just not at this moment.*

What did seem to matter, now? Raising money! *That's what mattered.* But people were more risk averse than they'd been before the summer – even Aaron. Aaron, yes! The call troubled him, and he couldn't work it out.

Earlier, as he'd climbed out of Moorgate underground station – the oppressive subterranean atmosphere bringing his perspiration levels to dripping point – he'd taken the call from his friend, Aaron Philips.

'Sorry, Finn,' Aaron had said, 'we'll have to cancel lunch at the tapas bar.'

Aaron, fifty-one, was Finn's business partner and the company's finance director.

'The Oxford train's running late,' Aaron continued, his voice agitated, with only the merest hint of apology. 'Apparently there's some signalling fault.'

'No problem,' he'd replied, '…another time, if you like.'

'No. You don't understand, Finn. I really needed to talk to you before the meeting…'

The signal faded.

'...Grayson's...   path...'

'Aaron, I missed that. The signal's crap. Can you repeat?'

Static.

The connection died. His stomach froze. But, shaking off the premonition before it materialised, he tried to re-connect to Aaron. He reached Aaron's answering service – it unnerved him.

So, tapas cancelled, he'd hurriedly dropped into a sandwich bar, to collect a working lunch. His briefcase and laptop were a dead-weight in his hand. He couldn't stop thinking about what Aaron might have been trying to say. He was trying to warn him about something, wasn't he? That was the agitation in his voice.

From the sandwich bar, he'd made his way to the office. At least here he'd gained sufficient respite to adjust his body and temperature to a more comfortable and dry state before the meeting. But he was on edge now. The call. Of course he'd tried Aaron's phone again, since – no luck.

The cooler, drier Finn glanced at his watch again. Where could the others be? He let his gaze drift out over the city, as he went about reviewing the main points of the forthcoming meeting in his head. *What had Aaron been trying to say?*

True, almost ten months on since Shufang's tragic death, the slow progress of the pilot operation in Peace River wasn't helping meet their objectives. Despite his positive recommendations of a number of potential candidates, the board still needed to agree on the appointment of a new operations director. The whole operation worked with a budget that represented a holed Dutch dyke – they always needed to move bits of cash around, to plug leaks, to get by. They were managing, weren't they? But with all the delays, low cash-flow remained an uncomfortable reality. They now met only essential operational costs. But the ever-hungry lawyers and corporate finance advisors still demanded their feed, as Tiger Oil prepared for its flotation on AIM, the London Stock Exchange's junior market.

Could Aaron's finance report be a problem? He'd been expecting the papers before the meeting, but Aaron, excuses at the ready, promised a full update when they met for lunch. But they hadn't met, had they...

Tiger Oil was looking to raise ten million pounds in the AIM float, to take the project forward from its fledgling pilot stage. It aimed to reach full production capability in the first of its small cache of four oil-field leases. But Tiger Oil merely intended to develop its technology sufficiently to attract a buyer, possibly Shell – a buyer who would have the clout and the funds to take the whole thing forward in large-scale. Ten million pounds did not make much of an impact in the oil business.

Agitated, Finn checked his watch again. Five minutes to go. His gaze set on the gothic-arch-like upper profile of the Norman Foster designed Swiss-Re building at St Mary Axe. He generally thought gothic, but, in the heat of the August afternoon, with growing financial turbulence being, in-part, acted out within the great glass and steel structure, *fried gherkin* gave a more accurate description.

Despite all the delays, he was proud of how far he'd come. He'd been born with rather limited prospects, in the small Yorkshire fishing town of Whitby. His long-suffering mother raised him as an only child, a product of her union with the type of man to whom charm appeared a gift and responsibility an anathema. His father was long gone, both physically and in memory. From there, from the two-roomed flat his mother had brought him up in, the only way out had been to go to sea – either that or the Army. Despite a mediocre education, the opportunity to learn a trade had not seemed worth the requirement to wear a green uniform. Now the company... *his* company, would soon place its first public offering of shares. That door to the garden was opening to him, beckoning.

A grin broke on his face, reflecting into the room, as he considered how much his shares would be worth when they listed. Although they had reined-in their valuation, they still looked to raise ten million for a forty-five percent share of the company. His shares would still be worth at least a cool three million. That, he told himself, will be a result. *It'll be worth all the effort and problems of the last years... a just reward.* It stood on today's agenda. *This afternoon the board is going to finalise the float timetable*, he thought. Perhaps there would soon be time for a long overdue holiday. His mind wandered – images of an October sunset across the Cote d'Azur appeared as fleeting, shimmering ochre mirages dancing beyond the glass of his cocoon-like office. Enchantment. He remembered the stories his mother used to read aloud to him.

He grinned at his reflection again. He loved the buzz of the city. It had all been new to him – a trying, learning experience. His naivety of city-ways proved a draw-back at times, but he learnt quickly. He could conquer this place – reap the fruits in the garden before him, beyond that small door, where only the few ever really passed. *Besides*, he mused, *it's much more fun than messing around at sea or in hot, dirty oil fields.*

The outer door opened onto the unoccupied reception area. Finn turned to see the tall frame of Grayson Barclay enter. Grayson, sixty-one and non-executive Chairman, quickly moved to hang up his superfine Monte Cristi trilby – a recent acquisition from Locke and Company on St James's Street. *That bloody hat!* They'd ALL heard about the purchase, the last time they'd met.

Grayson walked up and took Finn's offered hand. Their eyes locked.

'Good afternoon, Finn.'

'Afternoon. . . how's the journey down?'

'No complaints… Look, Finn, I won't beat around the bush with you. I have cancelled the meeting.'

'Pardon…' Finn wasn't quite sure he'd even said the word pardon, let alone made sure his inflection turned the word to a question. It sounded more an involuntary statement. His expression became one of puzzled incomprehension.

'I called David and Jonathon over the weekend,' Grayson continued. 'We spoke with Aaron in a conference call yesterday. We all agreed…'

'You agreed what?' interrupted Finn. A chilling realisation dawned on him – they'd left him out of the loop on whatever they'd agreed. Whatever *it* was, *it* did not bode well for him. Finn's expression washed over with disbelief.

'I'm sorry it's come to this, Finn, but we've all reached an agreement… you should go. We want you off the board. I chose to come here today to tell you personally, rather than just call you. It is the least I could do.'

'The least you could do? What do you mean, *the least you could do*? This must be some kind of…' But Finn didn't finish. His mouth shut, slowly.

Grayson kept speaking, but Finn did not hear, he simply kept looking at Grayson. Finn raised his hands, finger tips spread across his forehead, and his eyes shut tight. He turned round, away from Grayson, to face the window again – as if a small boy, by closing his eyes and looking away, he would be safe from the trouble confronting him. Grayson talked on.

Finn regained his composure. 'What are you saying?' His eyes opened, but he continued to face the window. His mind raced. He needed to focus. *Fried fucking gherkins.* 'You're sacking me?' he said. The words ricocheted off the glass.

'No. You know we can't do that.'

'So what exactly *are* you fucking saying?'

'I understand you must be upset and disappointed, Finn, but we want you to resign as chief executive and director. I know

9

it's been a difficult year and, with the death of Shufang…well, it can't have been easy for you. But this is a business, Finn. I did not put up half a million pounds to see us still waiting today to get our listing on AIM. You are the Chief Exec and the only measure of a good CEO is one who gets things done. You know my stance on responsibility, Finn. It goes to the top – it goes to you.' Grayson's voice held a cold edge. 'And we are still waiting, Finn… I am still waiting.'

'SO!' snapped Finn, sarcastically, '…you're not taking any responsibility yourself? What about all your objections to getting a new ops man in place? You telling me I should've been on-site, supervising? And here, working the city at the same time? Come on, Grayson. You might be past an executive role yourself, but…'

'No need to be so personal, Finn…'

'Oh shut up, Grayson. You know what's involved in all this. We want public company status, to get access to institutional investment. You know there's a huge cost in all of this stuff we're doing.' Adrenaline pushed Finn's response with a passion. 'It ALL costs time and money. You… sorry, the frigging Board… well, you can go stuff yourselves if you want me out. I founded this company with Shufang and Aaron, and I still own twenty-five percent. You can't fire me. You'd better put what you want in writing. …Goes for the board as well. Now get the hell out of here.'

'Finn, we all know you own a major stake in the company. We want your shares as well.' The tone of Grayson's voice held no promise of friendly quarter.

'YOU WANT WHAT?' shouted Finn, spitting the words out.

The shout surprised Grayson, momentarily. 'Errr… We just feel because you've not delivered us to AIM yet, then when we do get there it won't have been through your efforts. We don't want you to profit from our success.'

'Your success?' said Finn, laughing in shocked disbelief, 'your success? ...Now I really know you're joking. . .' His voiced trailed off... and then recovered. 'Just get out,' he shouted. His hands shook with rage.

Grayson hadn't moved since earlier taking Finn's hand. He turned and walked to pick up his hat. He walked forward and opened the door to leave, but, pausing by the open door, he turned to face Finn again. 'I am taking control of the company finances. I have instructed Aaron not to advance you any more on your loan account without my authority. Talk to him if you like, Finn. Perhaps he will get you to see the way it should be.'

Having delivered his final blow, Grayson turned, exited the door, then closed it solidly behind him. Finn stared at the closed door. Astonishment numbed his senses; he could feel nothing. Then, from deep within, a wave of nausea-tinged sadness crashed against his beached soul. He saw, with an immediate clarity, there could be no arguing against the dogmatic Grayson. Grayson had just destroyed all sense of trust. What could he fight for? *There's no point in a fight*, he thought. He sat down hard on one of the chairs. With his head hanging over the table, he closed his eyes again. Anger had carried him through the confrontation with Grayson. Now he could only sit there in shock. Over three million pounds worth of shock.

NO! No, he couldn't just give up – not on everything he'd worked for! *For Christ's sake*! *I can't not fight*! He had to wrestle the shock first – he needed to get to Aaron. Aaron knew – didn't he? Of course he bloody did. That's what he'd been trying to warn him about, wasn't it? He eyes closed, he could just make out, at his feet, an almost imperceptible chink of light shining through the key hole of that small door.

THREE

FINN NEEDED AIR. The hour had just turned three o'clock. He left the office where he'd sat in stunned silence for some time, and walked out, trance-like, turning down Moorgate in the direction of Bank tube station. He couldn't think straight. He fought the shock that pervaded his senses. *What the hell just happened?* The question circled his mind – it tore at his consciousness, a relentless pain.

He felt rather than heard his phone. Instinctively, his right hand lifted it from the breast pocket of his jacket. He slid the cover open.

'Finn Jackson.'

'Finn, it's Aaron…'

'Christ, Aaron… What's going on?' Bewilderment leadened his voice. It lay like a thick veneer of panic across each word he spoke. But he was on auto-speak. He was listening to himself – in his state of shock, he sounded weak and pathetic. His naivety shone, stripped bare to all who cared to notice. This wasn't him. He had to snap out of it.

'Look… Where are you? Let's meet up… Where are you?'

Finn looked up. He'd stopped walking to talk and now he sought his bearings. 'Just into Cornhill…'

'Go into the Counting House. I'll be there in ten. You

sound like you could do with a drink.' Aaron ended the call.

It took Finn more than a few seconds to close his phone and return it to his pocket. Having put everything into Tiger Oil, he'd entered a dire strait. All his assets supported the business – his house, his savings policies. They all secured borrowings, most of which he'd sunk into developing the firm. He existed on credit. *Christ!* Three platinum credit cards out to their max. Grayson's move pushed him through the strait and he could only see sharp rocks ahead. There was no retreat, no possibility of turning. How the hell could he make payments this month, if he couldn't draw funds on his director's account?

Finn reached the Counting House and entered the cavernous, soaring city basilica, in its former days a NatWest bank. Any other day and Finn would have drunk-in the atmosphere – it was his sort of place. Aaron knew that. He slunk forward, as if captive in a dream, toward the immense island bar under the huge glass-domed roof... Wood, brass and marble lay everywhere; Finn loved the simple beauty of wood.

'Christ, Finn, I'm really sorry about all of this...' Aaron's voice punctuated the vacant space in his mind. 'Taxi got me here quicker than I reckoned. Look, go grab a table on the mezzanine. I'll go get us a bottle of something and a couple of glasses... White all right?'

'Yeah. Thanks,' he said, without thinking.

Finn went for the steps. He knew he should be livid with Aaron too, but he could see that Aaron wouldn't have had any choice in the matter and he needed a friend right now. A large light suddenly shone, in his mind, unseen by anyone else. *No!* That wasn't it at all. He didn't need Aaron's friendship – he just needed to know why. Aaron knew. He'd tried to warn him. Finn needed to know.

He climbed to the gallery and went to sit at one of the many small tables dotted along it. This Wednesday afternoon it wasn't busy. But, then again, the pub could soak-up an entire Friday-lunch crowd of suits without Finn feeling crushed. It provided the sort of experience where lunch would frequently turn into dinner.

Normally, Finn would people-watch from the gallery but, today, his mind drifted elsewhere and nowhere – a confusion of emotion spiked by fear and dread. Why hadn't he seen this coming? *Why?* His mind raced. The light? Anger wouldn't do – it wouldn't get to the truth – he needed to keep calm. *Naivety* he thought. He would play on it. He would court Aaron's sympathy and see where it got him.

Aaron approached with a bottle and cooler in one hand, two glasses in the other; a lap-top case hung from a strap over the shoulder of his city-stripe suit. 'Here you are.' Aaron placed the cooler and glasses down, removed the case from his shoulder and took the seat opposite. Mechanically, Finn poured two glasses.

'When did you find out what Grayson wanted to do?' asked Finn.

'Friday night. I'm sorry – I was hoping we'd get lunch. I wanted to warn you. Damn phone battery.'

'Friday? Jesus, Aaron!' he said. Deep furrows appeared on his brow. His eyes rolled. He wanted to scream *you bastard…* but he curled his toes viciously, letting the pain dissipate his anger. He wanted to reach out and grab Aaron by the throat. 'Surely you could have warned me earlier – the weekend?' he continued, anger seeping into his voice. 'I could have at least got an argument ready. Now…' he paused to draw on the cool Sancerre. 'Now I have no option. You know that. . . Why?'

'Simple, Finn,' said Aaron, matter-of-factly. 'It's his money we've been spending – he's impatient for a return.'

'That's crap, Aaron, you know it,' he said, swallowing bile, '…what the hell does he expect?'

'When he called me Friday evening, he'd been livid. He

ranted on about misrepresentation – he wanted to sue us over lies in our business plan.'

'But…'

'No buts, Finn, both you and I know there are no lies. But that wouldn't stop a man like Grayson. He has deeper pockets than you or me, and we simply can't afford to take him on in a fight – it would lose us everything. He is pissed about all the delays. I've spent the weekend trying to talk him out of this. I thought I could.'

'*He's* pissed? Christ!' he said, then downed his drink – as if the cool wine would douse his anger. He stared at the empty glass. 'This isn't doing a thing. You should've got some large whiskies. …Anyway, what does he fucking expect, this is an experimental development. He certainly hasn't helped in getting someone else out there to pick up from Shufang.'

'I know. But getting at Grayson won't help. I don't think there is anything you can do. He wants your blood… Look, you know how short of cash we are. Perhaps if I can get him to front up enough to get you thirty grand, would that help you out?'

'I need more than your sympathy, Aaron. He wants my shares too – he wants my bloody shares.'

'I know, Finn, but he can't just take them off you. Let me talk with him. He's done his deed, perhaps I can reason with him now.' Aaron reached for the bottle and poured another two glasses. 'You now what Machiavelli said, don't you?'

'No. Go on.'

'When he wrote his CV for Lorenzo de' Medici, he'd written something like *The innovator makes enemies of those who prospered under the old order. He can expect only lukewarm support from those who would prosper under the new.* Grayson is old-school, Finn. He's been swayed by the promise of great profit. But I think the delays have given him time to see how new all this stuff you're doing is – how risky it really is. He can't handle it.'

'No buts, Aaron. If we get this right, we'll revolutionise the whole process. Everyone will want our business. We'll be worth a fortune and we're nearly there. I can feel it, Aaron.'

'I just think he wants to back-pedal on it all. He's probably thinking to resell the well and the other three leases to Shell.' Aaron took a long drink from his glass. 'Given the price of oil at the moment, it would be economical for Shell to work them now, even if they cost more to buy back from us than they sold for.'

'So he makes a small profit. Bully for him. Doesn't he know what we will all make out of selling the company later, once we've cracked it? Jesus, Aaron, the stock broker is putting a market value of over twenty two mill' on us when we float.'

'Grayson's not thinking long term, Finn.'

'What's to stop me just leaving and setting up again?'

'Come on, Finn, you can answer that yourself. Can't you?' The wine wasn't staying in the glass long and Aaron reached the bottom of his second. He reached over and topped Finn's glass up, and gave himself another small amount. 'It all comes down to money. If we had it… if you had it, we could all keep going.'

'Yeah. I know.'

'Look, Finn, I think…' Aaron paused. 'Look… before you do anything you should get legal advice. I know a small firm here in the city. I went to school with the senior partner. There're only two of them, but they have a good reputation. They do mainly commercial stuff. Why don't I give them a ring and set up a meet.'

'Thanks,' said Finn, biting on his anger. He swallowed more bile. The desire to throttle the life out of his friend heightened as he heard the acquiescence drip through his own voice. He continued to wrestle with his state of shock and his naïve responses covered his feelings well.

'No problem, anything I can do to help, just call me, OK?'

16

One side of Aaron's mouth curled upwards as he gave Finn a half-smile. 'Sorry, Finn, I have to get to another meeting. Why don't you just sit here and gather your thoughts? Finish the wine. I'll get Hillary Keaton at Keaton-Jones to call you. They've an office over by Holborn. He will talk it all through with you.'

Aaron rose from his chair. Standing, he finished his wine, then gathered his case from under the table. 'You know, Finn…' he paused; 'it will all get sorted. Let's get you some money flowing. I'll call tomorrow.' He turned and left for the stairs.

All get sorted, he'd said. *Money flowing,* he'd said. But Finn knew, until he reached an agreement over leaving, Grayson would make sure he didn't receive a thing from the company. He'd been well and truly stuffed. Aaron may have sounded sympathetic, but he wasn't promising to be helpful. *Machiavelli? Old order? What the hell's that about?*

He was livid. Could Grayson's agenda really be to close the business, and resell the leases to Shell? But Grayson had still mentioned the AIM float, hadn't he? Could selling to Shell, now, just be a ploy to get his shares away from him? Until they floated, as a private company with no revenue – never mind no profit – the shares weren't worth a great deal. Floated, they stood to rise significantly, particularly on the back of the rising oil sector. He needed to hang onto his shares if he could.

Finn downed the last of the wine. Anger welled deep within him; he needed to get even, but how?

Where the hell did Aaron figure in all this? …On the fence? Right now, Aaron incensed him. He tried to consider the reverse. If it had been Aaron axed by Grayson, what would he have done? Would he have fallen on his own sword for Aaron? Would he have risked it? They'd needed Grayson's finance; they still did. If Grayson decided anything, then he'd probably have had to go along with it too. But it didn't feel right. Mentally, he started to kick himself. *Not much of a frigging strategy that... Play dumb?* Who was he kidding? He'd wasted an opportunity.

He needed help. He wasn't going to be able to count on Aaron for much. He sensed that, but he did still need Aaron in his camp. He needed to keep Grayson in focus also. He wanted to kick out, hard. His eyes narrowed at the thought.

FOUR

FINN HAD NEVER experienced a week like it. He'd returned straight home after his meeting with Aaron, catching the five o'clock GNER train to York. Any normal week, and he would have spent around three days in the city before returning, but he needed to get back and take some steps. Now, with no possibility of money going into his bank account, he needed to prevent the inevitable haemorrhaging of cash that would occur later in the month.

Of course, he had rights. The law required the company to pay him. But he knew the accounts. He knew how little cash remained. If he took it to court, a successful action would destroy the company. There would be insufficient cash to pay out any tangible level of compensation. It would leave him with nothing. No one, least of all himself, wanted to destroy what they'd all spent the last years working on. Grayson frigging Barclay knew that, and he was playing on it. *No,* he thought, *he would need to box clever.* Grayson had tied strings to him and now dangled him, marionette-like, over a gaping abyss.

On the Thursday, Finn went on-line and cancelled all his direct debits and standing orders. At least he could control the rate at which money would leave his account. He would respond only to those creditors shouting at him the loudest.

He went to his bank and explained the situation, but they'd been completely unhelpful. He'd wasted precious time there...

'...your overdraft has already reached its maximum, Mr Jackson,' said his so-called *personal banker*. 'I can only suggest that you make a formal application for a larger limit – it will take a week or two to process,' she invited.

'I don't have a week or two,' he'd replied in frustration.

He'd called the credit card companies, loan holders and the mortgage company. He explained the situation with increasingly forced patience. He grew ever more irate, passing through the security checks and speaking off-shore to people reading limited response scripts in thick, over-clipped accents that made understanding difficult, if not impossible. They'd passed him from pillar to post until he'd ended up with various collection departments. Still, when it came to it, despite all his debt, he hadn't yet got into arrears, and...

'...sorry sir, I see your account is up to date. You're not in arrears and therefore you don't have a problem we can help you with,' said the arrears consultant.

Perverse! 'You mean to say I have to get into trouble before I get out of it?' said Finn.

'Yes, sir.'

'Listen to me. I *am* in trouble. I can tell you that by the end of the month I will owe you. Can you please make a note of this call, so I'm on record as being a responsible client and, being a responsible client, I've informed you of the circumstances of my default?'

'Sorry, sir, but the system is not aware of your default, so I cannot make any arrangements on your behalf. Please call again later,' said the arrears consultant.

'But you are going to charge me for non-payment by the end of the month,' said Finn.

'Yes, sir. I am sorry, sir, but I cannot do anything for you until you appear on my system.'

The calls, on seven major finance agreements, took their toll on Finn. All ended in frustration, as he put the phone receiver down on his study desk with increasing degrees of force. *They can shout for their bloody money*, he thought.

At least Aisling kept to herself. But he felt sick. *Why the hell has our marriage gone like this?* He wanted her affection, her support, now. He'd tried talking in the past – she wasn't interested. At least the girls gave him hope.

Hillary Keaton called late Thursday afternoon.

'Hello, Finn. I've just spoken with Aaron Philips. I hear you are in a spot of bother.'

'Yeah. Thanks for calling.'

'I would be happy to take a look at this for you. Why don't you jot down some notes? A bit of a time-line if you like, covering what you see as the key points at issue. I will take a look… revert to you with some questions. We can talk more when we meet next week.' Hillary paused… and when Finn didn't say anything… 'How does next Wednesday sound?'

'Fine,' said Finn. 'Sorry, I didn't mean to be short with you. It's a bit of a trying time. . . As you can imagine.'

'I understand. Aaron has given me some details, but I would like to hear your take first, before I comment. Can you get the info to me by the weekend? Just don't go and resign.'

'Yeah, sure. I don't have much on my plate now. Oh… and don't worry, I'm refusing to resign.' Finn sensed the note of defiance rise in his voice. Tell me, Hillary, what is the process from here in? This is a first for me.'

'Well, it's all quite straight forward really,' said Hillary. 'We need to agree terms for a formal Compromise Agreement. What you need to do is be happy with the basic terms, and we will make sure the agreement is watertight, so they cannot rescind on it…'

Finn didn't respond.

Hillary continued '…Effectively, once you sign a compromise agreement in exchange for some compensation, you have no rights to take any further action against the company. There is a whole raft of legislation that's covered, but I'll go through it all with you when we meet.'

Having exchanged a number of e-mails and telephone calls, Finn found himself at the offices of Keaton-Jones LLP. He sat opposite Lyneth Jones, the exceptionally successful litigation partner in the firm. *She must be in her mid thirties*, he thought – a stunning brunette.

'You know Grayson is alleging you misrepresented the state of the project development at the time of his investment?' said Lyneth.

Welsh without a doubt. Her accent, though soft, confirmed the origin of her name. But there was an edge. *No shy, retiring type*, he mused. 'Yeah. I know. He's saying I lied.'

'We prefer to use the word misrepresented… it's less dramatic,' she said, with a wink.

'But, I copied you in with the consultant's report,' said Finn, brushing past the come-on in her eyes.

'Yes,' she said. 'I've been through it quickly. Very useful, thanks. The report's independence squashes Grayson's threat. Plenty of ifs and buts to keep an army of us lawyers engaged for a long time.' She smiled; a broad grin broke out. 'You know what we lawyers are like.'

What a smile. Was she flirting with him?

'His allegation wouldn't stand up in court,' continued Lyneth.

'So, I have a case?' he asked. *Good God, she's attractive*, he thought.

'Yes, a good one. Clearly it's building up to a constructive dismissal. We could take them on…'

'And win?'

'Eventually? …Yes, Finn. We would win. I have no doubt.

But, from what Hillary has told me, that's not really an option. Is it?'

'No. It would topple the beast. I can't afford that, not while there's hope.'

'Then all we can do is get you to the point where you can sign a deal as quickly as possible. Have you any thoughts?' Again, the smile.

'Aaron has talked it through with Grayson, and he believes he can get me a thirty grand payout. It's something to do with the maximum tax free limit. Is that the case?

'Yes,' said Lyneth.

'But they'll only settle on that if I agree to sell them the lion's share of my shares at par value.'

Her riposte was emphatic. 'Bastard!' she hissed.

The sudden edge in her tone surprised him. He could have sworn her eyes abruptly went from warm to cold steel. Is this the same woman? Every vestige of her smile vanished. Her colours as a legal Rottweiler unfurled before him. She seemed to be spoiling for a fight.

The change in her eyes reversed as quickly as it had occurred.

'God, I wish I could take him on,' she said.

'I wish we could too, but I'm no more than a puppet to Barclay. He could cut the strings and let me fall, and he knows it.' As he spoke, he saw the smile return. He was glad of having Lyneth on his side. *She'd be useful in a fight*, he thought.

They continued to discuss the drafting of the compromise agreement for another half hour. 'How much is all this going to cost me, Lyneth?' he asked.

'We'll work something out. We can't do it for free, but I'll talk with Hillary when he returns from court. I am sorry he wasn't here to meet you today, but this is more my line in any case.' More smiles. 'We can probably keep it under a grand. It really is straight forward, and, if you are not going to be able to improve on the terms, we should be able to get the draft out by the end of the week.'

'Anything you can do to help would be great, Lyneth. Thanks.'

'We'll be able to get you all signed up next week and money in your bank.'

'When we brought Grayson in, he bought-in for twenty percent at half a million pounds. A month later, a bunch of his friends put up another half mill' for fifteen. My share is now down to twenty-five percent and Grayson wants me to sell all but two and a half.'

'What will that give you, Finn?'

'Next to nothing. With the state of the company finance, Grayson is saying the shares have little value. Truth is, he's right.' The tone in Finn's voice lowered. 'I can't fight this, can I. . .' *That was a dumb thing to say* he thought, as his voice trailed off. But he'd got no nearer to working out any other angle.

His thinking carried him out of the meeting with Lyneth. Even the intellectual property for the oil-extraction process they'd developed held little value until they'd proven it. He'd secured patents for the modification to a hydrocarbon solvent-based extraction process, but he'd done it in the company's name. How the hell could he regain ownership and take his ideas forward? The question hovered in his mind, relentlessly spurring his anger.

*

Lyneth had been true to her word. The taxi pulled up on the corner of Clerkenwell and Hatton Garden, outside the office of Keaton-Jones LLP, at around two o'clock the next Thursday afternoon. Finn paid the driver and entered the building, resigned to signing the compromise agreement. He signed-in at reception and collected a badge.

When he'd first read the draft agreement, it took him aback. Twenty pages of obligations, warranties and legal stuff and most of it directed against him. It seemed more about preventing him from taking any possible action against the company, or its directors, than giving him anything. It gagged him, bound him and, in return, what? Shackles! It required him to sell his shares at par, back to the company. In return, he would get a thirty grand settlement, drip-fed to him in monthly instalments. Big deal. OK, he could pay the mortgage, and he could meet his other payments if he managed cash tightly, but he would need to wait some time to see if the remaining two and a half percent holding came to anything. What the hell was Grayson playing at? Begrudgingly, he supposed he owed Aaron some credit. At least he had the thirty grand coming – Grayson hadn't been in any mood to give him a bean.

Finn exited the lift at the seventh floor and buzzed the door to Keaton-Jones. The solenoid on the lock clicked, releasing its hold over the door, reminding him of that other door now, seemingly, fast retreating to the distant horizon. He opened the door before him. Lyneth stood there ready to greet him.

'Lovely to see you again, Finn,' she beamed. 'Just sorry it's the sort of situation it is. Look, why don't I take you for a bite to eat later? We could meet around five-ish, when I've finished here. We could have an early dinner if you like?'

'Yeah, I'd like that. Thank you,' he said, half smiling.

'Grayson and David Kail are already here. They're in the meeting room. We've coffee laid on, but this won't take long, Finn. Let's just get it over with and perhaps you can get on with life.' She smiled again. 'Come on then,' she said, as she turned to lead the way.

Again, true to Lyneth's word, the agreement-signing thing transpired to be a short, almost silent, ice-cool process – almost. Grayson stood throughout. He was edgy – visibly impatient. *No surprise there*, Finn mused. Grayson spared little time for formality. David was the "almost" surprise.

David Kail, at fifty eight – in many ways looking a younger, shorter version of Grayson; he too with a full head of white and grey hair – sold his services to many companies as a professional non-executive director. He'd over thirty years in the oil and gas industry, most of it in senior management roles in major companies operating in the European, South American and Chinese sectors. Finn always took David to be a consummate professional. But, today, David also seemed to be visibly on edge. He was noticeably nervous. *Surely it couldn't be because… No, there's something about the whole affair that's unsettled him*, he thought. *What was it?* Finn pondered the possibilities, but neither Grayson nor David had much to say. He pushed the notion of David's troubles away for the time being. He had his own to contend with.

A steely-eyed Lyneth busied herself passing the various copies of the agreement between the parties, opened at the appropriate pages for signature. And, as the ink of the last signature dried, David spoke…

'What are your plans now, Finn?' he said, directing most of his words down onto the table top. 'Have you something to go to yet?'

'No, David. This has all come as a bit of a shock. It's all happened too fast. I'm going to need time to get my head round it all.'

'Yes, I suppose…' A noise interrupted David. Grayson had grunted something – David responded to the unsubtle hint. 'I suppose we'll be away now. G'bye, Finn.'

'Yeah.' Finn hadn't wanted to embellish his goodbye.

Grayson collected his precious hat and left without further acknowledgement. David followed. Finn's feeling of defeat lifted a little as he watched David leave. It had just turned two-thirty. He looked over at Lyneth – her smiled warmed him.

'You go get a coffee or something,' she said. 'I'll phone ahead and book an early table at Rowley's. Fancy a good old-fashioned steak and chips?'

'That sounds like good comfort food to me – thanks,' he said.

*

'Do you get many like this?' he asked. Finn sat opposite Lyneth. Three hours had passed since the signing.

'Cases you mean?' Lyneth held her head tilted slightly to her left side, elbows on the table and hands held together under her chin. She looked at him thoughtfully – she didn't wait for him to affirm. 'Not so many that are over as quickly. I prefer a good fight.'

'I can tell.' *Cat and mouse.* And no mistaking her role. She didn't leave any impression of being a small, cowering, timorous creature.

Finn's gaze took in the surroundings. For the first time since Grayson confronted him, he seemed to be relaxing his mind a little. The vast mirrors and elaborate ceilings of Rowley's interior showed off the Victorian charm of what had been the original Wall's butcher shop. It had been a restaurant for going on thirty years and he always enjoyed coming up to the West End for its steaks. It'd been too early for a full dinner, so they'd both settled on a single course of the trademark entrecôte and French fries.

Finn sat pushing the few remaining fries around his plate, soaking up the last of the herb butter. 'If you weren't my lawyer, Lyneth...' Finn checked himself. 'If you weren't my lawyer, I would have to say I'd find this all quite romantic. Even at this time of day, it's a nice place to be. It certainly feels later than it is.'

'So, what's it going to be now?' Her voice held none of the hard edge he knew she could muster in an instant. Quite the reverse, her soft Welsh lilt touched him like the feel of warm satin on the raw wound of his day. The light of tiny oil lamps, scattered around the closely packed small tables, threw flecks of sparkling diamonds skipping into her eyes. ...And those eyes shouted to him, a single word – trouble.

'In truth? I want to get it back, Lyneth. Tiger Oil is all I have known for the last four years. I got the idea for it doing my MBA. I just don't feel as though I can simply move on – it's unfinished business. I want to get even. There *has* to be a way to regain control.'

'Yes, but that would take money you just don't have, Finn.'

'If it goes public I will lose any chance I might have. At least if I can delay or even stop the AIM float, I can buy myself some time. Something might come up.'

'You're an optimist then?' she said, laughing. Her question was rhetorical.

Her remark stung. 'What can I do to stop them, do you think?' *Another stupid question* he thought, but in keeping with a naïve front. Jesus! Whom was he kidding? He *was* naïve. He hadn't a clue – but he wasn't going to give up.

'I'm the wrong person to ask. I love the law. I don't see you can do anything, legally. I'm sorry, but even the agreement you signed today restrains you. It's a double-edged sword.'

'What if I spread some news around…' He hesitated over the half-formed question, not wanting to sound too pathetic.

'What do you mean, Finn?'

'I've made a lot of contacts since setting up Tiger Oil. I could drop a few hints… maybe suggest the patents are weak… That sort of thing…' *He was fishing.* 'Maybe even hint the project results are shaky…'

'Listen to me, Finn. That's dangerous. You know what

sort of man Grayson is. If he got wind you'd done anything slanderous against the company, he would have the full force of the law behind him. You've the moral high-ground for now. Don't spoil it.'

'Yeah,' he said. *And high morals don't pay bills.*

'You are still too angry, Finn. Please, for me if not for you, put some time between you and Tiger. Grayson seems a right bastard. I don't think you're thinking clearly yet.'

His gaze locked with hers and they fell silent for a moment.

'You're married aren't you, Finn?' asked Lyneth, breaking the spell.

'Yeah.'

'So there it is – no contest. For the family, too. Just sit tight. I'm sure something will come along soon. If I think of anything in the meantime, we can see what we can do then.'

Finn considered what she'd said for no more than a few seconds. *Family? Right!* He didn't hold the thought. 'And you? Do you have a partner?' he asked, with no expectation in the question, just idle curiosity, his mind still on the day's event. He'd lost, hadn't he? No, not yet – David's demeanour meant something, surely.

He was aware Lyneth still spoke to him. He sensed rather than heard her words.

'…I've never really found much time for relationships,' she had said.

Finn filled in the blanks he'd missed. *She's single.* But she tried to move the subject on, back to him, and he wasn't getting it.

Suddenly he tired of this *getting to know you* line. Alarm bells tinkled in his head, as if the bells lay in the path of a gentle, but increasing wind – a tinkle yes, but still an alarm. Why should this stunning Welsh brunette be interested in him anyway? Any other time he would be flirting with a woman like this.

'I am sorry, Lyneth, but do you mind…' He lowered his

gaze to his glass. He lifted the glass and drank to the bottom, replacing it on the table with slow deliberation, twisting the stem through his fingers as he did so. 'Dinner's been good for morale, your company's perfect. Another time. . .' He glanced at his watch. Just gone seven-fifteen. 'I could do with some thinking time,' he said – maintaining his lacklustre tone.

'Yes of course, Finn. You go. I'll get the bill.'

She watched him as he rose, following his every movement.

'Thank you, Lyneth,' he said. He smiled at her and turned, leaving her at the table. As he reached the door to Jermyn Street, he made a mental note not to retain her legal help now that he'd concluded the compromise deal. She'd wanted to flirt – wanted to get him to talk. Why? She wasn't going to help him with anything if it wasn't straight down the line legal, was she? And he needed to pay his bills.

*

He'd texted Carole as he left Jermyn Street. Yes, she was free and yes, she wanted to see him. It had been some time.

He took the tube from Piccadilly to Embankment before grabbing a Circle Line train to Tower Hill. As he travelled, an expectation grew deep within the well of his stomach – Carole had called it butterflies, when they first met.

He got back to his room in the Tower Hotel by eight and she arrived within minutes of him. He opened the door to her knock. She stood there a moment – a smile broke, parting her full, glossy, but not overly coloured lips. He let his eyes travel up from her heels. He noticed the short, but not cropped, silk top she wore. It exposed just a slight amount of her deliciously-flat midriff, above a long flowing white skirt.

As his gaze drew up over her curvaceous lines, Finn reached

out. His right hand deftly found her exposed midriff. Like a heat-seeking missile, his hand skimmed the surface of her warm skin. His fingers curled round her waist, pulling her into the room. As they tangoed backwards, he closed the door with his free hand, his other now completing its passage round her back. His fingers slid upwards, drawing her, firmly, even closer, forcing the warmth of her breasts through the marriage of silk and the thin cotton of his shirt. He looked down into her dark eyes, wanting to reach inside them. Then, lowering his lips to hers, he kissed her open mouth. She responded in kind. Their kisses became deep, and, in the warmth of the late summer evening, words did not seem necessary. Their passion maintained its steep and rapid ascent.

*

The sex had been good. It had been some time for both of them. They'd kept enjoying each other.

They lay there, still entwined… spent… the drapes open on a dark London sky. The natural light had long since faded on Tower Bridge, replaced seamlessly by the warm yellow glow of floodlights. The sky had morphed before them, from a blue to a black canvas. Neither had spoken much, words had remained unnecessary. They'd just been happy, being close.

By two a.m. Carole lay on her side, fast asleep. Her long, lustrous auburn mane cast adrift, floating away on the pillow. But, despite their earlier exertion, Finn could not find respite in sleep. His mind remained too active.

Despite his own obvious faults, he didn't believe himself to be a bastard. There was no guilt over Carole. Regret, yes. Regret that his relationship with Aisling had got into such a state. No doubt, he was difficult to live with. No doubt, he'd hardly been there for Aisling and the girls. But, when he *was* there, she showed no interest in his physical presence. Not for them. For everyone else, yes. For the outward appearance of a marriage, yes. Talking never helped. He'd found Carole… she helped.

Guilt, no. A bastard, no. But now? Now, seemingly, a board full of bastards had shafted him – or at least one and a number of cowards. Would he now have to behave more like them, just to get even? What had Lyneth said? *You have the moral high-ground for now.* But he couldn't see a clear path ahead. *Smoke and mirrors* – a crap cliché, he thought. Though, for the moment, he could not think beyond it. And the smoke troubled him deeply.

He fell into a shallow, restless sleep.

Suddenly, he found himself awake, in a field. It was peaceful and green. Silence reined. He saw trees, many trees.

He turned round, slowly – taking in the panorama before him. Abruptly, a shiver ran the full length of his body. It started between his shoulder blades, radiating deep within, travelling outwards with the speed of a lightning bolt to all his extremities. His face drained of colour. His mouth gaped open. Shufang stood there before him. She was some distance from him and he could not see her face clearly, but he knew it was her.

All of a sudden Shufang started to lope toward him and, frightened, he turned to dash for the trees. He ran hard, but could not make much ground – his feet felt leaden.

He reached a river bank. The fast flowing current raged below him. The safety of the trees – visible before coming upon the river – now lay beyond his grasp. He turned to face Shufang scurrying up on him…

Finn had woken with a start. The first-light of early morning streamed in past the still open drapes. He'd lain a while on his back, motionless. A chill swept across him as the cold

32

sweat formed during his dream evaporated from his naked body. The single sheet provided no barrier to the cool breeze from the air-conditioning unit that ran in the background – the constant hum reminding him of his reality. He lifted his arm and checked his watch. Six thirty. He crooked his head a little, glancing to his side, but she'd already left.

Christ. Why Shufang?

Finn rose, showered and left the hotel early. He'd had enough of the city this week. With the agreement signed, he'd managed to secure some income. But the best he could think of, for now, would be to establish a new office somewhere close-by. Perhaps he could line up some consulting work to keep him going, and wait for an opportunity to strike.

He could do little else. He returned to King's Cross station and caught the next train to York. All the while he could see nothing but the turbulent waters of a swollen Peace River flow past his life. They were drawing him in.

FIVE

'YOU'RE NOT THINKING clearly, Lyneth.' This Monday morning, August twentieth, Hillary Keaton, fifty one and the senior-half of the Keaton-Jones partnership, leant back in his chair. He held his arms raised, his hands clasped behind his neck. 'How long have we known each other?'

'Enough…'

'Exactly. I *know* you, Lyneth.' Hillary sounded his superior, chauvinistic self. 'You took a fancy to Finn, didn't you? Sorry I wasn't here to help you keep your distance. The Wilson case kept me in court far too long.'

'All I'm saying is I want to keep in touch… to give him a little advice every now and then. He needs a friend.'

'And we need our fees, my dear.'

Over the weekend, she'd reflected on her dinner with Finn. Despite failing to get him to talk about anything but the case… well, yes – she admitted to herself – she did fancy him. He's attractive: her height, five-nine at least; maybe a little over-weight, but he did have great eyes… when his gaze had caught hers… Oh yes, and he looked like he *needed* a friend.

Finn had been stitched-up good and proper. *Grayson Barclay's a bully*, she thought, and she didn't like bullies. Period. She wanted to help Finn, but not to the extent that she would help

34

him break the law, or risk more trouble. She loved the Law. The Law gave her a reason to be. Another admission, she told herself. The Law lay at the roots of her own problems – the Law, in effect, supplied her only life.

'Aaron asked me to do a favour for a friend,' said Hillary. 'He did say Finn wasn't going to be a rich seam of fees, but Aaron and I go back a long way, Lyneth. We were at Marlborough together. I only agreed to help Finn as a one-off.'

'I suppose you're going to say our current clients give us more than enough to work on.'

'Exactly, my dear. I can't have my junior partner swanning-off on personal mercy missions, now can I?' Hillary leant forward as he spoke, unclasping his hands and pushing his arms out before him, hands face-down across his desk. He looked straight into her eyes.

Lyneth knew Hillary's measure well enough not to counter directly. 'OK, so no *pro bono publico* then,' she conceded. 'But Finn did say when the company floated there would be a lot of value in it. Over twenty million he reckoned. What if there is something there? Don't you think we could get something out of it – fees I mean?'

'Come on, Lyneth. You're a bit slow on this one. Finn must have *really* floated your boat! Where's your cool logic now?' he chided. 'Aaron's an old school friend. I'm hardly likely to sit and watch my friendship destroyed for your sexual gratification.'

She didn't balk at the truth of the comment. 'Since when have you bothered where our fees have come from?' She'd grown accustomed to Hillary's more than occasional bluntness over the years she'd worked with him. She could give as good in return. 'But isn't Aaron Finn's friend also? If there were something behind all this plotting of Grayson's, wouldn't Aaron side with Finn? We would all gain… surely.'

'Lyneth,' said Hillary, his tone patronizing. 'Aaron called me late Friday to thank me for helping Finn. Of course I said it was all your doing…'

'Thanks.'

'But he said something else. He said it could have all got rather messy. Apparently, Grayson does have something on Finn, but he didn't want to reveal it at the time – to save Finn any embarrassment, Aaron said.'

An expression of puzzlement crossed her face. *Surely not? What could Hillary mean by that?*

'Now, Lyneth, can you please give me a run down on your other work this week. This is supposed to be a case review.'

*

Later the same day, at around six thirty, the phone on Finn's desk rang. He stood in the study of his home near York – a converted barn with a half-acre paddock adjoining open fields and close by the village of Husthwaite.

'Finn Jackson.'

'Hi, Finn, it's me, Lyneth.'

Even her voice sounded to be smiling, he mused.

'Look, Finn, I'm not sure what your thoughts have been over the weekend, but I just want you to know if I can do anything to help at all, I'll happily lend an ear, and… Well, I promise I won't charge you too much.' Lyneth paused, giving a little laugh. 'Well… maybe dinner occasionally.'

'You lawyers are all the same.' It was good to speak to a friendly voice, though she still sounded unmistakably flirtatious. He could do without that.

'When are you next in town, Finn?' Perhaps we can grab a coffee or lunch or something?'

'Didn't you have enough of my talk at Rowley's?'

'It was a bad day for you... you did keep on a bit... about getting even with Barclay I mean.'

'I know... sorry,' he said, warming to the sound of her voice. He found her easy to listen to; listening to her Welsh lilt had become a pleasure.

'No. Don't apologise, Finn...'

'I just want to get even with Barclay. I reckon he's stripping me of over three million.'

'But, really, there's nothing I can think of, legally speaking.'

'I know. I do appreciate your offer, Lyneth, honestly, but I just think your legal principles might clash at some point.' He was alert; why was Lyneth so interested in staying close to him? His guard remained raised.

'But if we can find a way, I'm interested in helping. I've been reading up on your business and I can see what you're trying to do.'

'Make money.'

'Yes, that... clearly.' She laughed briefly at his quip, and then switched to a more serious tone. 'But your process of extracting oil is also friendlier to the environment, and *that* appeals to me. I've seen the pictures of fields where they're just digging the stuff up. They're just destroying loads of trees and fields, Finn. At least what you're trying to do doesn't lay waste to the land. It's so beautiful out there.'

'It is.'

'What about lunch, Finn? We can talk some more now you're thinking clearer.'

'I'm down Wednesday if you're free?' It was dark beyond the bounds of his campfire. The only way he could see was to invite any strangers inside his circle. 'Tell me, I'm curious...'

'About?' asked Lyneth.

'...your interest in helping me?' His alarm bells still rang.

'I just am, Finn... Do you know Finsbury Avenue? I heard there's an Italian there worth a visit. Gatti's, I think. Do you fancy that?'

'Yeah. OK, sounds good to me. I should be able to get there for around twelve thirty. I'll meet you inside then?'

'Good. I'll look forward to it… Bye, Finn.'

'Yeah, bye, Lyneth.' Finn replaced the phone on its base unit. She's a fighter, he reasoned; she's certainly not giving up, but why? Suddenly, a noise swept his thoughts aside. The sound of girls screaming. The door of his study flung wide. Two girls, Becky, eight, and Jane, nine, flounced into his space, fighting over some doll or other.

'GIRLS!' he shouted, louder than he should have, but it stopped them dead in their tracks.

Becky and Jane could have been twins. They stood there, their arms dropped to their sides, a doll hung by a leg from Jane's right hand. Becky's lip quivered as her small, round, chocolate eyes filled with tears. Jane held her head high in defiance.

Jane swivelled round and took her younger sister's hand. Now best of friends again, Jane led Becky, her tears stifled, out of Finn's study and towards their Mummy standing in the spacious hallway.

'Don't worry, girls. Daddy has a lot on his mind. I'm sure he didn't mean to snap like that.' Aisling Jackson, thirty-nine, looked over the top of the girls' heads. Her gaze locked briefly with his. There was no such understanding in her connection with him.

Slowly, Finn closed the door to his study again.

Nothing worth having comes without payment of some kind. Even family. Of that, he'd been convinced a long time ago.

His thoughts returned to Lyneth. He still suspected her motives; is she friend or enemy? He would need to get closer.

*

Alexa Stuart did not excel at cooking. A boiled egg perhaps; an omelette at a push; a simple steak would be asking a lot; but a Sunday roast? Impossible! On the cooking score, she would contentedly hold her hands up and accept domestic defeat. Neither could any other form of domestic activity enamour her.

Alexa had been born for a city apartment life – it lay in her genes, she'd been convinced of that from an early age. She'd travelled to London at sixteen, running away from her native Edinburgh, where she'd taken to apartment life with never a care for the consequences. Her soft Edinburgh accent was rarely discernible nowadays. At forty-four, she claimed contentment with many aspects of her life. It did not distress her that she'd never had a child; a number of nieces and nephews blessed her, and she would see them on her sporadic trips to the home land.

Yes, she thought. She enjoyed a good life. Even her husband did not interfere too much. She enjoyed her space. She had learned to cope with her lot and could find what she wanted, when she wanted. She had a beautiful apartment in London's St Katherine's Dock and a cleaner to help keep some form of domestic bliss. Oh yes, and she had a husband who could cook, and, on Monday's, he was generally at home to cook them a fabulous dinner.

Monday evenings always pleased her – they had become something of an institution. From the kitchen adjacent to the massive open plan lounge area, separated only by a large, polished-granite-topped island unit, sounds of Aaron Philips cooking dinner punctuated the playing of Claudio Arrau and the London Philharmonic in a recording of *Krakowiak, the Concerto Rondo in F, Opus fourteen*. Yes, these Monday evenings pleased her.

'How are things at RedWood, Darling?' asked Aaron, as he

occupied himself stirring something. It smelt good. It usually did.

'Fine,' she said, her voice raised slightly, against the music. 'At least we have good clients, they pay on time. They also listen to what I tell them.' It was a slight dig at Aaron – his own clients were always awkward in that regard, part of being an accountant, she'd reasoned. "You remember I'd taken on another consultant, from one of the big PR firms?' she prompted. In one, gentle, sweeping movement, she ran her right hand around her neck and through her long, thick auburn hair, letting it fall across her shoulders.

'Which one?'

'The one from Smithfield's. A young girl who worked on their Rothschild account. She'd been there about two years.'

'Yes. Bit of a coup for you, that one?'

'Yes, I think so. She's shaping up well, despite our small size.'

Dinner was a carpaccio of salmon to start, followed by a warm salad of tamarind and orange roast duck with pear. They didn't do desserts. Alexa was proud of her fine figure; desserts were an unnecessary risk to her curves.

The August-light faded fast as they reached the finish of their meal. The dining table looked out over the marina, as did most rooms in their apartment, and reflections of the lights of the moored boats, large and small, danced fleeting images across the water.

'How are you about the meeting I set for you with Grayson Barclay tomorrow?'

'Fine, Dear.'

'I thought a new client would be useful to you. You know the problem we've had with Tiger Oil, and of course you know Finn – we went to their barbecue in May.'

'Yes.' Alexa recalled the last time she'd met Finn and Aisling. They'd enjoyed a good time, staying in a local pub and meeting for lunch the next day. They could have become good friends, if they'd only lived a bit closer.

'We fired the last financial PR firm last week. The board wanted a new angle to overcome the impact of market delays and, of course, we need some sensitivity in handling the announcement of Finn's departure. We're only looking at around two months before we go for our float on AIM, and we can't afford any poor publicity.'

'No, Aaron. I'm happy with the brief. I know it's a shame what happened to Finn, but I guess the board considered its reasons justified. Grayson is coming round to my office around two tomorrow.'

The Bose sound system worked its magic with a Chopin nocturne, as the sound of *Vivace number three, Opus fifty-one in G flat major* filled her ears.

'He can be a bit prickly – just let him think he's got his way and you should be OK with him.'

'Fine, Darling.' The two bottles of *1996 Chateau Clerc Milon* they'd managed to work through between them, had induced a deep, warm glow inside her now.

Aaron continued to tell the background story, to which she only half-listened.

'...Shufang's accident last year... it has already delayed our float and the pilot project in Canada is still unfinished... the last PR firm did a good job with the launch publicity... well, you know how fickle the press can be. ...The markets are volatile at the moment.'

'Sorry, Darling, what did you say? I wasn't really concentrating. It was a lovely meal and I'm a little relaxed.'

'The markets, Dear. They're a bit volatile.'

'Yes.'

'I suppose I shouldn't really give you so much wine...'

'But I like it, Darling. It works magic,' she said.

'I've got an early start in the morning. I have a car arriving at six, for a Heathrow flight. You do remember?'

'Of course, Darling, six-thirty.' Her eyes closed; her head rolled back; she continued listening to the music. 'I'm sorry, Darling. It's the wine and music... and you're off early.' She opened her eyes and, head forward, looked at him. 'Can't we leave the work-talk out of this? Truly, I'm happy about what you want of me tomorrow. You know that, don't you?'

'Yes... you know me though, just checking details.'

'You accountants are all the same.' She smiled at him in good nature. 'You'll want an early night again?' she said, knowingly. Aaron's early nights and early departures had long-ago ceased to frustrate her with disappointment. She rose from the table. 'Well, Darling, the cleaner can do the dishes in the morning, I have a date with a book. Are you coming too?'

The opening notes of Chopin's *Lento sostenuto Opus twenty-seven in D flat major* followed the pair from the table to their bedroom.

*

It transpired to be a professional challenge. Alexa's meeting did not turn out quite as she expected. Grayson Barclay had been gruff, though formally polite – a bully if ever she'd known one. His politeness, she thought, could only have been the thinnest of veneers.

It soon became clear to her, Grayson Barclay wanted more than Finn's departure; he wanted Finn to suffer a loss of credibility. She found it difficult to convince him that what he wanted would only make the situation look worse for the company. They needed to keep the event of Finn's departure as low-key as possible. It would not look good if they'd appeared to sack him. Grayson Barclay's blinkered, old-school

42

mentality, shone through in spades, face up for all to see. He'd kept insisting any press release should at least damn Finn with faint praise. Reluctantly, Alexa had agreed to draft the press release for Grayson's approval, and she'd agreed to take Tiger on as a new retained client.

Alexa had begun to think that with Finn, not all might be as it seemed. She certainly liked him, having met him socially with Aaron a few times. She just couldn't see what the issue could be, but she did get a sense of the difficulty Finn must be facing now. She confided as much to Aaron later that Tuesday night, after he had returned late from a Brussels flight.

'Alexa, I know Finn stays at the Tower Hotel when he's in town. Why don't you fix to meet him? I think he's there tomorrow.'

'Thanks, that's a good idea,' she said.

'He's agreed to cooperate in drafting any release about his departure. His cooperation is a condition of his pay-off. Maybe, to soften the Grayson blow, you can work on something Finn will agree to.'

'Yes. I'll do that,' she said.

*

A short distance across the marina basin from Alexa's apartment, in a third-floor room of the Tower Hotel, Finn looked out over the yachts moored beneath him. In his mind, he could hear the strings of a sea-harp, of halyards pinging gently against alloy masts, as the boats swayed on their mooring lines to the breeze, fenders squeaking as they rubbed against each other and the quayside. He loved boats. One of his character flaws, he mused – expensive toys.

He'd decided to advance his trip to London to that morning.

It had been an uneventful journey. Despite their financial troubles, GNER seemed to be doing a good job on the East Coast line.

The house – its atmosphere – had become unbearable. Aisling had not taken the whole episode of his losing Tiger Oil well, especially on top of his constant trips away. She'd stressed-out with it all.

Once he'd got into town, he'd spent the rest of the day arranging for a new office. He needed to be here in the city. He needed to be able to react to any opportunity to fight back.

He'd stood many times looking out over the yachts in the St Katherine's Dock marina. *Thirteen acres of land for thirteen knights* – recalling the fact that over one thousand years ago, Kind Edgar gave the *Knighten Guild* a jewel in the crown of London. He'd believed, one day, with the hard-won fruits of his labours, he'd have at last got his own yacht to add to those below him now.

We don't want you to profit from our success. Grayson's words echoed around inside his head, trampling on his thoughts. Christ! They wouldn't even be this far if it wasn't for my ideas, he reasoned, amongst the crescendo of Grayson's still echoing statement. *Sod them. Sod them all!* Even Aaron stood aside and let Grayson do it. Sod Shufang for dying. *Oh Christ, why did she have to die?*

He couldn't afford to stay in this place much longer; he needed to cut his costs. He'd done cheaper city hotels before, but he'd grown sick of waking up with the sense of being in some foreign country, sick of lying awake at night in rooms possessed of the air of a trucker's motel. He'd worked his way to the city and developed a taste for what came with it. He'd seen through into the enchanted garden – he belonged; he just needed to get through that door. He wasn't going to give up on it all so soon.

'The girls have had a bad day at school again today, Finn. I need you here to help me…' Aisling had said when she'd called earlier. 'I've just put them to bed and they were both in tears. They sense something is wrong.'

'I know. . .' he said, not able to think of what else to say; tiredness had washed over him – a tsunami, its steep waves crashing, menacingly, over a gently shelving beach.

'One of Becky's friends told her you'd been given the sack. Who've you been talking to, Finn?'

'Just tell them no one can sack Daddy, he owns the company. Just say…' He had no bright ideas. '…Just tell them if any of the other kids say anything, they can say I'm starting something new.'

'What?'

'God knows, Aisling.' He wanted to shout. 'Don't you start on me,' he said, in a raised voice. Anger welled up inside him. 'I can't do this sort of conversation on the phone – you know that.'

He'd spent another five minutes trying to ebb the flow of tears he sensed rather than heard. He'd agreed to return home as soon as he could.

I could really do without all this family crap happening now.

He fell into a troubled sleep.

*

It was so peaceful. Around him, the grass grew so green. He could hear the birds – their chorus a sound of tranquility. Trees, a bounty of aspen and poplar, separated the green from blue, a border of evergreen on his near horizon.

'F i n n . . .' said the voice – the word drawn out, the wind accelerating each nuance of sound past his ears. The horizon slid through his vision as he turned, first his head, then his body, until he faced her again.

The shiver, this time half expected in the semi-lucidity of his dream, ran the gamut of his spine, radiating to all points of his soul – a thunderbolt of alarm. Now though, in this expectation, his face no longer drained of colour and his mouth no-longer gaped wide. But he stood, momentarily paralysed with fear. Shufang, her slight frame shrouded in white, ran forward, towards him.

The panic of alarm broke his paralysis and Finn turned to flee from her advancing, faceless form. He ran hard for the trees in the distance. His legs were heavy and cumbersome – as if running through sodden marsh-land. He arrived at the river bank and turned to see Shufang almost at him. The fast flowing river raged below.

In the dark of a three a.m. silence, Finn woke in a cold sweat. What had he been running from? What is he running from …home? …business? Did the dream hold a message? A message to turn and fight? He couldn't answer his own questions.

Perhaps, he thought, if he could just solve his professional life then maybe he would have more opportunity to work on the rest of it. Maybe *then,* he would understand… He knew he needed to get it all sorted – he didn't want to lose Aisling and the girls.

SIX

FINN HAD SLEPT little and, with the August dawn still breaking early, Wednesday morning came to meet him on the coat-tails of Tuesday night. By ten o'clock, he considered he should have been leaving for the evening.

He sat, at the empty light-oak coloured desk, in the small but newly refurbished office he'd arranged to hire the day before. He'd thought of the Finsbury area after Lyneth suggested they meet for lunch at Gatti's. There had been no sense in going far from the buzzing financial centre he knew. He looked around and found a serviced-office facility on Worship Street, behind Finsbury Square.

Finn had been fortunate this time. Due to a fresh insolvency, he managed to secure two days a week in a small single-desk office. This was far better than having to make do with the more open plan hot-desk space usually free at short notice. The service-company required the first three months paid up front. There was little space on his credit cards, but he needed an office. The room offered no view to speak of, but at least he had a base – every Wednesday and Thursday. Importantly, he now had a London business address and phone number. He could go ahead and set up some form of project consulting business to tide him over. Hope would not pay his mortgage.

Hope was not a strategy for survival.

It had just turned nine-thirty when Alexa Stuart called.

'Hello,' he said, forgetting the usual formality of introducing himself.

'Hi ...Finn?

'Yeah, Finn here.'

'This is Alexa Stuart... Aaron's wife. We met before.' Alexa always used her maiden name professionally. 'Is now convenient?'

'Yeah, fire away. How are you anyway?' He remembered Alexa, a tall, elegant and good looking woman, with lovely thick hair she wore long.

'I'm fine, Finn, and you? I know you're having a rough time of it – Aaron's kept me up to date. Not with the full details of course...'

'I'm alive and kicking, thanks. At least I'm not bankrupt yet.'

'Yes. I'm truly sorry to hear about it all. How are Aisling and the kids?'

'Aisling's not taking the uncertainty of it at all well. But we'll cope. Thanks for asking.'

'The reason I'm calling, Finn, is Tiger Oil have retained me as their Financial PR agent. I had a session with Grayson Barclay yesterday. I must say I'm not keen on him, as a person, but Aaron asked if I could help out.'

'Not keen? You're telling me!'

'The first thing I need to do is work on a press release about your exit. Are you free to meet this evening? Aaron mentioned you usually stay at the Tower – our apartment is over the marina too.'

'Yeah, I gather... Sorry though, I'm afraid I have another meeting this evening, and I could do with keeping some time free.'

'Yes... of course, Finn. How about now? I can manage an

hour for coffee. Where are you?'

'Behind Finsbury Square, Worship Street. Do you know it?'

'Yes… Look, why don't I buy you coffee at the Royal Exchange? Say… after ten?'

'Yeah. That'd be good. It would be lovely to see you again, Alexa. How about 10.30, at the Bank end? I'll try and get one of the balcony tables.'

'OK, see you there soon.'

'See you,' he said. He slid his mobile shut, and placed it on the empty desk next to his silent Blackberry. Aside from meeting Alexa for coffee, he had no real idea of where to go or what to do next.

One step at a time, he told himself.

He'd resigned himself to Grayson Barclay's desire to see him suffer. David Kail, and Jonathon Long, forty-eight – the other non-executive director – had made themselves conspicuous by their respective silences. Only Aaron seemed willing to say anything, and his words were largely ineffective. Aaron had called offering verbal support on a number of occasions – but that was all.

Finn had no idea what they'd all said between themselves. He'd lost all influence at Tiger Oil. To cap it all, his compromise agreement obliged him to sell the majority of his shares prior to the company's float on AIM. Aaron had confirmed the flotation would happen early in December. *When the shares are gone… what then?* The thought triggered a wave of nausea.

Finn stood and took his jacket from the back of his chair. He swept up his phone and Blackberry from the desk, and left the building. He went along Worship Street then turned down City Road in the direction of Moorgate. Despite his scurrying for the interludes of shade offered by the taller buildings he passed, the mid-morning sun beat down upon him. Sweat began to reveal beads of dark colour spotting through the pale blue of his tie-less shirt.

Finn arrived at the Royal Exchange at around ten twenty-five and, checking around to see if Alexa had already arrived, he went straight up to the Mezzanine. He managed to grab a table in the first balcony – just as another couple were leaving.

The Royal Exchange served as a favourite haunt for many meetings. Looking down over the other tables in the central atrium, Finn thought he could count a number of head-hunters plying their incongruous trade, enticing further suspects to add to their surreptitious short-lists.

'Hi, Finn.'

Finn turned in his seat to see Alexa. She smiled in recognition as she came up to the table, her long legs making quick work of the short distance from the stair top. She wore a burnt orange blouse beneath a classic cut, mocha suit. His memory had not failed him; she looked a match for any other women in the building.

Finn stood to take Alexa's hand and, simultaneously, went to kiss her offered cheek.

'Hello, Alexa. Lovely to see you again.'

'Yes… and you, Finn. Just sorry it's not what we'd all talked about when we last met. It would have been good to all go over to the villa in Piemonte for a weekend, to celebrate the float. I'm sure you and Aisling would have loved it out there. The local wine is fab too – we've got Barolo, almost on tap!'

'Yeah. One day perhaps.'

Finn offered a chair to Alexa and she sat down as the waitress came up to the table.

'Two coffees please, and some sparking water,' he said to the young girl dressed all in black. He turned to Alexa. 'Sorry, Alexa, is coffee OK for you? I should have asked first.'

'Fine for me, Finn.'

He saw the warmth in her smile, then turned to nod confirmation to the waitress. He retook his seat.

He found Alexa to be easy company and they chatted

about many unimportant things as the coffee and waters were brought over. The informal conversation continued, with neither Finn nor Alexa making much of an effort to turn to business. It felt good to just relax.

Alexa looked at her watch and gave a coy, little-girl laugh. 'Good grief, look at it. It's gone eleven and here we are discussing anything but press releases.'

'Yeah, fun isn't it.' Finn laughed, feeling genuinely relaxed. 'You're the second woman to be distracting me from business.'

'Pray tell...' she said, raising her eyebrows.

'Do you know Keaton-Jones? Aaron put me onto them, to sort the agreement out.'

'No, never heard of them. Doesn't surprise me though, Aaron keeps an awful lot to himself. You know, he's involved with lots of businesses. Too many, I sometimes think. He's hardly in the city, or at home these days.'

'Well, they've got a razor-sharp lady litigator there. She took me out to dinner, after I'd done the deed and signed my business away.'

'Mmm... nice!'

'Well, to be honest, given what'd just happened, I wasn't best company.'

'S'pose not...' Alexa giggled – her mood playful without any hit of being flirtatious, just honest friendliness. '...Does she bite?'

Finn laughed. 'I didn't stay to find out. I made my excuses and left.' His expression fell serious again. 'I'm not sure if she's after me, or has been set a task to watch what I am up to. You know? ...the *keep your enemies close* sort of thing.'

'Why do you say that?' Alexa looked puzzled.

'It's a feeling. I just think the whole compromise agreement turned out to be a one-sided thing. You ever been involved with one before?'

'No. Only the fall-out – like this. I've done a few press

releases for clients who've sacked senior staff, and needed to control the news.'

'Well, the agreement protects the company more than me. I just wonder what hands played in the damn pie before it got cooked.'

'I see what you mean. I'm sure there's nothing sinister going on. Aaron has been unusually up-front talking to me about it. I don't think there is any real issue, just a cantankerous Barclay.'

'I suppose you're right.'

'Just keep your eyes open, Finn.'

'I will. I am seeing her for lunch again today, at Gatti's, a little Italian.'

'Mmm... nice!' She smiled again, teasing him.

Finn laughed. 'What, the little Italian? Or... good grief, Alexa.' Finn feigned shock. 'I'm a married man with two kids and a field full of my wife's horses to worry about.'

They both laughed.

'What's on the menu d'you think?' asked Alexa.

'I feel like I want to get even with Barclay. He's stripped me of over three million pounds...'

Alexa whistled. 'Wow. I had no idea, Finn.'

'Yeah, that's providing they float on the market of course ... which now looks confirmed for sometime in December.'

Finn paused to drink some water. 'Lyneth... that's the litigator's name...'

'She's a Welsh rarebit then...' Alexa giggled playfully.

'On the button.'

'Mmm, nice!'

'Stop it, or I will have to find a *new* new friend.'

Alexa feigned a hurt expression – but she didn't hold it long.

'Lyneth has some high legal and moral principles. Strange for a lawyer, I know,' he continued. 'She's interested in the green angle of the business, and seems keen to help me find a legal way to regain control at Tiger.'

'Finn...' said Alexa. Her tone had fallen serious. 'Listen. I like you, as a friend, and of course I'm sorry to see you in this position, but I'm not going to condone anything that's going to affect Aaron's role too.'

'I know.'

She reached out and touched his hand briefly. 'Just be careful, Finn.' The smile returned. 'Why don't you pop round to my office, before your train tomorrow, and we can work out the draft press release then? Maybe we can get the whole thing sorted by the end of the week.'

'Yeah. That'd be good, Alexa.'

'I've got to dash, Finn.' She pushed her chair back and collected her handbag from the floor. 'I'll get this.' She reached over and kissed his cheek. 'Pop round about two-ish.' She smiled and walked over to the bar in the centre of the Mezzanine.

Finn watched her pay. She turned and smiled at him again. Then she walked past the bar, to the opposite exit. He checked his watch. Eleven thirty. He would walk up to Finsbury Square, slowly.

*

After some of London's Italian restaurants Finn had been to, Gatti's proved to be a welcome relief. He'd found the many faceless, up-market chains to be an anodyne experience. Today though, as he entered, he saw a dining room packed with personality. But it wasn't a little Italian. *You could do big deals in this place.* Despite his precarious position in life, again he felt the buzz of just being in the City.

Finn followed the *maitre d'* down to the bar area, where Lyneth's table lay behind a wooden partition, in a booth-like alcove. Having arrived ahead of Finn, Lyneth had already ordered a bottle of wine, which now sat in its cooler, aside a single red carnation in an off-white bud vase. The setting for lunch appeared cosy.

'Hello, Finn.' Lyneth's face beamed as she looked up at him. She remained seated but stretched out her right arm, offering her hand.

'Hello again.' As he took her hand, he couldn't help but smile. Her hand-shake was warm, sensuous even, but firm and positive.

Lyneth looked every inch the sexual, confident woman he believed her to be. He'd noted the heads of a number of suits check him out. They'd clearly seen her enter, and now engaged themselves in sizing up the competition. Despite his wariness, he fed on the satisfaction that other, flashier suits had seen him with such a woman. He took his seat as Lyneth poured him a glass of the straw-yellow wine.

She nodded at the bottle, inviting his gaze to follow. '*More Maiorum*, I hope you like it.'

Lyneth had taken control. He didn't mind, she wasn't pushy, just confident. He lifted the glass, rotating his wrist as he did so. He lowered his nose over the rim, pushing into the aroma now rising from the cool wine.

'Cheers, Lyneth.'

'Mud in your eye,' she said.

They both took a drink.

'Not something I've tried before,' said Finn. 'I've never been good at picking whites. You saved me from having to think about it.'

Lyneth smiled at his riposte. There'd been no way he could switch control on that one. 'What do you think?' she asked.

'Fiano, isn't it? I like it. Definitely some honey in there… and some spice too. Quite complex…'

'Like me?' She laughed. 'I can tell you're a bit wary.' She

smiled, her head tilted to one side.

'Do you have an apricot and orange finish too?'

'Touché.'

'Or a nutty after taste?'

They laughed.

The waiter brought the menus. They both considered their choices and enjoyed further sips of wine.

'I'm afraid I don't like anything too heavy at lunch,' she said. 'I'm just going for the *insalata caprese di bufala*. I just love it. It's so simple. You go for anything, Finn. My treat.'

Finn considered his menu a moment longer, then closed it with a snap. The morning had been good to him and conversation with two women, both likeable, but poles apart, gave him renewed confidence.

'Easy, *rigatoni arrabbiata*! I like spice with my mozzarella.'

The meal was exceptional, and they failed to talk about anything Finn expected. The wine flowed. They'd already called for a second bottle when the food had arrived. Finn realised the ever-confident Lyneth retained full control. He was on her agenda – whatever that could be.

'Are you trying to get me drunk?' he said, laughing, as she poured more wine to his favour.

'Well,' she winked, '…maybe a little.'

Lyneth began to ask about his home and family, and about life in Yorkshire. Finn's guard lowered in increasing amounts.

After a while, he grew conscious that he'd been talking rather a lot. He tried to regain a distance from her questions. 'Where are we going with this, Lyneth?' he said.

'Just trying to get to know you… if we are to work together.'

'But we're not exactly working on anything. Are we?'

'Not yet,' she said, and winked again.

By the time the second bottle stood empty, he'd revealed more than he would have liked. His lapse of control at her prying questions irritated him. But, she'd been good company, and he hoped his annoyance didn't show in his expression.

'It's been a lovely lunch, Lyneth...'

'It's over?' She smiled.

'I can't afford your fees. If you're going to keep treating me like this, I reckon I'll have to let you get to the office.'

'Well, if that means it's not the last time then... I guess we both have things to get on with.' Lyneth turned her head towards the bar, where a passing waiter had just come into view. Her slight movement triggered more than the waiter's acknowledgment, as the heads of several suits also reacted. 'The bill please,' she mouthed, rather than said, to the waiter.

The waiter brought the bill over and silence reined as Lyneth completed the transaction at the table. She'd paid for the meal on a personal credit card; Finn had managed to read that much upside down. He glanced briefly over to the bar area, to some of the unlucky competition. A couple of tall, dashing-looking, alpha-grade suits noticed Finn looking in their direction; they turned their heads to resume their conversation. Another man, a short, heavy-set man, tie-less – as many were these days – in a dark city-stripe, had taken a position by the bar in full view of where he and Lyneth sat. At least the short man had not appeared to be eyeing Lyneth up. *No competition there,* he thought.

'Right, Finn, care to walk me out?' said Lyneth, breaking the silence.

They both stood. Lyneth offered her arm to Finn. He knew damn well she'd caught on about the other male attention – attention she attracted with every move she made. She was letting him milk it. They walked together, arm-in-arm, to the door. They took their time and talked of more, inconsequential things. On reaching the street, she turned to him and kissed his cheek. 'Bye, Finn.' Her smile was generous. 'Let's do this again... soon,' she said, and gave him another wink.

Finn watched Lyneth walk away in the direction of the

Moorgate tube – he watched her movement. *And, she knew it.* After a few moments, he turned to start his walk to Worship Street.

Two minutes later, Scott Lindon emerged from Gatti's. Under the shade of the recessed portico, he reached for his phone and selected a number.

'Scott here.'

A pause while the other party answered.

'I couldn't overhear what they'd said, but it looked like a cosy chat for two… She's a beauty that one. She attracted a lot of attention, from the waiters and others… What do you want me to do?'

A further, longer pause.

'I don't think so. I couldn't tell for sure.'

A short pause.

'OK,' he said.

Scott closed his phone. Deep in thought, he looked down onto it for a moment, before replacing it in his pocket.

*

Lyneth was sitting in her office at Keaton-Jones by a quarter to three. The city-bound afternoon heat had become oppressive. She removed her Souster and Hicks tailored peak-lapel jacket and hung it over the chair back. She sat down at her desk and reflected on her lunch date. Clearly, Finn didn't see how she could help him for the moment. That had partly been her fault, she mused, for staying on the family line too long. But it *had* been interesting.

Although Finn let his guard down with the wine flowing, it had risen again by the time they'd both walked out of Gatti's. Had they parted at night-time, she might have tried for a proper kiss. She smiled to herself.

Her office door opened, abruptly. Hillary Keaton stood there, leaning, one arm raised and resting on the door-frame.

'You're looking a bit smug, my dear. I guess you've seen Finn Jackson for lunch.'

'None of your business, Hillary,' she retorted.

'I just hope he paid.'

'No, *I* did… on my *own* card. And don't worry your little head, I'm not using our fee-time either.'

As she watched him walk away, she mused over the relationship between her and Hillary. It had grown from one of mutual respect of each other's legal prowess, to one of love-hate, based on their familiarity of each other. Clearly, Hillary wasn't taking kindly to Finn. Hillary was right though… they did have many clients who paid handsomely. *No*, she thought, she couldn't help Finn just yet, not with two sources of conflict – Finn himself and Hillary too. She needed to choose her battles carefully.

Hillary re-entered the open doorway, interrupting her thoughts.

'Oh… I forgot to mention. Just before you came in, I took a call from Grayson Barclay at Tiger Oil. Apparently, they have a letter-before-action, from the family of a Chinese girl killed in an accident on their site in Canada last year. It seems the family is considering a charge of corporate manslaughter against the board. Barclay wants us to take it on. One for you, I think.' Hillary's face contorted into an over-smug expression. Sarcasm reached into his tone. 'I guess you'll need to stay away from Finn now… In case there's a conflict of interest, dear. You understand.' He turned and left.

'Shit!' she said to no-one. How the hell could she further any sort of relationship with Finn now? 'Shit… Shit,' she hissed.

*

That night, much later – quite what the time was Finn couldn't be sure – he lay beside Carol. She slept soundlessly beside him. He savoured the warmth and closeness of her body. She lay with her arm across his chest.

The day had been interesting, though not productive – certainly not if he counted it as the first day of his future. The new office at least located him in the City, and he'd begun to feel the buzz of city life again, for the first time in the past weeks. The multitude of microcosmic worlds, all going on around him in the cafes and restaurants provided a background of white-noise to his new-found world of deceit and trial. He *would* find a way out of this dark passage, and through into the garden he could taste on the breeze flowing through it.

But, ultimately, it had been a day without achievement. He still had no idea quite what to do next. He'd no plan, just an objective. In taking his place in the garden, he wanted to get even.

One step at a time.

The pretence of seduction practised by Lyneth was interference, albeit an attractive kind. He didn't like to mix business and pleasure – it could be dangerous. Mixing business and pleasure only ever led to clouded, dumb judgments. He liked to put some things in boxes, to control them where he could. He would need to be cautious about any further meeting with the lovely Lyneth. He'd said too much private stuff at lunch, and that worried him. But she did have something about her… something sublime. He *knew* he'd been attracted, caught on a barbed-hook.

Alexa surprised him. Whereas he could listen easily enough to Lyneth, he could talk to Alexa; they communicated on some other level. Sure, she'd been sympathetic, but she wasn't afraid to say when something bothered her. He liked that. He wished his other friends, Aaron for instance, could be the same. He always considered Aaron's conversation a little shallow at times.

Carol stirred. She rolled away, her arm slipping from his chest. He was disappointed at losing the intimacy of her contact, but he consoled himself remembering their earlier closeness.

He couldn't sleep; there were just too many strands of thought – his dream for one. The dream's lucidity haunted him. He'd been aware, but he had no idea of its meaning.

What am I supposed to be running from? Why Shufang? Surely I'm not running from her?

The idea and ideals that drew Shufang together with him and Aaron, almost four years ago – when they met doing their MBA – lay shattered. They lay like the scattered, broken shards of a mirror dropped to the ground, reflecting pieces of what might have been back at him, taunting him with glimpses of a future – the enchanted garden – now lying, seemingly, beyond his grasp.

He remembered the coming together – it had been October 2003. They'd all joined a two-year part-time course at Lancaster University Management School.

Shufang had been twenty nine, petite, long jet-black hair, and highly intelligent. She possessed a brilliant control of the English language, even if Americanised from her earlier studies in Texas. Shell Oil had put her on the MBA course; she'd worked for them for a number of years and, at the time, she'd been working on a project in the Peace River region of Alberta. Shell had set eyes on her for great things. It considered a UK degree would broaden her capabilities still further. Fully funded, she'd found her own well of success.

Aaron had arrived as an experienced energy accountant.

60

He'd previously been FD in a number of European oil-exploration companies. He'd gone on to co-found Henley Oil Consultants, taking them to the OFEX market. He'd made himself a handsome return. He still served as a director there, and he held a number of other oil-related non-executive directorships. Without a doubt, Aaron's expertise lay in corporate finance; he'd joined the MBA *for something else to do*. Finn, naively perhaps, had been impressed by Aaron's city stories, and of his role in consulting to a number of the smaller, emerging East-European governments.

And he, Finn?

Well, he'd been "in between" things…

'What brings you to this course?' Shufang had asked.

'Well, long story, but I started off in the Merchant Navy. Worked on Shell tankers most of it, getting to first Engineer by time I got to twenty-nine. But I'd done enough oceans by then. I left for a shore-based job with Saudi Aramco, in ninety-one. Did a bit of North Sea stuff, ninety-eight to nine, then got the chance to join a small UK outfit, on a contract for Petróleos de Venezuela… the PDVSA.'

Aaron, who'd sat quietly to that point, had suddenly chirped-up, laughing, 'You're an engineer, I guess?'

'You could say that. Yes. I like building things and fixing things. Quite creative when I put my mind to it.'

'But doing an MBA now,' Shufang had said.

'Yes. PDVSA became a problem. It'd been great at first, and it paid well. I got to move to a nice big house with a field. But I would have to pick the one country the oil-shock messed up this year.'

'The national strike?' Aaron had asked.

'Yes. Hugo Chávez fired over a third of the thirty eight thousand workers, and he split PDVSA in two to weaken it. He sent the company reeling.'

'I remember,' Aaron had said. 'Most of the workers

supported the strike, hadn't they?'

'Yeah. Our company got out and we wound it down. I got away with enough to pay for this course. I'm doing some project consultancy work on the side.'

'What do you want to do after this, Finn?' Shufang had asked.

'I reckon a crash course in business and I will have a go at something myself.'

'That's what I fancy, sometime,' she'd said. 'It's in our Chinese blood... business.'

That was then. The introductions over, they'd started the course; three with a common interest: oil – and, of course, making money. They agreed to syndicate on any project work, to work together to see where they got to.

And now? First, Shufang's death last year, then his exit. Events had beached the plan – he the ideas man, Shufang the geologist, and Aaron the financial expert with the city contacts.

There are too many open ends. Too many parties holding cards he couldn't see – he'd never enjoyed playing cards, not with money on the table.

Despite the friendship, he couldn't rely on Aaron because of his continuing majority interest in Tiger Oil. It seemed strange, he thought, but the only person he could confide in appeared to be Alexa. Her skills as a PR professional were valuable. He knew the value of PR – he'd learnt that early in the city. Everything appeared to be about perception. Now even more so, he mused.

I'm not going to condone anything that's going to affect Aaron's role too. Alexa's words echoed inside his head. He would need her help – he could see that. He also needed to take the offensive – rather than to sit and react to events as they unfolded. He drifted into a fretful sleep, only to meet Shufang again.

SEVEN

THE THURSDAY BEFORE the August Bank Holiday, and the city seemed quieter. August was a silly-season – traditionally less busy than most months in the city, because of extended summer holidays. Many suits had left, and now curious tourists appeared to take their places. Coloured Hawaiian-style shirts and Bermudan-style shorts replaced the city-stripes. They mingled and explored the environs of the great *City of London*, the financial hub to many of the world's great enterprises. Now, Thursday, with the Bank Holiday in their midst, more suits had taken their leave. With many of their colleagues already departed, they took the opportunity to start the break early.

Alexa had been at her desk in her sixth-floor office in Birchin Lane, just off the Bank station, from eight that morning. With no Aaron around the apartment, there had been no one and nothing to distract her. She'd come in and spent the morning dealing with e-mails and reviewing the previous day's client releases. There had been several e-mails with overnight cuttings to review and get out to her clients, but her staff could easily clear the remainder.

The telephone rang. The light on the phone showed an internal call from reception.

'Miss Stuart,' said the young voice, 'there's a Mr Jackson downstairs for you.'

'Please, Michelle, can you go and bring him straight up… and can I have coffee for two please?'

'Certainly, Miss Stuart.'

Within minutes, there was a knock on the door. Michelle showed Finn in. *Yes, it added up to a good morning.*

'Hi, Finn, you found us OK?' she said.

'No problem. Didn't realise you worked this close to the Royal Exchange. I've just been sat there having lunch.'

'Really? You're not that broke then.' She smiled.

'Yeah, I am – only had enough for coffee and water. I just watched, greenly, while others ate oysters at the bar. I'll grab a sandwich on the way home, or even one of those Cornish pasties at King's Cross. I love the steak and stilton.'

'Oh, you do know how to slum it.' She laughed.

Michelle returned with a cafetière of coffee.

'Yeah. I've even taken carnation cream in coffee because we ran out of milk.'

'Desperate a little, weren't we?'

'Yeah, s'why I always drink it black now – I don't want to get caught out again. By the way, I *am* impressed! Real coffee.'

'Thank ye, kind Sir,' she said, in mock deference. 'So what have you done this morning, Finn? How's the new office?'

'Between you and me, my boss gave me the morning off… I didn't check out until twelve. Then I walked over from Tower Bridge.'

'Likewise; I always walk in. That's why I set up here.' She paused. 'Well, Finn, I guess we have to draft a press release.'

'The sooner it's out of the way I can draw a line.'

'I've looked at the pre-float release you let out in May.'

'Yeah, a little premature, given the delays in getting the float going.'

'But you did only say *hoping to float in September*.' She pushed

a copy of the press release over to him. 'As long as you…'
she stopped. 'Sorry, Finn, as long as Tiger Oil is seen to be
making progress, a positive release for September will pander
to expectations.'

'I guess.'

'The markets are jittery about the sub-prime and there's a
certain expectation of delay building in any case. We just have
to put a positive angle on your exit from the company. It will
blow Grayson out. He won't like it, but I'll handle him. He
wanted you hung out completely, but to castigate you in any
way would be too negative'

'Thanks. I appreciate that, Alexa.'

'You'd made a big thing about the patents and their value in
the May release. Was that to cover over the delays in the pilot
caused by the loss of Shufang?'

'Yeah. I guess the last PR guys took the same view you're
taking now. No offence, but I thought they'd done an OK job.
I can't quite see why the board sacked them.'

'Me neither. But, every cloud. . .' She stopped to consider
her words. 'We can play on the patent angle, since the value is
there regardless of whether you are or not.'

'I see what you mean.'

'Yes, the patents have effectively securitised your vision.'

'My loss,' he said. His shoulders pitched up in a defined
shrug.

'Sorry.'

'Not your fault.'

'Right, Finn, where do we go from here?'

'Mmm…'

'Take a look at this. Some words I've been playing with
this morning… I've included some of Grayson's already.' She
passed another sheet of paper to Finn.

He read it quickly…

TIGER OIL PLC ANNOUNCES DEPARTURE OF FINN JACKSON

Tiger Oil plc announces that its cofounder and Chief Executive, Finn Jackson, is to step down as director after a successful three years as head of the London-based Tar Sands Experimental Oil Extraction business.

Although Mr Jackson leaves the company as director and hopes to takes things a little easier, he will continue to provide consultancy services to Tiger Oil as well as to other organisations in the sector.

A spokesman for the board of Tiger Oil comments, 'Whilst the departure of Mr Jackson will be a sad loss to Tiger Oil, this will however enable the business to move forward with a clear directive coming from the Management team as well as a more strategic input from the directors. Our people are our best asset and it should be them that have a say in what direction the business takes, this will ensure we have a sound growth plan with greater opportunity for profitability.

The spokesman further stated that, 'The company's FD, Aaron Philips, will step in to the CEO position to lead Tiger Oil's IPO planned for December this year. The selection of a new Chief Operations Officer to replace the geologist Shufang Su who died in a tragic accident last year is well under way, and an appointment is anticipated next month. With solid patents in place, the new COO will be expected to waste no time in further developing the pilot project in Peace River. Reports, there, are that local management are progressing well. Following the departure of Mr Jackson the company still maintains an impressive Board of directors.

'You've been busy,' he said.

'What do you think, Finn?'

'Couple of points, really. Not sure about the *little easier* bit, sounds a bit like I've left through stress.'

'I see what you mean.'

'Also, the consultancy to Tiger Oil, I can't see Grayson buying that.'

'He won't. But it's good to leave something in for him to take out. It'll make him feel better.'

'Yeah. I like your thinking there. I think the middle bit's a bit boiler-plate. About people being an asset. We... they don't have many staff... Again the *sad loss* bit will probably have to come out; and lastly the end bit's all a bit tongue-in-cheek for me.'

'But? ...I sense a *but*, Finn.'

'No buts. Over-all I can go with this as a first draft.'

'Thanks, you've made my job easier, agreeing so quickly.'

'No. You've put some thought into it. I can see that.'

Alexa understood. She'd gained a good feel for the difficulty Finn faced – after all, she'd earned her spurs as a financial analyst. Initially she had worked for a small city bank, then in equities research at James Capel for a number of years, before she left to go into PR.

Alexa and Finn brainstormed the finer detail of the text for another half-hour or so. They needed to bend the text to Grayson's will, or he would not release it, and Finn would not receive his first payment. In the end, while Finn hadn't been completely happy, they'd at least agreed to a compromise version. Alexa e-mailed it straight out to Grayson. Finn sat with his cup, having filled it with the last of the now cool coffee.

'I've suggested the release for tomorrow afternoon, Friday. With the Bank Holiday coming up, there'll be an extra night for it to get lost in the wires,' she said, as she hit the return key on her key board.

They sat in idle chat for a few minutes. Grayson was quick to acknowledge receipt, with a short message sent from his Blackberry.

'He's promised to respond by the end of the day, Finn,' she said, reading the e-mail from her computer screen. 'There's nothing more we can do now. Why don't you catch an early train home? I am sure Aisling and the girls would be happy to see you.'

'Thanks, Alexa, I s'pose you're right, really.'

'You know I am.' She smiled at him.

'Thanks for your help.' He drank the dregs of his coffee and put the cup down. 'I'll let you get on now,' he said, rising from his chair.

'You're very welcome, Finn. I'll call if I hear anything.' She rose and walked with him to the door, and on out to the lift.

The lift arrived and Finn stepped into it. As he did so, he turned to face her. 'It's been good to see you,' he said.

'You too, Finn. Take care, and have a good weekend with the family.'

The lift doors closed and she turned to go back to her office. She was nervous. There had been something about the final text, but she couldn't put her finger on it. It was a feeling; it could have a barb in it, she just hoped it wouldn't be the case. *I'll need to think of a contingency if I'm to do all I can to help him.*

*

Saturday morning, and it had just turned eleven-thirty. Lyneth felt sluggish. She sat, alone, in the deep, soft leather of her couch. She wore her teal satin pyjamas. Legs tucked up under her, and cradling a mug of coffee, she cast her gaze ahead. Her apartment – a bright two-bedroom conversion – lay in one of Harley Street's fine period buildings. The large lounge faced the street. Three windows threw a cascade of late-August light onto a polished oak floor. She surveyed her little piece of heaven. Her calculating logic reminded her that she even owned a share of the free-hold in the building. *Such a great asset for a girl's bottom drawer*, she mused. She'd worked hard to get it.

Yet another weekend alone. Yet another bank holiday. Crap!

She didn't do holidays joyfully. She usually slunk herself away, with all the petulance of a spoilt teenager having to go visiting family. She would hole herself up with a bottle of good Polish vodka.

She liked *Zubrowka* the best.

'...you like?' The waiter had spoken in his clipped, hesitant, Polish-English.

'I like very much,' she'd replied, mimicking his accent. She'd given a smile that disarmed the Pole in an instant; he'd taken no offence. The start of a great relationship.

She had stumbled upon the *Stara Polska* restaurant, one Saturday lunchtime, and she'd immediately taken to its hand-made feel.

'I like very much,' she'd repeated, for the fourth time during her lunch that day. 'Another glash please.'

It should have been Poland, she thought, though she'd never been – it made her want to visit.

Lyneth acquired a taste for the vodka there, particularly the *Zubrowka* with its blade of Bison Grass. She reached a deal with the owners. In exchange for her regular custom, they would keep her supplied with the odd bottle or two, at cost. She'd struck a good bargain.

Lyneth occupied her weekend with loads of hot baths, and quite a few good books. Television never figured for her; she despised the quality of contemporary programming, all food for the masses.

Only after lunch – she loved her bed, with or without, but preferably with, a man – would she venture out and browse the shops on Marylebone High Street. She conceded that shopping, like for many girls, remained a passion for her. *Marylebone Village* is a *nice* place to be, she reminded herself.

The man bit? Good question. She'd not been in a decent relationship for over a year, and the one before only lasted six months. Now, with instructions for the Tiger Oil corporate manslaughter action imminent, she couldn't see how she could further any sort of relationship with Finn. She'd firmly set her sights there, married or not. Well, she mused, he didn't seem at all happy, from either a business or personal perspective. That much she'd found out.

Why the hell did he affect her so much? She rose from the couch and went to lie in her bed. Maybe one too many vodkas last night, she thought – she'd clearly woken in a more introspective mood than normal. She lay under the summer-weight duvet, cosy, but saddened.

Her journey through to professional success had not brought with it anyone to share her life with. She'd been clear in her mind for some time – she wanted someone. She wanted the happy home coming; wanted the security of knowing there would always be someone to turn to, no matter what things were like, no matter how things evolved. She wanted to share the good and the bad. But she'd not found anyone. Like the Alchemist's search, she'd not found what she left Wales to look for. She had not found what she'd developed herself for – becoming the sort of woman who would be in a position to meet the sort of man she wanted to meet. She hadn't considered she would meet him in Wales. The irony shone through. The closer she got to the men she admired, the further she got from being able to relate to them. They were uncomfortable with her success.

It had to be some form of desperation at the root of her

attraction to Finn, she reasoned. She'd learned a lot about him in the short space of lunch, despite his closing down at the end of it. She wondered why he'd done that.

Rationally, she thought, Finn's unhappy family life might leave an opening for her. He *was* attracted to her, she could sense that, but something wasn't right and she couldn't weigh it up. Logically? What could there be to stop Finn engaging with her? He looked the flirtatious type – there was something in his eyes.

She needed to keep alert. Could there be... would there be... just possibly... something stemming from the impending Tiger instructions she could bring to Finn? Something to give her an opportunity to win him over? She decided to go shopping.

*

The Flying Scotsman hurled Finn down the tracks of the East Coast mainline. The schedule for the GNER train that carried the badge of its great ancestral namesake put Finn into the city shortly after nine a.m., where it would stand to collect its passengers for the traditional ten o'clock flight to Edinburgh. Finn had taken a phone call from Aaron on the Sunday afternoon, amid the peace and tranquility of his copy of the Sunday Times. The paper lay with its sections spread liberally across the large pine farmhouse table in the centre of the kitchen. The Aga, still on despite the heat of the summer – summer days could still turn cold this year – dissipated a warm, cosy feel around the place.

'Hi,' he said, casually announcing himself to his caller.

'Finn?'

'Hi, Aaron. How's the weekend shaping up for you?

'We'd thought about the villa, but Alexa wanted to do some work here for some reason.'

'We've been having a bit of a barbecue again,' said Finn. 'Any excuse. A few friends came over. Been cleaning up most of this morning.'

'Sounds fun. How are Aisling and the kids?'

'Fine, thanks. They're all out riding. I've some peace and quiet for now. Just going through the paper.'

The weekend had been passable at home. Despite the usual threat of British summer showers and heavy breezes, the area's micro-climate proffered its local support, even offering the hamlet of Husthwaite sight of the sun. A little sun lifted everyone's spirits.

'The barbecue got the Pimms flowing,' he'd said. 'And the neighbours helped lighten the day. We even got some laughter going here.'

'Good. I am sorry it's worked out like this, Finn. I did try to talk Grayson out of it, but he wasn't for it.'

'Aisling's taken it badly of course, and the children sense something, but their friends have been round playing in the fields. . .'

'That's good.'

'Things are a bit easier, for now. Thanks, Aaron,' he'd said.

Aaron had been his usual supportive self.

'What are your plans now? Alexa told me you have a new office in the city.'

'Yeah, I'm going to try and do some consulting. Like I had been when we met. I figure, with the new contacts I've made in the last few years, I might be able to stretch a bit more out of it.'

'I wanted to mention that, Finn. Can I ask you not to contact any of our advisors, or anyone else Tiger are involved with.' Aaron did not wait for a response. 'You know how the city can be. There will be a lot of questions about your departure, and we don't want to upset anything before the float, do we?' Aaron paused, but he'd remained silent.'

'It really is in your interests too,' Aaron had continued. 'I know you'll only have a few percent left after you complete the sell, but those shares will still be worth something. Let's try to keep the launch price as high as possible. OK?'

'OK. I guess,' he said. Aaron had succeeded in stripping the edge off the weekend. He'd swallowed hard.

'I've been thinking, Finn. Alexa and I should come up to visit. We could take you and Aisling out for dinner next weekend. How about that?

Finn had lost all interest in Aaron's shallow attempts to stay concerned. 'If you feel like it...'

'You sort a baby-sitter out, and I will talk to Alexa.'

'Aaron, I've got to go, the kids are here; they're fighting outside.' There had been no-one in Finn's view out of the kitchen window by which he'd stood.

'Just a final one, Finn. Alexa's been beavering away in her study all morning; she left here about an hour ago.'

'And?' He had been interested then, but he maintained his lack-lustre tone.

'She seemed excited about something. She left saying she'd been working on your future. She asked me – if I was to call you – to ask you to pop into her office, if you're down next week.'

'Tell her I'll call. I'll probably come down Tuesday.'

'Rightio. Will be seeing you, Finn. Remember, baby-sitter!'

Having spoken with Aaron, and hearing of Alexa's request, he'd decided to catch an early train down.

Finn sat in the standard class. The near-field scenery lining the tracks tore past his vision too quickly to focus on. He sat reviewing the latest copy of *International Oil Economist* he'd received that weekend.

The Tiger Oil press release had clearly not been available

to make the issue's editorial date. But he'd printed off a few bulletins he'd found on the internet wires, during the weekend – the release had gone out unchanged. It depressed him to read it. It objectified his misery, but at least it should help draw a line under the separation, he thought. It should allow him to move forward. *Should!* But he kept his burning desire to get even.

Finn's eyes buried into an article in the IOE.

CHINA TO EXPAND CANADIAN OIL SANDS PRESENCE AIMD GREEN CALLS FOR INVESTOR REVOLT

BEIJING, July 31 (Hu Su) – China National Petroleum Corp. is to expand its cooperation with Canadian partners in developing Alberta's oil sands. However, following the drafting of a major new report that claims the carbon intensive processes involved represents an unacceptable environmental risk, green lobbyists are calling for investors to shun the controversial oil extraction projects.

China National Petroleum has concluded an extensive oil sands resource study and, earlier this year, acquired exploration leases for eleven oil blocks in Alberta, CNPC said in a statement on its Web site on July 20 2007. It marks the first time a Chinese firm has gained control of a Canadian oil sands project.

Alberta's tar-like reserves may contain 175 billion barrels of recoverable oil, second only to Saudi Arabia's 259 billion barrels, according to the Canadian Association of Petroleum Producers. But an advance draft of a forthcoming joint report from Co-operative Investments and the WWF, seen by this reporter, claims projects to extract oil from tar-soaked sands in Canada will not only result in nearly eight times more carbon emissions than conventional oil production, but will also use three times more water, destroying large tracts of the Boreal forest region.

China National Petroleum was awarded more than 250 square kilometres of oil-sands leases in northern Alberta, the Globe reported in June, citing Zhang Xin, director general of external affairs for the state-owned company, who spoke at an energy conference in Edmonton. "We will jointly explore mutually beneficial collaboration in oil sands development" CNPC said in a statement released July 20 2007.

Nearly all major oil companies remain committed to oil sands projects with Shell having announced its plans to produce over 650,000 barrels of oil daily from the Alberta oil sands by 2020. The oil majors maintain that while unconventional oils remain more expensive and carbon intensive than conventional oil, rising energy demand means a significant source of energy situated in a politically stable region cannot be ignored.

The forthcoming lobbyist's report is however aimed at generating significant support from institutional investors in the hope of increasing pressure on the oil majors, such as Shell, and now China National Petroleum, to halt plans to expand tar extraction projects.

Something, the seed of an idea, took root at the back of his mind. He busied himself for the rest of the journey finishing his copy of IOE.

Just leaving Peterborough, as the train relentlessly sought to regain its cruising speed, Finn called Alexa. She was pleased to hear from him and they arranged to meet for coffee at the Royal Exchange, at ten o'clock.

Fifteen minutes late. The Flying Scotsman slowed on its

entrance to King's Cross, pausing for nearly ten minutes in the tunnel section outside the station, waiting for a clear platform. A late departure blocked the Flying Scotsman's scheduled platform. Helpfully, at least GNER staff made information available to their passengers.

Finn mused over the interconnectedness of things. Perhaps the butterfly flapping its wings in Argentina had caused a freak gust of wind in a London suburb – a wind that prematurely scattered leaves on a pavement. After a late summer shower, the now wet leaves caused an elderly person to fall on their slippery surface, only days before she'd been due to take a train to some unknown destination. The unfamiliarity of having to travel with a wheelchair, led to a delay on platform five, as the train crew provided assistance. The inbound Flying Scotsman waited. And what of onward inter-connections? The suits, now delayed fifteen minutes – maybe more? Connections on flights to Argentina, lost? Perhaps. Perhaps not. Who could know? The delay prevents the butterfly collector, on a planned trip to Argentina, going to catch his prey.

The train restarted. The station welcomed it.

Finn decided he would take a taxi. He left the train and walked down the platform. He turned left at the barrier, to make his way to the taxi rank.

Unnoticed in the swarm of commuters and other travellers, the innocuous, heavy-set form of Scott Lindon merged with the migrating crowd a few paces behind Finn.

As Finn reached the taxi rank, Scott Lindon made judicious use of the hustle and bustle tactics of crowd-warfare. He manoeuvred himself into position just behind Finn. They mounted their waiting cabs almost simultaneously.

What had Alexa been working on during the weekend? What could she be excited about?

Finn considered the possibilities. The increasing Chinese interest in Alberta? *Christ!* He wished he'd had the IOE article in front of him when he met Grayson for the board meeting. Damn Aaron! Why the hell couldn't he have warned him... he'd known days before. Those two things would have prepared him to argue against Grayson.

Christ, I've been so naïve. Then, '...you can stop here,' he called to the cabby. They had gone past St Paul's, into Cheapside and drawn roughly opposite Old Jewry – slowed by traffic heavy. 'It'll be safer than the Bank junction.'

'Right on, Sir.' The cab pulled over.

Finn paid through the slid-back glass window and climbed out of the cab.

Twenty-five metres behind, Scott Lindon re-enacted the scene in an identical black cab. For such a heavy-set man, Scott moved with the lightness of a ballerina. As in King's Cross, Scott moved deftly through the crowd as it weaved down Cheapside in the direction of Bank.

They slowed as the crowed pulsed its way over the crossing outside the Bank of England.

Finn stopped at the lights. Traffic flowed by quickly. Crossing on the red man just wasn't worth the risk.

Behind him, Scott Lindon drew up close. Others hustled and bustled at the side of the road, waiting impatiently for a lull, or for the lights to change.

Scott judged the flow of traffic and picked his moment. A white van with no markings approached from the right. With his hands held low before him, shielded from onlookers by the crowds, Scott pushed at Finn's back.

Finn never knew what hit him. The impact with the van flung him against the barrier to the left of the crossing. He fell to the ground. His head hit the pavement with a dull thud – unheard in the background noise of the busy morning rush.

Scott slid to the right as eyes went left. He faded from sight as the crowd froze, their gaze now only on the motionless Finn.

A small pool of blood formed on the pavement under Finn's head. It seeped, slowly spreading out to the size of a dinner plate. The spell of shock, holding the crowd momentarily in its grasp, broke with the sound of a single, piercing, scream.

EIGHT

October 2007

'THE BRAIN IS A MYSTERY.' The voice suddenly rang in Finn's mind; he'd gained an awareness of sounds near him. Awareness of quite what, he could not be sure. *The brain is a mystery.* The voice again. This time, he thought – *female and young.* For some reason he could not fathom, the voice echoed still.

Darkness hung ubiquitously, like thick, heavy, treacle-covered drapes – but not quite… he sensed light, but he did not see it. He lay in bed. Still. *That's it, I'm asleep!*

'At first, there'd been little change,' the young, female voice said. 'But, you kept talking to him and he'd turn his head and look at you. That was a great step forward.'

'I know,' said a voice he remembered – another female… older this time.

'Aisling, why don't you go and get a coffee from the canteen? I'm on shift for another couple of hours. I'll come by and fetch you if I see any change.'

'There won't be any, will there.' The older voice sounded utterly dejected. 'There never is. But…'

'But, just in case, I'll come and get you. I promise.'

Aisling? He knew the name. Why? Why wasn't anybody listening to him?

79

Finn's awareness grew. More comings and goings happened around him. Light? *But, I'm in bed.* Where?

Someone… the young female voice, perhaps? …someone busied himself or herself around his bed. He felt a gentle disturbance.

He heard the noises, but, strangely, he couldn't respond in any form. He just lay there. Everything was curiously immobile. *A hangover? I'm recovering from another hangover, another late-night-early-morning drinking session in the village pub.* But he couldn't remember anything of last night. If he moved now, the room would start spinning again… wouldn't it? His head would start to thump and, no, he didn't want a thumping head. Best stay still. Don't move.

If I move, I won't like it.

Finn remained motionless.

It went dark. For how long he didn't know. The sounds faded. Voices, hushed, some not so hushed, came and went. Some talked to him, some to each other.

It grew light. Gradually. *Why is it taking so long to get over last night? Surely, someone must think it odd I'm still in bed.*

'How are you this evening, Mr Jackson?' The young voice returned.

You must think I am so rude not answering.

'Your wife will be here soon for her visit. You know? … she's been here every evening.'

Wife? Visit? Evening? He became conscious of someone touching his bed again, the sheets, and …him. Why?

'Just make sure you're all tidy for her,' said the young voice. More touching. 'There… You have a lovely wife, Mr Jackson.'

Footsteps? Then, 'No change I'm afraid,' cooed the young voice to… whom? 'His eyes have opened occasionally, but that can happen in a minimally conscious state.'

'Thank you, Mandy. I'll just sit a while,' said the voice he remembered.

The brain is a mystery. The echo. *Christ!* Move, won't you. You can't lie here all day. It must have been one hell of a night. Now *move,* you lazy bastard.

*

Finn lay motionless as Aisling took his hand yet again. She didn't know how much longer she could keep this up. Tears welled in her eyes. Silent tears fell for herself and her girls, defining rivulets down her pale, washed-out cheeks. She didn't want to bring the girls to see their Daddy lying here, like this.

He'd lain the first three weeks following his accident in the acute brain injury unit at London's National Hospital for Neurology & Neurosurgery, on Queen Square. There had been little sign of recovery. He'd sustained heavy bruising from the collision with the van and the barrier, but no broken bones. He'd also collected a hairline fracture of the skull from his flying contact with the ground. He lost a lot of blood from his head wound, but overall he'd been lucky not to hit harder. Although his wounds healed over the weeks, and Finn would occasionally open his eyes, he hadn't shown any response to stimuli. He'd entered a coma-like state of minimal consciousness.

It had not been a challenge, to convince the doctors at the NHNN to give him time to wake. Finn was relatively young and healthy, and his injuries hadn't been anywhere near as traumatic as many of their cases. With the blood-loss at the scene of the accident, it had all looked a whole lot worse. The coma-like condition appeared to be just Finn's body controlling – pacing – his recovery process. All they could do was wait.

And they waited.

After three weeks, the kind National Health Service

transferred Finn to his local hospital by ambulance. The NHNN could do little more for him. He'd arrived at York's Hospital on Wigginton Road, on the twenty-first of September. Aisling visited every evening since. She'd grown tired. Every teatime she left the girls with her parents; she would read them a short story before leaving for the hospital.

They all waited. The waiting was hard.

The kind NHS had given Finn daily therapy to stimulate his brain and keep his body in action, ensuring they exercised his muscles and joints. He would need that to recover fully.

'Aisling, why don't you go and get a coffee now? I'll watch over him for a bit. You look tired. I'll come and fetch you if I see any change.'

Aisling looked at Mandy, the question heavy in her eyes.

'I *will* come and get you, I promise,' said Mandy.

Aisling left to get her evening coffee. Finn lay motionless.

*

The brain is a mystery. He heard the young woman's voice repeating the phrase over and over. It seemed to him like some sort of alarm clock.

Move, you lazy bastard.

He made a quiet, dry, rasping noise. Finn's eyes opened, more in surprise than with any intent.

I've said something? He'd intended to say something. *OK, I'm awake!* he'd intended to say to the voice. But, whatever the noise, the effect on the voice became palpable.

'Pardon!' The surprise in the young voice shone through – sharp and clean, like morning sunlight streaming through an undraped window.

'Oh, my God! You're awake!' The young voice morphed

from cooing dove to frenetic, joyful child. She was clearly pleased. 'I've got to find Aisling,' she blustered. 'Lorraine!' she shouted, 'Come here and sit with Mr Jackson. …Talk to him, I need to get his wife here… Oh! And call the duty doctor.'

Lorraine hurried to Finn's side. 'Follow this, Mr Jackson,' said Lorraine, as she moved her raised thumb across the line of his vision.

His gaze followed Lorraine's thumb, slowly.

'Mr Jackson, you've given us all a bit of a turn.'

'Whe—re … am… I?' The words staggered and slurred their way out of his mouth – they made a quiet, dry, rasping noise. It didn't sound like him. *Jesus! My mouth's dry.* He tried again. 'Whe–re am… I?' More volume this time, but only just. For some reason it strained him to talk. He closed his eyes. Something wasn't right. But, he *had* made himself heard.

'You're in hospital, Mr Jackson …in hospital,' said the kind voice.

She might be smiling at him, he thought, but he could not see.

'Don't talk,' she said. 'Take it easy, the doctor will be here in a moment.

But I want to talk. He tried again. Eyes open. 'What happ—ened… pub… last night?' Again, the dry rasping, his voice straining, his words slurred. And he still found it difficult to hear what he'd actually said.

'Pub?' quizzed Lorraine. She looked puzzled. 'A van hit you in a road accident, in London. Do you remember?'

'No…' he said. He closed his eyes.

*

A man arrived – he heard him speak with Lorraine. Mandy

83

returned with Aisling.

The voices merged. They all seemed to be talking to him. Then at him. Then to each other. So many words, so many voices. 'Some—thing's …wrong. . .' he tried to say, but again… noise.

'He's coming round,' said the man.

A doctor? Lorraine had said doctor.

'His words are there…' the doctor continued. 'They're very slurred, but they are there, Mrs Jackson.'

Crying now. *Somebody is crying.* Someone took his hand; he remembered the touch – this hand had held his before. *The hand's wet… tears?*

Finn's eyes opened. His head still, he managed to move his eyes a little. His vision was blurred, but his gaze took in what he could, slowly. *So many people.*

His eyes closed. *No. Sleep. . . Sleep now.*

*

Gradually the periods of light and dark merged. It had been two days since he'd first managed to make himself heard. He'd passed two days like this, drifting between light and dark – two days since the alarm, his alarm. *The brain is a mystery.* Not so many people in the room now, he thought, gladly.

The blonde woman, with the voice he remembered. *Aisling?* She still held his hand. Her touch warm, not wet now, inviting memories he'd long forgotten. *Aisling.* His wife. He remembered.

The kind nurses had given him sips of water and he regained some measure of control over his voice.

'Hi. . .' he managed to say. It still strained him to speak.

'You're awake again.' She rose from her chair and stood

looking over him. She smiled. He sought her eyes and they held each other's gaze.

Aisling.

'Yes,' he said. His voice sounded unsteady, but the words came less slurred. 'How long?' he said, each syllable drawn, as if stretching out damp, coarse cloth. He'd not seen her smile for some time, he thought.

'It's been eight weeks, Finn.'

His eyes closed. 'I'm confused… What… happened? Why… why am I here? His eyes, still closed – the little boy, still trying to make it all go away.

'You were in an accident, in London. It was just after the August Bank Holiday. Do you remember?'

'Eight weeks. . .'

'Yes, Dear. You've been in a coma, you got knocked down.' Aisling recounted the story, as she knew it.

'Sleep.'

'Yes, Dear,' she said. 'You sleep. I'll be here when you wake.' She took his hand.

He drifted into sleep.

*

As the week progressed, Aisling saw Finn regain his faculties, slowly. He had no recollection of the accident, whatsoever. Gradually, he remembered other things, first the train journey and then, backwards in time, to the reason he'd been travelling. He remembered *they'd* squeezed him out of Tiger Oil. And, as he remembered, she could see the pain inside hurt him. He stayed silent for almost an hour after she'd helped him with the detail of that one.

His memory recalled jumbled thoughts.

Aisling cried. Her tears were joyful. Finn had seen her smiles through her tears, but she could read his face: he was wondering why.

To Aisling, it looked like Finn wondered *why* a lot. He'd said as much on one of her visits.

'I wonder in the dark and in the light,' he said. 'Why the hell has my life taken this turn?' His questions were rhetorical – she kept quiet. '*OK, so the going got tough…*' he'd said, 'but we'd been working things through. We all stood to get rich… Didn't we?' She did not answer him.

And then…

'When is it?'

'What, Dear?' she said. The lack of light outside suggested evening, but she had no idea of the actual time. She sat there, next to him, in the chair that had become a second home to her. She'd slept in it, read in it, eaten scraps of meals in it, and she'd cried tears in it.

'When is now?'

She could see Finn trying to get his mind to work. He needed details.

'It's Tuesday…' she paused, but sensing Finn wanted more… 'It's Tuesday, thirtieth of October.'

Finn stayed silent. But this time his eyes did not close. He stared ahead.

'It's taking you time, but you *are* getting stronger, Finn,' she said. 'The doctors are saying you might be well enough to leave in another week or so. I want you home, Finn.' She lay her face against his and kissed him. 'What's the matter, Finn? Talk to me.'

Finn's silence in his coma-like state had demoralised Aisling. His silence, now, unnerved her. She pulled away from him and dropped into the chair. She sat, waiting for the inevitable. It came.

'I've lost, haven't I?' he said, finally.

She did not answer. Tears re-appeared, swelling her red eyes.

'I've lost it all. All I worked for.' His words came clear now. He'd gained some strength in his mind at least. The body would follow.

'I don't know... I don't care.' She didn't shout. She was tired, past caring. Her voice fell quiet through the silent tears.

Finn remembered Tiger Oil. He remembered Grayson Barclay and Aaron. He remembered Lyneth and Alexa. He remembered the company float due towards the end of the year. When exactly? Aisling didn't know.

'It's nearly November,' he said. 'I have to get fit... get well. I have to get out of here. I can't do anything from here. No phone, no Blackberry. Nothing.'

Finn fell quiet. To Aisling, it seemed as though he cringed. It had struck him. He'd spent almost two whole months out of action – time he would have used to get at *them*. Two whole months. She saw the remembering set him in a depression.

'They'd demanded the sale of my shares before the float. ...It can't have happened yet,' he said, to no-one in particular. 'I have some time – don't I?'

Aisling didn't want to listen. He'd been on his way to see Alexa; she'd wanted to tell him something. There were too many women she didn't know.

'I need to see Alexa,' he said. 'She will know what's going on.'

Aisling looked across at the wall opposite. A small hair-line crack in the plaster gave her focus.

'I need to sleep,' he said. She turned and saw he had closed his eyes again.

She drew her knees up under her chin and rocked, back and forth, on the chair – like one of those child's toys. She didn't say anything. Her tears of joy morphed into tears of sadness as she sat and watched Finn's focus return. He hadn't even asked about the children.

'Jesus, Finn,' she whispered, her voice laced with hopelessness. 'The girls…' Her voice broke. Her tears streamed heavy and silent.

But Finn lay asleep.

NINE

TWENTY STEPS TOWARDS the rest of his life. Finn walked those first twenty, tentative steps on the Wednesday. He ate pureed chicken and mashed potatoes, and he began to talk with more confidence. He'd asked more questions about the past two months of his hospitalisation – he'd begun to fill the void in his memory.

'He's making miraculous leaps and bounds,' the doctor said to Aisling on her visit that night. 'Everything's returning to him. It really is like someone's hit the reset button.'

'Finn?' she said, smiling. She'd returned, resigned to her lot in life, merely another disappointed wife who lay second to her husband's career.

'Hello, Love.'

'I've brought you some books and things,' she said. She unpacked a small bag and placed its content into the locker at the side of his bed. 'I'll bring Becky and Jane tomorrow afternoon. The doctor says it'll be fine.'

'Yeah. That'll be great. How are they?' he asked, with genuine enthusiasm.

Prompted, Finn showed he *did* care about the children. He did love his daughters; she knew that.

'I've missed them,' he said.

He didn't lie; she knew that too. 'Aaron called...' she started to say.

'And?' interrupted Finn.

'He wants to come up and visit this weekend.'

'OK. Can you tell him OK, please?'

'Yes, I will,' said Aisling. She knew Finn would be hoping that Aaron would bring Alexa with him.

*

Alexa got her chance to speak with Finn. She learnt he'd continued making great progress through the week. By the Friday, he could get up, dressed and move around without assistance. And some kind soul removed the wheel-chair – the ungainly addition to his room's furniture, which appeared the previous week.

The girls visited each evening with Aisling and, although the visits got shorter – to get the girls to bed for school the next day – they got better. So did Finn's morale. The girls clearly took *fun* with them to visit. *No tonic could be better than the happy smiling faces of little children*. Finn's strength had gained daily.

The Saturday afternoon, Aisling had brought her and Aaron in to visit. It was a warm reunion. She hugged Finn and kissed his cheeks. Aaron's handshake looked a warm, two-handed affair.

'Good God, Finn,' said Aaron, 'we thought we'd lost you. You look great for someone who's been out of it for so long.' He smiled. 'You look a lot better than I reckoned you would.'

'Yeah, they've really been good to me here,' said Finn.

'Aisling called last week, to let us know you'd woken.' As he spoke, Aaron glanced over and caught Aisling's gaze. 'I've been checking in with her ever since the accident.' Aaron looked at Finn. 'Thank God you're out of it now.'

'It's great to see you up, Finn,' said Alexa.

'He's been pestering the nurses already.'

'I'm sure that's not true, Aisling,' she feigned, her retort delivered through a broad grin aimed at everyone.

Aaron hadn't needed to persuade her to join him visiting Finn. She recalled, just before Finn's accident, she'd been nervous about that press release. She'd continued to think about Finn's position ever since, but as it transpired, Finn's accident overshadowed whatever issue might have arisen. As far as the industry took any notice, Finn's exit from Tiger Oil passed as a non-event.

'Did you travel up this morning, Aaron?' asked Finn.

'Yes. Aisling's going to look after us tonight, then we're off in the morning – I've got to return to the city for an early meeting on Monday.'

'Don't remind me, Aaron.'

Alexa watched Finn's eyes flash shut, as if a sharp, stabbing pain had hit him. A little of it hit her, too.

'Sorry, Finn,' said Aaron. 'I'm not good at this sort of thing.'

'Oh, he's all right,' added Aisling. 'He's been doing nothing but talk about work. He just wants to get cracking on something soon.'

Alexa thought the touch of sarcasm in Aisling's tone went unnoticed. She stepped back, trying to hide her frustration at not being able to talk privately to Finn. Not while Aaron and Aisling were both present. Over the weeks, she'd grown concerned for Finn and his family. Although she didn't know them well, she wanted to support Finn. Despite her implicit stake in what remained her husband's business – now her client too – she wanted to help Finn get out of his mess.

'It's about time they released you, isn't it? You could have done us a barbecue since we are here,' said Aaron, attempting to lighten the effect of his previous comment.

'Don't be silly.'

'No, Alexa, didn't you know Finn will barbecue any opportunity he gets?' said Aaron.

'Yes, he's always been a bit strange that way,' added Aisling. 'He's been out in the snow with an umbrella before now. The girls think he's mad.'

'I have to be,' said Finn, laughing. 'Have you seen what happens to me occasionally?'

No one knew, quite, whether to laugh or not at his quip. Aaron broke the silence.

'Aisling, you look beat. Sorry for saying so… Can I take you for a coffee? Alexa will keep him company for a bit.'

'Yes. Thank you, Aaron. I could do with a hot drink.'

She looked like she needed a break too, thought Alexa.

'I'll be fine, Darling,' said Finn. 'You go and sit with Aaron for a bit. But watch him, he's a bit of a charmer.' They all laughed.

'Gosh, Finn, it's great to see you,' she said, after Aaron and Aisling left them. 'I've been really worried about you. How are you? Really. How are you?'

'Fine. Honest. I get headaches, but the medication's controlling them. Some big bruises, but they're fading fast, and I think my hair's growing back over the crack on my head. I had to get a haircut the other day!'

'Oh? Which one?' she asked, mustering all the apparent innocence of an angel. The ice broken, they laughed together.'

'It's great to see you too, Alexa.'

'What happened, Finn?'

'I've no idea at all… I know I'd been on my way to see you. I remember calling from the train, to say I'd be there for coffee. Something delayed the train, so I decided to take a cab. I don't know why, they're not so quick – just a whim I guess. Then… well, …then I just don't know. I can't remember a thing afterwards. It's all a perfect blank.'

'I had gone into the Exchange from my office side. I heard sirens, but there are so many nowadays I didn't give them a second thought. You just didn't turn up. I sat there for nearly an hour. I tried to call, but your phone just kept ringing.'

'How did you find out?' he asked.

'I really worried. I knew something must have happened because you'd called earlier. It wasn't until early afternoon when I got the news from Aaron. I don't know how he knew. I assume Aisling. . .'

'I guess.'

'But that's not important now.' She took his hand and squeezed it, pausing briefly before she let go. 'What are we going to do now?'

'We?' he asked, quizzically. Their gaze locked on each other for a moment.

'I know, *I'm a married man with two kids and a field full of my wife's horses to worry about,*' she said, mimicking one of his earlier comments, from before the accident. 'I mean, *we*! I want to help you get on your feet again, and out of this mess. Aaron's distracted by the Tiger Oil float. And anyway...' She shook her head once, freeing her long hair and letting it settle comfortably across her shoulders. '...it would be a conflict of interest for him. I think you need some support in the city, if you want to get into something new. Don't you?'

'Yes.' Finn shrugged.

'Well! No question then. We can be a team.' She gave Finn one of her best impish smiles – broad and generous.

'So, how's it going in Tiger Oil?'

'Ooo..., Finn Jackson, are you asking for inside information?' She laughed.

'Still a share owner here.'

'I know. Well, the flotation is scheduled for twenty-second November.'

'Christ...'

'Finn!' She hadn't expected his reaction. 'Surely you're not thinking…'

'I can't help it, Alexa, I'm always thinking,' he said, sadly. 'It's only a couple of weeks away. I guess I'm going to have to complete signing my shares over before then.'

'I know. I am sorry, Finn, I truly am.'

'It's not your fault, Alexa.'

'What's happening will happen, Finn. Don't fight *it* – fight to get better. Fight for Aisling, the girls and…'

'And?' interrupted Finn.

'And fight for me.' She smiled warmly, taking his hand again. 'I want to see you out of here – doing something productive with your life again. You're better than any Grayson Barclay.'

'You don't know me, Alexa.'

'I know you won't let me down.'

'Thank you,' he said.

They talked quietly some more, before the sound of footsteps reverberating down the corridor drew their gaze to the doorway. Aaron and Aisling were returning.

'Get well, Finn, and come and see me when you're in town,' she said. 'We'll get a plan together. Anything you need to help – just call me.'

'Alexa?'

'Yes?'

'I was travelling to see you. Aaron said you wanted to speak to me about something.'

'Yes.'

'What was it?'

'It doesn't matter now, Finn. Things are different now.' She turned to the doorway. 'Hi, you two… Do you feel better for that, Aisling?'

'Yes thank you.' Her thanks sounded genuine; her cheeks possessed more colour than before.

'I think we could all give Finn some rest now,' said Aaron.

'We can pop by quickly when we leave tomorrow.'

Typical, Alexa thought, Aaron didn't like spending time in hospitals. Just enough to say hello was his limit.

'Thanks for coming, you two. Thanks, Aisling,' said Finn.

Alexa and Aisling took their turn giving Finn a kiss on his cheek.

'Tomorrow,' they all managed to chorus.

Gathering their things, they left Finn to rejoin a book he'd been reading earlier.

*

On Wednesday, November seventh, around 8.00pm, Lyneth still sat at the desk in her office at Keaton-Jones LLP. The large, undraped, arched windows, seemingly suspended beneath the tall ceilings of the top floor office suite, brought inside something of the dark, forbidding, cold and wet atmosphere that lay in wait, beyond. She could see no incentive to go home. No incentive existed to tempt her to leave, not even while she could still reasonably expect to buy dinner somewhere on the way. Even the cosy, home-made appeal of her pet Polish restaurant could not draw her from her work. The warming vodka would wait.

Keaton-Jones received their instructions from Tiger Oil only a few weeks previously. The action, muted by Shufang Su's family, now took its form in legal due-process. Each side wrote their letters. *A lot of letters!*

The family's lawyers faced a problem, she reasoned. Parliament hadn't yet passed into law, the much vaunted Corporate Manslaughter and Corporate Homicide Act of 2007. Countless amendments had delayed its enactment. But, even so, it would restrict private prosecutions to deaths occurring in the UK and territorial waters only. It was unlikely to be retrospective; and Shufang died in 2006. Then of course, she mused, they would need to persuade the Directorate of Public Prosecutions to permit a private prosecution – no mean feat.

No, the lawyers representing Shufang's family had embarked on a pre-action fishing trip. They sought disclosure on facts they only *hoped* they could use to gain a conviction. And that would have to be under the existing common-law offence of manslaughter by gross negligence.

There was a chance – they knew it. To do this, the family's team first needed to establish the company owed a duty of care to Shufang. Unfortunately, for Tiger Oil, their employment of Shufang provided the only justification required. The complication arose because the Company's insurer refused to award the family the full amount of death benefit. They cited, in their defence, Shufang's culpability. The accident report claimed Shufang had been on site, out-of-hours, and without appropriate safety cover. *That,* Lyneth mused, *provided the real reason for the action arising now, and not following the accident.* There would have been little to gain in an earlier action. But, now? Now, with the company floating on the stock market… well, now, it was a different matter entirely. Tiger Oil would be able to pay.

Lyneth looked through the background notes again. Shufang had been the ops director – an oil-professional, experienced and qualified. She would have been fully aware of the site safety protocols; she'd clearly flouted them, and to her peril. Tragic, yes, but the insurance company's refusal to make a full payment, while unsavoury, didn't break any law. They'd made an offer of fifty thousand US dollars, plus the costs incurred in repatriating Shufang's body. The family took insult – they had suffered a severe loss of face.

Lyneth reflected on the family's team. They would have a job proving anything beyond a duty of care. Gross negligence meant they would need to prove Tiger Oil's conduct had been criminal. But *The Law...* her law, required a guilty mind when committing a criminal offence. How on earth did they expect to establish a guilty mind? Who could they pin the guilty badge on?

Lyneth stood up from her desk and walked over to the book case lining the entire right-hand wall of her office. She moved along it slowly, deliberately – her right hand raised, fingers outstretched, touching the spines of the books as she glanced at their titles. She knew what she looked for and where to find it. But she continued, slowly, enjoying the sensation as – in passing them – her fingers caressed each of the bindings in turn. She loved books.

Her tattered university copy of Mozley and Whiteley's Law Dictionary covered neither *guilty mind* nor *controlling mind*. Next, she went to her precedents on manslaughter. She found the test set out in Lord Denning's 1956 landmark ruling in case of *HL Bolton (Engineering) Co Ltd v TJ Grahams & Sons Ltd*.

> *A company may in many ways be likened to a human body. It has a brain and nerve centre which controls what it does. It also has hands which hold the tools and act in accordance with directions from the centre. Some of the people in the company are mere servants and agents who are nothing more than the hand to do the work and cannot be said to represent the mind and will. Others are directors and managers who represent the directing mind and will of the company, and control what it does. The state of mind of these managers is the state of mind of the company and is treated by the law as such.*

The family's lawyers must be trying to taint the whole company with an intention. But, on what basis? Whom did they think of as the controlling mind? *Yes, they fished!* Their letters suggested nothing more than a concoction of circumstance, idle threat, assumptions, hearsay and leading questions. It never failed to amaze her: professional lawyers, all having been through similar training and qualification to her, resorting to such methods in the lack of any proper evidence. They appeared to be spinning the thing out; it would cost the family dear. Oh, yes, she'd take a good bet on it.

The only possible route lay in Denning's caveat. While it made it virtually impossible for any business over a reasonable size to be successfully prosecuted, it was not so for small companies – those with easily identifiable management structures. Tiger Oil is a small company, she reasoned. If they could pin anything on any of the directors, or cast their credibility in doubt, they may just have a case. They would certainly have enough to tie the firm up in adverse publicity for some time. She needed to be convinced none of the directors had anything to hide.

News of Finn's accident devastated Lyneth. It'd been over two months now, and she'd done what she did best – she buried herself in her work. Only when she sat at home, did she dwell on the might-have-beens of yet another potential relationship.

In the last two weeks, she'd been working hard on collecting evidence to counter the expected Shufang Su claim. But, now, she worked on a delicious high. The previous week, when Aaron Philips called her with some information, he'd mentioned Finn coming out of his coma, and his progress since. Aaron said he'd be going up to visit him at the weekend.

That was last week.

This Wednesday evening and the high hadn't abated. She knew she needed to keep alert to anything arising from the Tiger instructions she could take to Finn. *He's going to need every bit of help he can get.*

So, there she sat. No incentive to return home, despite knowing she could take her papers with her – at least some of them.

It got later. Lyneth now sat studying the accident report from the Canadian authorities. The report presented a time-line of events, of sorts. The investigating officer went to interview the Tiger Oil managers in their Peace River hotel, the morning after the accident. The officer had interviewed Scott Lindon, who she didn't know – apparently a sort of roving technical manager who spent much of his time on site in Canada – and Jonathon Long.

Aaron had provided her with a little detail on Jonathon Long. Jonathon, a close friend of Aaron's, also worked with him as a consultant at Henley Oil. Jonathon, with almost thirty years in the oil industry, first entered as a technical apprentice before going on to university to study geology. He'd worked extensively in the UK and Netherlands' sectors of the North Sea, and played a key role in the appraisal success of the Ravenspurn North gas field. More recently, Jonathon consulted for BHP Biliton on the exploration of a major oil field in the Algerian Berkine Basin. Aaron brought Jonathon into Tiger Oil as a technical non-exec. He'd held a similar role in a South African company.

An innocuous accident report. She tossed it onto the desk in front of her. Leaning back in her chair, she played "what ifs" in her mind. What if this? What if that? What if someone had lied? If the other side could establish the report's conclusions had been based on lies... then what? *What if either this Scott Lindon or Jonathon Long had lied.*

Lyneth reached for the report again. Something lay in the dark recesses of her mind. She read:

> *At approximately 2.15 p.m. MST, Mr Jonathon Long, a director of Tiger Oil, called his fellow director, a Mr David Kail, in the UK. He informed him of the situation...*

Why? Why not Finn, the CEO? Or even Barclay? Why call another non-exec in the first instance? Or did he try the others, and simply couldn't get through? If she could ask the question, she damn well knew someone else could too. Then the time, Canada time, Mountain Standard Time no less – it sounded grand, but what difference did that make?

Lyneth turned to her computer and Googled *MST*. She received her answer quickly: GMT less seven hours – around nine-fifteen our time. Why so late? Couldn't he get through from the actual site to report the accident? Did he have to wait until he reached the hotel in Peace River?

She had questions for the board of Tiger Oil. Hadn't Aaron mentioned David Kail being away on a fishing holiday in Scotland? If there could be any chance the opposition might prove a director lied to the Canadian authorities during their investigation, then... well, *then there would be a real case to answer*. At this stage, the question of whether such a case could bring down Tiger Oil's board remained mute.

Christ! If the board could be culpable in some way, could Finn be? He'd been CEO at the time. The family's manslaughter action could draw him in, just by implication. The possibility catapulted Lyneth into a dilemma. Should she cut her losses and forget her interest in Finn? She fought her emotions with rationality.

No! No facts suggested Finn was involved. Nevertheless, she did need to get some answers to her questions, and it would be best if she proceeded quickly. ...Quietly though, without raising anyone's suspicions. *Well, I can at least tell Finn about the possibility of a case*. With the company floating soon, any rumour of a court action would affect the share price. *Maybe Finn can use that knowledge to his advantage*.

Like a legal Rottweiler with a new bone to worry, Lyneth smelt blood.

The inhospitable darkness lying in wait outside seemed to

creep, inescapably inwards, towards her. It reminded her she still had to get home. She checked her watch – gone ten. *Home and vodka!* She needed to do some more investigative work yet, but at least she now knew in what direction to go.

*

On Saturday morning, Aisling drove Becky and Jane into the car park of York's Wigginton Road Hospital. They left an hour later with Finn.

He'd made excellent progress and, barring the recurring headaches, now thankfully on the decrease, he felt able to recommence life. He looked forward to returning home.

The doctor's last words echoed in his mind. *Just take it easy. Come in mid-next week, and we'll see how you've fared at home. If you're OK, I'll consider writing you up fit for some light work. Just take it easy. If you get tired doing something – stop doing it. No sense in killing yourself recovering now, is there?*

'Daddy's home, Daddy's home,' the girls erupted in chorus as they sat in the rear of the Landrover Discovery, the large vehicle a necessity for pulling the horse-box.

'Ssshh. …Quietly girls, Daddy isn't so far from you. You needn't shout at him. Remember Daddy still gets headaches. So please, girls. Quietly please.'

The family, at least the children, seemed glad to have him in their fold again. He reached his right arm out and rested his hand on Aisling's thigh. He closed his eyes for the journey to the house.

'Home sweet home,' said Aisling. 'We're here, Dear.'

His eyes stayed closed.

He heard the sound of Aisling getting out of the Discovery, then the sound of her attending to the girls. The rear doors clunked. Little footsteps crunched the gravel of the drive, as Becky and Jane ran round to open his door for him. Home.

*

By Tuesday, thirteenth November, Finn began to feel sorted – both mentally and physically. He'd gained strength; he was less weak by evening times, even after spending time with the girls, when they had returned home from school.

But, as Finn grew stronger, he grew edgier. That Tuesday afternoon, at around two-thirty, Lyneth called his mobile – new phone, old number; the old cell smashed when he'd hit the ground. Disorientated for a moment by the unfamiliar layout, he let it ring more than he intended – the shrill tone threatening to invoke a headache.

'Hi, Finn. How are you?' asked Lyneth, with a clear note of concern.

'Fine, how are you? …You heard then?'

'Of course. You don't think I've been ignoring you, do you? I've tried to hold off calling – to give you time to recover. … It's just Aaron mentioned you were up and about now. Thank God. …I've worried about you, Finn.'

Weariness overcame Finn. He recalled his annoyance at failing to keep a distance from Lyneth the last time they met. This was his home and he wasn't comfortable talking to her. He caught sight of Aisling looking through at him, from outside his study door. He felt even less comfortable.

'Lyneth, it's a little difficult to talk right now.'

He could see his body language and guarded conversation weren't lost on Aisling. He knew she couldn't hear the full conversation, but he suspected she knew it was a woman. *Aisling's mind is probably in overdrive.* It had been, before the accident. He knew that – his frequent trips to London did not help matters. *She suspects something, but she doesn't know anything.*

'Sorry, Finn, I couldn't hold back much longer. I had to say something. Tiger Oil is completing its AIM float next week. You do know, don't you?'

'Yeah, I know.'

'Well, did you know Shufang's family is considering bringing an action against them for corporate manslaughter?'

'Aaron mentioned it, but I've not seen anything public about it.'

'You won't. But it seems likely there *is* a case to answer.'

'There's a what?' The surprise shook him. 'How come? . . .' He fell silent for a few seconds only. 'But, I thought...'

'I know what you *might* have thought, Finn. I'm pretty sure the others are thinking the same also. Damn it, it'll be risk-assessed in the flotation documents. But if I can find a chink in the armour, I'm damn sure the other side will find it too, if they haven't already.'

'What are you saying, Lyneth?'

'I'm saying... I expect the other side to lodge an action with the court before too long – though probably not until after the float. They'll have worked it out... they can cause more damage waiting until after.'

'Christ!'

'Yes, I know.'

'How sure are you?'

'I'm gathering more evidence at the moment, to prove it either way. But, in any event, I'm sure there might be enough of an argument to create a significant entanglement in the courts, at least until they sort it. I'm thinking six months to a year.'

Finn whistled.

'If they raise the action and there is no case, it would still have an effect. I think, with the court's workload at present, it might take a month or so just to throw it out.'

'This is inside information, Lyneth. Why are you telling me?'

'You mean despite my high legal principles, Finn?'

'And some.'

'I don't like bullies, and you need a break. Simple.' Lyneth fell silent a moment. 'Listen, Finn, I know it's not easy to talk now, and God knows this is not the sort of conversation we should be having on the phone… When do think you'll be in town next? We could meet,' she said. She sounded hopeful.

This time he could see a meeting would be good. He started to doubt his earlier wariness. Maybe he'd been wrong to suspect Lyneth may have been working for Tiger Oil – as he'd first thought. Or is there some other, bigger game in play?

He wanted to see where all this would lead, but he would still be cautious with Lyneth. After all, he mused, he had practice in keeping an emotional distance from attractive women.

'I have a check-up next week. If that's OK, I'm planning to get down sometime soon.'

Finn's head buzzed. He now possessed some real inside information. He might be able to use it.

*

Finn spent the rest of the week alternately resting and working in his study. He tried to keep occupied; he needed to get his brain working again. The news about Tiger Oil set him on a path of hope.

He recalled the article on the increasing Chinese interest in Canada, and re-read it. Surely, it could only be a good time for Tiger Oil, couldn't it?

He stood convinced there could be no case to answer in the court. He'd seen the accident reports; the board had discussed them in detail. The directors were all present and they'd all concurred, it had been a tragic accident. Shufang should not have been on site at the time of her accident. They'd all been at a loss to understand why she'd been there at that early hour. The family could not hold them – Tiger Oil – collectively accountable for the actions of the Insurer. Even the lawyers advising on the float had accepted the low risk.

He mulled around an idea. Let it go to court. Tiger Oil would bounce back all the stronger for the Chinese interest and the increasing price of oil. Any impact of the misjudged legal action would be short lived. He saw a window to work in. He had a God-given opportunity to get at Grayson Barclay.

'I might have known,' said Aisling; her words held a bitter-sharp edge that sliced cleanly into the silence of his study. She stood in the doorway, glowering. 'For Christ-sake, Finn, can't you just accept it?'

'I suppose you'll never be happy with me.' His voice held a strong note of resignation. He'd given up, in his mind, a long while ago.

'Why can't you just get a job locally, Finn? Why? I need you here – the kids need you here! But, OH NO! All you can bloody well do is sit here in your crappy little world – *Finn, the great businessman!*' Her head shook as she spoke. 'You lost, Finn. Accept it.'

'I can't.'

'I thought you'd got it when I took you to sign your shares over yesterday. What did the guy say? Your accountant, wasn't he? *Two and a half percent left you on track for nearly three hundred thousand when they float next week.* That's a result, Finn; can't you be happy with that.'

'They've taken three million from me, Aisling. It's all I've worked for – it's all *we've* sacrificed. Those last shares only cover our mortgage. And we won't be able to touch them; they're locked-in for eighteen months.'

'Great bloody cop-out, Finn. You're just oblivious to us, aren't you?

As oblivious as you have been of me… he wanted to scream at her.

'Oblivious to what we need…' she continued. 'We don't figure, do we?' Her anger subsided, in its place she, too, displayed resignation again. 'You don't know how much I prayed you'd wake a different man, Finn. Every night I prayed, as you lay there. I wished. . .'

Tears welled in her eyes – he heard them in her breaking voice. She turned and left him to his space.

Perhaps, if she didn't spend so much time with her frigging horses… *If she wants to keep them, she's going to have to let me get on my feet and earn a living again.* His thoughts welled inside him, like a sudden and unwelcome bout of indigestion spiked by conscience. He needed to get away from the house. Aisling hemmed him in. *She's never been good at controlling her stress.*

He needed to get to London to meet with Lyneth and Alexa, to find out what they knew. Christ, how long to that bloody check-up?

TEN

THE CITY BUZZ welcomed Finn like an old friend. It reached out and grabbed him. It hung on with the passion of an over-large, unshaven, unkempt Russian barman greeting a long-lost, favoured customer with a huge bear-hug and kiss. He'd seen that happen, at sea – in the days of a communist Russia. A big bear of a Russian seaman, overjoyed at the friendship he'd found in the bar of Finn's ship. The Russian went round each of the British officers in turn. Finn, a young cadet at the time, stepped back in fear of the Russian crushing him with kindness. He thought, a little sardonically, he really wouldn't welcome a bear-hug and kiss from any Russian – even now.

Finn liked the City. He liked it a lot. It held his promise of enchantment. After years of travelling at sea, and across some of the world's great oil fields, he was strangely at home in London. Even his house in Yorkshire didn't quite feel like home; it certainly didn't feel warm now.

He loved the anonymity of it all. The city. It was what he couldn't see, hear or know that fascinated him – the enchantment of the garden he could, as yet, barely glimpse. The unknown attracted him; it held his attention. The comings and goings of people enmeshed in the complexity of the big city's life. The meetings, the deals ...the assignations even. He smiled to himself... London, where you could find just about anything going on – if you knew when and where to look; everything could be found here, all going on right under everybody's gaze. Many people simply didn't know where to look, didn't need to look, or simply chose not to look. But he was not part of that garden yet.

He held his own theory. What you didn't know, but attracted you, held the secrets of progress – and the risks. *Why are we attracted to anyone or anything?* It all boiled down to there being someone... something we wanted to get to know better. Someone or something we didn't know, but we *felt* we needed to. Feelings came before knowledge, before truth. *But I didn't feel this coming, did I?* A wry smile touched his lips.

The city buzz, though, reflected a tightening collar – a pull on the leash from the great Gods of fiscal constraint. Finn read it in the Financial Times; he heard it spoken in Starbucks. But, despite the growing fiscal fuss, London maintained its aura as a king amongst financial capitals – a sublime temple to excess. The danger inherent in *the* City lay in wait, ready to pounce on the unprepared. Risk. Finn admitted it to himself – he thrived on risk. It had been why he hadn't sensed his fall coming. He'd not been open to the feeling. He'd already been seduced by the enchantment. Three million for starters – some seduction.

Risk has two sides, he mused. Just over two months ago, he'd been on the verge of claiming himself a multi-millionaire, well... at least on paper. He'd made it; the door started to open before him. In his mind, he could see his yacht in St Katherine's marina, the mortgage paid and, yes... time for the family again. He hadn't been looking to feel anything bad.

And today?

Today, Thursday, Tiger Oil shares opened for their first day's trading on AIM. He'd checked that morning, on the train.

They'd opened, as expected, at twelve and a half pence a share, valuing the company at just shy of thirty million pounds. The company had placed one hundred and two million one-penny ordinary shares at a price of ten pence. They'd raised a cool ten point two million pounds for Tiger Oil.

Finn now held only two and a half percent, but they amounted to a respectable three hundred and ninety grand. Not bad. But, a mere two months ago, he'd owned twenty-five percent and, at today's price, he'd have been worth nearly four million pounds. Today it became concrete. Grayson Barclay: *thief.* He'd stolen over three and a half mill' from Finn – half a mill' more than he'd first calculated. He'd felt sick on the train travelling to King's Cross – sick to the core. His Blackberry screamed the price at him. Taunting him. Goading him.

Risk. Yes, risk had two sides to its equation, and he now sat on the wrong side of the divide; the door locked before him. He *felt* bad now. And, moreover, he knew it as a truth.

*

Finn had called Lyneth on the train journey down; they decided to meet at Gatti's. As he climbed out of Moorgate tube station, the chill of the late-November air slid round his neck, snake-like, as if a constrictor, curling itself about its prey. He instinctively gathered himself further into his overcoat. He was cold. He tried not to think about doctor's warnings – about not pushing himself too hard, too quickly.

The neurologist gave him a tentative OK on Tuesday, two days ago, and only ten days after his release from hospital. *OK'd for light work.* Finn wasn't sure what constituted light work. He'd horrified Aisling, telling her he'd be going down to London, but she'd concluded, a long time ago, when he set himself on something, it would be best to just give him enough rope.

'. . .One day you're going to hang yourself, Finn, and I won't be there to bury you,' she'd said.

'Just take things easy, Mr Jackson,' the neurologist said.

Now, Thursday, he entered the restaurant. It didn't feel like two months ago. It seemed a lifetime since his last visit with Lyneth. Suddenly, his heart raced, as if struck by a panic attack. He became conscious of a strange, detached sensation, as if he stood watching someone else step, with trepidation, into the unknown.

Settling himself… 'I have a lunch with Miss Jones, Miss Lyneth Jones. …I believe she has a reservation.'

'One moment please, Sir.' The *Maitre d'* checked his reservations. 'Ah, yes …I see she is already here. …Please, Sir, follow me.' The *Maitre d'* turned and led the way.

This time Lyneth did not remain seated.

By some fluke – or, he thought, it could have been her looks and a flash of her eye lashes – she'd procured a table in the same off-bar alcove, this time opposite to their last table. He didn't know how, but she'd done it.

Lyneth stood up from the table. She almost ran the three metres to meet him; brushing the *Maitre d'* aside, she took Finn's hand. She couldn't stop her smiles, as broad as he'd seen from her. As he'd noted the last time they'd been together in the restaurant, her lithe movements were not lost on the other customers. Again, he felt the growing sense of pleasure from the situation in which others saw *him* as an object of envy.

'You look great, Finn.'

'Thank you – then I should probably feel stronger than I do,' he said. 'I reckoned on OK… perhaps middle to average.'

He let his gaze traverse the room; the motion of his eyes beckoned Lyneth to do likewise. She did, with no hesitation. She smiled, knowingly; the effect of her sudden movements on the other men were not lost on her, either.

'Do you think...' whispered Finn, as he stepped forward to hold Lyneth's chair for her to sit again. 'Do you think they...' his gaze traversed the room again, '...would want to be in my shoes this morning ...having just lost three and a half million?'

'Maybe,' she sang, striking a philosophical note with her musical, Welsh lilt. 'Maybe they're thinking, if they've just lost so much, there's nothing more to lose bumping you off to get me. People have killed for less,' she said, laughing.

They were through their single course and down to the last two glasses of wine before either broached the inevitable topic of Tiger Oil's potential court case.

Fatigue plagued him. *Surely Lyneth can see I'm tired.* Yet there she sat, looking as though she wanted to eat him. Maybe she'd just expected the worst; seeing him would surely have been a relief. She'd certainly seemed thrilled to see him again. Did she sense his weariness and understand? If she did, it would explain why she seemed happy just to talk about this and that. *But, now...*

'You do see, don't you, Finn? What I've told you about, could have a great impact on Tiger Oil, now it's a public quoted company.'

'You sure it's not general knowledge yet, or at least public info somewhere?'

'Yes, I'm sure. The other side wouldn't want anyone to know just yet, since they're still preparing their case. They've been struggling with facts, but I've received another letter from them this week. It looks like they've picked up on the same questions I did. The accident report relies heavily on the statements of Jonathon Long and a Scott Lindon. Do you know Lindon well?'

'No, not really. Met him a couple of times out there, on-site and in oily clothes, or wearing a thick Parka — that sort of thing. A stocky guy I think, but I'm ashamed to admit I probably wouldn't recognise him in front of me now. One of the others recommended him, and Shufang did the hiring out in Peace River.'

'Well, the other side are looking to undermine the credibility of Jonathon and Scott Lindon, so they can argue the report is some form of whitewash. I reckon they are just lining their ducks up at the moment. It won't be long though, before they come out with their duck guns blazing.'

'Christ! You sure you're sure?'

'As sure as I can be in this town,' she mimicked, in a western accent; she made a poor substitute for a female John Wayne. She laughed at her inept impersonation.

They both managed a look into each other's eyes, smiling. Lyneth's head slightly, and now characteristically, tilted to one side. The look lasted longer than Finn would have credited. It became uncomfortably long. He broke eye contact first.

'I've been thinking of an idea,' he said at last. 'The oil price is rising and, with Tiger Oil, there's the added interest of China in the Canadian oil-sands; the share price is going to be fairly solid, if not on the up.'

'I agree. I'm no financier, but what you say is logical.'

'But this...' He paused to take a drink, weighing up whether or not he really should be having this conversation with Lyneth. He relented. She'd brought the information to him. 'But this is big enough to rock the price of Tiger's shares – it's such a young company. Despite its capital position now, a big case would severely dent its cash resources. I'm sure Tiger's insurance covers were minimal, if they existed at all. We had trimmed all our expenses.'

'What are you thinking, Finn?' Her eyebrows dipped as her eyes narrowed. She looked at him quizzically.

'I take control of the situation,' he said.

'By?' she said.

'Well, if you're right about there being enough doubt

to initiate an action, then before long it will be common knowledge. An announcement will need to be made and we can expect a negative shock to the price.'

'And?' Lyneth, with her logical mind, appeared to be following his argument. A look of acute interest replaced her quizzical expression.

'Suppose we had shares to sell. If we sold a big bunch when the news became public, it would set off a panic reaction. Others would sell and drive the price further down.'

'You want to short Tiger Oil!' Lyneth rocked back in her chair and gave an almost imperceptible whistle. She fell silent.

'Look...' he said, leaning forward. He spoke with an unnecessary air of defiance. 'I was CEO at the time. I've read all the reports. We discussed it all in detail at board level. There is no case. But, as you said, it could take a month or so to clear up. While it's being sorted, all the doubt will play out in the market and the share price.'

'But what... just... well, what if there is a case, Finn? I mean... I told you, I had questions. The other side have questions. What if either Jonathon or this Scott Lindon lied to cover something up?'

'Cover what up, Lyneth? Have you found anything? I'm telling you, there can't be anything. This could be a perfect short.'

'I dunno, Finn...'

He heard concern dragging in her voice, like the heavy feet of booted Welsh slate-miners dancing in a dewy meadow.

'I just don't want to see you hurt any more,' she said. 'Don't get me wrong...' She looked like she wanted to reach out and take his hand. 'I don't think the legality of shorting with inside knowledge is a problem here,' she continued. 'I think we can work that out...'

'And your principles?'

'I've told you, Finn, these guys are greedy bullies. They

thought nothing of stealing your shares from you. But the stakes are higher now, Finn. Much higher.'

'Yeah, the company's value is standing at around thirty million now.'

Lyneth gave another little whistle. 'Geez, Finn. Are you sure you still want to be messing around with them? They have much more to lose now, don't they?'

'I don't know what else to do, Lyneth.' His tone held a note of desolate sadness. 'It's a cancer eating at me. I just have to cut it out. I have to get even somehow.'

Lyneth reached out and put her hand on his. The instantaneous warmth of her touch reached into him. She held it there, briefly. She took her hand away again, slowly; it looked to him as though she'd surprised herself. The chemistry between them made him uncomfortable. *There's risk here, with this woman.* He sensed that he had affected her, too. …Shorting stock on insider knowledge? *She would never have condoned that a few months ago. What's happening here?*

'There's a problem,' he said, breaking the spell.

'Sorry, Finn, I got distracted, my Blackberry just vibrated.'

It had been a quick response from her, he thought, but she'd lied about the Blackberry. 'Yeah… there's a problem,' he said. 'I've no idea how I can get hold of enough shares to short.'

'Some problem.'

'Guess so. If I could get hold of ten to fifteen percent I think I could work it.'

'But what do you know about dealing?'

'Problem number two, I'm afraid. I know diddly-squat, zero, zilch, nothing in fact. But I can learn.'

'Christ, Finn, you're an optimist,' she said. 'And what about financing? I know you borrow shares to short, but that will still cost, won't it? And you've got no money.'

'Numero trois!'

'You've thought it all out then,' she said, laughing.

114

'Yeah, still working the fine points through.' He smiled.

Lyneth seemed to consider his idea for a moment. 'You're serious about this aren't you, Finn?'

He made sure he held her gaze; he wanted her in no doubt about his intent. 'Yeah,' he said.

Lyneth looked thoughtful again. What was she thinking? Were her feelings playing tricks, like his? She was a logician – the logic of legal argument. She was the legal Rottweiler. *This is crazy.*

Lyneth broke the spell this time. 'Well then, I will do what I can to help.'

She looked like she wanted to touch him again.

'What next, Finn?' she asked.

He smiled at her again. A grin broke out. His lips parted and widened. His eyes shone brighter than they had a right to. He was ready for a fight. 'Next we attack my problems. One, two, three! Have you met Alexa?'

'Alexa Stuart?'

'Yeah.'

'No, we've not actually met yet, though I have exchanged a couple of e-mails. She's handling Tiger Oil's PR, isn't she?'

'Yeah.'

'Won't it be a conflict for her?'

'That's for me to handle. In theory, yes, but I had a good chat with her the other week, when she and Aaron visited me in hospital. She wants to help me too.'

Was that a look of jealousy flashing through her eyes? *Interesting.*

'Help is one thing, Finn. Helping you to bring the value of her husband's company crashing down is another.'

'It's only a short term thing… I just need to get something more for my loss. I won't be attacking the company directly. Once the action clears the courts, as you say, and the share price rises again, I will have made a few bob more than

115

Grayson bloody Barclay intended! Not perfect, but it'd be a good result. All their shares will bounce back. I'll be profiting through legitimate trading, not at Aaron's expense.' He felt good. He was thinking now. 'Lyneth?'

'Yes, Finn?'

'Thank you.'

She blushed slightly. 'I'm going to the ladies,' she said. '…I'll get the bill. Honestly, Finn, you should probably get some rest. Are you going straight home, or staying down overnight?'

'Thanks. I guess I'm looking tired. …Still recovering really. No, I'm staying down tonight. I'm travelling light though.' He didn't have a case with him.

Lyneth got up and left him with his thoughts.

He'd enjoyed the meeting, more so than anticipated. He'd not expected her receptiveness to his ideas; he'd imagined her principles would have intervened.

For him, this was no question of morals or ethics, but he did feel up against his own risk appetite. It was a big bet the share price would slide before recovering. He had no cash, and little chance of gaining any form of credit. He would need to find someone willing to trade the position for him. Who the hell could he get? He knew, with few friends in the City, he could only really turn to Alexa; she held the potential key. He just hoped…

Lyneth returned. She'd paid the bill. She came up, past her seat, to his side. He stood. Buoyed by the moment, he moved closer to her. She placed an arm on his shoulder, drew closer and kissed his cheek. He turned his head imperceptibly closer to return the kiss. His lips brushed her cheek. His arm involuntarily moved to her waist and, the muscles in his arm contracting, he drew her even closer.

They both released, the electricity of the moment passed.

'Call me,' she cooed, her voice now deeper and sexier than he'd heard it before.

'I will,' he said, without hesitating.

She turned and left. It seemed as if the gaze of a thousand eyes followed her out.

He took a deep breath, sat down, and lifted the phone from his pocket. Sliding the cover open, he selected Alexa's number from the address book and pressed call. He let out a deep, slow sigh. He waited for the call to connect.

'Hello, Finn,' bubbled Alexa. 'This is great …just thinking about you.'

'Hi, Alexa, I don't believe that for a second.'

Despite the telephone being an intermediary, he could feel her laugh at the other end of the line. *She's a real tonic*, he thought. 'Are you free later?' he asked.

'Oh dear. Sorreeeee, Finn, I've just fixed to meet another client. Damn! Oh, if only you'd called earlier…'

'Can you talk at the mo? Is it convenient?'

'What's on your mind, Finn? You sound quite chirpy – sorreeeee again, didn't mean it in a bad way.' Her laugh deepened.

'I want to ask you a favour.'

'Of course, Finn, you know you only need ask. Fire away.'

'I know you're well connected in the city. I'd like to tap into your network if I can.'

'Who do you want, Dear? Go on, rub the lamp and ask!' She was ever playful.

'I need to talk to someone who can help me short some stock.'

Silence. Alexa's ripostes usually came as quick and as sharp as a rapier. The silence spoke volumes.

'Finn! You want to short Tiger Oil, don't you? What do you know? Jesus, Finn, it's Aaron's company… I know you're upset, but…'

'You can't… you won't help? …It's OK, I shouldn't have asked. I'm sorry.'

'Anything else, Finn, *anything*. I just can't, you know… don't you?'

'Look, I'm really sorry; I shouldn't have said anything on the phone. I wanted to meet with you, to tell you…'

'Finn… no.'

'I wanted to tell you how it would all work; it won't hurt Aaron. He's my friend. You're my friend. Christ! I'm so sorry, Alexa. . .'

'I'm sorry too, Finn. I just can't see it. I can't see it,' she said.

He'd upset her; he heard the change in her voice. He'd upset her because she couldn't help. He'd been wrong to presume.

'I'm in town tonight. Let me call you tomorrow, Alexa. See if we can meet for coffee or something?'

'I'm sorry, Finn, I have to get going.'

'OK. I'll call?' He felt as if he'd had to ask.

'Yes.'

Alexa ended the call. Finn took the phone away from his ear. He sat a moment, looking at it in his hand. 'Christ! What now?' he said to himself.

ELEVEN

ALEXA'S KEY SLID into the lock of her apartment door, silently. It was six-fifteen. She'd had enough of the office for the day; she hadn't achieved much since Finn's call. Her mind lay awash with emotion: anger, disappointment, regret. They stirred within her, concocting a froth of sadness. It rose throughout the afternoon; from the pit of her stomach, it brought a bitter taste to the back of her throat. Why, Finn... WHY? She'd wanted to help – anything but this.

Her immediate reaction to his idea had been to imagine the effect of a falling share price on her husband's shares. Despite being an ex-analyst, she hadn't been able to objectify Finn's plan in the space of that short telephone call. It had been a crap afternoon. She'd done nothing, thought about nothing, since. She knew it could have worked as Finn suggested, and now she'd failed him.

Feeling low, she turned the key and opened the door slowly. As she crossed the threshold to the apartment she heard a voice in conversation, but not loud enough or distinctive enough to hear the words being spoken. She wasn't alarmed, just surprised. She wasn't expecting Aaron to be at home this evening. She'd set her mind on some music, a bottle of wine, and perhaps one of the M&S ready meals she kept in stock.

Alexa entered quietly, not out of deference to Aaron's conversation, merely through the practised, graceful movements of someone used to effortlessly floating around. She placed her handbag and keys on the small console table in the apartment's hallway. She removed her coat and placed it on its hanger on the adjacent coat stand. She hadn't called out; she didn't want to disturb Aaron. She could hear him talking, through the open door to the lounge.

'…we can't try it again, for Christ's sake.'

Aaron sounded irritated – his words discernible, now, as she approached the doorway. She slowed her forward progress, curious. She possessed a natural proclivity for nosiness, and she'd a God-given opportunity in front of her at that moment.

'We got lucky. The damn fool over-stepped the mark. What did he think he would achieve? Did you give the go ahead?'

This is getting interesting.

'What was the brief?' snapped Aaron.

Whomever he has on the other end of the phone must have pissed-him off a bit. It wasn't usual for him to be so short with anyone.

'Christ, but it was so busy… The bloody idiot.'

He hardly ever used profanity either. *Mmmm….* The more she considered his words, the more interesting it all seemed. She backed up a little, instinctively, in case she needed to retreat into one of the bedrooms. She leant against the hallway wall, just close enough to hear Aaron's words. *He can't have heard me come in.* He would never speak on the phone about business with her in the same room. He would go for a walk.

'Look, we're businessmen, not crooks. We made a mistake last time. You know I voted against it. We can't go round acting like that every time we get a problem.

Last time? What on earth did he mean, last time?

'I know judgement was taken in the heat of the moment but…'

Last time? What did he mean, *last time?* Of course he's a

120

businessman, she thought. Surely he's not got himself mixed up in some shady deal. She knew Aaron poked many fingers in many pies. He held board-membership of at least seven offshore companies. For the most, he'd set them up for wealthy clients who sought tax-efficiency.

Her mind worked overtime, conjuring all sorts of possible scenarios out of the snippets she heard.

'You mean *their* stories,' said Aaron.

Their stories? Well, I guess if he's been advising clients on the edge of legality, they'd better have their stories straight. As a financial analyst, she'd always been good at looking for inconsistencies in narratives, to ensure she wasn't recommending anyone back a loser. Story consistency was critical; inconsistency was a red flag to her.

'Yes, I believe so. We all have a lot riding on this,' said Aaron. 'Everyone knows we can't afford a slip up now. As I said, we simply can't afford to try *that* again. It would be madness. We just need to watch.'

Oh Jesus, he's playing round with shares again. I wonder how much he's in for this time. She'd been annoyed earlier in the year. Aaron made a large investment – fifty thousand – in a start-up mining company. The company's claim to have discovered new mineral deposits quickly turned out to be premature. Aaron only just managed to get out on the plummeting price, but not before losing twenty-seven grand in three days. *He's a crap analyst. Corporate financier, wheeler-dealer, yes; but no analyst.*

'No, I said I don't think we can. Too risky. Alexa's close to it – we will be able to see how things pan out.'

Alexa's... Christ! What did he just say? She rocked. If she hadn't already been leaning against the wall, she would have hit it, alerting Aaron. *Christ!* Her mind raced. She swayed with dizziness.

'Thanks,' said Aaron. 'It just came to me. Figured we needed an ace up the sleeve.'

Alexa's mind went blank. The surprise was complete. She had no inclination of what the hell was going on. For once, she wished her mind hadn't gone off on its tangents as she'd listened. What had been said? She tried to remember. She couldn't.

'I will,' said Aaron, still unseen.

Aaron's voice stung her ears. *Alexa's close to it.* The phrase echoed. It ran circles through her mind. It interrupted any chance of thinking clearly. *What the hell am I close to?* Christ, what's going on here?

'Look, just stick to the plan...' he was saying. 'I laid it before you all. Stick to it and we'll manage this. ...Right?'

Through her confusion, she sensed she needed to move. The conversation was going to end. *Move girl.* Her senses screamed at her.

'Remember who started this,' he said. 'I came to you, you recall.'

Move yourself!

Alexa backed away down the hall and reached for the handle of the outside door. She opened it with more effort at working quietly than usual. She paused. She closed the door loudly. She went forward again and retrieved her keys, again quietly. Her mind lay in turmoil. *What on earth am I close to?* She dropped the keys on the table. They made a noise as they landed. *No, don't say anything. That would be suspicious.* Quickly, she went to the bedroom door and entered. She paused only to kick off her shoes. She went through to the dressing room, into the en-suite. She closed the door behind her and sat on the edge of the bath. *Christ!* Her heart pounded; it was as if she'd just come off a sprint finish after a half-hour stint on the rowing machine at her gym. Her head spun. She reached down, thankful for the support of the bath – she needed it.

'You there, Alexa?'

Faintly now, she heard Aaron's words through the closed

door. 'Yes…' she said, catching the tremor in her voice. She tried to check herself. *Easy girl.* 'Yes, Dear. Just on the loo,' she shouted, trembling.

'I need to go out to a dinner tonight… all right with you?'

A rhetorical question. It wouldn't have mattered much if she did mind. 'Fine, Dear,' she shouted. She had more control now.

Calm, girl. Don't panic. It's just the shock of the unexpected.

She started to analyse the situation. The context. That's it… her name in the context of half a conversation. *What did he say?* Now try to remember everything. *Damn it!* She shook her head, her long, thick hair heaving, on mass, about her shoulders. She couldn't remember.

Damn racing ahead of him, thinking of possibilities. *I wasn't listening.* What the hell did he say? *Alexa's close to it.* What am I close to that he's also involved with?

Suddenly she grasped it, the reason why, subconsciously, the words shocked her. The trigger pulled back. *Tiger Oil! It's the only thing I deal with that Aaron does too.* We never talk of each other's clients.

What else did he say? Think girl, think!

'I'm off now,' shouted Aaron, from outside the door. 'I'll be home around midnight. See you later, Darling.'

She heard the sounds of Aaron getting ready to leave the apartment. The apartment door closed behind him. She still sat on the edge of the bath, rooted. A shiver traversed her spine. Involuntarily, her knees started to bounce as her forward weight came to rest on the balls of her stockinged feet. *He can't have known I heard something.* She breathed out, as if she'd been holding her breath the whole time. Relief washed over her.

Tiger Oil! Whom had Aaron been talking to? *Tiger Oil?* But I'm no closer to the company than anyone else there… am I? *Close to it?* The hammer went forward and the cartridge fired

123

its round off inside her head – a gunpowder-bright flash of realisation. *Oh Christ! What's going on?* NO! Finn? It can only be Finn. *What on earth's going on?* She was utterly confused. It was as though someone had tied her feelings to the carriage of a rollercoaster ride, in full gravity-defying progress.

All afternoon her mind had been in turmoil. She'd felt guilty turning down Finn's request for help. Now, *this*! Christ, what's going on. *Please… somebody… tell me.*

She needed to think – to think clearly and carefully about her next move. She stood. Colour returned to her ashen face. No, no panic. *Think girl, you're the analyst.* Finn might just need her more than she'd first thought.

She considered calling Finn. No. She needed to clear her mind first. She needed to get her mind straight. She knew just who to speak to – the time had come to call in a favour.

*

Across the water of St Katherine's Dock, Finn lay on the queen size bed in his fifth-floor room in the Tower Hotel.
After his lunch with Lyneth, he'd gone round to Worship Street, to his serviced office. He spent a while going through the story of his accident, to satisfy the whims of the management team there. They'd been curious about his apparent disappearance. No one had told them, but, with the office prepaid for three months, no one had been the least bit bothered – just curious. After a number of ooohhs and aaahhs from the two girls on the reception desk, he finally found himself in his office.

He'd sat in the empty space, at the empty desk, but he'd been unable to think clearly. The two glasses of wine provoked more of an effect on him than he'd expected. To cap it all, his failure to get Alexa's support bothered him. It left him feeling

124

low. He knew he shouldn't have built his hopes on Alexa, but...

He'd left for the hotel shortly after.

Finn glanced at the digits of the clock face embedded in the television, across from the foot of his bed. Six twenty-five. He reached for his mobile phone from the bedside table. He slid the top cover up to expose its keys and selected *text, new text*. He entered his message, one-handed, his left arm lying up round behind his head.

Hi. U there? he typed.

He entered Carol's number and pressed *send*. He didn't leave her number in his address book – one of the few numbers he made the effort to remember.

About a minute later, the phone buzzed in his hand. He opened and read the incoming text.

yes. gr8 2 hear from u. missed u. can we meet? xx

The text conversation continued:

not yet. soon. promise. still tired after hosp :(u ok? x
yes. frustr8'd. want u :(when do u think? xx
want u 2. may b 'nother week or 2 :) u take care. x
an u. txt soon. xx
will do. x o x

Finn selected *delete all messages*. He slid the cover closed and replaced the phone on the bedside table.

The end of his first full day working out of home and he was tired. He'd also developed a massive headache by the time he'd arrived at the hotel. As he got to his room, he'd taken a Percocet to ease the pain. The neurologist had prescribed Percocet when he'd been for the check up – for occasional use only, he'd stressed! The prescription warned him of its opiate-like addictive nature, and he'd managed to avoid taking it, most times, but not this one. Drowsiness crept upon him. He closed his eyes.

'F... i... n... n...'

'F... i... n... n...' The wind again accelerated each nuance of the ghostly sound past his ears, drawing the word out as he turned his head to face its source. The vivid colour of the grass below him, and the distant aspen and poplar, were now a familiar sight.

He faced her. *Shufang*. He tried to call out to her, but no sound came to his closed mouth. He shivered, not from the cold wind, but from the apparition before him. *Shufang*. Why? He dropped to his knees in the tall, damp grass, the moisture seeping into his soul. His eyes grew swollen with tears he could not understand.

But Shufang did not chase. Inexorably she moved slowly forward, calling his name.

'F... i... n... n...'

She was giving him time. Playing with him.

Run. You have to.

Tiredness ate at him. He didn't want to run, but knew he must. Shufang expected him to.

The shiver spread. His whole body started to shake before the advancing apparition. His mouth was dry, his eyes wet with tears. He lifted himself from his knees. *Nooooooooooowwwww!* he wanted to shout, but his mouth was too dry.

I can't.

But he knew. He had to. It was expected.

He stood and turned to run. The grass turned to marsh below his feet, slowing him. He struggled as he reached the water's edge and stopped. But he didn't stop – he fell. He fell headlong into the raging water below him.

Christ! The shivering real this time. The bed was soaked with sweat.

Finn lifted his hand to his face – the luminous pointers on his watch suggested four-thirty. *Christ!* He knew it to be a dream. *But why…? Why Shufang? Why the river?* He lay on his back amid the damp bedclothes. He lay still, trying to rationalise, but he couldn't. Finally, he drifted into sleep.

He rose quickly at eight a.m. The alarms on his Blackberry and mobile had broken into choral disharmony. He'd not been as strong as he'd thought. His body needed rest; he remained weak. He knew he needed to get home now.

On the train, he contemplated the risk in what he needed to do. He needed to win something back, to get at *them*. He just had to try Alexa again. He had no other choice.

*

Alexa first met Ozzie Medwin about two years earlier. He'd been her first contact when she'd decided to take the plunge into her alter-world of sexual encounters. She'd read – where, she no longer remembered; it might have been some random magazine at her hairdressers – of a web-site for people who sought introductions of an illicit nature. Yes, her life wasn't a bad life. But, two years ago… well, then it had been a different story.

It took her a couple of weeks to pluck up the courage to sign up to the web-site. She chose her nom-de-plume with care; she called herself *Honey Ryder:*

> *Hi, I'm Honey Ryder. I'm an intelligent, confident and attractive girl who's looking to regain the passion and excitement in life. I enjoy the good things life has to offer, and like to think I'm adventurous. I work hard and travel from time to time.*

I have long auburn hair, brown eyes and a smile that's always there. I am 5' 8" tall and slim, but with curves in all the right places. I like to keep fit and active. I take care in my appearance and my clothes vary according to the occasion, but always stylish and feminine. I love sexy underwear.

I'm looking to meet someone to make me smile and laugh a lot, to make me feel special. I want someone who brings a sparkle into my life. I want someone who I can have fun with, flirt with, tease, challenge and enjoy getting to know. I like style on the outside, but what's on the inside also counts.

I'm looking to meet a man who takes pride in his appearance with good looks and a personality to match. I'm looking for good conversation as well as someone to treat me in that very special way. I'm looking for a "romance & fun", "see how it goes", type of relationship.

I love life and believe you only get one chance at it, so we should enjoy every minute of it. I enjoy many things, from spending an evening in the company of friends with great conversation over a good bottle of red, to getting out in the open air blowing the cobwebs away. I am married and intend to stay that way, so discretion is a necessity.

She'd been shocked with the response. Dozens and dozens of e-mails, some with vulgar photographs clearly taken with mobile-phone cameras held to display the writer's private parts. She'd received e-mails from players, those seeking another notch in the bed-post of their mind.

She received e-mails from some suitors she found to be interesting. She even replied to a couple and, after an exchange with one particular author, tentatively arranged to meet him in a crowded coffee bar. The meeting never happened. Oh! She had turned up all right, but her prospective paramour hadn't – a time-waster, clearly. One who'd no intention, or, more likely she thought, no balls to carry through with what he might have wanted. His loss.

It took two months of false promises; two months of wading through an inordinate amount of extremely tacky photography; two months of reading the writing of plebs that left nothing to the imagination, before she came across *Trader Guy*.

Ozzie Medwin turned out to be a curious individual. He possessed the air of a geek, yes, but one with certain *film star* looks. Quite what film star she couldn't guess, but she could have easily watched him in any film, over and over again. He stood two inches taller than she did; she'd grown particularly comfortable in his company.

From meeting on-line, they went on to meet in person, in a café, and then they met in bed. Several times. They enjoyed good meetings; everything she could have wished for from a paramour. Her one disappointment remained her need to go *off-piste* to get such satisfaction. If only she could have found the same with Aaron, but there had been no interest there for some years.

Alexa and Ozzie met each other frequently over the next twelve months. There had been plenty of opportunity – Aaron continued growing more absent during the working week, with many stop-overs and foreign trips.

At the time, Ozzie had been working as a derivatives trader for Merrill Lynch. Too geekish to find a normal relationship, he'd decided to follow a life of *anonymous sexual encounters*. But he wasn't a bed-post kind of guy. Ozzie had never made her feel as if he'd merely given her a place in his stable, along with others – only for him to ride at his pleasure.

They had both accepted the rule. NSA – no strings attached. As soon as their relationship threatened to become more than sexual, Alexa called time. They both understood and respected the rule, and they stopped seeing each other for pleasure; but they retained a friendship based on mutual respect and common interest.

Ozzie had reason to call on their friendship within a few weeks of Alexa calling time. Alexa, as a PR guru, helped him to negotiate his exit from Merrill Lynch. The company's IT staff had discovered his particular use of the internet at work. He'd been careless looking for a replacement for her.

On the Sunday morning Alexa called on Ozzie. Since leaving his position at Merrill's he'd taken to working from home. It had been one of those pure coincidences; Ozzie lived in the same block of apartments as Alexa and Aaron. Alexa had another rule, *not on her own territory*. She broke that one. Once they'd worked out how close they lived to each other, it'd been too late. In their minds, they'd already decided to go ahead. They'd both accepted the risk.

Unlike Alexa's comfortably-chic apartment, Ozzie's came sparsely furnished. The most striking aspect revealed itself on entering the lounge. Two large semi-return desks took up an entire sixteen-foot section of rear wall, between the door and right-hand corner of the lounge. Side-by-side, the desks formed a large wrap-around workstation, on which a bank of computer screens stood, alive – even on a Sunday – flickering with colourful neon-like intensity. Five large wall-mounted clocks, the type that sit in classrooms, hung above the desks, each indicating a different time: New York, London, Paris, Hong Kong and Japan. Alexa counted seven screens.

'What are all these for, Ozzie?'

She couldn't quite take it in, despite her knowledge of finance and investments. The screens showed a variety of charts and other financial data. Two of the screens displayed twenty-four hour news services from CNBC and the BBC. To all intent and purpose, Ozzie owned a mini-trading floor.

'The three central ones are my trading platform,' said Ozzie, gesturing in the direction of the screens. 'I'm running a ShareScopePro system at the moment – though I'm considering changing it...'

'Sorry, honey, too much information for me,' she said, giggling.

'K,' he said, returning a look of disappointment.

Ozzie loved his system, she could tell, and he clearly loved to talk about it. *The lovely geek.* At thirty-seven, he remained the still-single, proverbial big kid with his toys.

'The other screens to the right have got news, and those two on the left are carrying chat rooms and analysis pages from the web,' said Ozzie, carrying on with his introduction. 'Cool, eh?' His face brightened again.

He looked hopelessly proud; his grin spread from ear to ear.

'I need your help, Ozzie,' she said.

Alexa had spent the weekend avoiding conversation with Aaron. It hadn't been difficult. They often passed time in silence, each in their own worlds. Music, the papers and a book hid her overactive mind. Aaron's words formed a constant, echoing and unwelcome companion to her mind. *No, I said I don't think we can. Too risky. Alexa's close to it. We will be able to see how things pan out.* Her skin crawled, she did not know why, and she did not like it.

Over the course of Saturday, Alexa concluded she would help Finn get his short position opened. Ozzie owed Alexa, and now she would call in the favour.

'I have a friend...' she said.

Ozzie winked at her.

'No, not *that* sort of friend,' she said, giggling again.

'He needs to open a short position on an AIM listed company. Can you help?'

'What's the firm, gorgeous?'

'Tiger Oil.'

Ozzie looked thoughtful for a moment. He still stood by his trading desk. He turned round to face the three screens arranged in a curve in the centre of the desk; a single key board fronted the screens, and mouse and two empty coke cans rested, haphazardly, close by. He moved the mouse and clicked a few times, the screen to his left-side flickered with movement. A graph opened. He clicked again and what looked like a page of data flashed up on the right.

'Now, let me see,' he said. He turned to the two screens on the far left, and their single keyboard. He typed Tiger Oil into a search engine; the two displays changed.

'Wow, clever stuff,' said Alexa, in genuine awe.

'Does your friend know something the market doesn't?'

'Yes.'

Ozzie turned to face Alexa. 'I know someone,' he said, launching yet another grin that continued to spread, reaching his ears within seconds of speaking. The Cheshire Cat personified.

'I thought you might,' she said, grinning.

'Has your friend got money?'

'No.'

'What *has* he got?'

'I think he's got a two and half percent holding already.'

Ozzie turned round and checked Friday's closing price. 'Steady at twelve and a half. I reckon they're worth at least three hundred and fifty grand.' He turned to face her again. He dropped the grin, revealing an expression of genuine seriousness.

'Can you help?' she asked.

'I'll need him to sign a blank share transfer certificate for his remaining holding, and I'll need his share certificate. I'll do it for thirty days maximum or until I have to cut out; it'll be my decision. No questions.' He was looking straight into her eyes.

'I'll have to check with him…' Had he read the plea for help that lay deep inside her. 'Thanks, Ozzie. Really… you don't know how much this means to me.'

'I think I do.' He smiled. 'I don't suppose… for old times sake…?'

'You don't suppose correctly, honey.'

They laughed together, warmly.

TWELVE

'THEN THERE'S SECURITY, Finn. Ozzie would need your shares as security for the trade.' Alexa paused to allow him to respond. He didn't. 'He's going to be doing this himself. If it goes bad, for whatever reason, he needs a fall back. …Finn?'

He'd considered the risk briefly. 'Yes, Alexa, I can see. It's just… well… it's a big call.'

'He will only cover you for a maximum of thirty days, after that your shares would default to him if you haven't closed the position in profit.'

'Those shares are all that's left of my mortgage and pension.'

'I'm sorry, Finn, it's the best I could think of.'

'No. Don't be sorry, Alexa.'

After feeling like crap over the weekend, he'd breathed a sigh of relief when Alexa called him first thing that Monday.

'It's my call. You've done great,' he'd said. 'I thought I might need to shelve the idea and get a job at Tesco's, stacking shelves.' *Gallows humour.*

He'd tried to laugh, but his mind hung on the down-side; the gibbet stared at him. He would be betting everything on making some money out of his inside knowledge. As an ex-analyst, Alexa would have known this too.

His mind had raced. If they could borrow fifteen percent,

sell, and buy with a margin of at least five pence, he could clear near a million pounds. He could bite his thumb at Grayson bloody Barclay, and move on to pastures new. It would all be over in a couple of weeks. He'd have returned with enough for a new stake in something – in control of his own destiny again.

'Finn?' asked Alexa, seeking a response.

'Let's do it,' he'd said. 'Let's do it, Alexa!'

At that point, his pulse raced to match his mind. The adrenaline of risk intoxicated him. It heightened his senses. No need for gambling, poker, roulette, horses – he'd never felt the need. *This was it!*

'You sure, Finn?' Alexa had wanted to be doubly sure.

'Yes,' he'd repeated. *The point of no return.* He would beat Barclay on his own turf.

After Alexa's call, he'd made plans during the rest of the Monday. He gathered the paper work and downloaded a blank stock transfer form from the Capita Registrars website. He'd travelled to London the Tuesday morning, going straight to meet Alexa for coffee at the Café Rouge in St Katherine's Dock. She'd taken him up to meet Ozzie Medwin in his apartment.

Ozzie's handshake had been firm. Finn liked a good handshake, but he made the mental recollection of Grayson Barclay's hand-shake – it had also been solid.

Another handshake – this time agreeing to the deal – and he provided Ozzie with the paperwork. Ozzie didn't waste time. He'd already called some people, as he'd said he would. Institutional investors held around thirty-seven percent of the company and Ozzie was confident he could borrow fifteen percent easily. His trading facilities and account could manage the transactions without a problem, and Finn's shares gave him enough security to protect his potential down-side.

Finn warmed to the geeky nature of Ozzie. The younger

man's boyish grin grew infectious.

He'd then gone with Alexa for another coffee, leaving Ozzie to prepare for the trade. They agreed Alexa would give Ozzie the nod when to sell.

'How are we going to do this, Alexa?' asked Finn, after the waiter delivered two cappuccinos to the table.

'I have some press contacts in a Texas agency,' she said without hesitation. She'd thought it all through. 'Ozzie will contract the shares this afternoon. It's going to be close and might arouse some suspicion, but with the Atlantic as a fire-break, we're sure Ozzie can defend himself. He's been collecting data on Tiger Oil and has a story he can push out – about how *he* worked out Shufang's family would lodge a court action. There's no known connection between Ozzie and me. I'm just helping it on a little.'

'You're no Essex-girl, are you?'

'No Scottish; Edinburgh to be exact. But you know...' She'd laughed. 'I'll take it as a compliment though, Finn Jackson.'

That had all been yesterday. Now, on this fine Yorkshire Wednesday, Finn sat at his desk.

His laptop was open and on-line. He connected to the Interactive Investor service and brought up the Tiger Oil page. He lacked the sophistication of Ozzie's displays – they'd impressed the hell out of him. But, the II web site gave him enough to see the plan clicking into place before him.

Ozzie didn't move until first thing that morning. He gave Finn a quick call around nine-thirty.

The late leak of information to the state-side oil press worked – some ex-analyst-colleague of Alexa's, at some nondescript agency, he couldn't remember the name. Over the previous night, e-mail trade bulletins in the States flashed the story to U.S. investors and day-trader chat rooms pushed the story around. Unless you'd been looking at the US, and specifically at the oil sector, you'd have missed it in the early-morning noise of Wednesday's opening London market. As the market opened, Ozzie hit the ground running; he put a chunk of shares out – waking people up to Tiger Oil.

Finn sat looking at the price, which, unlike Ozzie's real-time info, lagged the market by around fifteen minutes; he smiled in satisfaction.

Finn's screen displayed mainly rises in oil related shares, with buyers buying across the sector on the back of strong oil prices. Tiger Oil stood out, it moved in the opposite direction, showing a fall to ten and a quarter pence.

Finn clicked on the recommendations page, the weighted average recommendation dropped from a *buy* to a *weak sell*. The institutions acted to off-load some of their holdings of shares, to reduce their exposure. The price continued to fall.

He checked the Discussion Board. Yes! Some guy calling himself *finalcount* had posted a note: *Jeez guys. Anyone seen the US reports on TIG.O? Someone's making a massive claim against the board for corporate manslaughter. Time to bail, guys.* Already, six follow-on notes had appeared in the discussion thread.

The market showed a clear perception, Tiger Oil faced a potential major loss. The chat even hit on the Insurance Company's refusal to pay out fully – all negative sentiment. It looked bad for Tiger Oil.

Finn checked the Users' Holdings page. He reckoned there were around seven percent of the shares in the hands of the volatile day traders. They'd reacted predictably – a degree of panic set in amongst them. By lunchtime, the shares had dropped twenty-three percent to a shade over nine and a half pence. Ozzie did his job well.

According to Lyneth, it would take over a month to clear the action through court – and they hadn't received it yet. He'd checked in with Lyneth after he'd returned from London the previous day. They expected to hear, formally, by the end of the week.

The next thing would be Tiger Oil issuing a press release to try to calm market fears, but Alexa stood ready primed for that one. She was going to caution Grayson Barclay against too strong a denial; it would only look worse for them once the family's lawyers lodged the action with the court. The board would need to retract any denial and that would lose them credibility.

He sat there, smiling solidly for the first time in months. It certainly looked like the fall had set in well. *There's plenty of time left for stock to drop further.* He would wait until Friday. With his profits, he could probably even buy back in. But, first things first, he told himself. *Watch your exposure!* Still, he could not fight against the rising image of the small door to the enchanted garden, as it started to open again. The light from within spilled over his feet, taunting him.

THIRTEEN

FINN'S MOBILE PHONE had rung around six the previous evening. He'd left the family at the kitchen table and gone quickly to his study, closing the door behind him. Aisling said nothing. She didn't need to. The look she gave him as he left the table spoke volumes about their failing relationship.

'Hi, Finn... it's Lyneth.'

'I guessed.' He couldn't mistake her voice – he didn't know too many Welsh girls. 'You were spot on,' he'd said.

'Yes. I saw the closing price. Seven point nine, wasn't it?'

'Yeah.'

'Something else you might like to know.'

She'd spun it out for him, building the suspense. 'Go on,' he'd said.

'I spoke with the family's lawyers this afternoon. The breaking news is prompting them to submit their action in the morning.'

'Wow! That's great. It'll hit the price further. Nothing for the board to deny now, is there?'

'No.'

'I owe you, Lyneth...'

They'd settled on lunch and he'd travelled down that morning to meet her. She had been in a flirtatious mood.

They met outside the Royal Exchange and Finn walked her round to Browns on Old Jewry, just off Cheapside.

He counted Browns as home turf. He took the lead and ordered a steak pie with chips – adding a bottle of the house cabernet sauvignon.

'You know how to show a lady a good time,' she'd said, following his lead with the steak pie. They both laughed at that. The waiter looked on, nonplussed. 'But no chips with mine,' she added.

Lyneth always dressed well for work. To Finn, the effect was classy, but entirely sexy. Her well-cut skirt suit looked to be of fine cashmere. The thickness of the material made no pretence at hiding the shapeliness of her figure. The large, soft bow at the bottom of the deep *v*-lined silk blouse led his eyes to notice a clear line of cleavage. *Yes, vereeee nice!*

In his mind's eye, lunch returned him to the first meal he'd shared with Lyneth. But this time he'd not dwelt in self-pity. This time he'd sought to rise to the flirtation. He noticed the flashing eyes, the tilted head and the full, parted lips; he noticed her face, smiling for all its worth. Buoyed by the success of the plan so far, he hadn't minded her questions. His wariness reduced to less than a background irritation. He'd enjoyed her company immensely.

Now in his hotel room, it dawned on him; Lyneth had only ever been interested in *him*. There had been clues. He had a vague recollection of her saying, *I've never really found much time for relationships.* He couldn't even be sure at which of their meetings she'd said it. A fog suddenly lifted before him. He felt... what? A missed opportunity? Even this lunchtime, despite the flirting, he'd been self-absorbed to an extent. He'd responded to her questions, yes, but failed to show interest... any real interest in her own story. He would change... next time!

Normally, Finn carefully compartmentalised his personal

140

and business life. He didn't like to draw the two sides together. It had been natural for him, he considered, to suspect Lyneth's motives for staying close. After all, Tiger Oil retained her firm.

Aaron had introduced him to Keaton-Jones, and, while he didn't tar Aaron with the same brush as Barclay, it was an uncomfortable connection. But, now! Now he knew Lyneth's interest had been on her own terms. She'd shown she only wanted to help him. She'd given him a way to get at them and, judging by the progress of their plan so far, he could see his way to achieving some pay-back. He would take his place in the city yet. *Sod you Barclay.*

He hoped the lunch hadn't put Lyneth off from pursuing him. He enjoyed the idea of a woman doing the chasing – quite a novelty!

Carol was different. They'd found each other, enjoyed each other and would continue to do so. They helped each other come to terms with what they missed in their own relationships. He missed her now, but now wasn't the time to pick up with her. Another week or so. He hadn't been in touch since he'd texted last week.

Lyneth, though. What to do about Lyneth? Despite her obvious attractiveness, and now welcoming her attention, he couldn't afford a relationship with her. He needed to play it all very carefully. She'd proved too valuable... but, *oil and water for God's sake*; business and pleasure – his thing – he didn't mix the two. He'd just never done it before.

He imagined the tightrope beneath his feet; imagined stepping out from the safety of his present foothold. He wanted to encourage Lyneth, to keep her on side, but he'd seen her edge. He didn't want... no, he couldn't *afford* to court her wrath. *A woman scorned and all that...* He'd one failing relationship to contend with, he could do without more complexity in his life.

The "family troubles" card, that's what he needed to play.

He needed time to sort things out, to keep some distance… and then? Lyneth? Who knows? *That's it… but…*

He got up from the bed and walked to where his jacket hung on the back of a chair. A chair? Really! …The over-filled desk – the television, leaflets, books, telephone. The chair's function was limited. He lifted his phone from his jacket pocket and found Alexa's number in the address book. He pressed call.

'Hi, Finn,' she answered.

'Hello, Alexa. You seen the price today?'

'Yes. I'm in the office now. Grayson Barclay's been on to me already, we have to release a statement on the Shufang Su action. The market's certainly jittery about the whole thing. It dropped another ten percent today. It's seven eleven now.'

'Look, I'm at the Tower again tonight. Do you fancy a nightcap on your way home? Or is Aaron expecting you?'

'Yes and no,' she giggled. 'Yes to a nightcap …be lovely, thank you. No to Aaron. He's in Stavanger, I think. Some North Sea meeting or other. I'm not expecting him home 'till late Friday.'

'When will you be out of the office?'

'It'll be a late one. I have a few things to do after this release for Tiger. Can we say around ten, in the hotel bar?

'Yeah, see you then, Alexa.'

He needed to guard his six-o'clock. He would let Alexa know of Lyneth's interest. He valued her counsel; she'd become as close a friend as he had for the moment. Aaron had taken a back seat. *Clearly, Aaron had a conflict of interest.*

*

Seven pence! Some result! Lyneth lay in her deep-filled bath; a large glass of cold vodka stood within reach. She relaxed; soap bubbles gently embraced her naked flesh, and the heat of the water contrasted well with the cold fire of the spirit. *Yes. Some result.* She smiled to herself and slid further down into the bubbles, before bracing her long, shapely legs; she pushed herself up into position and reached for her drink.

She smiled again at the day. She'd enjoyed lunch. OK, so Finn merely answered her questions, but he *had* warmed to her. He'd noticed her. She'd seen his eyes drawn to her. She wore the blouse especially for him, for the affect it would stir in him; she'd not been disappointed.

Her arms moved fluidly. Her hands, crossing themselves, moved impulsively to her breasts, cupping them. Feeling them. *Yes. A result!* She slid further down the bath again, letting the heat of the water work its magic caress on her body. It reached over her shoulders, warming them. It reached round her neck – a delicious feeling that sent a tingle down her spine – the feel of a lovers kiss. Her hands now gently kneaded, her fingers stroked. Slowly her hips gyrated, thighs gently squeezing in time to the swelling, rocking ripples of the water, amplifying them – amplifying the sense affect. Her right arm lowered. Slowly, her hand slid over the surface of her flat stomach, settling between her thighs. Her eyes closed. Delicious thoughts carried her away…

Lyneth's shoulders broke through the surface of the water as her legs braced again – her reverie lifted. Her eyes opened and her hands both rose above the water. The ripples died away as she reached over and took the glass. Cupping it with both hands, she raised it to her lips and drew long on the cool liquor. The ice, melted now, had done its job.

She'd *smelt blood* on the Shufang Su case. Despite the sense of attraction and her feelings for Finn, her passion as a litigation lawyer kicked in – the proverbial and argumentative dog with a bone. Her face flashed over with seriousness, lifting the smile of seconds before; the ice in her eyes now more visible than the ice in her vodka had been.

What if? *What if the facts do implicate Finn in all this?* Could he be culpable in the manslaughter charge? The legal action, now with the Director of Public Prosecution's office, would soon have the police involved, re-interviewing everyone. If there were some discrepancies, they would come out soon. Had she been right not to voice this concern to Finn?

Yes. She'd no answers yet, only questions. Seeking answers, yes, but she wasn't there yet. Formally, she needed to act in defence of Tiger Oil; it would be counter productive to play any other card for the time being. She'd been right not to say anything. *Let it play out as it will – just be prepared, girl.*

There are premises, no conclusion. Argue each premise first. Get the premises right. Be prepared. When the time is right… move. You'll get to the answer if you stick to the logic girl. *Disinterest, that's the key.* She'd always been glad of her interest in philosophy; philosophy helped with rationality when she could find no clear direction. Disinterest wasn't uninterest, she mused. She needed to disinterest herself in Finn for a little while.

He's hooked. Once she'd collected evidence, to support her belief he wasn't involved… *then she could have him… enjoy him.* Moreover, she would. But, for the time being…

Lyneth replaced the empty glass on the side. She closed her eyes and again slid slowly down until the bubble-covered water lapped her chin. Her hands moved to feel the warmth of her body. The water caressed her skin rhythmically, tuned to the slowly increasing caresses of her hands. She slipped into her seductive reverie.

*

'Seven pence,' she said.

The bar in the upper foyer of the Tower Hotel gave a panoramic view over the yellow-cast, sodium-lit Tower Bridge. Neither Finn nor Alexa took notice.

'*Seven pence! Finn,*' repeated Alexa. She felt like an excited child. 'It's great, isn't it?' she said. 'And it still looks like falling. I don't think the release I've drafted will make much of a difference tomorrow. Everyone is going to wait for it to be sorted out in the courts.'

'I know,' he said. 'Lyneth told me it might take another week – even before the DPP's office takes its first steps. They're so overloaded at the moment, apparently.'

'Have you spoken to Ozzie?'

'Yes, I called him quickly, before you got here. He'd drip-fed some stock at the top end of the fall, but got rid of most of it at about ten pence. He reckons it may drop to six by market-close on Friday, settling down to as little as four or five next week. I'm going home tomorrow morning; I'll monitor it from there. Ozzie reckons to close the position late next week, or early the following week.'

Alexa looked thoughtful for a moment. 'Yes,' she said, '...a two week maximum is probably OK. Just keep a close eye on it, Finn. I'll keep you posted on anything I hear across my desk.' She laughed. 'Grayson's running around like a headless chicken at the moment. I reckon they'd thought it would all blow over. He called me trying to reach Aaron. He's hopping mad. One to you, I think, Dear.' She took a drink from her glass, emptying it.

'Here, let me.' Finn lifted the bottle out, clear of the cooler, and poured her a second glass of the non-descript white he'd chosen. He recharged his own glass and replaced the bottle. 'Not quite sure why I went for this one,' he said, nodding at the bottle. He smiled, sheepishly.

'As long as you choose your women with better insight,' she said with a giggle. 'At least Aisling seems a catch.'

'All that glitters. . .' he didn't finish the saying.

'Surely…' began Alexa, with concern in her voice. 'Isn't everything OK at home?'

'No,' he sighed, 'not really. The stress of all this hasn't helped. We've grown distant over the past couple of years. All the travelling; the accident; my coming down here so much…' He took a long drink, trying to drown the regret. He forced a laugh. 'Perverse, isn't it?'

'What do you mean, Finn?'

'Well, now I have the lovely Lyneth chasing me.'

Alexa's eyebrows rose. 'Lyneth?' she said, the surprise genuine.

'Well, I'm not quite sure. Maybe she's desperate. She's clearly very single.'

'Don't knock yourself, Finn. Desperate is possibly not the right word. But, I mean… Lyneth?' She leant forward and took Finn's hand. 'Tread carefully, Dear. From what you've already told me about her, she sounds a bit of a man-eater!'

'I wouldn't go that far… maybe… but thanks for the word of caution. I've decided to play it a bit cooler with her in any case. I just need to keep her on side to help.'

'If she *has* strong feelings for you, she could be more trouble than you need, Finn.'

'I know,' he shrugged. 'I do get myself into trouble sometimes.' He smiled.

'Just be careful, Finn,' she said.

He hadn't quite known what to expect from Alexa; but he'd wanted to tell her about Lyneth. He wanted someone to know. He knew Alexa was right.

'Yes,' he said.

'If Aisling ever suspected anything, I'm pretty sure, from what you've just said, you might have more trouble on your hands. The last thing you need right now is a divorce.'

'We've been bumping along that bottom for some time. I just think we've reached a kind of status quo with having the girls. She has her horses. I have my work. We sort of meet in the middle, with the children.'

They both fell silent, cradling their drinks in their hands.

'Right, Finn, I'd best go get my beauty sleep. Thanks for the drink. We'll get this all sorted and you back on the road to success!' She finished her wine. 'Call me next week. I promise I'll call if I hear anything.' She got up and reached over to kiss his cheek.

'Thanks, Alexa.'

She winked at him, gave an enormous smile, and left.

He drank deeply, finishing the last of his wine. *Stormy waters!* He'd totally exposed himself financially; he'd little, if anything, left to protect himself. Despite his appetite for risk, he was nervous.

FOURTEEN

'OH SHIT! WHAT the hell is this?' she said to no one in particular.

It was late Friday afternoon, Lyneth stood by the side of her desk. A letter lay in her hand. She had just picked it up from the top of a pile of mail on her desk.

The last thing I need. She'd just returned from a client lunch. One of those working lunches where it had taken an interminable length of time to get her points across. The client drank too much, pre-lunch, and then, when they'd got to the business of the day he'd been over the top, not listening to a word she said. But he was the client she'd reminded herself. She saw the lunch through to its end, gritting her teeth, thanking God that Friday afternoon came just before Friday evening. And Friday evening rolled over into Saturday – a bath and chilled vodka awaited her.

The morning's mail, already opened by her secretary, had lain there to greet her as she'd entered the room. There, at the top, she'd seen the Tiger Oil letter-head, recognising the logo instantly. The letter contained Jonathon Long's response to her questions.

The oil-man cum non-exec director had been at Peace River at the time of the accident. He'd written clarification on a number of points she'd raised over his testimony in the accident report. And there, appearing like bold neon type flashing incredulously before her eyes, in the first few paragraphs, Jonathon wrote about independent corroboration of his schedule. He could confirm, through phone records, the timing of the call made to his colleague David Kail at precisely two-fifteen p.m.

> *I returned to the hotel to make the call. I was aware David would be unavailable for the entire afternoon (UK time), due to his fishing holiday in Scotland. I had been unable to contact either our Chairman Grayson Barclay or Finn Jackson, despite leaving voice mail messages, as my itemised phone bill will show if required.*

Plausible… completely plausible. *Shit!* In truth, she hadn't known what to think, or what to expect. She just… well… She thought that maybe there was something – a chink of an untruth. *But no!* It appeared Jonathon Long could cover his story. 'Shit!' she said, aloud.

She found nothing else of relevance in the mail. Certainly nothing either from, or pertaining to, Scott Lindon. Even Jonathon hadn't referred to Scott Lindon… but, shit! This blew out her earlier conclusion. It looked like Tiger Oil might not have any case to answer at all. Did the lawyers for Shufang's family merely jump the band wagon? *Christ! Was there a case?* Or were the other side just playing a game to screw as much fee income as possible from the family?

The letter left her in a quandary. If there was no case to answer, the court was sure to throw the action out as soon as they got to it. Once the police re-interview Jonathon Long, his telephone records will hold up and it will be clear no one lied – that no one took part in any form of cover-up. The accident report would hold and the action fail. It would restore market confidence and the share price. *Christi Should I tell Finn? What if I'm wrong?* The letter troubled her.

She needed to call the DPP's office. She picked up the phone on her desk and got straight through to her secretary.

'Claire, can you get me James Green at the DPP please?' She'd known James for a few years; he'd even shared her bath with her on one pleasant occasion. She loved to stack up favours.

'I've James on the line for you, Miss Jones.' Claire had not taken long.

'Hi, James?'

'Well hello, gorgeous. When do we get a re-run?'

'We don't. But you could help me out a bit, if you like.'

'I'll try. As long as it's legal. Immoral's OK, but not illegal. Someone might be listening.'

'If they're listening, you've already lost your job, sunshine!'

'Do you know any good lawyers?'

'Ouch,' she said, more in relation to the poor standard of humour than any hurt, feigned or otherwise. 'Tiger Oil.'

'What about it?' asked James.

'You know it? It's a private prosecution action... corporate manslaughter... Chinese family called Su, from Hong Kong.'

'Just a mo. I'll take a look.'

While Lyneth waited for James to return to her, she considered the situation. If James could just confirm the state of play; even with no case to answer, it might remain in the system for weeks yet...

'Ah! Here you go,' said James. 'Are you still there?'

'Listening.'

'There's a record of receipt entered yesterday, but no case details yet. The system hasn't even assigned a case number yet. You'll be lucky if you see any progress this side of Christmas. We're down on clerical staff as it is. Colds and stomach bugs. Do you want me to flag you if there's any change?'

'Yes, that'd be great, James. I owe you.'

'Well then, gorgeous…'

'No. I can see where you're going. But I *will* let you take me out for a Christmas drink.'

'OK, I'll settle for that. Nice to speak to you again. I'll call soon.'

'Thanks, James. Bye.'

She replaced the telephone handset on its cradle. She felt happier. *With the action only just entering the system, there'll be time enough yet.* She hadn't paid much heed to Christmas, but there it was, looming upon her! She reckoned, even at a push, the DPP wouldn't expect anything from Keaton-Jones in the matter of *Shufang Su v Tiger Oil* for another ten days or so. She still stood ahead of the curve.

Lyneth thought about it some more. She didn't really act like this often, but, in her view, she hadn't undermined her principles. It all boiled down to the end justifying the means. A bit Machiavellian perhaps, but she could live with it. She would hold back her thinking from everyone, and continue to fit with due process. Her idealism allowed this. She still believed a greater injustice lurked below the visible facts, and if a slight wrong would surface it, then so be it. *If the DPP does throw the case out, it will be well after Finn closes his short position.*

*

Beethoven's Symphony Number Two came on. The horns and woodwind grated on her. Alexa wasn't in the mood for Beethoven this Monday evening. She'd been listening to it at times over the weekend, as she'd busied herself around the apartment doing the chores that absolutely needed doing – the ones she couldn't avoid. She hated the chores. The passion and exuberance in Beethoven's work proved useful to get over her distaste for such domestic activity.

She'd switched the CD-player on random-play, and now Beethoven returned to haunt her. 'No. Not Beethoven, not now,' she said. She got up from her chair at the dining table and went over to change the CD.

'What was that, Dear?' asked Aaron. He stood in the kitchen area, where he busied himself preparing dinner. He was nothing if not a creature of habit.

'Nothing, Dear, just talking to myself.' She pressed a CD selector, cancelling the random-play. She didn't yet have an iPod, and was still using her aging cartridge-loading Pioneer player. She had a number of cartridges pre-loaded, each with six CDs for different moods. The present cartridge, her favourite of the last few months, contained a selection from her large collection of classical CDs. *As steals the morn upon the night* came on.

'Good,' she said, with some satisfaction. She'd remembered the location of the right CD, a compilation of Handel. 'That's better.'

December had broken with nothing but endless cold and wet. Certainly, there had been no promise of either a white Christmas, or much cheerful exuberance in the air. Even looking down from the apartment into the marina basin didn't elicit any of its usual romance.

Earlier, Aaron had opened a bottle of 1999 Pol Roger Brut. As Alexa returned to sit at the table, anticipating the meal, she noted the near-empty bottle. A red now sat next to it, open to breathe. The label faced away from her and she couldn't arouse sufficient interest to see from which of Aaron's wine cases it came.

By the time they'd finished their meal, unusually, Aaron had produced a third open bottle. Alexa felt decidedly heady – a little too relaxed.

Aaron's increasing absence from the apartment had been particularly noticeable, almost since the time of Finn's accident. Apart from the Monday dinners, an odd mid-week pass at breakfast, a few weekends, and the trip to York to see Finn, she'd hardly seen him.

Of course, there had been the dreadful conversation she'd overheard... it had kicked her out of her stasis and into helping Finn.

'How's Finn?' Aaron's voice interrupted her thoughts.

'He's fine. He's made a great recovery. I was talking to him only last week. ...You know, just before the accident, he'd got himself an office down here? He was planning to spend a couple of days a week drumming up some consultancy work in the city.'

'Yes, I remember.'

'Well, he reckons he's strong enough now to pick it up again,' she lied, thinking of the words impulsively. *At least it's plausible – partly true perhaps.*

'I know I've not spoken with him recently,' he said. 'Things have been heating up for me. Grayson Barclay's on me like a ton weight with this legal thing Tiger Oil's been hit with...' He paused in contemplation. 'I probably shouldn't have so many directorships. Now funds are so difficult to raise, each deal I'm working seems to be taking far too much time.'

'I've noticed,' she said, smiling sardonically as she closed her lips on the last syllable. 'At least your absence has never really bothered me, Darling. I quite like the space.'

'I know.'

'Yes. At least Finn's draw-back from the business will probably help his marriage.'

'Oh?' Aaron's interest appeared aroused, though he'd tried not to show it.

'Yes,' she continued, 'Aisling never really liked him being away so much, even though she married him knowing he was

153

the travelling sort. Just like you!'

'They having problems?' he asked.

'They *were*. The accident slowing him down will give him some time with her. I think it'll help them both.'

'Either that or it will break them,' he said, lifting his glass from the table. 'So, when did you learn all this?'

'We've been keeping in touch. I offered to help him re-establish himself in the city, using my contacts.'

'Good of you.' He drank deeply from his glass before topping-up their drinks from the now half-full bottle. 'I can't help much, because of the conflict of interest.'

'I know,' she said. 'I just have to keep him away from Lyneth.'

Alexa could feel the rapidly increasing effect of the evening's drinks, despite having eaten a reasonable amount. A filling, wild mushroom risotto lay more heavily in her stomach than she would have credited.

'Pardon…' said Aaron.

Again, Aaron had tried to sound as if he'd merely missed her words, rather than the words knocking him back. 'Finn thinks Lyneth…' she began.

Too late! She saw the look of alarm flash past Aaron's ice-blue eyes. What had she said? *Bloody wine!* Her mind raced – fighting against the haziness imparted by the alcohol. *Three bottles?* 'Finn…' she tried to say. *We never do three bottles.*

Panic.

'Finn thought…' She tried again, '…Finn *thought* Lyneth was keen on him …when they'd worked on the agreement.'

Had it worked? Alexa looked for any sign her words might have calmed the alarm in his eyes. He hadn't said anything. Outwardly, he looked the same Aaron who'd been sitting in front of her the whole evening – chatting amiably about things, as they did. The same Aaron she would climb into bed with later. Her husband. But, she knew she'd betrayed a confidence. Aaron hadn't known Lyneth and Finn were still in touch. Oh God, what had she said? First, that dreadful conversation she'd overheard. Now this? Christ! What on earth *was* going on?

The rising tension in the skittish strings now playing *Mozart's quartet number twenty-two in B flat* made a surreal backdrop to the emotion now welling inside her. *Judas!*

'I feel… sick,' she said. She did not lie.

'I'm sorry I poured you that last glass, Darling.'

Alexa did not see the half-smile play on his lips as she left for the bathroom, hurriedly.

She retched uncontrollably for what seemed an eternity but which lasted, in reality, mere seconds.

She stood in front of the mirror, her face drained of colour. A bitter taste of bile mixed with alcohol invaded her senses. She splashed water on her face and rinsed her mouth.

'Are you okay, Darling?' Aaron came up behind her. He passed her a hand towel from the warmer by his side. 'Why don't you get yourself to bed? I'll finish up in the kitchen and be through in a few minutes.

'Yes,' she said, unable to think of more to say.

She saw Aaron standing there, as if completely unaware of the turmoil now in her mind – as if, to him, everything was normal. It wasn't. Not to her.

'Can…' she gagged slightly, 'can you get me a glass of water please?'

'Yes, Darling, I'll bring it through.'

Alexa went from the bathroom to her bed, removing her blouse and trousers. She paused only to knock the scatter cushions from the bed-head to the floor, before climbing under the duvet. Her head spun, but it wasn't so much the alcohol now.

What's going on? She lay on her stomach, head to one side, facing away from the bed – away from where Aaron would take his usual position beside her. She shivered.

The spinning of her thoughts gave way to the spinning of her equilibrium. She'd fallen asleep before Aaron returned with the water.

*

The end of a long week of watching approached – a nervous watching; a twitching, on-edge, pacing, coffee-drinking watching. Lord only knew how much coffee he'd drunk. His blood-caffeine level caused his hands to shake uncontrollably at times. He was glad he'd never turned to cigarettes – it would have cost him a fortune in chain-smoking.

Throughout Monday to Thursday, Finn made daily contact with Ozzie, reviewing the exposure of the position. There had been further falls in the share price – it dropped to four point seven by market close on Tuesday. But, for the rest of the week, he saw little additional movement.

Four ten in the afternoon. Finn noted the time on his computer screen and checked it against his watch, rehearsing a movement he'd carried out a thousand times since breakfast, surely. Both computer and watch showed the same time. No difference. As if he'd expected one! His nervousness was palpable. He sensed it – tasted it, even.

The falls on Monday and Tuesday were minor after-shocks. The various bulletin boards and chat rooms commenting on the press release and other analyst reports had triggered them. With a lack of clarity on the issue, it seemed that investors now waited for the DPP to issue its findings. Lyneth had called to reassure him the action remained stuck in the system. She would let him know of any impending change.

The only thing not according to plan had been Alexa's

worried call on Tuesday morning. She'd wanted to speak with him, but not on the phone; a personal matter she'd said. She hadn't been too happy when he'd insisted he needed to keep his eye on the ball currently in play.

'Can it hold 'till next Monday?' he'd asked.

Reluctantly, she'd agreed, but, unusual for Alexa, she sounded troubled. The call worried Finn, but he'd needed a clear head. Selfishly, he didn't want to get involved with Alexa's personal issues. Not yet anyway.

But, to be safe, just in case, Finn called Ozzie on the Tuesday morning – earlier than he would have done, and only shortly after he'd spoken with Alexa.

'Everything OK your end, Ozzie?' he'd asked. He was conscious that Ozzie's real-time indications were around fifteen minutes ahead of his data. His screen had just popped another sell order, showing a further small drop in price.

'It's fine here,' Ozzie replied, 'predictably fine. You need to stick with it a couple of days.' Ozzie exuded confidence. 'Look, Finn, I'll buy in again the moment an upswing occurs, if it does,' he continued. 'But, if not – as I expect it won't – I'll close the position out first thing on Monday.'

Ozzie wanted to squeeze the pips on this one. Moreover, he seemed to know what he was doing.

Four-twelve, Friday afternoon. He'd just checked. The market would close within the hour and the price, steady at four point seven pence, would be the price they bought into, on Monday. Even if they only achieved five pence, having sold everything before it dipped below ten, they'd have made their target five pence margin on each share. Ozzie managed to dump nearly nineteen million shares. Finn did a quick mental calculation. They would make just south of a million – somewhere near nine hundred and fifty thousand pounds. The seconds couldn't tick away the minutes fast enough.

He tried to call Ozzie again. He'd tried a few times during

the day, but there had been no answer. It only set him to seek more solace in a greater quantity of coffee. He just got edgier as the day progressed.

Aisling had stayed out of his way all week. That afternoon, at around three fifty, she'd returned from collecting the girls from school. She'd come through to his study. 'I'm taking the girls through to mum and dad for the weekend,' she announced. 'On Saturday morning,' she added with equal brevity.

Her parents lived the other side of York. He didn't raise an eyebrow.

He sat at his study desk, phone to his ear. Where the hell was he? Ozzie's phone just rang out at the other end.

He'd left messages before, of course; another one now wouldn't help. He considered calling Alexa, but decided against it. She would be at her office. She wouldn't be able to check in on Ozzie easily, not until she left for the evening. He checked the screen. Steady at four seven.

He'd been trying to reach Ozzie, to get him to close the position that afternoon. He couldn't spend a weekend like this – caffeine high. The price held steady, the market appeared to be anticipating the worst – a case to answer in the courts. He knew differently. How could anyone be culpable? It had been a terrible, tragic accident.

Finn decided to go and get some more coffee. Time progressed.

In the kitchen, he placed the kettle on the boiling plate of the Aga. His mobile phone rang. He felt the vibration also, through the thin material of his trouser pocket. He retrieved his phone and slid it open. He didn't bother to check the number showing on screen, but lifted the phone deftly to his ear.

'Hi. Ozzie? You finally returning my calls?' he said, trying to sound nonchalant. He wasn't convinced he'd had the desired effect.

'Oh, Finn…'

It wasn't Ozzie. He'd heard Alexa, sobbing as she spoke his name. This wasn't what he expected.

'Steady, Alexa… Tell me, what's wrong?'

Aisling, who been standing at the sink washing vegetables for the evening meal, stiffened. She stopped what she was doing. She snatched a tea towel from the handrail on the Aga, to dry her hands. The sudden change in his tone had alerted her. Her expression shouted at him – *what now?* She stood with her back to the sink, arms folded before her. She looked icily across at him.

'Something's wrong,' Alexa sobbed through unseen tears.

She sounded completely unlike the Alexa he knew, the clever, confident, chirpy Alexa – Alexa, the financial analyst, PR-wiz and friend. It wasn't even like the concerned Alexa of Tuesday's call. No. This was different. His senses pricked.

'Alexa, just tell me what you think is wrong. What's happened?'

'I've just come off the phone with Grayson Barclay. He rang me to get a release published immediately.'

'What release?' Now Finn's concern solidified. It dropped to the bottom of his stomach like a concrete block.

Aisling stood there, in staring, abject disapproval at what seemed to be happening before her – her husband, comforting an upset woman on the phone. *Whatever bloody well next!* Her body language kept shouting the phrase at Finn. But he stood, too engrossed, listening too intently to notice her.

'Finn, they've withdrawn it…'

'Withdrawn what? Who? You're not making sense, Alexa.' The sound of her sobbing made her words difficult to understand.

'The family… Shufang's family… they've withdrawn the action… no reason! I just don't understand, Finn,' she cried.

Time stood still.

Four thirty-five. The whistle blew loud on the boiling kettle. It pierced the sudden silence. Finn reacted.

'Where the fuck is Ozzie?' he shouted into the phone. His face drained of colour. 'Where is he, Alexa? Where?'

'I don't know, Finn. I tried to get him myself. He's just not answering. What's going on, Finn?'

'And another thing, Finn!' shouted Aisling, joining the melee. 'Get your own fucking dinner! I've had enough of this!' She threw the tea towel to the floor and marched through to the hallway. 'Girls,' she shouted. 'Now! Get your coats, now! Just leave the TV... we're going to Granny's, now!' She turned to face Finn through the open doorway of the kitchen, her tone no softer. 'I'll come and get some things tomorrow. I'm not staying here. You sort it out. Whatever *it* is. It's your bloody mess. I'm leaving. I can't take this anymore, Finn. I just can't.'

The girls started crying. Aisling's own tears burst as she helped Becky and Jane with their coats, buttoning them against the dark, cold outside.

Then they were gone.

The pressure in the still whistling kettle blew the cap off its spout. Silence.

Finn stared at the door in disbelief.

'Finn, oh no... Finn!' Alexa had heard the exchange over the phone.

'I can't talk. . .' he said, slowly.

Finn slid the phone closed and stood there. He moved the boiling kettle off the Aga and stared after the front door. It had closed on the dark night before him. It sealed him inside, awash with emptiness.

It took him some time to move, but, eventually, he left the kitchen, his face ashen, trying hard to come to terms with the events of the past... what? Ten minutes? It couldn't have been much longer, surely? He checked his watch. Four forty-five. No. It hadn't been long at all.

How? Grayson frigging Barclay again! What's happened? *The family — Shufang's family — they've withdrawn the action... for no reason!* Alexa's words ricocheted of his mind's eye, blinding him. How had they suddenly and without explanation withdrawn their action? How could it have happened? No warning? Lyneth would have known. No, she *should* have known. *She should have called!*

Finn went to the drinks cabinet in the lounge and took out a bottle of malt, a Laphroaig. He needed a drink. He collected a glass from the tray on top of the cabinet and moved through to his study and to his desk.

He sat down hard on the leather chair and poured himself a large measure. Heady fumes of peat and Germaline rose from the hand-cut crystal glass. They were a far distant concern to him. He glanced at the screen, nudging the mouse to clear the screen-saver. Its dancing pattern gave way to the Interactive Investor service with the Tiger Oil page still showing. He clicked *refresh screen*. The price had closed at four point seven.

Finn's jawed dropped, whatever colour remained on his ashen-face, faded. The sudden realisation, above the shock of all that had just happened, hit him hard between the eyes. Tiger Oil would not open at four point seven on Monday. Panic gripped his throat like razor wire.

He'd sensed *it*, as the conversation with Alexa unfolded. He pushed *it* away as Aisling reacted. And now, there before him, *it* hit him in all *its* reality. He held a lot of borrowed stock and he couldn't reach Ozzie to react. Now he couldn't get the position closed without a major loss. Ozzie would take his last remaining shares to settle his debt. He'd lost his last hold in Tiger Oil. He'd lost his mortgage and pension security. He had nothing left. . .

Finn drank the measure of whisky in one, and reached to pour another. He sat staring at the now three-quarter full bottle on his desk. Again, he reached out for the glass.

FIFTEEN

December 2007

THE WHISKY BOTTLE stood one third full, but the glass on his desk still held a good two-fingers of the viscous, amber fluid. Friday night? Saturday morning? Finn possessed no clear idea of the time. His head felt heavy, his eyes heavier – as if they strained against their sockets, seeking release. He lay forward in the chair, slumped over his desk, head resting on folded arms. He'd been asleep; that much he could be certain of. The rest...? Nothing.

Finn grew aware the lights in the house still shone; the kitchen, hall-way and lounge, his study... the whole, a beacon of light amidst the cold, dark December fields that lay, threatening and mute, beyond the glass and stone boundary of the house.

Finn's eyes remained obstinately closed. His mouth was dry – dehydrated with the volume of spirit he'd drunk. His head, though, tried to come to terms with the nightmare situation he'd attempted to leave. The nightmare had not left him, despite his attempt to drown its very being. But he did not want to move; he did not want to relieve the dryness of his mouth, even though the dryness worked its way, inexorably, down his throat, gripping him from the inside, as if the Devil himself stood ready to tear out his tongue.

It had been a long week – a long week during which he'd become increasingly edgy; a long week during which he still had to admit to himself he hadn't fully recovered from the accident, though his headaches occurred less frequently, and less intensely. He knew he remained unfit. The shock of hearing Alexa's news, and Aisling's reaction, hit him full-square. Everything became, in that instant, just too much...

He opened his eyes, slowly. He blinked, erratically, trying to force his focus. The bottle of Laphroaig stood in front of him, within his reach, a silent, menacing challenge to an inevitable duel. No, it did not stay silent. It shouted at him, *Coward!* He moved his right arm from under his head, stretching it out, his fingers inches from strangling the neck of the bottle, the back of his hand brushing against the glass. *Choose your weapon*, the pair screamed at him.

Finn withdrew his hand slightly and turned it to grasp the glass, drawing it closer to his head. Adding an alcoholic accelerant to his depression could never be a good idea. And he did not feel good. He struggled to lift his head, but did so, feebly. He drank long from the glass. All his effort expelled, his head dropped onto his arm; his right hand lurched to pour another glass.

He'd lost... lost... lost... lost everything! All his remaining shares. His contract with Ozzie. The blank share transfer certificate! Ozzie would be safe – that's why he'd wanted the security. Ozzie would be in profit even. Damn him. Damn Alexa. Damn Lyneth. *Damn himself!* Those shares had been his security. They would have paid his mortgage and would have given him a small pension. Now he had nothing left. Christ, he didn't even have a family now.

Finn struggled, again, to raise his head and drink. And again, he drank deep and swift, gulping at the viscous, fiery liquor. He paused only to pour another and down that one too.

He'd no job; his expenditure in trying to recover his situation was outstripping the pittance he'd gained as compensation. 'Go and get yourself a job,' Aisling said, when it had all started – a lifetime ago, now.

Go and get yourself a job. The ominous echo in his head was palpable.

'Yeah, right!' he'd shouted. 'And where the hell do you think I'm going to find one of those around here! You wanted to live here, close to your family, close to your precious horses.'

'You're always away, Saudi, the North Sea, Venezuela… and now London. I needed some people around me, especially when Jane was born, and then Becky. I need people around me now. You're no help; you're never around. It's my family that helps.'

'Well, don't expect bloody miracles,' he'd answered, angrily. 'At least London means I'm not away for weeks on end. Just days. I've tried my best, Aisling. It's all I bloody know. There's nothing for me round here. Nothing. I've got to try and get it back.'

A bloody job? Yeah, right! He'd worked for himself now for the past five years; he couldn't go backwards, it just wasn't in him. *Christ*, he thought, through his growing whisky-induced stupor, *she's going to hit out at me now. If she divorces me. . . ?*

The thought trailed. Again, he lapsed into sleep.

'F… i… n… n…'

'F… i… n… n…' Again, the wind accelerated each nuance of the ethereal sound past his ears, drawing the sound of the word out. Again… but, somehow, different this time.

He was already running – running hard toward the aspen in the distance. He ran through sodden, lush vivid-green grass.

'F… i… n… n…'

'F… i… n… n… n… n… n… n…'

He turned his head to look over his shoulder, seeing the faceless apparition of *Shufang*. Her white shrouds billowed as

164

she raced towards him.

S T O P P P P P... he wanted to shout. But, again, his mouth uttered no sound. Instead, he gasped for breath. The effort of running with leaden legs burned his lungs. He ran for the safety of the tree line. But the river? The river! The river lay before him. The river was the only way. It was not the trees. The aspen, the poplar – there was no safety there. He needed to cross the raging water.

'*Finn...*' Shufang's ghostly voice resounded inside his head. '*You can never enter the same river twice. Enter the river.*'

E... n... t... e... r... You have to. He knew – she expected him to! E... n... t... e... r...

He slowed at the water's edge, stopped and turned. Shufang still advanced, but no longer quickly. '*Enter the river. You know you have to.*' The wraith-like echo in his mind reared as an invisible, advancing wall of sound, pushing him involuntarily backward towards the water's depth. A shiver tracked outward from the depth of his soul. It raced with the speed of a bush-fire. His whole body shook as he stood, bent forward, breathless before the slow, advancing apparition of Shufang. He knew what he must do.

Through breaking tears, the green before him faded to grey as he slowly turned his head to face the water. Noooooooooo! he wanted to shout at the voice in his head, but he possessed no control. Panic erupted within him.

'*Enter the river. You know you have to.*'

He knew he had to. The sound of her voice – the impenetrable, crushing wall of sound – pushed at him, relentlessly. He knew. His body turned as he pitched forward. The froth on the racing water rushed to meet his tears as he fell into the turbulent depths, his extremities flailing against the current.

He tried to lash out, tried to gain some sort of rhythm to his movement. He spun round and round with the force of the swirling water.

His head broke the surface and, through stinging eyes, he saw the bank side. Its mountainous rise from the water's far edge set a final barrier to his safety. He needed to reach it. He must reach it. He kicked out. A quick glance behind. Shufang was standing at the river's edge, staring at him as he clawed his way across the raging water. '*You can never enter the same river twice, Finn, never.*'

Blackness.

Peace.

Everything rendered dark, quiet.

*

Finn opened his eyes slowly, his head pounded – regular beats on a kettle drum. He moved slightly, his pulse-rate increased with the effort. The beating of the drum quickened. *Bad idea.*

He lay in bed, aware that all he now wore was underwear. The warmth of the bedclothes laid a small measure of comfort against his near-naked body. How long had he lain there? Slowly, gingerly, he tilted his head on the pillow. He glanced at the clock by his side. The digital display threw a sharp, red, incandescent five-twelve at him. His eyes took the catch and his mind staggered at the sharpness of the sudden objectivity. What day? Monday? Monday! It could only be Monday.

Finn remembered a little. He had not finished the bottle. Somehow, against the odds, he'd won the dual. He'd picked the glass not the bottle, and he'd won. Sometime during the Saturday... or Sunday, perhaps... he could not recall – it didn't seem to matter, not for the moment – he at least managed to get himself to bed. He'd slept through, though he had a sense of drifting in and out of consciousness. He was never quite well enough, never quite conscious enough, to be motivated to do anything about his state.

The thought came to him – it explained his winning over the bottle. His rundown condition after the accident had brought on this period of enforced rest. But, with the rest accelerated by the whisky, he felt rough – sick. The constant beating of kettledrums compounded his nausea.

The dream pervaded; a constant companion. It wasn't a nightmare. Reality was the real nightmare. *The now* – the nightmare happening to him now. No, the dream, lucid and ethereal; it meant something, he was sure. But it did relate to *the now...* didn't it? To give up or continue the fight? At the point the water reached out to him for perhaps the ninth time that weekend, he'd woken. The time, five-twelve. Had the water released its prey to fight? *Fight could be the only answer. But how?* He felt ill. He needed caffeine.

Despite the early hour, he managed to rise and get himself down stairs. He picked up the Saturday copy of the Financial Times. He'd found the paper lying on the small table in the hallway. Aisling. *Christ!* She'd been round during the weekend, and he'd slept through. The thought triggered his memory. The house was empty, desolate, without Aisling, without the children. Even at this hour, in this state, the memory bore heavily on his senses.

He got himself to the kitchen. There he struggled, but eventually made a cafetière of coffee. His senses stabilised, gradually. He took a couple of Paracetamol, staying away from the Perocet. He was bad enough, but he didn't need the overkill of a narcotic analgesic on top.

He turned to the paper. The markets were not due to open for another three hours or so. It was all over, wasn't it? The fat bloody lady had stopped her singing, hadn't she? He checked the Companies and Markets section, going straight to the back page.

He hadn't quite expected to see Tiger Oil in the FT – it wasn't a well known stock. It hit him further to see it there, black on pink, head-lining the Small Cap section. *Extinction Threat to Tiger Removed.* He didn't need to read further. He couldn't. He waited for the coffee to work its magic. He couldn't concentrate to read. He simply scanned the headlines depicting the rest of the increasing gloom in the financial sectors. Curiously, his mood lifted a little. There was a lot of shit going on out there. A lot of angst building. Nervous people were turning any bad news, suddenly and irrationally, into tragic proportions.

As the caffeine kicked in, clarity returned slowly. And so did thoughts of his worsening situation. Christ, his interest-only mortgage stood due to come off its fixed-rate at the end of the year. Any new rate would hit him – even if he could remortgage. But he had no job. He ran on financial fumes and he could feel the ugly B-word beckon.

Bankruptcy. No. Surely not. He'd no assets to speak of, but it didn't mean he couldn't pay his bills, did it? Technically, the deal with Ozzie only lost him his security, not his income. But now he'd nothing left to trade, and only about two months cash available to him in reserve. He needed some answers. Where the hell had Ozzie got to? Why did Lyneth not know what was happening? Worse! Did she know and just not say anything? And Alexa? *She'd wanted to speak with him, but not on the phone.* The conversation came to him again. *It was personal, she said.* Suddenly, he remembered – Alexa had not been happy. *Can it hold 'till next Monday?* It was Monday now.

Finn lifted his head from the paper. Cupping his refilled coffee mug in two hands, he glanced over to the fridge. There, written on the small magnetic white-board attached to its door, a simple message. *We need to talk – I want my life back. A.*

SIXTEEN

LYNETH SAT IN SILENCE. She'd been in the office since seven a.m., shrouded in quiet solitude. She sat troubled, watching the struggling dawn rise on a bleak December city morning. She watched as the detail in the buildings opposite came to life – gradually picked out in the meagre contrast of the dull, austere, morning light.

It had been a lousy weekend, full of doubt and regret. Neither shopping nor vodka eased her conscience or placated her. Regret, doubt, then regret again; her mood swung with the motion of a pendulum. At eight a.m. the phone had rung – an expected call, but dreaded all the same. Finn.

'Hi, Lyneth,' she heard, the tone of his voice matter-of-fact.

'Hi,' she replied. Did he suspect something?

'You know what's happened...' Again the matter-of-fact tone; more statement than question. '...or at least you will when the market opens in about half an hour.'

'Yes, Finn. God, I am *so* sorry, Finn.' She stressed the *so*, over compensating because she was restricted to the telephone; Finn would not be able to *see* how sorry she was. 'Alexa called me straight after she'd called you. She'd been totally fraught... I didn't know what to say or do. I tried to call you, later, but didn't get any reply.'

'S'OK, Lyneth,' said Finn, his tone softened. 'I've been a bit dead to the world this weekend. Hit the bottle I'm afraid. I never even checked my messages. But I'm a bit more alive to it all now. I think coffee, a long hot shower, and more coffee did the trick.' It sounded a sad attempt at trying to lighten the situation. Emotionally, the banter translated as anything but. Then... 'Didn't you get *any* idea what was happening, Lyneth?' he asked, at last.

Lyneth hesitated a moment, not quite sure whether to blurt out her theory on the evidence. But no. *I'm better than that.* She had no answers... no confirmation even. James Green at the DPP had not been in touch, and he wouldn't be in his office yet. No. No concrete answers. And she wasn't about to lead herself into any confession, not yet. She did feel partly responsible, yes. But it was only a feeling, after all... wasn't it?

'I don't know,' she said, having settled for a half-truth. 'I've just got into the office, and I can't reach my DPP contact just yet. He's got some explaining to do. He was supposed to be on top of it all. He should've called me if anything changed.'

'It did change, didn't it,' said Finn, his voice heavy with sarcasm. 'So much for friends in places.'

'I know. I do trust him... something else must have happened. I'm truly sorry, Finn... Look, I'm glad you phoned, there's something I need to say to you. I just need to find some answers first. Can you come down today?'

'Yeah, later,' he said. 'Call me around eleven. I should be able to get a train soon; they run hourly. I just have to get changed. See you.'

Finn ended the call without waiting for her response. 'OK,' she said, to the dead connection.

At around eleven – a little before, or a little after, she couldn't recall such trivial detail – she'd called Finn again. They could meet around twelve thirty; he expected the train to get to town for about twelve.

'A sandwich OK?' he'd suggested. 'I don't fancy anything much after this weekend.'

'Fine for me. Meet me at the office,' she'd replied. 'Call at reception, and I'll come down to you.' She didn't feel like being in a restaurant either, but for different reasons.

After she'd called Finn, she went through to see Hillary. It had been pointless going to see her partner-at-law before then. He didn't usually show up in the office until ten-thirty. Of the two partners in the small law firm, Lyneth pulled the most weight these days. Hillary Keaton merely kept in with some well heeled clients, most of whom he'd apparently been at Marlborough, or Oxford, with. Hillary did not impress her much of the time – he had done, but no longer – though his clients did bring her some interesting litigation cases, cases that had propelled her far from her humble Welsh beginnings. In truth, they needed each other, and they each knew it.

'So. I guess you've come to let me know you're taking some time off?' he said, reclining in his oversized, leather swivel chair. A smug grin spread untidily across his face, like a child having spread strawberry jam on some toast – most lumped in the centre, little of it reaching the edges.

'How...' she started.

'How did I guess?' He didn't wait for an answer. 'Because, my dear, you look beat. What's a matter, didn't get much sleep over the weekend, did we?' He winked at her.

He sprang forward in this chair – the sudden movement, uncharacteristic. Lyneth flinched. 'No. Not *just* that,' he continued. 'I've just taken a call from the DPP. They confirmed my weekend phone conversation with Aaron Philips. They've pulled the case... Shufang Su's family. You know that, don't you? And with no case, your work load just got lighter... so, you thought you'd take a quick break and catch some rest.' He paused, his smug grin even smugger – if that could have been possible. 'I'm right, aren't I, Dear?'

'I guess,' she replied. She did feel tired.

'So, lunch with Finn?' he goaded. His expression remained faithful to the sleazy persona his character had more recently adopted in her presence.

Too tired to react, Lyneth rolled with the metaphoric punch. *Where the hell did that come from?* 'Pardon?' she said. *It's getting time to move on*, she thought.

'I suppose you're going to meet up with Finn now?'

'I guess.' No actual point in denying anything, not now. But it came as a complete surprise – a fast-ball of a comment, not in the least expected.

Dulled a little through tiredness, but still sharp enough for Hillary, her mind set on it. Hillary had been quiet on the subject of Finn, ever since they heard about the accident. She'd assumed that her recent contact with Finn escaped his attention. She knew how her partner's mind worked. Never a man to forego innuendo in his conversations with her, the least suspicion of an aspect of her sexual life would provide a nugget for Hillary to test his bite on. So, if he had not known of her contacts with Finn over the last weeks, why did he know now? *More bloody questions.* She turned on her heels, her back facing him squarely. 'I'll see you tomorrow, Hillary,' she said over her shoulder. She left him for the privacy of her own office.

Lyneth picked up the phone, called her secretary, and managed to get James at the DPP.

'Yes, gorgeous,' chirped James, '...the family dropped the action.' And then '...no, they offered no reason for doing so. There are still no details on our case admin system. I doubt it has been anything we've said or done. I'm sorry, Lyneth,' he continued, '...but I can't offer anything to help explain why.'

'Thanks anyway, James. Call me for that Christmas drink.'

At twelve twenty-five the phone rang; the internal ring signaled Claire's call. 'Finn Jackson has just arrived, Miss

Jones. He is waiting in the reception area.'

'Can you take care of my desk please, Claire? If there are any calls, you can hold them over to tomorrow morning. Just say I'm at court this afternoon. Hillary can take anything urgent. Thanks.'

Lyneth replaced the phone on the desk, gathered her briefcase, handbag and coat, and left.

*

Lyneth saw Finn as soon as she exited the lift. He was standing, centrally, in the lobby area. She went straight over and, with a half-smile she didn't really feel up to giving, she gave him a quick, uncharacteristically sheepish kiss on his right cheek.
'Hi, Lyneth.'

'You look like I feel today, Finn'. She quickly checked herself, '…your expression, I mean.' Finn looked nicely but not expensively dressed, she thought. He sported a crisp white shirt with a plain pink tie under a navy blue suit. The suit had a fine white stripe – not the quality of some suits she bustled alongside during her city career, but he did look handsome. She'd be damned if she let herself lose him just yet. 'You look great,' she added. She exaggerated the cast of her downward gaze, along the length of his figure, allowing her smile to develop more fully this time.

'Thanks. It's from Jaeger, but I had hoped to have changed my tailor by now.'

'It's lovely to see you, Finn,' she said, relieved at the slight touch of levity in his response.

They left the building and walked down Clerkenwell Road.

'I know a cheeky little sandwich shop just down here,' she said, after they had walked in silence a while. But her own

173

attempt at a little levity failed to elicit a reaction from Finn. It reminded her of the gravity of the moment.

They turned down Turnmill Street, towards Farringdon tube station, and walked on, again in silence, until reaching a Pret A Manger.

'In here,' said Finn.

They entered to a relatively light, lunchtime rush. Finn selected an innocuous salad and sparkling water. Lyneth picked some sort of chicken wrap – she didn't look too closely at it – and a blackcurrant smoothie. There were still a few seats left vacant at the window bar and, after they had paid for their lunches, they took two adjacent stools.

'Bit different to Gatti's, isn't it?' she joked, feeling a little more relaxed, despite the present difficulties. With no instructions remaining with Tiger Oil, the idea of helping Finn settled easier on her conscience.

'Needs must. ...just don't feel like eating much at the moment,' he replied. 'My head's OK, but I downed a lot of whisky this weekend, and my guts are not quite right...' He turned to face her; the gaze from his bright blue eyes pierced her being. 'What *was* it you'd wanted to say to me, Lyneth?' he asked, matter-of-factly.

'I kinda think things have been overtaken by events, don't you?' she replied. She'd opted not to tell him of her earlier fears over the validity of the litigation case. She tried to change the subject. 'Where does all this leave you now?' The look she gave him showed genuine concern, as genuine as the attraction she felt toward him. She experienced a pang of guilt knowing that, had she said something, she might have enabled Finn to close the short position earlier. *But, damn it, he's the man I want. I'm not going to risk upsetting the possibility of a relationship.* Needs must – her thoughts echoed Finn's words for an entirely different reason.

'What went wrong, Lyneth?' he asked, evading her own

question. 'Surely you must have known something? You're counsel to Tiger Oil. I can't believe you didn't know anything...'

'All we know, Finn...' She paused to take a quick drink from the bottle of highly viscous purple liquid. 'All I know is the family requested the action be withdrawn. They gave no reason. Apparently, according to Hillary, the family didn't even give their lawyers a reason. I confirmed it with the DPP's office this morning – they just received the instruction to pull it. No questions. No reasons. I'm as much in the dark as you, or anyone else for that matter.'

'But you sat on top of all the information? He turned his head to look directly into her eyes again, his gaze as sharp as a Toledo steel rapier. 'If anyone could see anything, you would have seen it, Lyneth.'

She could not deny the statement. Her principles told her so. Finn's rapier-like gaze held her, in that moment, to account. He sought her truthfulness. Of course he didn't know anything – how could he. But his challenge was direct and immediate. She knew if she continued to deny any suspicion, and something came out, as it could, she would have destroyed any hope of a relationship with him. And it could come out, with so many unanswered questions still. There, at that precise moment, as he sat looking into her eyes, trying to read her, she relented.

'I received a letter...' she started. Finn looked content for her to continue. '...A letter, the Friday before last, from David Kail. He'd written in answer to some of my questions. I really thought Tiger Oil had a case to answer. Until that letter, I could find nothing to corroborate either Jonathon Long's or Scott Lindon's version of events. Without corroboration, I truly believed the other side would attack their versions of the events, and allege some form of cover up. So I asked questions.'

'And the letter... David's letter?'

'He offered the evidence available in his telephone records, saying it would confirm the various times I questioned. The letter washed my argument out.'

'So, you knew there wasn't a case?' said Finn. His voice was calm, measured even; not the raised pitch of her fears. He turned his head, slowly, away from her, transfixing his gaze on the comings and goings in the street – black cabs, red buses, white vans, people. Many, busy people. He fell silent.

The silence unnerved Lyneth. *Why can't he be angry or shout at me. I could handle that – I could shout back, hold my own.* But silence? It killed her inside. She hurt.

'You could have told me. I could have closed the position. A week, Lyneth. A whole damn week when I could have got out.'

He sounded dejected. She'd hurt him, and she knew it. It hurt her too.

'What can I do to help, Finn?' *Dumb question.* She realised as soon as she'd opened her mouth.

'I think you've done enough. Don't you?'

'I'm truly sorry, Finn. As soon as I got the letter, I checked with the DPP. The action wasn't going anywhere; it stuck in the system. Even without there being a case to answer, it would have been Christmas or, most likely, after, before it would have been thrown out. You would have been long gone. I just thought...'

'You thought wrong.'

'I know, now. I'm truly sorry . . .' Her voice trailed off, she didn't know quite what else to say.

Damn him, why can't he show anger, I can deal with anger. She couldn't say sorry again. It wouldn't help.

'We don't know why, Finn,' she said. 'We have no idea why. It can't simply have been the fact there's no case to answer... Shufang's family would not have used that. They would not have known about the letter. We would have got some wind

176

from their lawyers. But we didn't. Nothing. Zilch.' She was frustrated. 'Look, Finn, there must be some other reason. This came from Shufang's family. No way could I have seen this happening. No way.'

Finn remained silent. He looked defeated. Lyneth moved her left hand, from where she had been playing with the edge of the packet still holding one half of her chicken wrap. She didn't feel hungry. She placed her hand on Finn's. He did not move to withdraw. At that spontaneous moment, a surge of aesthetic electricity caused her heart to miss a beat. Finn withdrew his hand, slowly, as if he had not wanted to.

They fell silent, both continuing to pick, unenthusiastically, at the remainder of their lunch. Finn reached for his BlackBerry, taking it from its belt holster. He alternated between pressing a few buttons and thumbing the little white track-ball.

'I don't understand?' said Finn, sounding confused. A puzzled expression broke over his brow, furrows tracking deep.

'You don't understand what?'

'Something's going on here. I... I just don't get it.'

There: life returning to his voice; she could sense it; a life not there moments ago.

'It's the MoneyAM website,' he said, in partial explanation, '...the intra-day stock chart for Tiger Oil. It opened at eleven pence this morning, I checked. But there's something else. The price did jump. With all the costs and everything, Ozzie would have exercised his option on my shares to cover his margin. I've lost them all right. No doubt. But...'

'Finn, for Christ sake, but what?'

'They've fallen back again,' he said, in a voice coloured with disbelief.

She could see his head shake, almost imperceptibly, but his disbelief was blatant.

'Not by much, but they've dropped away,' he said. 'With all the US and Chinese interest in the sector, and in oil-sands extraction, I expected them to climb to where they were. I expected around twelve or even higher. But no, they've tailed off again, down to nine and a half pence. Something else is happening here, Lyneth.'

'What do you mean?'

'There has to be more to this than any of us knows right now.'

'It's what I've been trying to say, Finn.'

Finn turned his head towards her, and held her gaze in his. She caught her breath. There: a glint, a brightness again, in his lovely eyes. His gaze was no longer rapier-like. *It's his damn eyes*. She smiled deep inside. They spoke trouble – the kind of trouble she liked.

Finn seemed to think a while; then spoke, more positively than she'd heard for sometime.

'Maybe... just maybe, Lyneth...' he said.

Clearly, an idea had struck him. He framed his words around it as it did so, speaking aloud.

'Just... what if...'

She could see him trying to articulate the right opening. She could sense his mind racing.

'What if the reason the price is staying low is that the market is fed up with a new share issue facing so many troubles early on? A lack of confidence, perhaps? Maybe there's frustration and anger over the management performance. Shareholders are not going to like being subjected to a roller coaster ride – not so soon after the company floated on AIM.'

'Yes, I follow. It's a plausible argument,' she said.

'What if there's poor confidence in the management of Tiger Oil?' He paused to drink the last of his water. 'A takeover bid,' he said.

'A *what*! Are you crazy?' she said, momentarily surprised. Her voice rose in volume and pitch. A few faces turned to look at her, but, as quickly, the interest of others faded.

'It could work,' he said.

'Shorting borrowed stock is one thing, Finn. You have to be kidding with a takeover. For a start, how the hell... No! *Where* the hell are you going to get funds to buy in?'

'I don't know, Lyneth.'

'Well then.'

'I don't know, but I've sure as hell got nothing else to do but think my way through this...'

She looked at him. His look, straight into the depth of her eyes, twinkled, disarmingly. *Trouble.*

'Haven't I?' he said.

*

Aaron called earlier in the day. He wouldn't be home for their dinner that night. *Would she be OK?* Of course she would. *Silly question, Aaron,* she commented to herself. But her mind troubled her. Over the whole weekend past, she'd been troubled, profoundly unhappy even. Her failure to keep the knowledge of Finn and Lyneth's potential relationship from Aaron, and the call from Grayson late Friday, disturbed her deeply. Grayson's call put paid to Finn's plan, and cost him the rest of his shares. And she, clearly... well, she couldn't claim to be an innocent bystander, could she? She, Alexa; she who recruited Ozzie's involvement; she who made it possible for Finn to get into this mess. Being unable to contact Finn all weekend, she'd felt his pain. She worried about him enormously. What had she done? *What had Aaron done?*

Before Aaron's call, Alexa had planned to use the evening's dinner to probe him further about Tiger Oil. After all, why not? As a marital asset, she could claim a vested interest in his business... surely? Now though, the probe would need to wait. Aaron! He was becoming more elusive lately - what did it all mean?

Although she could not remember thinking much about it in past years, an air of secretiveness had always pervaded Aaron's businesses and, for that matter, his frequent absences from home. *Just a part of business life* she'd previously told herself. *Nothing more.* Before, she'd never found a reason to question anything in his life. In truth, she hardly ever discussed her own business with him. But now? No! She could no longer be sure about anything, not now. From Aaron's joining with Finn and Shufang, and getting Grayson Barclay involved, she now grew quickly, and acutely, aware how little she knew about Tiger Oil plc.

She tried to speak to Aaron over the weekend. Trying to play it all low key, just the occasional question, interspersed with their normal weekend routine. For the main part, they busied themselves with their separate activities. She read, listened to music, took a quick trip out shopping; he sat at the dining table, working on some deal or other.

'I've a great deal of difficulty with Grayson Barclay, you know?' answered Aaron, in response to one question. 'Ever since Shufang's death he has been trying to micromanage his investment in us. He's only a non-Exec chairman, damn it! You know something else? I think Grayson really engineered Finn's exit. Grayson called everyone to cancel the meeting that day. *He* took the decision to tell Finn to leave, not us.'

Alexa could not be sure her questions appeared as innocent as she hoped they would. She had no real way of knowing. Aaron answered her questions naturally, without any difficulty. Everything seemed plausible enough. But, her senses screamed the opposite to her.

'When I met Finn after his run in with Barclay,' Aaron had continued, '...I'd mentioned Machiavelli's theory about the old order not welcoming the new. I just feel the experimental

180

nature of the project got a bit too much for the old goat. I really think, at the time, Barclay's feet got cold on the idea of floating. He just wanted to cut his losses.'

Everything Aaron said over the weekend just seemed so… well… so *organised*.

'All the Chinese interest in the Canadian fields, and the rising oil price of course… It all appeared to fire him up to chase a quick profit. I guess Barclay reckoned on using his contacts in Shell. He probably imagined he could sell the well subleases back to them for more than we'd originally paid. He would have been in profit. We all would. Even Finn would have made money. I do think Finn's been a bit silly.'

'What do you mean, silly?' she asked, trying to speak with an indifference she certainly hadn't felt.

'I gather he took a bet with his shares, on the falling price caused by the Su family legal claim. You know, the one Grayson got you to issue a statement about on Friday?'

'I've no idea,' she said. 'I haven't spoken to him this last week,' she lied. Lying to her husband came easily. It had become something of a norm in their relationship – certainly in recent years. In fact, ever since she decided to regain her life. It kept things on an even keel.

'You know, Finn's accident was a complete tragedy. I could have worked with him, to see him through the AIM float, so he could have made something out of it all. But now? Now I reckon he's got himself burnt.'

Aaron's words did not give her any comfort.

No, on reflection, it had certainly not been a good weekend for her. She poured herself a glass of wine from the bottle resting on the coffee table in front of her. She retrieved her phone from where it lay next to the bottle, and reclined into the comfort of the couch. She dialled Finn's mobile.

'Hello, Finn. Can we talk?'

'Yes, it would be good,' answered Finn. There was an odd,

unexpected brightness about his voice.

Alexa's spirits picked up. Finn certainly did not sound the same as he had on Friday night. *His family? . . .* she remembered. *What about his family?* But she didn't ask.

'Why don't you come round to my office tomorrow morning, you know, Worship Street? Say eleven?'

'Yes, Finn, I'd love to. Eleven. See you then. Bye.' Her relief was obvious. *But what is going on?* She drank swiftly, replaced the glass and phone on the table, and again leant back. This time she closed her eyes and slept.

SEVENTEEN

'LADIES, I HAVE A PLAN.' A bold statement, considering he had no detail to suggest. The two girls looked at each other. If any sense of rivalry existed between them, an observer would not have detected it.

Early December, and in a couple of weeks it would be Christmas. The financial markets continued to behave with volatility; they appeared fragile at best. And there he found himself, with nothing to bargain with but his wits. He had little income to speak of. His credit cards stubbornly butted at their limits and, if he stopped to think about it long enough, he stared divorce in the face. He had lost everything. So, he reasoned – in the space between lunch with Lyneth yesterday and meeting the girls today – if he continued to go down, he would go down in style.

Remarkably, he felt refreshed. The weekend's alcohol-induced rest clearly served him well. He thanked God he'd not finished the bottle, as intended, on the Friday evening.

As soon as he left Lyneth after lunch, he had gone round to the Tower Hotel where he'd managed to get a room at short notice. He then went to sit in the Café Rouge for the rest of the afternoon. He drank coffee and scribbled notes on some paper he retrieved from his pocket. He tried to recall who held what shares in the company. Whom did *he* know in the institutions? He managed to recall a few names, from introductions Aaron had made during the initial preparations for the AIM float, back in April. If he could swing it, who, he asked himself, might be favourable to seeing a management change?

Later, well after it turned dark, and after the reflected lights of the apartments and the hotel opposite started their dance of sparkles on the water's wind-rippled surface, he had sent a text to Carole.

It had been on the off-chance. He held no expectation of whether or not she might be free. Her husband frequently travelled away with overnight stops, but never predictably. Neither Finn nor Carole took anything for granted. But, last night, the husband had stayed up in Manchester. Yes, she could get out. Babysitting never appeared problematic – he never asked how. She would see him, but would not stay all night.

When Carole arrived, they decided to prolong the anticipation further. They enjoyed room service first – a shared club sandwich and a bottle of house champagne. A slight extravagance perhaps, but then heck! Why not? Their brief repast concluded, they turned to each other. They made as much use of the rest of the room as they could. For them both, the affair gave them each what they sought – fun. And it had been a while since they'd enjoyed some real fun, tactile sex.

They lay a while, naked, legs entwined, her head on his chest and his arm around her, drawing her close. The sheer silky touch of her long, thick auburn hair, as it lay across his arm, pleasured him. He decided not to mention anything.

They agreed, when they first met the previous year, after telling each other the basic facts of their situations, there would be no need to bring the subject up again. As long as they both remained clear about what they wanted from the relationship – their little, parallel slice of life. As long as they respected each other. They both knew that at some point it would end. Neither wanted to change their marriages. But now it had ended. Finn knew, as soon as Aisling left him. He represented a threat to Carole now. But he did not say anything. The night remained theirs.

He would text her. She would understand. He tightened his arm muscles slightly, drawing her closer to him. He kissed the top of her head to the sound of a contented murmur. She nuzzled closer in response.

Yes indeed, the night was ours.

The girls arrived at eleven that Tuesday morning. Before he left her the day before, Lyneth agreed, they would meet at his office – the fewer people who saw them together the better. Lyneth offered to pick up some sandwiches on the way. He called her earlier, at nine. There would be three of them.

Although Tuesday wasn't a day allocated to him for the office, he managed to secure another small meeting room from ten until two. This close to Christmas, the meeting rooms frequently went unused – the short notice had not been a problem.

'What sort of a plan?' they asked, almost simultaneously. They looked towards Finn. For Lyneth and Alexa, the meeting gave them the first opportunity to be in each other's company. They knew each other, of course. They spoke frequently, and e-mailed. After all, they were both retained advisors to Tiger Oil.

Though he felt stronger and more positive – perhaps more so than at any time since before the accident – if he wanted to mount a takeover, he would need to throw himself into it. He would need all the help he could get.

Finn recapped on the Tiger Oil share price movement he'd seen the previous day.

'I do think you're right, Finn. There does seem to be some underlying lack of confidence in the business model,' said Alexa.

'But a take over...' said Lyneth, joining the fray. 'I asked yesterday, how the hell do you expect to achieve a take over? You have nothing, Finn.'

'She's right,' observed Alexa. 'How can you possibly hope to mount a takeover? It would take loads of planning, not to mention the fund raising you would need. If you tried anything, the board would be sure to suspect something. It's a small company.'

'But we know from Ozzie Medwin, around forty five percent of the shares are out with institutions and private investors...'

'Has anyone seen Ozzie? asked Lyneth.

Finn looked at Alexa, 'No,' he said, answering for her, too. He paused to check the scrap of paper he'd scribbled on in the Café Rouge. 'Ozzie reckoned there are around fifty or sixty investors in the mix, with around ten institutional investors. There are two key ones at seven and five percent, but the remaining stakes are all small. If I can talk to these about selling their holdings then...'

'What about funds, Finn? OK, let's assume you *can* talk a bunch into selling. What on earth are you planning to buy them out with... smoke?' Lyneth clearly doubted the efficacy of the plan. 'It just doesn't make much sense to me,' she said.

'I can see that if you could fund it, then it *is* a potential option...'

'Thank you, Alexa,' he said, as he remained looking at Lyneth for a short time. Then he turned to engage with Alexa. 'That is where you come in, I'm afraid.'

'Don't be afraid, Finn,' giggled Alexa. She looked to Lyneth at her side, and winked at her. 'I supposed you only wanted me for my little black book.'

'Yes,' said Finn, grinning broadly.

'But how?' asked Lyneth.

'And this close to Christmas,' added Alexa.

'I'm not sure, Lyneth. That is about the extent of my plan, so far.'

'You need our help badly, don't you, Finn?' concluded Alexa, hitting a serious tone.

'Yes. I do. I need you both.'

'Well…' said Lyneth, as she looked to Alexa. 'I guess we'd better deliver this time.'

Chalk and cheese. Both tall, shapely, sexy. Both impeccably dressed. Lyneth, in her mid-thirties, a brunette; her long hair tied behind her in a ponytail today. Alexa in her forties, her long auburn hair flowing free in thick, crashing waves across her shoulders. Both sharp minds. Lyneth, a Rottweiler of a litigation lawyer, hid her sharpness behind a thin veneer of ice cool, translucent smiles – smiles, Finn knew, that could come and go at will. Alexa's sharpness, soft in comparison. She possessed a further ten years of life experience on Lyneth. Alexa could play the politics of any situation. He knew that, if necessary, she could act dumb to get close and learn, before she reached any conclusion. But she, too, could strike with precision. *Yes*, thought Finn, *this is a team*!

'Well,' said Alexa, in giggles again, '…for a start, we have every card we might care to think of, stacked neatly against us. Christmas is looming and the City is depressed. There's a weird early party-mood around, since no one has anything better to do. The champagne and bonuses are not flowing quite as much, but you can get beer and wine from dawn to dusk.'

'You make it all sound so easy, Alexa,' said Lyneth.

'Well,' said Alexa, 'I s'pose my point is there isn't really *any* time for a normal fund raising. We can't just get a plan together and walk it around a few funds and institutions. We need to interest someone with serious money – and fast.'

'Any ideas, ladies?'

'How much do we need, Finn?' asked Alexa.

'I reckon eight mill' to make a decent offer, slightly less if the share price falls away anymore…'

'We can hope,' said Lyneth.

Finn looked again at the scrap of paper in front of him. 'But that only buys us thirty percent. Under the City Takeover Code, we would then need to be prepared to buy the rest of the business out.'

'Another…?' asked Alexa.

'Another, say, eighteen million,' he said, a little hesitantly.

Lyneth whistled. 'How?'

'Banks,' said Finn. 'It's all I can think of at the moment. I doubt we'll get an individual stumping up for the full amount, and I don't buy lottery tickets.'

'So, you need to raise, say, ten million cash? And then get one or more banks to extend a twenty million facility?' said Lyneth.

'About sums it up,' replied Finn. 'Any ideas, Alexa?'

Both Finn and Lyneth looked expectantly at Alexa, waiting for her response.

'Well, I love a challenge,' she said, playing with them.

'But have you any ideas?' asked Finn and Lyneth, in unison.

'I only know of two or three people who we could approach on this. It's all foreign money.'

'I don't care, really,' said Finn.

'As long as it's not illegal, Alexa,' chimed Lyneth.

'Never asked,' laughed Alexa. 'I can check?'

'That'd be a good opening line. Yeah… can just see that one!' said Finn.

'OK, OK, just don't tell me – I'm a lawyer, remember.

'Well, it would not be from normal people. I don't think too much due diligence would help matters.' Alexa had noticed Lyneth's eyebrows rise, but she carried on. 'As far as I know, they're all respectable businessmen in their own countries, but…' she looked straight at Finn, 'we can't afford to cross such people.'

'I know. But the end will justify it. Who are we talking about?' asked Finn.

'You would probably need to offer most of the upside to whomever might help. It would mean you acting more as their employee, than partner.

'Any gain now would be a win for me, Alexa.'

'OK. Paper!' said Alexa. 'Let's draw up a short list. I can work on a presentation over the next couple of days. I can use the company's AIM admission document for most of it.' She turned in her seat to face Lyneth more directly. 'Lyneth, can you do a quick verification on the presentation, just so that it will hold up to initial scrutiny.'

'Yes. Sure thing, Alexa.'

'Right. I'll go get some paper.' Finn rose and left the office, closing the door behind him.

Lyneth and Alexa turned to each other. Alexa broke the silence first.

'You like him a lot, don't you, Lyneth?'

'Yes.'

Alexa, too, saw what Finn had seen before: the coolness of mind lurking beneath the veneer of Lyneth's smile. But she didn't feel threatened. 'Just don't hurt him,' she said.

'I don't plan to.'

*

Every nation has them. There are businessmen – and women of course, but in truth mainly men – businessmen who, under certain circumstances, one might class as "shady characters".

In general, one would not want to think of such men as crooks. Certainly, one would never talk openly in such terms about them, to anybody. One might merely think… Such men and, occasionally, women, simply appeared to be successful without apparent logic.

And so it was that Alexa drew up a list of three names. Neither Finn nor Lyneth deemed it appropriate to ask the "whys" or "wherefores". When they first read the list, they considered it would be the basis for a good joke. Alexa had written the names of an Arab, a Chinese and a Russian. Neither Lyneth nor Finn recognised the names, let alone gave a correct pronunciation of them.

Yes, every country has at least one. Fahad Al-Shahrani, Chan Chao Xiang, and Grigoriy Moshkovich.

'These are the only ones I can think of whom we could approach quickly. They all have money – I think mainly mining and steel interests. They might look on the Canadian oil sands as a useful diversification. We can at least try,' said Alexa, as she transferred contact details from a small note book.

That had been last Tuesday, when they met in his office. Now, Wednesday afternoon, and despite the flush of enthusiasm produced by last week's meeting, Finn sat in his Worship Street office, alone. The city would effectively close in a few days' time – close for the Christmas holidays. He sat in quiet solitude, having made no forward progress.

He counted himself fortunate in having met two out of Alexa's three contacts. Alexa revelled in the financial analysis she clearly excelled at. She'd done a great job on putting the investment presentation together, based on the perception that Tiger Oil was ripe for takeover. Lyneth gave it the OK. From an investment prospectus perspective, she's been happy the presentation contained no statements an investor could hold out as misrepresentation, if the company could not achieve its projected performance.

The presentation put forward the idea that Tiger Oil lacked visionary leadership. It suggested he, Finn Jackson, would be the best person to continue to develop the new patents and the business. Without Finn, there would be no technical leadership, and the firm's true potential would not be realisable. If they backed Finn, they could expect a strong performance in a valuable sector, set against rising oil prices.

During the previous Thursday and Friday, Alexa had made the arrangements for Finn to meet with Fahad Al-Shahrani and Grigoriy Moshkovich. Chan Chao Xiang declined. He'd clearly been too busy with his inscrutable preparations for a return to China, while London slept on its fat Christmas belly. Chan Chao Xiang reduced their list to two.

He met the Arab for coffee on Monday afternoon, in the bar area of the Hyde Park Hilton. Fahad Al-Shahrani was able to spare an hour between meetings, "…on account of the introduction being from Alexa". Again, Finn did not ask any questions.

'It is not a great deal of money,' said Fahad, in his perfect, but noticeably clipped English. 'Why should such a small deal interest me?' The worry beads in Fahad's hand looked dangerously close to making a noise. He toyed with one bead in particular, moving it back and forth with a thumbnail. The movement provided the sort of continuous motion that annoyed Finn – like the incessant clicking of a pen top, or the tapping of a foot.

'It is the potential in the patents,' said Finn, struggling to overcome this unexpected objection. It was certainly no small deal for him. 'When the extraction process is proven,' he continued, '…it will open up the more economic development of the fields, without tearing nature apart to get at the oil. There is a lot of concern…'

'In the West, yes?' interrupted Fahad.

'In the West, yes,' repeated Finn. He considered Fahad,

191

briefly. In his late thirties, Finn thought. But he spoke with the authority of a much older man. Here sat someone the like of whom Finn had not personally encountered before; someone used to playing for high stakes and who, quite clearly, usually won. He was someone who clearly owned a large part of the enchanted garden Finn sought entrance to. The authority in Fahad's voice, and in his words, did not proclaim arrogance. It was merely the high confidence born of continued success.

'There is a lot of concern over the damage to the environment caused by other methods of extraction,' Finn continued. 'The Tiger Oil process will overcome that. It will make most of its money through licensing the technology around the world.'

'But there is a risk?' *Click. Click.* The worry beads finally broke through. 'The technology is not proven?' *Click.*

'It is a matter of time. Once I can get control, I can bring the project back on track.'

'Then, what is to stop me buying…' *click!* '…the company when that has happened? I could afford to. There would be little risk then, no?'

Finn could not counter Fahad's argument. He was out of his depth – ill-prepared. As he sat contemplating this result, he saw the entrance through the door to the enchanted garden become further distant.

The Russian met with him earlier that Wednesday morning, at the Royal Exchange. The Russian, too, contributed to his overly reflective mood. Finn arrived first; he occupied a balcony table overlooking the atrium bar. As he waited for his guest to arrive, he watched a throng of city-stripped suits commence their Christmas cheer. There were seemingly fewer deals and interviews going on. People stood, drink in hand, winding down in the run-up to the holiday.

The Russian arrived. He was about Finn's height and age. Grigoriy Moshkovich looked as though he spent a good deal of time exercising. Finn's initial reaction had been to run through the list of acronyms in his head: KGB, GRU. *Where did guys like this come from?* He could not fathom it.

As well as Arabs, Finn had met many Russians in his past, particularly during his time at sea. The Russian did not intimidate him. But, for all the Russian's imposing frame, Grigoriy came across as a charming individual, although his distinctive East-European accent and economy of words did counter the effect, somewhat.

'You will tell me plan,' said Grigoriy. Everything Grigoriy said sounded like a command. Finn learned to accept this brusque manner a long time ago. It did not put him off; Grigoriy had not had the benefit of a wealthy Arab family paying for an English boarding-school education.

And, just as with Fahad, Finn talked through a paper copy of the presentation with Grigoriy.

'I see problem,' said Grigoriy.

'Yes?' responded Finn. He looked across the table at the Russian; his eyebrows rose in a quizzical expression.

'When you need money?' The Russian's eyes narrowed. His forehead creased.

'Soon,' said Finn. 'The company is weak now. We need to move quickly. Maybe a month... six weeks at the most?'

'I like it. I like idea. But problem. I think time short. I need speak to my people.'

Grigoriy's response spoke volumes to Finn. Despite the appearance of wealth – and Finn held no doubts about Alexa's belief in that regard – the Russian before him held no authority to deal. He sensed Grigoriy would not be able to deliver. Clearly, Grigoriy could not make a decision himself. But for the plan to happen quickly, Finn wanted to be talking to a decision maker at that moment, not in another few weeks time.

Finn leant back in his chair. Now, Wednesday afternoon, and the clock continued to tick the seconds into minutes, the minutes into hours, the hours into days. And there were precious few days left within which he could achieve his plan. He needed to make progress while the market's perception Tiger Oil's weakness, persisted. He could be sure of one thing: Grayson Barclay and Aaron would not sit and let that perception remain for long. They must be looking to do something. *But what?*

Who could he find? Who might have an interest? *Think.*

Finn leant forward, his elbows on the desk before him. His hands went to his head, fingers splayed across his temple, eyes shut tight in concentration. *Think damn you, think.* WHO?

What had he achieved? What had the Arab and Russian really told him; what did they hide between their spoken words? To work within the City Takeover Code, he knew he needed to set up a Concert Party – a team to make the bid. They needed the necessary funds for the acquisition of thirty percent of the business. This would then trigger a mandatory bid for the rest of the company. He needed to make sure they could fund the purchase of the other seventy percent, in case the other shareholders decided to take up the offer as well. But the funds might not all be needed. It could even be possible that none of the additional funding would be required.

They should buy Grayson Barclay out of his share, if possible. He would insist on that. He wanted to be sure Barclay fell on his sword. *It might cost around three mill' – but worth every penny.* The others? Well, he could work with them. *David and Jonathon are only non-Execs and Aaron's a friend.* But he wanted Barclay's blood.

When you have no money, funding something is always difficult. A truism, certainly. First, he needed to finance the initial thirty percent. The Russian's main objection had been the time-scale. Fahad Al-Shahrani had also been concerned about the requirement for the follow-on funding, to cover the compulsory bid issue. Finn's belief that he could convince

194

a bank to extend a large credit facility in the current climate failed to sway either Grigoriy or Fahad. Fahad had been courteous and outwardly friendly, but he left the meeting with no commitment to even further talks. *Arabs!* Honourable, but you never quite knew where you stood with them – well, at least *he* didn't. He needed to find another potential source of funding quickly. *Arabs.* Who did he know? *Think!*

Suddenly, the ideal name occurred to him ...*That's it! That's who! Arabs. Abdulrahman Shah.* A half-smile broke out, playing at the corners of his mouth.

EIGHTEEN

ALEXA STOOD, UNDER the window of her office, with her back against the room's single, large radiator. The welcome heat seeped gently through the fine, high-twist worsted wool of her trouser suit. The view from her window, looking down over the narrow Birchin Lane, afforded little of interest. As she cast her gaze over the Rothko prints suspended from the room's traditional picture rail, she found further solace in the warmth of the backdrop given by the dusky-pink-painted walls.

The offices stood quiet. No sounds of daily toil emanated from outside the door to the rest of the RedWood office suite. She had let a number of her staff go early for Christmas – those travelling to the extremities of the country, to stay with families they had not seen, perhaps, since the previous Christmas. *Christmas: a time for family.* She flinched at the idea.

Not a family-orientated person herself, her thoughts embraced Finn's family. Aisling *had* left him. He'd confirmed as much when they spoke on the phone the previous night. Things did not look good for the Jacksons. She felt for the little girls, Jane and Becky. She remembered them from earlier in the year. They were out riding a Shetland pony, in the field adjacent to Finn's house. She recalled thinking, at the time:

what a wonderful family setting, so much unlike her own, brought up in Edinburgh, without a father herself from the age eight. Yes, she felt for the girls now.

Finn had given her a rundown on the two meetings. They had not gone well for him. He merely confirmed her suspicions – she expected as much. She had not wanted to spoil things for Finn. She enjoyed seeing him enthuse about the prospects, enjoyed seeing the life return in him – so she never mentioned her doubts about his ability to raise such a large amount of money so quickly. She sensed Lyneth held the same thoughts also. *He needed to work this out of his system. It would hurt no one if he couldn't raise the funds, only his pride.* Barclay had already done the damage, surely. Besides, it didn't cost anything to put people in touch, to effect the introductions – so she'd gone along with it all.

But she had her own problem now. The whole episode set her to thinking about her position in life. Like Finn perhaps, she could not see her problem going away easily. She would be forty-five next birthday. Creeping doubts slipped into her mind, like rolling balls of mercury escaping from a shattered thermometer, gathering inside her head, expanding to take up a new, toxic form. Conceivably, it wasn't enough to be content with only *some* aspects of her life. It wasn't children. She remained damn sure she would not be going down that path – and particularly at such an age. Even if she changed her mind, it would not be fair on a child. No, neither she nor Aaron harboured any regrets on the child front.

Aaron. Aaron. Aaron. What the hell was going on with him? *If the problem possesses any roots at all, then Aaron lies in the thick of them.* Her unease grew over his role in Tiger Oil. The overheard conversation? Could it have been Grayson Barclay? And, her betrayal of Finn's confidence didn't sit at all well with her. Now, she was sure unseen games played out in front of them – long, complex games, yet another thing she kept from

197

mentioning to Finn. He had enough on his plate for now. She needed to deal with Aaron. She knew that. Only she stood close enough to Aaron to understand he lay behind at least some of the goings on within the company. And she felt increasingly guilty about it all. But it was still only a gut feeling. She needed some proof. She would need to watch Aaron, for Finn and for herself.

The more Alexa considered the situation, the more she centred herself emotionally, away from Aaron and towards Finn. *A sort of maternalistic worry,* she mused. Though she held no conception of what maternalistic might properly mean. She merely assumed maternalism, in place of any other emotion. It wasn't born of a sexual attraction. She just felt for him and enjoyed his friendship. *We both just seem to… well, to … click, I suppose.* A warm smile spread across her lips, like colour filling a flower at sunrise. Besides, she hated to see a victim continue to lose. She admitted to a little idealism at times.

Aaron often chided her about her idealism over the years they'd been together. To Aaron, she always championed the underdog. She took on clients in difficulties, instead of focusing on the successful – as Aaron did all the time. Natural enough for an accountant, she supposed. He'd been pleased when she started her own agency, but he doubted it would last long. *'You will take on too many bum clients, Darling,'* he'd said.

But Aaron had been wrong. Yes, she did take on seemingly poor clients but, in PR, it's what she considered the core. She saw the good, however deeply hidden, and made it her goal to get the story out. She loved to help her clients realise their full potential. Yes, in truth, she felt protective towards Finn. In some way at least, she was responsible for being blind to what lay directly in front of her: Aaron and Tiger Oil.

So what did it all mean at Tiger Oil? Despite being their PR agent, neither Aaron nor anyone else on the board, for that matter, provided her with any material of substance.

Everything seemed suspiciously low-key. She merely responded to specific releases when asked to draft them.

Why didn't the shares bounce back fully after the withdrawal of the litigation action? She could see as well as Finn that, despite the overall sense of doom in the financial markets, the oil sector remained buoyant. Oil prices seemed to be heading upwards and, with the rising price, Tiger Oil's technology should be carrying a premium – but it wasn't, was it? Why?

From where she stood, still warming herself against the radiator, she cast her gaze towards her desk and over the graph on her computer screen. Taking out the rapid movements aligned with the overall market fluctuations, and the trough of the recent legal action, the underlying movement of Tiger Oil showed a downward trend. But, since the company's market listing had been recent, there was insufficient data to show any sustained trend. She just considered that she would be able to trace the decay in value to the time of Shufang's accident – if data had existed.

It's strange isn't it? There's been little activity in the company itself. Well, at least from what she could tell. Aaron hadn't even been out to the site in the past year. Everything, including the AIM admission, appeared based on technology, and the patents the company held, and not on any operational activity. It appeared to be the nature of Tiger Oil's "more-economic" and "less-environmentally-destructive" oil-sands development process, driving the investment potential. But, so it seemed, investors already had their doubts. They appeared to be losing their confidence in the management, daily. Perhaps all the noise of the banking turmoil, and of the credit crunch, hid Tiger Oil's lack of momentum – just long enough to get them their AIM float... *If so, luck had ridden with them.*

What Alexa could see before her gave her cause for hope. The Tiger Oil narrative lacked substance. It *had* to be a question of confidence in the current management. Clearly, a lack of any negative news at this time provided no substitute for positive news. *Finn's belief must be right, Tiger Oil is weak.* And she knew, then, what she could do – what she needed… NO… *had* to do. She also knew it would be a catalyst for her own issue. She would deal with that as and when it came up. Now, though, she would act for Finn. She would take up the offensive for him. She would undermine Tiger Oil. She would make it weaker. She would resign RedWood's agency, and no longer provide the financial PR the company relied on to report to the city.

Slowly, Alexa lifted herself from the warming comfort of the radiator, and sat down at her desk. She cleared the screen of its graph and opened the word processor. With a degree of resolve she didn't feel entirely comfortable with, she typed a letter of resignation and a draft press release – her final one for Tiger Oil. With a final press of the return key, she sent it by e-mail to both Aaron and Grayson Barclay. This, she told herself, would reflect further on the state of management at Tiger Oil. The resignation was a notifiable event. It would raise more questions with the watching city analysts. It would hit the share price. Aaron would not be happy, nor would Grayson Barclay.

*

Later that same Thursday, at around ten thirty in the evening, Lyneth sat cross-legged on the off-white, oversized shag-pile rug adorning the centre of the polished oak floor of the lounge in her Harley Street apartment. Earlier, she had drawn the heavy drapes closed against the inhospitable December night. She wore an exquisitely-embroidered kimono she'd bought some years ago, from a stall in a Kowloon street-market, during a visit to Hong Kong. Having just emerged from a deep relaxing bath, she found the sheer-silk kimono by far her preferred lounge wear. A glass of vodka balanced on the lengthy, thick-wool pile of the rug, close to her hand. Case papers lay, spread liberally around the floor, most arching in a semi-circle around her, spread with the deftness of a croupier. She lifted the glass and took a sip of the ice cool *Zubrowka.*

She had talked briefly with Finn during the morning, only to hear he had not got far with his fund raising meetings. There had been no news from Alexa. Lyneth did not work on financial figures and market perceptions. Her expertise lay in logic and argument. *Some news from Alexa would have helped.*

After speaking with Finn, she decided today would be the last work day before her holiday. Even so, she did not leave her office until seven, when she went to meet a few friends for a pre-Christmas drink. But, throughout the small-talk of friendship, she felt detached. She felt engrossed, entwined in an unseen battle in a parallel world. She needed to return to it. Sure, others around her also faced problems, but she knew most people lived their lives in blissful ignorance of others. *We all,* she mused, *live in parallel worlds – it is just that they only occasionally collide.*

Now, though, she no longer needed to fight for Tiger Oil. Her conscience rested easier, her helping Finn no longer posed a conflict. Sure, Tiger Oil continued to retain their firm, but as Keaton's client, not hers. She lent only her litigation expertise to the party. Her own system of ethics stood, satisfied. She could help Finn, and in the end get him for herself. But first… the help.

She sat, restudying the collected material on Tiger Oil. She failed Finn the last time. She would not do so again.

Lyneth took another drink from the glass of vodka, letting the cool fire burn her throat. All the time she scanned the papers before her, her gaze seeking patterns or interruptions in patterns. *When in doubt, scan!* Her motto. Earlier, she had opened the case file, separating out the tabbed elements of correspondence. Finn had also provided her with copies of some relevant articles. The case cover, with its title: *Tiger Oil – Su Family Action*, lay on the extreme left of her arc.

She placed the glass down on the floor, checking its balance on the thick pile. She picked up the small stack of papers provided by Finn, placing them across her knees. They included some photo-copied newspaper articles, mainly from the Financial Times. All concerned the oil sector. *Back-ground stuff, in the main – useful, but not particularly relevant at this time.* She glanced at each one quickly, and cast it to a separate pile on the left, next to the case cover. Unimportant. At the end of the stack, a copy of the *International Oil Economist,* September's edition. Finn had placed a Post-it, flagging one of the pages. She opened the journal at the flagged page and scanned the headline:

CHINA TO EXPAND CANADIAN OIL SANDS PRESENCE AMID GREEN CALLS FOR INVESTOR REVOLT

BEIJING, July 31 (Hu Su) – China National Petroleum Corp. is to expand its cooperation with Canadian partners in developing Alberta's oil sands. However, following the drafting of a major new report that claims the carbon intensive processes involved represents an unacceptable environmental risk, green lobbyists are calling for investors to shun the controversial oil extraction projects.

More background. She reached out and placed it, open at the article's page, on the background-info pile. She picked up her glass again and drank deeply, finishing the clear, cold liquor. *Speak to me.*

Lyneth got up and went through to the kitchen, to recharge her glass from the bottle she kept in the freezer. Returning, she retook her place at the centre, scanning the documents as she re-crossed her legs. *Nothing. Everything is as it is.* Nothing appeared out of the ordinary – the accident report, the David Kail letter; minutes of the meetings, during which the board discussed the accident; and the insurer's claim report. *Nothing. Speak to me.*

She swung her gaze, methodically, from top left, the case cover. Round, through the arc, she took in the top sheets of the tabbed inserts. Then, like a typewriter carriage return, she swung back to the pile of background notes, and the top one, open at the article: **CHINA TO EXPAND CANADIAN OIL SANDS PRESENCE AMID GREEN CALLS FOR INVESTOR REVOLT** *...BEIJING, July 31 (Hu Su)...*

BLOODY HELL! Lyneth's gaze, now wide-eyed, almost staring, lifted from the article to the cover: *Tiger Oil – Su Family Action* and then to the article: *BEIJING, July 31 (Hu Su).* Surely not! It couldn't be. She had no idea about Chinese names. Did Su figure as commonly as Smith did? *There...* it screamed at her, a potential connection. A connection to what, she had no idea, but it certainly seemed like the reporter possessed the same family name as Shufang. *Christ! If only I could get hold of the reporter who'd written that article...*

Lyneth went straight over to the laptop that sat, semi-permanently, on a small dining table in the corner of the lounge. She Googled the name "Hu Su" and got over twenty-five thousand hits, too many to go through. "Hu Su" and "oil" did little better, over one-and-a-half thousand. She tried "Hu Su" and "reporter" – seventy one, much better. She went through each entry, scanning for signs she might have found the reporter she looked for. *Nothing. Damn it!* It would be no good calling the journal office – she would find it shut at this time. *Where next? Think girl! Where could you try next?*

203

Lyneth began to rationalise the problem. Journalists don't mind their names in the public domain, do they... they relish it. *Where would I go?* She remembered her LinkedIn account, the social network for professionals. She avoided Facebook but, from time to time, she did visit the LinkedIn site. Maybe...? She typed "LinkedIn" into Google search and, once guided to the site's correct address, she gained entry to her account quickly.

Twenty two personal connections linked Lyneth to over two million names, each of whom she could contact directly. She entered a search for "Hu Su". Only two hits, and neither person existed in her network. There existed a Hu Su working as a trader in Taiwan, the other... BINGO! Hu Su, a freelance reporter. The LinkedIn site would not give her any contact details, but she could send a message through the system, inviting contact. She could only hope she would receive a reply. She sent a short, one sentence message, adding the e-mail address of her private Hotmail account. *Please respond in connection with Shufang and Tiger.* If the other party made the connection they would get in touch, she was sure; if not, then no issue. The innocuous message would mean little to anyone else. Now, she needed to wait. *Patience girl!* She could do nothing more for the moment. But, she could not resist smiling.

Progress! She had just scored a small victory in the unseen, other-world battle. She got up from the computer, fetched the glass from the floor where she had left it and drank its contents in one. She went to the kitchen to pour another.

Back in the lounge, she stood for a moment, looking at the papers on the floor. *YES!* She stepped backward, to sit on the couch behind her. With one hand on her glass, she pulled a cushion up in front of her, drawing it tightly into her heaving breasts, her pulse now racing in anticipation. She sipped on the cold liquor, letting the fire take hold. The cold heat of the vodka raced down her throat, pushing her whole body deep into the couch.

She surveyed the mess of papers, festooned, arc-like on the floor. She had no idea what she would find out next. She just knew there had to be more. She continued to smile. She smiled to herself. The Rottweiler just dug out another hidden bone. On Sunday, she would travel to Wales, but for the next couple of days she would relax.

*

Christmas Day. Finn just wanted to sit in a corner and roar at someone. Since returning from London the previous Thursday, he had received a visit from his father-in-law. Finn respected the man, who now adopted a new role – go-between. With an amicability Finn did not expect, his father-in-law suggested the whole family should spend Christmas in the house, for the sake of the children. Finn glossed over Aisling's planted sub-text – of course, it would make looking after the horses easier. His father-in-law stressed he and his wife would "come along" too. He suggested their presence would "keep things on an even footing". Finn did not disagree. Selfishly, he was relieved. Christmas would happen around him, and he would at least have the tranquility of his study available.

They – Aisling, her parents, Jane and Becky – all arrived on the Saturday afternoon, but, despite the children's obvious pleasure at everyone being together, no adult really enjoyed themselves this particular Christmas.

Finn could not say the time passed intolerably. However, an undercurrent of tension ran its tentacles throughout the mesh of everyday activity. It did not leave him feeling comfortable about the situation. Quite naturally, the question of survival preoccupied him. Family politics simply bemused him, and their presence, at best, presented an unwelcome distraction.

Finn had spent the majority of the time since the previous week's meetings, trying to track down Abdulrahman Shah. He trawled through all his copious notes and diaries, looking for contact details. He went through boxes of business cards, all collected over the past four years. He checked out the internet, and, eventually, reached him on the Monday. Some people did not stop work just because of Christmas.

He had eventually traced him through a Swiss press contact of Alexa. A brief call and, yes, Abdulrahman Shah did remember him, fondly, and yes, he would be delighted to meet for coffee at the Langham on Tuesday, eighth of January, two p.m. Finn bit his tongue. He felt grateful, but the delay... *Tuesday eighth of January at two p.m.!* He needed resolution, fast. The mere fact that Christmas – and therefore his family – interrupted him, turned him feral, like a bear with a sore head.

NINETEEN

January 2008

HIS FOOT TAPPED, soundlessly, against the thick pile of the grey striped carpet. He checked his watch. The date counter showed the figure eight, the time, now two-thirty. Finn desperately needed to make progress, but he continued to sit, feigning patience. His lightly tapping right foot – the sole betrayer of his true feelings – appeared to mark an involuntary reaction to an imaginary tune running through his head.

Finn had sat, just so, for over twenty minutes. Around him, the drawing room of the Langham's Infinity Suite looked surreal. He had not known what to expect, having never experienced such opulence in a hotel room before. It was another tantalizing glimpse into his enchanted garden.

The experience assaulted his senses from the moment he stepped, from the corridor outside, through the open doorway, and into the private inner lobby. It seemed to stretch out forever. It came to rest only at a large abstract sculpture – a guardian sat, innocuously, upon a wooden plinth-like table. The sculpture, made from glass, caught the light of the drawing room beyond, throwing it out into his path, challenging him to step beyond the deep purple silk walls – the colour of ripened aubergines – into the rich brightness of the room ahead.

Beyond the sculpture, through the double doors, a large

semi-circular drawing room ballooned, outwards, from the dominance of an eccentrically chaotic chandelier hanging above a small dining table. The chandelier shone a mess of fibre-optic light, adding warmth to the January daylight streaming in through the curved wall of huge arched windows. Large planters lay outside, at the foot of each window. It all suggested the room did, indeed, reach out to infinity.

He had arrived a little ahead of the appointed hour of two, and remained in the hotel's lobby, soaking up the atmosphere. At a minute to, he announced his arrival at the reception desk. The clerk there informed him Abdulrahman Shah's personal assistant would be down to greet him shortly. And, indeed, so she had.

A beautiful, tall, elegantly dressed young blonde woman approached from the lift – Finn thought late twenties, or early thirties. A nomadic concierge directed her to where Finn stood. *German, but with faultless English – possibly Swiss, given Abdulrahman Shah's residential status.* She introduced herself as Heidi Mahler – no frau, a definite fraulein, in Finn's humble opinion. She escorted him up to the suite and, as the shock of the assault of opulence gave way to mere awe, she had invited him to take a seat.

'I'm afraid Herr Shah is engaged on an urgent call for the moment. He apologises for the inconvenience. He may be a little time,' said Heidi, mirroring the apology in her tone. 'Please, do sit down…' She cast her hand in a generous sweep, taking in the entire centre of the room and its comfortable-looking seating. 'Can I get you something to drink, Herr Jackson?'

Heidi's use of the Germanic salutation on an Islamic name, let alone his own, added further to the already surreal experience. 'Thank you… err… coffee please… black, no sugar,' he replied.

Finn removed his overcoat and handed it to Heidi. He

crossed to sit in one of the overly-large armchairs, also covered in dark purple velvet. The chair itself faced a large, walnut looking hollow-square coffee table. Atop the table rested a huge ceramic bowl, filled with oversized ceramic eggs. *Yes, everything here is oversized.*

There he sat. To his left, and over his shoulder, through one of the large arched windows, Finn could clearly see the clock face on the gothic spire of the All Souls Church opposite. To his right, two large floor-to-ceiling sliding panels, topped with a kimono-shaped relief, formed the focal point of the rear wall to the huge bow-fronted room; *presumably housing some large flat screen TV.* He glanced over at the clock on the tower. It showed the same time as his watch, two-thirty. He glanced down at the table, to where the cafetière of coffee now stood, half-empty. He considered Abdulrahman Shah, not for the first time in the past twenty minutes. Could he simply be making sure Finn knew who held control of the situation? *Unnecessary.*

Clearly a wealthy individual – certainly judging by his taste in hotel rooms – Abdulrahman Shah remained a little-known and private individual. From his previous knowledge, Finn knew him to be a secretive and highly successful investor. When he first made his acquaintance, Finn had not been aware of his name, though that wasn't surprising in itself. At the time, Finn, Shufang and Aaron had just established the company, receiving the promise of initial funding from Grayson Barclay, an acquaintance of Aaron.

As part of their executive MBA, and as a syndicated exercise, the three of them reviewed a feasibility study that Aaron's consultancy, Henley Oil Consultants, had undertaken. They had presented the findings to the clients. Abdulrahman Shah, a key investor in the client company, had been at the meeting. At the time of the presentation, not even Aaron could offer the name of the quietly-spoken, diminutive Arab of Persian descent. As Finn later learned, Abdulrahman Shah could trace his lineage directly to the Yamini tribe, descendants of the last prince of Persia.

It had been during research for the presentation when Finn identified an old 1978 patent languishing on the internet. The feasibility study they'd reviewed had been a project to renew efforts to extract the oil from oil sands, using steam-assisted gravity drainage. The SAGD technique proved to be a major breakthrough. It allowed a high recovery rate – up to sixty percent of the oil in place. Because of the economics of SAGD, and its applicability to a vast area of oil sands, the technique effectively led to a quadrupling of the North American oil reserves. It allowed Canada to move to second place in world oil reserves, after Saudi Arabia. The study sought to review methods for increasing the efficiency and scope of SAGD, to provide for better returns in the more difficult areas. It had been Finn's ideas from the review, which led to the three of them – Aaron, Shufang and himself – establishing Tiger Oil to exploit a variation on the SAGD theme. He'd based the variation on a modification to the 1978 patent he had identified.

The presentation: the first, almost perfunctory, meeting with Abdulrahman Shah passed without note. Another more meaningful meeting occurred some six months later, at a small London conference on green oil issues. Finn gave a short paper on the environmental benefits of the Tiger Oil process. On this occasion, Abdulrahman Shah sought Finn out after his session. Finn impressed him. The two were of a similar age.

'You have come far, Mr Jackson, since your presentation. I am glad to see someone has taken up the challenge. Unlike many of my fellow countrymen and, of course, many I see in this industry, I have a keen interest in maintaining the world we live in. Not all of my homeland is a desert – I feel we have too many deserts in the world. Would you not agree, Mr Jackson?'

'Very true, err…'

'Abdulrahman Shah, at your service.'

'I'm sorry…' said Finn, 'I remember you from the presentation. You asked me some pertinent questions. Please forgive me for not remembering your name,'

'No. There was no reason for you to do so. Perhaps it is I who should apologise to you, for not introducing myself just now,' he said, his smile genuine and warm, and his hand-shake solid. 'I am interested in your venture, Mr Jackson. Tell me, are you looking to raise funds currently?'

'Finn, please. Call me Finn.'

'Thank you… err, Finn. And please, you may call me Abdulrahman. Perhaps… of my question… are you looking to raise funds currently, Finn?'

'Well, we are not seeking further funds just yet. We have recently raised seed funding through our family and a few friends. I am sure you will appreciate, to raise too much, too soon, would mean we would dilute our own shareholdings far more quickly than necessary.'

'Yes, I understand perfectly,' said Abdulrahman, flashing his warm smile, yet again. 'I think you have a good solution in mind, and it is perhaps a shame I find myself a little late for the party.'

'There will be another time, I am sure,' said Finn. 'It has certainly been a pleasure to meet you.'

With the passing time since his first meetings, Finn's memory of Abdulrahman Shah's interest faded – that was, at least, until the moment in his office, the week before Christmas. *There will be another time, I am sure.* He'd never been so pleased to hear an echo from his past.

'Finn, it is very good to see you again.'

The sound of Abdulrahman's voice broke Finn's reverie.

'You look well, my friend,' continued Abdulrahman, with

a smile as warm as Finn remembered it. He'd marched up to Finn's seat before Finn could react.

'And you too, Abdulrahman,' responded Finn, slightly embarrassed that he only just managed to stand in time. He took the proffered hand. 'Thank you for agreeing to see me again.'

'It is my pleasure, Finn. Please…' Abdulrahman motioned with his hand for Finn to retake his seat. 'I am sorry I have been a while. My bankers in Switzerland are an interminable bore.'

'Necessary though, I should think,' said Finn. Again, a streak of envy flashed into his mind, as he gained a further glance through the door into the enchanted garden.

'Yes. As you say… a *necessary* evil.' Abdulrahman went to sit on the large cream sofa. The light from the windows behind him rendered his dark skin, darker in appearance. 'Thank you for the presentation notes you sent to me, Finn. I have had an opportunity to read them. First though, some fresh coffee?'

'Thank you… yes.'

'Heidi? Please,' he said, as he glanced across to the dining table where Heidi had discreetly taken a seat, shorthand notebook in hand.

'I was shocked to learn what has happened to you this last year, Finn. Are you all right?'

'The accident? Oh yes, thank you. I still have some headaches, but they are getting fewer.'

'He who has health has hope, Finn. If you have hope you have everything,' he said, with a knowing smile. 'And the business? I understand you did not desire an exit in the manner achieved. A plan not of your design, perhaps?'

'You are well informed, Abdulrahman.' Finn smiled this time.

'I make it my business to find out about things of interest to me, Finn.'

Abdulrahman Shah spoke with a matter-of-fact delivery, but the statement left Finn in no doubt. The man in front of him could, and would, do anything he wanted to. The equality in their ages seemed to be about the only commonality between the two of them. Yet Finn remained deeply conscious of a level of connection between them that, for the moment, he could not fathom.

'No, the exit was not my wish,' said Finn. 'It brings me to the reason why I sought your counsel. When we last met, you spoke of your interest in Tiger Oil. I believe there is an opportunity for you now, with my help, to gain control of the business.'

'I do not normally seek to control the subjects of my investments, Finn.'

Finn caught his breath. *Normally.* He felt he could be direct. 'And in this case, Abdulrahman?'

Heidi's return, with a small silver tray of fresh coffee, interrupted the conversation. She poured two cups as Finn and Abdulrahman remained silent. Looking up, Finn caught the glance of Heidi's eyes, as her gaze fell on and caught Abdulrahman's in return. *Interesting, is PA the only thing in Heidi's job description?'*

'In this case, Finn,' said Abdulrahman, 'I have to say that while I can fully understand your desire to pursue this course of action, it is not one I feel I can support. It is not the money. The cost is a side issue of no real importance to me. Tiger Oil is a small company.'

A wave of disappointment again crashed against the beach of his soul. He swallowed the palpable lump that had risen in his throat.

'Neither is the idea... your idea, Finn,' continued Abdulrahman. 'I do like the Tiger Oil proposition. I believe it has great potential. It would fit well within my portfolio, and there would be clear synergies with some of my existing oil interests...' Abdulrahman paused, appearing to sense Finn's disappointment. 'My friend, I would wish you to understand, there is too much emotion in this proposition, as it stands.'

Finn sank, almost visibly, into the deeply upholstered chair, the contrast between the deep purple velvet of the chair and his pale skin became perceptibly enhanced.

'Please, drink...' Abdulrahman motioned towards the cups of fresh coffee, so far untouched by either of them. A most charming host, he appeared to delight in seeing to his guest's comfort. 'I can understand your disappointment, as I would understand my brother's were he, as you are now, before me.'

'I suppose it was wrong of me to assume...'

'No, my friend,' said Abdulrahman, taking a sip of coffee, '...it was not wrong. We should live our lives like brothers, free to be friends as we are, free to speak as we do, but we should do business like strangers.'

'Thank you, I understand,' said Finn. He reached for his coffee and drank deeply.

'Finn, may I speak to you, as I would to my own brother?'

'Of course... you honour me, Abdulrahman.'

'Dwell not upon your weariness. Your strength will be according to the measure of your desire,' he said, smiling broadly. 'That is, of course, an old Arab saying. But, I think you should look at the basis for your judgement.' Abdulrahman glanced quickly to his left, to where Heidi had returned to sit at the dining table. 'My friend, I am reminded by my ever watchful assistant that I have another appointment. I regret my earlier call has left us short of time. Please, let me make amends. You would honour me if you would dine with me, here in the hotel's restaurant, on Thursday evening. Shall we say eight?'

Finn sat motionless, momentarily struck dumb – his audience seemingly over, almost as quickly as it had begun. To compound his lengthy wait, he'd gained nothing; yet, here sat

Abdulrahman Shah offering him dinner in two nights' time. '...Thank you, I should like that,' he said, using the only words he could think of to say.

'Please, do bring a guest. I shall have Heidi join us. It will be a nice evening, to talk as brothers talk, yes?'

'Yes,' replied Finn, managing a half-smile. He hoped his host did not take him to be ungracious.

'Herr Jackson, your coat please.' Heidi miraculously and silently appeared next to Finn.

Finn stood and took the offered coat, as Abdulrahman rose to show his guest towards the lobby.

'Heidi will show you down. Finn, I will look forward to our dinner on Thursday.' The enigmatic Abdulrahman Shah paused slightly, in reflection. 'Please, some final words, we Arabs are fond of our sayings.' He held his hand out to Finn. 'Examine what is said, not him who speaks.' He smiled as Finn shook his hand in farewell.

'Thursday evening,' confirmed Finn. He turned to follow the shapely Teutonic figure of Heidi Mahler, as she gracefully led the way, down the lobby, to the door that reopened onto an entirely different world – his world, his reality.

For God's sake, where next. The door closed silently behind them.

*

A dinner at the Landau restaurant in the Langham was not an opportunity for a girl to pass up, especially with a wealthy Arab as host, one whom she now knew to be perfectly charming. As soon as Finn called her, she had detected his down-beat mood. She listened attentively to him recount the brief rejection from his quarry.

215

'Listen, Finn... you say he's invited you to dinner?'

'Yeah, but...'

'But nothing, Finn. He wants to talk... And you say he's asked you to take a friend? No question then. I'm coming with you.'

'I'd thought of Lyneth...'

She brushed off his half-finished suggestion. 'What's this PA of his like?'

'Young, beautiful. I guess she's around thirty.'

'Then, there's no sense in baiting her with competition, is there, Finn? You don't want her talking to her boss now, do you?'

'Guess not.'

'Settled then. Pick me up at seven. I'll arrange for a taxi.' It was as though she left a more up-beat Finn by the end of their phone conversation – but she couldn't be sure. *No problem,* she'd mused.

The dinner proved to be a most relaxed and particularly western affair. Clearly, Abdulrahman Shah had adopted a great many of the proclivities of the western capitalist life a lot of his countrymen frowned upon. He did not shout his wealth, but she could see it there, in everything he said, did or touched. *And that included Heidi Mahler.* She was a lovely looking girl who could not be much more than half his age. *Lyneth would have set her on edge.* She looked across at Heidi. *Yes, I gave Finn sound advice, for sure.*

From the glances their host gave her throughout the evening, Alexa knew she had chosen well. She wore her favourite little black number, a daringly sheer, long-sleeved jersey dress by Emilio Pucci. She felt Abdulrahman's eyes sear into her back as he'd helped her to the table. The dress featured a wide neck, dropping low behind her, unhindered by the exquisite backless body she wore beneath. From the front, through the sheer jersey material, the hint of lace detail in the body, set against

216

a bronze panel, reflected the merest hint of promise. The whole effect created, as intended, an understated sexiness. The simple blue and green print detail on her cuffs and neckline provided just the right amount of colour. *Yes, a good choice.*

Alexa could not fault the excellent and discreet service in the Landau. She had chosen a breast of quail with red-onion and truffle bonbon to start, followed, for her main course, by a peppered loin of venison and spiced red-cabbage. The others all chose similarly wonderful sounding and presented meals. She wondered at the set piece "Trou Normand", an exquisite apple and calvados sorbet, and, by the time the desserts and coffee stood finished, everyone looked to have enjoyed themselves immensely. They had not uttered one word of business. To Alexa, it was as if two brothers and their partners luxuriated together in their first meeting in years, catching up on their respective lives.

'So, Alexa,' said Abdulrahman, as he turned his head to look into her eyes. 'I see Finn enjoys the company of beautiful women.'

He could have been referring to Finn, engaged in deep conversation with Heidi, but he wasn't; she caught his inference and blushed, slightly. She held her eyes steady.

'I am intrigued. You resigned your company's association with Tiger Oil?'

'Yes,' she said. The attractive, charming man before her knew his facts – a wise, attractive, charming man; honesty would the best policy for her. 'I considered my desire to help Finn stood in real conflict, and my relationship with some of the other directors lacked the openness I would have wished for.'

'But your husband? said Abdulrahman. 'Did you not have a duty to protect his interests?'

'Duty is not a word I would use. But, yes, I struggled with the idea I might be acting against his interests,' she said, truthfully. 'It hurt me to think my husband might have been involved with what happened to Finn.'

'Ah! A chameleon does not leave one tree until he is sure of another.' Abdulrahman's smile lit dancing lights in his deep brown eyes. 'In your heart you no longer trust your husband, do you?'

'No.'

'The failure of trust is always a terrible shame… but all too common, I fear.' The smile faded slightly, his voice taking a more business-like tone. 'So, you stopped acting for Tiger Oil. I see their shares lost another five percent when the news came out.'

'You have done your research, Abdulrahman.'

'As I have said before, to Finn I believe, I make it my business to find out about things of interest to me.'

'So, you *are* interested,' she said. She tilted her head to her left side, slightly, as she tried to follow the sparkle playing in his eyes, captivating her.

Abdulrahman's smile broadened again as he noted her reaction. 'I, too, am such a chameleon. We two are alike in that respect.' He glanced over to see Finn still in deep conversation with Heidi. 'I hoped I would see you this evening. It pleased me to see Finn had invited you.'

'How…?' she began to ask, feeling more than a little puzzled at the revelation.

'Do not worry how, Alexa. I have been interested in Tiger Oil since I first met with Finn and his colleagues. I had been interested in investing before, in the early days; but I arrived a little late to join the party.' His voice held no tone of regret. 'Patience is beautiful, do you not think? Still, it is strange what coincidences do occur from time to time. Your husband called me before Christmas; he sought to gain my interest, to assist with raising additional funds. He looks, even now, I believe, to acquire more capital equipment and well leases. I met with him and Grayson Barclay, yesterday.'

'I don't understand...' she said.

'As my interest in Tiger Oil is tangible, I felt it an opportunity I needed to investigate. I am afraid, while I found your husband, Aaron, to be a charming man, I found the arrogance of Mr Barclay most unwelcome. If you forgive my language, Alexa. Arrogance is a weed found growing, in the main, on a dunghill.' He smiled.

'So, you held back with Finn, on Tuesday, until you had met with the others.'

'Precisely,' he said, with a flash of his eyes.

'And tonight?'

'Tonight has been for brothers to talk.' The smile broke into a grin. 'As you have done, I shall do also. I am now sure of the tree I shall move to.'

Abdulrahman raised his glass to Alexa, pausing, inviting her with his eyes to do the same. She needed no verbal encouragement, and raised her glass without hesitation.

'Friends and brothers,' he said, in toast.

'Friends and brothers,' she replied.

'It has been a lovely evening, Alexa. I shall leave it to you to give Finn the news. I would like to finance him. He should know that when what he wants does not happen, he must learn to want what does.' He spoke next to the others also, raising his voice slightly. 'My friends, please – this evening has been a great pleasure for me.' His gaze again briefly entwined with Alexa's, before turning to set on Finn. 'Tomorrow is another day and there will be much to do.'

Finn looked quizzical.

'Alexa,' said Abdulrahman, '...why don't you give Heidi a call in the morning. She will give you some details about what we discussed.'

Alexa saw Finn turn to look at her, but he clearly knew not to say anything, for fear of appearing ungracious before his host. She could see the puzzlement growing in his eyes. She was elated, giddy – it took all of her self-control to remain seated and demure – her sense of power at that moment was overwhelming; *almost better than sex*, she mused. She had the power to remove Finn's cloud.

Heidi passed Alexa a business card. It bore Heidi's contact details. 'Tomorrow, Alexa, please do call when you can.' Heidi's smile held only friendship.

'Thank you, Heidi.' Alexa looked at Abdulrahman Shah, still giddy. She sensed a pay-back would be required, perhaps not yet; but she held no doubt – it would be for her to pay. She looked across at Heidi. Clearly, Abdulrahman Shah liked his women. She could see no problem there – it would be her pleasure. She turned to smile, again, at Abdulrahman.

*

He had been gob-smacked in the taxi ride to St Katherine's Dock. 'How the hell…' he stammered, '…what are you saying, Alexa?'

'He wants to back you.'

'But I thought…'

'He'd been playing you a little, he needed to make his mind up,' she told him. 'I guess, once he realised you'd gained the support of other friends, it convinced him. He's always been keeping an eye on Tiger Oil and I think he reckons you're the better person to take it forward.'

Finn had been on a high since. He hardly slept in the hotel room on the night of the Landau dinner. After walking Alexa to her apartment door, he returned to his room, sat at the desk and tried to make notes. But it all proved to be too much on top of the excellent meal and the wine. He'd just lain on the bed and let the consequences of the evening and the ideas race around his head, seeing the possibilities – the opening of the door.

Alexa had called Heidi the following morning, to get details. Abdulrahman Shah's basic terms of offer would provide Finn's new company with a convertible loan note for ten million pounds, for eighty percent of the shares, and with few conditions. Abdulrahman Shah wanted Alexa to join the board as an executive director, and he would nominate one of his own advisors as a non-executive. The money would be conditional on its use to fund a takeover of Tiger Oil plc.

Given the promise of the Abdulrahman deal, Finn had busied himself contacting a number of investors whom he judged to be sufficiently divorced from the current board. He wanted to sound them out about their potential interest in selling their shares at a premium. Now, Wednesday, January sixteenth, he sat at his desk in Worship Street.

Over the Christmas, since Alexa's PR company had resigned, the Tiger Oil shares had been languishing at around eight point three pence, with no sign of a recovery, despite a background of increasing oil prices. Analyst recommendations turned from hold to sell, as market perceptions of a lack of confidence in the management team increased. The penny-share chat rooms of the day-traders threw out increasingly emotive comments, as their authors' frustrations grew. The shares now traded, consistently, at less than their flotation price of ten pence.

It had not been too difficult to find sufficient investors willing to discuss an offer of eleven-five. Such a price offered them a greater than thirty percent gain on where the share price currently stood – a fifteen percent gain on its flotation price. By lunchtime Tuesday, he received the firm expressions of interest from thirty percent of shareholders, which would require him to make a formal bid for the whole company.

Finn's mobile phone rang.

'Hi, Alexa, how are you getting on?'

'Good, Finn, we are almost there with the loan-note agreement. I got your comments first thing this morning, and have taken them up with Abdulrahman's lawyers. I've managed to get Lyneth to go through it too. She didn't have much to add, it's all standard stuff really. We should be ready to sign the note off this Friday. Once we have the money in the bank we should be ready to make some commitments.'

'That's great, Alexa. I'm just troubled about the rest of it now. We need to secure a facility for anything up to another eighteen million to underwrite the formal takeover bid. I don't for one minute think we will need to buy up the total remainder, but since we are trying this by stealth, we need to make sure we can finance the whole thing if necessary. I've spoken to the banking contacts I know, but no one seems interested in this deal at the moment.'

'I've spoken to some people I know too, Finn. It's an issue all round.'

'Christ, we can't give up now, we are so close, Alexa.'

'I know. I'm scratching my head here.'

'I've been thinking, Alexa, given all the progress we *have* made, and it's all positive, I think we've no other choice but to go back to Abdulrahman Shah. What do you think?'

TWENTY

SHE HAD RETURNED from her parents' home in Usk on the second of January. It had been a pleasant holiday – away from the bustle of city life. Lyneth enjoyed the large-village, small-town atmosphere of the place she grew up in – the ruined Norman castle, the narrow cobbled streets, the architectural variety, a place of true character.

The old market town provided the shelter of a number of warming, welcoming pubs. But, in truth, she never, truly, felt at home there. Few school friends remained in the area – most having gone their separate ways from university. Although she loved her parents dearly, she would walk out each day, into the middle of the town, to Twyn Square, with its Victorian clock centre-piece. She would secretly wish she could transport herself to work, to her apartment. She needed a focus in life, a challenge. Usk stood tranquil – beauty of a sort. A place for between challenges.

Her Blackberry remained uncharacteristically silent all Christmas. Her few, true, London friends sent her occasional phone texts along the way. They told of their exploits, their conquests and their drink tallies – all fun, all responded to in kind. Her text replies – news of her own conquests – necessarily bordered on the fictitious.

Lyneth had got into London, and to her desk, on the third of January. With the office quiet, and with Hillary still out of the way, she called Finn and Alexa to update herself on their progress raising funds. She had been holding her breath, and, of course, her own news about Hu Su.

When she returned to her apartment, on the Wednesday night, she had checked her Hotmail account, the one she used to e-mail Hu Su. She found the usual mixture of junk – sex tips for unmarried women? Yeah right! Little blue pills for lagging libido; urgent warnings to update account details with banks she never knew existed; and follow-on marketing from various on-line stores she previously shopped with. But there, near the top of the list, received that morning – according to the date-time stamp – she saw the message from "hsu@hkmail.com". Lyneth caught her breath. She clicked on the message to open it.

> *Please, if you have information relating to my sister, Shufang, who died in an accident in Canada in October 2006, can you identify yourself and your interest? I would like to talk with you.*

Lyneth showed no hesitation; she followed with a quick reply.

> *I am a British lawyer working on behalf of interested parties. I am investigating the accident. I believe there are unanswered questions surrounding your sister's death. I believe it would be in our joint interests to discuss our mutual concerns and, if appropriate, see how we might work to resolve matters. To verify your connection with Shufang, I would be grateful if you would confirm to me the significance of the events of December last. With regards, LJ*

The reply came equally quickly, as if Hu Su had been hanging on his computer, desperate for any information regarding his sister.

> *Dear LJ,*
>
> *I have eternal gratitude for your interest. At the beginning of December last, while I was in Canada doing research for an IOE article, my parents, who now live in Hong Kong, received a visit from someone out of the UK.*
>
> *They will not tell me the exact circumstances, nor will they tell me any of the detail of the visit. They are proud people. What I do know is the visit became the catalyst for them dropping their action.*
>
> *I have included my cell phone number below. I shall be en-route to Canada again later this month and could arrange to stop over in London a short time.*
>
> *If you can help me with any information, perhaps my sister's death will no longer bring such heartache to our family.*
>
> *KR Hu*

YES! Damn it! She had been right. *Someone has some explaining to do.*

Now? Thursday, January seventeenth, and... *who in the hell would have visited from the UK?* ...The question had hovered in her mind ever since opening the e-mail. It hung there when Alexa called for assistance in reviewing the loan-note agreement, earlier in the week. Now, Lyneth stood in the arrivals hall at Heathrow's Terminal One. The screen display listed Hu Su's Hong Kong flight as having arrived and its progress as "passengers in the baggage hall".

Lyneth had made short work of the e-mail exchange with Hu Su. If he could drop into London on his way to Canada... Why mess around? After a few additional, equally short e-mails, during which Hu Su asked for her identity – to which she'd happily obliged – she placed a telephone call to her new

Chinese contact, inviting him to stay over at her apartment.

Her mobile phone rang and, as she lifted it to her ear, she noticed ahead of her, a tallish, thin Chinese man of about thirty, with a thick mop of gelled black hair. He waved, cheerfully, in her direction. 'Hello,' she said, speaking into the phone, 'Hu Su?' She kept her sight on the approaching figure, who, she could see, also held a phone to his ear. The Chinese man's cheerful face broke into a huge grin. 'I see you,' she said. She could not help it, but, as if spread by some air-borne infection, she felt herself breaking into huge grin also.

Hu Su reached her, and grabbed at her outstretched hand, shaking it enthusiastically with both of his own hands. His grin did not relax for a moment. The two bags he carried, each suspended off a shoulder, looked in danger of falling between them. 'Lovely to meet you,' he said, in excellent – albeit Americanised – English.

'And you, Hu Su. I hope your flight over was good. My car is in the car park. Let me get you out of here and we can talk about things over something to eat. Do you like Polish food?'

'Thank you. I'm glad you didn't say Chinese.' They both laughed.

Lyneth led the way. The level of background noise in the busy terminal area curtailed any real conversation, but they soon retrieved the car, and headed out of the airport, towards the city.

'This is the first major break I've had, Lyneth.'

The low-toned, quiet-seriousness in his voice took her by surprise. While his smile and grin could disarm anyone, she understood. Hu Su possessed a more complex character than initially met the eye. Of that she could be sure.

'I've been covering the Oil Industry for a while, and you learn quickly how dirty the business can be,' said Hu Su. 'Something ain't right about this. I know my sister would never have flouted safety regs. Not as the insurance company and investigators have claimed. That wasn't Shufang. No. Something ain't right.'

'I know, Hu Su,' replied Lyneth, keeping her concentration on the road ahead of her. 'But, I think we can work this out together.'

As she sat, driving her passenger into London's failing, late-afternoon light, she considered Hu Su, at heart, must be like her, another dog with a bone – a dog of the oil press corps, a kindred spirit. *Who could have been the visitor to Shufang's family?* The thought persisted.

*

Alexa agreed with him. The only option had been to go to Abdulrahman Shah with the positive note of their initial success. They checked Companies House records; the current board members held twenty-seven-and-a-half percent between them. The promise of thirty percent, and the inevitability of gaining at least a proportion of the remaining shares from a compulsory bid, would secure a vital controlling interest in Tiger Oil.

Surprisingly, Abdulrahman had not been dissatisfied, quite the opposite. To Finn, it seemed Abdulrahman had anticipated his call, expected it, welcomed it even.

'Do not worry, Finn, only the tent pitched by our own hands will stand. We shall have no need of banks; let us put our hands together,' he had said.

When Finn volunteered Alexa's offer to go over her analysis again, just to confirm the value of the proposition with him, Abdulrahman simply brushed the offer aside. No. He remained content to proceed and, furthermore, he would underwrite the entire bid at the offer price of eleven-and-a-half pence.

'Finn, my wish is for you to buy-up as many shares as possible. I would prefer us to gain total control, to take the company private again.' Despite the clarity of the wish, Abdulrahman remained as enigmatic as ever.

The single issue remaining for Finn to deal with that week came out of a call from his solicitor in York. *Could he come into the office and discuss a letter from his wife's solicitor?* Finn left for his home late on the Wednesday afternoon, shortly after speaking with Abdulrahman. His soul lay heavy with premonition.

He spent the morning, Thursday, with his solicitor. It had not been a comfortable meeting. Besides the inevitable feeling of being stalked by a large, unseen fee-clock – its mechanism ticking away more minutes than he cared to imagine – it became clear he would need to write off a considerable part of what remained of his income. He would also lose at least whatever equity there remained in the family house he still occupied.

The Christmas truce had merely persisted until New Year's Eve, when Aisling returned with the children and her parents, to their rambling house on the other side of York. Her solicitors wrote, putting forward their proposal for a formal separation. He had no stomach for a fight with Aisling. In truth, their relationship ended a long time ago, and he did not want to cause the children more pain than they had already. He would pay and would not contest the house. He instructed his solicitor to offer what Aisling sought, on the condition that, since she presently stayed with her parents, he would have a period of six months before he needed to vacate the property.

The only bright side to his meeting that morning, had been confirmation of the agreement that he could have the girls to stay with him every other weekend. This weekend would be the first.

He picked up his desk phone and called Alexa at her office. 'Hi, Finn, how did it go this morning?' she asked.

'OK, I guess. I'm going to be giving the house up eventually. I've got the girls sorted though; I'm having them this weekend – over night Saturday. How's the loan agreement?'

'It's just about finished. I've agreed to go in and sign it at his lawyers' City office, at eleven tomorrow morning. They will wire the money across from Switzerland, to our account. We should be in funds by three at the latest. We will be able to roll on Monday.'

'Great. You and Lyneth have been brilliant. Thanks, Alexa,' he said, hoping his gratitude reflected through into his voice. Without the pair of them working together with him, it would have taken far longer, if it could have been done at all. It would certainly have cost him dear. Now he had Alexa as a director of his new firm, and he felt far stronger. 'Look, there's not much point in me coming down tomorrow… unless you want me there? I'm happy that we're all on track and we can start making our formal approaches on Monday. I'll come down first thing Monday. I've booked in at the Tower, so we can work late, close to your place if we need to.'

'No. No need to come down tomorrow, Finn. You rest up and enjoy the weekend with Becky and Jane. I'm happy to handle the agreement. I know I'm not seeing eye-to-eye with Aaron at the moment, but I can see this should help his shares. Are we going to keep him on the board, Finn?'

'I'm not sure, Alexa, to be honest. I think there *is* a role for him – maybe as a consultant. But, I do think he has too much on his plate just now, too many other directorships. I would have to question his commitment to us.'

'Yes, I think so. He's away again, for the moment. I'm not even sure if I expect to see him this weekend. I think he's up in Norway at the mo.'

'Give me a call if anything crops up. I'll call you later tomorrow afternoon – I'll be checking the bank account. Probably glued to the screen,' he said, giving a slight laugh.

Things seemed to be looking up, at last.

'OK. Bye, Finn.'

'Speak soon,' he said.' He pressed the call cancel button, and replaced the receiver on its desk unit.

Finn worked on at his desk a while longer, before checking his watch. Four-twenty. One more call. He picked up the receiver and dialled Lyneth's office. The call went out to her PA. Did he want her to take a message? Miss Jones was out of the office for the moment. No. He would try her mobile thanks. He cancelled the call and dialled a second time.

'Hi, Lyneth? It's Finn.'

'Hello, Finn.' The lovely Welsh lilt came through distorted by background noise. She spoke loudly to compensate.

'You out driving about?' he asked. 'I thought you didn't need a car in the City... Thought I might have got your answering service, with you stuck down some God-forsaken tube, or something.'

'Or something! No, Finn, we girls have to get out shopping sometime,' she laughed. 'I'm on hands free, so fire away.'

'I've checked in with Alexa, and all's OK with the agreement. We should have funds in place late tomorrow.' He still felt a need to walk the tightrope of her feelings. 'I'll be in the city on Monday. Why don't we all meet up?' He wanted Lyneth on his side, but he couldn't be sure about the relationship-thing she seemed to be pursuing with him.

'Sorry, Finn, got other clients, you know.' Again the laugh, teasing him. 'You're not my only beau you know.'

'OK, what about later in the week? he asked, '...I'll be pretty busy pinning down the purchase of the first bunch of shares during the early week, but we should have some results by Thursday. I wanted to talk to you about a position on the board of the new Tiger Oil, once the bid is public – sort of company counsel. Would that suit?'

'Wow, Finn, you know how to charm a girl, don't you...

Look, what about Tuesday lunch? I have some time then. Why don't you take me to Brown's again? I quite liked it there. Let's just meet inside this time.'

'Yeah, that'd be great.' Despite himself, the possibility of a relationship with the beautiful Lyneth attracted him – and he would formally separate from Aisling soon. 'How about a table in the open? Can't have you seducing me in an alcove again.'

'Finn!'

The mock surprise in the tone of Lyneth's reply, tinged with laughter, told him he had the measure of seduction right. 'OK. Tuesday then. Have a great weekend. Don't shop too much.'

'Bye, Finn.'

The line went dead and Finn cleared the call, placing the receiver down. He could do nothing more for the time being.

*

'Sorry about the Polish food,' said Lyneth. 'I didn't think they would have a private party on.'

'Don't worry, Lyneth.' Despite his good, American-English, Hu Su seemed to have a little difficulty in getting the right pronunciation of her Welsh name. His Chinese heritage showed through. 'Pizza's fine. I live on it when I'm in the States,' he said.

They both sat cross-legged on her lounge floor, the furniture pushed further aside, giving them more space in the centre of the room. Pizza boxes – two empty, one part-occupied – lay spread amongst various files and papers on the floor.

Earlier in the day, before she drove out to the airport, Lyneth took the opportunity of Hillary's lateness to go through the archive files, in the small room off her partner's office.

She discovered two files in particular, amongst others with different company names, all filed under *Philips, Aaron*. The file drawer, in a cabinet at the rear of the room, held the mark: "pre-2000", way before the 2003 date that she had joined with Hillary in setting up Keaton-Jones. The draw contained files dating back to at least 1985.

The two files Lyneth found related to litigation actions raised by families of employees who had suffered accidents in Aaron's employ. One, a large global company, in which Aaron had been regional finance director, showed the action settled out of court by the company's insurers. The second file, like Shufang's case, told of an action in which the plaintiff withdrew their claim, with no reason given. These files now lay open before them.

'You know, Lyneth? queried Hu Su, 'in both these cases you've found, all the witnesses are saying the same thing. The accidents occurred in the employee's own time, while they should not have been at work on site. It must be more than a coincidence, surely.'

'I know. The reports conclude that the accidents had been the fault of the individuals; that it had been their own fault in being on site without safety cover. Just as with Shufang.'

'But the cases are around eight years apart. Different companies, different continents. No wonder there's never been any question,' said Hu Su.

'Not until now. Three cases — we have your sister's to consider now.'

'But it still covers a total of eighteen years, and now three continents and three companies.'

'But we have some big fat common denominators now, don't we!' remarked Lyneth.

'Yes,' he said, grinning broadly, '…we do.'

'There's my partner, Hillary, the lawyer defending each company. We've also got Aaron Philips, an executive director in each of the companies. And then we have this Scott Lindon, who was either a witness of the accident…'

'…or, as with Shufang, he found her body,' interrupted Hu Su. 'I've brought some of the stuff I've collected with me.' He reached to his side, to lift a grey canvas shoulder-bag onto his knees. Fishing inside, he withdrew a single manila folder and placed the bag to his side again. 'I've tried to build a profile of the board. Got a sheet and some cuttings on each, here. We ought to go through Aaron's; he's the only one who counts as common.' He passed the folder to Lyneth. 'You've done some work on this yourself, haven't you?' he said, casting his eyes over the array of documents on the floor.

'A little… I lead a sad life really,' she said, laughing, a little self-mockingly. Taking the folder, Lyneth leafed through the tabbed entries relating to Aaron. The first one showed a single, US-letter size sheet with a printed bio. It listed some factual dates and company names. Second, came a series of press cuttings.

'The cuttings have taken me sometime – they're mostly local press,' said Hu Su. 'Whenever I've been to an oil town, I've done a search on the directors' names – just in case.'

'A lot of travel!' said Lyneth. She had already noted the headings on a number of cuttings, all printed in different type-faces, presentations, styles.

'The job has helped. I do get around a bit as a freelance. I'm just chasing oil stories, mainly.'

'What's this one?' The question had been rhetorical, as she separated a photocopied sheet from the folder, holding it closer to read.

'I'm not sure,' said Hu Su, as he tried to look over to see which cutting she had withdrawn. 'Without a context, I haven't known what to look for.'

She read the title aloud, '**OIL EXECUTIVE SAVES COLEAGUE'S LIFE.** It's from the Daily Record, Glasgow,

Scotland, from 1987… It goes on…' She continued reading a little more. 'It goes on to say a Mr. Aaron Philips, a visiting company executive, saved the life of a rig worker… He managed to grab the worker before the man plunged from the top of the North Sea rig when, in a freak accident, a cable whipped back, knocking the worker from his feet.' She looked up from the paper, towards Hu Su. 'It seems like Aaron managed to grab the guy before he fell off the rig.'

'The guy?' asked Hu Su, looking somewhat puzzled.

She looked down at the paper in her hand again, scanned it quickly, and raised her head again, slowly. 'S c o t t   L i n d o n,' she said, equally slowly, stressing each syllable of the surname in growing realisation. Christ, we have another link here, Hu. This is great!'

'So, first man saves second man's life, and second man figures he owes first man.'

'Sums it up. I'd call that a connection,' said Lyneth. 'And a damn fine one too.'

'But, who is this Scott Lindon? Apart from his name in the accident reports, as an employee of Tiger Oil, and now this article, we don't have anything. No description. Nothing,' said Hu Su, scowling.

'You didn't know of him before, then?' she asked.

'No,' said Hu Su, '…do you think…'

'That he could have been the visitor to your parents?'

'Yes.'

'Well…' she started, looking at the photocopied newspaper cutting in her hand, '…if he was, it would answer one hell of a lot of questions. It would directly implicate Aaron Philips in the possibility of a cover up. We need to find out who this guy Scott Lindon is. We need a description.' Her mind was racing ahead, joining dots, considering the implications of the facts before her. 'But we can't afford to alert anybody here to what we're doing… Can you get a description from your parents?'

234

'I can try,' said Hu Su. 'They've said nothing so far. It's a question of face. If they admit anything to anyone, even me, it will shame them for not standing up to whomever it was – for not standing up for their own daughter. But now, if I can say we believe there has been a cover up, and we have some proof... well, maybe...'

'It's got to be worth a try, Hu Su. If we can prove the Scott Lindon connection, we should have enough to get Shufang's case, and the others, revisited.'

'Don't we need to show the guy in Peace River and the guy in Hong Kong is one and the same?'

'Yes,' she said. Her eyes twinkled. 'I think we should check out Peace River. I think this is possibly too big to let blow without being sure of ourselves. If we talk to anyone here, we are bound to alert the wrong people.'

'We need to go over there,' said Hu Su, the inflection in his voice turning the obvious into a question.

'Yes... I think we do,' she said. 'And soon!'

'I can phone my parents.' He checked his watch. 'Ten-thirty; breakfast will be in another couple of hours.'

'Good,' said Lyneth. 'Let's look at flight times. My laptop's on the table, logged in. You have a look... do you like Polish vodka, Hu?' She was glad she'd decided not to let on to Finn about Hu Su. For the moment, she thought, the less Finn and Alexa knew, the less danger they might attract.

TWENTY ONE

THE DARKNESS PERSISTED. *Friday,* she thought. Alexa opened an eye and glanced at the clock by her beside. It glowed red, throwing a ghostly haze across the books and empty wine glass also positioned on her bedside table. Six-forty. *No need to get up just yet.*

The RedWood business ran smoothly. Her only real task of the day would be her eleven o'clock meeting to sign the Abdulrahman Shah loan agreement. *A ten million pound transaction.* She smiled to herself, closed the open eye, and pulled the duvet up over her shoulders. She dozed.

The sound of the alarm broke her drift into deeper sleep. Her hand darted out and slapped the top of the clock, sending the irritating sound crashing into silence. Another nine minutes. *Probably get away with another couple of those, and surface around half-seven.* She pulled her arm under the cover, into the warmth of her bed.

Suddenly, she was alert. Alarmed! Something? A shiver tracked through the length of her spine. Darkness plagued the room. A darkness that now formed a blanket of heavy trepidation. It weighed down on her. Her eyes widened in panic, but she did not move. *Something's wrong.* Fear grabbed at her. She lay still, her racing heartbeat the only sound she could hear. She fought to hold her breath. She fought to lie as quiet as she could. Listening. Listening for the sound that had triggered the sudden shiver. The clock cast its eerie red glow about. Her pupils, now widely dilated, took in the growing contrast in the shades of black and dark grey surrounding her. Familiar shapes... but!

...Christ, there's someone there! A shadowy figure in the bedroom doorway, where there should have been no shadow. She slept alone last night. She went to bed alone. Panic and fear rose in her belly. She felt sick.

Someone, there in the room, there with her. She dared not move. The icy chill of the shiver did not let up its grip on her soul. *Oh Christ...*

'You're awake then,' said the shadowy figure. The voice was not friendly, the delivered statement even less so, but she knew the voice. She cowered. *Aaron!*

She turned in her bed, slowly. She came to lie on her back, her arms braced by her side, ready to sit bolt upright.

The shadowy figure moved. An arm reached for the light switch and a sudden bath of light swamped the room. Her eyes flinched, closing tight at the shock. She opened them. The light revealed Aaron, standing there, starring at her. He projected none of the charm that had been her bond with him.

'What the fuck have you been up to, Alexa?' he shouted, with unrestrained anger in his voice.

Alexa sat up. She drew her knees up tightly to her chin; her arms wrapped themselves equally tightly round her legs. Involuntarily, under threat, she tried to make herself as small as possible, tried to shrink away from Aaron.

'You stupid... stupid... stupid bitch,' he said, spitting the words out. Ice appeared to form in his eyes. 'What the hell has Finn been doing with Lyneth? And why the fuck did you resign your agency? You've got to know...' he said, this time sounding almost pleading. 'I know you've been spending time with him… And who, for Christ-sake, is that bloody Chinaman with Lyneth?'

Alexa couldn't move. Fear rooted her to the spot, struck dumb and pinned down by the barrage of rapid-fire questions. The sudden assault shocked her senses. Her mind raced to catch up with her heart-rate; her rapid breathing, almost hyperventilating. She was totally and utterly confused. Chinaman? What Chinaman? It just wasn't making sense. Nothing made sense. She couldn't speak.

'You stupid bitch… What the hell have you done?' Again, he spat the words out. He turned and walked away from the door.

Alexa sat still – petrified. She heard the sound of Aaron's footsteps as he reached the outer door, opening it noisily. The door slammed. Silence. He'd gone.

The tears streamed. Rivulets collected and rolled down her cheeks. Her stunned immobility turned to a racking sob. She cried.

*

Finn checked his watch. It was late Friday night – nearly ten. Earlier, around eight that morning, his mobile, ringing and buzzing incessantly by the side of his bed, dragged him out of his sleep. It had been Alexa, in tears, terribly upset.

Through her sobbing, she managed to tell him about Aaron's outburst. He wasted no time in insisting she came up to Yorkshire for the weekend. She didn't feel safe in her apartment with Aaron acting in such a manner. She needed to get out of London.

'But you've got the girls,' she sobbed.

Christ! He hid his anxiety. 'I'll sort it,' he said. 'Don't worry, Alexa, Aisling will understand,' he said, not believing himself.

They arranged for her to pack a few things for the weekend and come up as soon as she signed-off on the loan agreement. That, and do whatever she needed to do at her office. He would go down with her on the Monday and stay with her for a few nights, until they could work out what to do next.

The girls! Aisling hadn't understood. He'd called her.

'Something's come up. I can't take the girls tomorrow.'

'Christ, Finn… It's the first time… and look what you're doing already. It'll tear them up.' She'd slammed the phone down on him.

He'd wanted to explain – but the truth would have been unpalatable. Aisling would not have accepted it. So he'd taken the hit – turned his other cheek. He was the bad boy. But he hadn't wanted another woman in the house with the girls there. They would not have understood. Aisling would not have understood. But he couldn't leave Alexa alone. *Christ! What next?*

Finn had picked Alexa up from York station, just after seven that evening. She looked beat; but he saw, then, her natural beauty. He'd offered to take her somewhere quiet, for something to eat. It looked as though she'd been crying on and off throughout the day. No, she hadn't wanted to eat out, so he'd gone to an Indian restaurant, on the drive out to his house. They collected a take-out.

'I'm sorry, Finn, I just didn't know what to do – or where to go.'

'It's OK Alexa, really. It's nice to have a bit of company. It's a large house with just me rattling around it.' He tried to make light of the situation, but Alexa still looked troubled.

'I know I've suspected something with Aaron,' she said. 'I hadn't mentioned it because I've not been able to pin anything down for certain. He's been so secretive about everything really. I'd overheard him on a strange call to someone. I think it might have been Grayson Barclay, but I can't be sure. I don't think Aaron knew I'd heard. It's all a bit weird. I'm frightened, Finn.'

He looked across at her. This girl, who'd showed strength for him when he needed it – she needed his support now. 'Well, you can stay here and relax this weekend,' he said. The vitriol he'd heard in Aisling's voice that morning, seemed a hundred thousand miles away.

They sat at a small table in the lounge. Finn began to clear the debris of the Indian meal. 'We can sort stuff out on Monday,' he said, '…get the locks changed on the apartment or something.'

'Yes,' Alexa replied, her voice quiet. 'But you've got a lot to do Monday… And the girls, Finn… you were going to have them this weekend.'

'It's OK, Alexa. Aisling was fine. The girls are fine. And we're all right. We're well on track with the deal. I checked the account; we have the funds in – all ten million pounds.' He smiled, warmly. 'We can have a little drink to celebrate if you like?'

Alexa managed a half smile. 'I could do with one… yes please.'

'Red wine?'

'Lovely.'

He checked his watch again. Ten o'clock. 'Why don't you switch the TV on? We can chill out with a bottle. I'll just finish clearing this stuff away and get one. The remote's over by the sofa,' he said. With a flourish of his hand, he waved in the general direction he thought he'd left it. 'I'm afraid I've become a bit of a slob on my own. Sorry about the mess.'

'Really, Finn, you wouldn't know,' she said, registering another half smile.

Finn took the debris to the kitchen as Alexa left the table

and went over to the sofa. She retrieved the remote and switched the TV on. She found the ten o'clock news just as Finn returned with an open bottle and two glasses. He sat them on the coffee table, in front of them both.

'There's a bit on oil prices. Turn the sound up, Alexa.' Finn poured the wine.

'…*of course, America's economy is a mess, but the currency cushion we currently experience here in the UK is not going to protect us from soaring energy prices. However, it will be much worse in the US…*' The TV reporter pulled no punches.

'It's just why Tiger Oil is so well positioned,' said Finn. 'Our timing is just right. Once we can get the project on track, we will be fine.' He took a drink from his glass.

'…*and the Chinese Government confirmed its interest in expanding their overseas influence today. Chinese demand for refined Alberta oil sand will create a lot of conflict with the United States. An economic clash may loom between Canada, the US and China…*'

'Exactly,' said Finn.

Finn sensed, rather than saw, Alexa stiffen. He glanced at her, next to him on the sofa. She stared at the screen. He looked forward and saw it too. His jaw dropped.

'*There is a lot of talk that Canada's Alberta oil sands will save the day. But there is much to resolve before it becomes clear whether this is the case or not,*' the reporter continued. '*The oil sands story is a valid and economically sound one. But the question is how best to get at the oil. I'm standing here with Grayson Barclay, Chairman of Tiger Oil, one of our own UK companies set to profit from the rapidly growing influence of the Chinese economy.*'

There, next to the reporter in a pre-recorded daytime news clip, shot outside some city building or other, stood the over-coated, fedora bearing figure of Grayson Barclay.

'*Yes,*' came the voice of Grayson Barclay. '…*the Canadians have been signing deals with the Chinese for years. But we are pleased to say, as a UK-based company, there has been significant interest in our extraction technology. It offers a far greater degree of environmental friendliness than other current methods, and we are expecting to do a deal with the CNPC, the China National Petroleum Corporation, within a matter of weeks…'*

Neither Finn nor Alexa heard the rest of the piece. The image of the smug face of Grayson Barclay burnt into their retinas; it persisted long after the news report moved on.

Alexa turned to face Finn – tears filled her eyes again. She could not speak. They both realised the significance of this news to the share price of Tiger Oil. By the time the markets reopened on Monday morning, it would be too late to buy in. The shareholders Finn received expressions of interest from would be unlikely to sell out now, not with such a major deal in the offering. The promise of a major contract with the Chinese would push the share price beyond their eleven-and-a-half pence offer. And, with the promise of riches to come, the shareholders would renew their interest in the company.

Shit! Not now!

After weeks of lows, and the lack of progress of a company languishing in the turmoil of a volatile market, Tiger Oil now looked to be a rising star. He could do nothing.

'E v e r y   b l o o d y   t i m e!' he said, mostly to himself. He saw Alexa's tears break, rolling down from her heavy eyes. Tiredness overcame her – the events of the day, just too much. He reached an arm out over her shoulders and drew her closer, comforting her. She melted into his arm, crying silently. He'd lost. He felt nothing. He had nothing more to lose, nothing more to feel. He stared at the television until long after the news gave way to the weather and the adverts. He knew the power of effective public relations – perception won over truth.

'Grayson frigging Barclay,' he hissed under his breath. His eyes narrowed… then closed.

TWENTY TWO

Saturday 19th January

ALEXA HAD GONE to bed in the guest room, the only respectably tidy room in the house. Finn returned to the lounge and knocked back a couple more glasses of wine, before he fell asleep on the sofa, the TV still on, playing to itself. Finn's Friday night modus operandi – an habitual practice. Even with Aisling and the girls in the house, and generally the result of a long week, Friday nights would frequently disappear into nothingness. He would often wake around two or three in the morning, notice a half-finished glass of wine on the coffee table, the television and lights on. It would mark the time for him to go to bed.

The incessant chatter of a girl in a short skirt presenting some all-night poker game, played out in the background. Finally, the chatter broke through his consciousness. He woke into the earliest hours of Saturday morning. This time, though, he could find no incentive to go to bed. He could find no incentive to do anything but lie there. He'd taken the cork from the cork-screw and turned it upside down, so he could wedge it in the bottle top. He didn't like waste, and the wine would keep a few more hours. He could still remember the aftermath of the last time Grayson Barclay shocked him. A vivid, raw, open wound. He harboured no wish for a recurrence of the whisky-fuelled backlash.

Where the hell had that come from? ...*We are expecting to do a deal with CNPC, within a matter of weeks...* No one could have seen it coming. He'd been watching the market reports and, yes, he'd seen the Chinese interest grow. But it all appeared at the Global-operator level, and within Governments. Tiger Oil? It was nothing more than a single-cell organism, in comparison to CNPC – an amoeba of the oil world. Christ, they never even talked about Chinese interest, at anytime. In fact, he recalled, the board made a point of staying away from Chinese money. Neither Grayson Barclay, nor Aaron, could find much time for them, despite Shufang's obvious knowledge, and his own interest. No! Grayson had led the other board members in rejecting any Chinese involvement. Grayson had argued the operations in Canada, and the interest of the US over the border, meant it would be counterproductive to talk to the Chinese. Both Finn and Shufang conceded Grayson's argument at the time; he made a strong case.

Now, though, a deal in a matter of weeks? It just did not make sense. How?

There would be no way the investors he'd lined up, would possibly agree to a sale now; not weeks away from a major contract win. They would hold on, or at least force the price much higher than he and the new team were prepared to meet. Again, Grayson frigging Barclay had screwed him over – stumped! And now? Well, now he held Abdulrahman Shah's money in the bank and, deducting the transaction costs, the ten mill' would already be reduced. He owed a wealthy Arab and you never get a second chance to let an Arab down.

A growing sense of panic welled in his stomach. If he needed to repay the transaction fees from somewhere, he could count himself down another fifteen to twenty thousand. *Christ! It isn't much, but I don't have fifteen to twenty thousand. If...* no... when... When Abdulrahman hears the news and calls

in his loan-note – as, inevitably, he would do, surely? ...
Christ! He did, literally, have nothing left. Technically, he was
bankrupt. He owed money he did not have and there seemed
to be no way out of this one.

He drifted into another troubled sleep.

'Finn.' A woman's voice. 'Finn. You awake? Here's a
coffee for you.'

Finn opened his eyes, slowly. He registered light. He still
lay on the sofa, dressed as he had been the night before.

'I managed to find everything for the coffee,' said Alexa,
smiling down at him. 'Hope I made it OK. I'm not used to
the cafetière. I've one of those things you just put a packet in,
press a button and hey presto, there you are.'

'I'm sorry...' he started.

'Don't be sorry, Finn. I think we both came off worse last
night. Did you manage any sleep?'

'I must have... just now...' he said, 'but it doesn't feel like
it. And you? Did you sleep?'

'No, not really,' said Alexa. Her voice sounded deflated.
'What are we going to do, Finn?'

He sat up, swinging his legs round to the floor. He looked
at the coffee, thoughtfully, then up at Alexa. Having never
seen Alexa in the morning, and despite her down-beat mood,
her appearance settled easy on his eye. 'I don't know, Alexa,'
he said.' He really had no idea. 'Well, I know one thing...
it's my problem... Abdulrahman's my problem... I just don't
know what to do about it.'

They both sat drinking coffee for a while, both emotionally
drained – incapable of thinking rationally.

'Let's get out of here,' said Alexa, breaking the silence of
their mutually assured depression.

'Pardon?'

'Let's get out of here, I mean, let's go away – somewhere
different... where we can think about it. I think we need to sit

somewhere restful, somewhere we can talk through it all, and get our options straight.'

'I'm skint, Alexa. I'm going to need every penny I've got.'

She smiled, softly – a little mischievous smile. The smile he'd come to recognise from her normally playful demeanour. 'I have a joint credit card on one of Aaron's bank accounts...' she said, grinning. 'I fancy the Lakes. Will you drive? We can stretch it into Monday, and get to the office for Tuesday. We can face the music then. What do you say?'

TWENTY THREE

MONDAY, JANUARY TWENTY-FIRST, and mid-evening, Mountain Standard Time; it would be a very early, cold Tuesday morning in London.

Lyneth Jones sat in the *Sternwheeler* bar of the Sawridge Inn hotel, Peace River, Canada. She sat with Hu Su. The sprawling, low-level motel cum conference centre nestled between Highway Two and the blocks of township buildings stretching, westwards, to the Peace River itself. The Sawridge Inn advertised itself as a full-service hotel and "executive" conference facility, providing them with a choice of two bars and a restaurant. But, to Lyneth, the alternative *Sharks* sports bar, with its array of pool tables, special deals for hunters, and its proximity to the burgeoning oil industry to the North East, made the word "executive" seem a little wide of the descriptive mark. *Not my kind of place.*

'You get used to it,' said Hu Su, seemingly reading her mind. 'I've stayed in far worse – anything from a corrugated tin shack, to the Waldorf. This is closer to the Waldorf than you might think, at least in a place like Peace River. I've used it a few times on trips.'

At least in the *Sternwheeler* bar they could get food from the restaurant menu. The idea of burgers, fries and suds, set against the interminable "click" "click" of pool balls ricocheting of each other, did not appeal. It had been a long trip out, and a long day fighting jet-lag and the frustration of trying to reach distant objectives within their short, self-imposed timescale. They were thankful the bar's billing of a *Las Vegas style atmosphere,* fell a long way short of the racket of a major gaming hall.

Lyneth had managed to late-book two economy seats on United Airlines flight 955. And, on the Saturday morning, they rose early, leaving Heathrow Terminal One at ten twenty-five, London time. They endured a long but uneventful journey, with a scheduled five-and-a-half hour stop-over in San Francisco. There, they changed from their Boeing 777, to a SkyWest Airlines Canadair 700. By the time they arrived at immigration control in Edmonton, they had been on the go for almost twenty-four hours, catching only short moments of rest on the two flights.

Despite their tiredness at Edmonton, they still faced nearly five hours of drive time ahead of them. Given the time of night, they passed through controls quickly. They sat, driving northbound in a rental car, by midnight Mountain time, taking turns to drive the near three hundred mile route, up Highway Two, to Peace River. They checked into the hotel for breakfast, on the Sunday. Around them, snow lay on the ground – it felt very cold. Mercifully, the roads stayed clear. As they learned on arrival, it had neither rained nor snowed since the previous week, the temperature even uncommonly warm for the time of year – a fact Lyneth had difficulty coming to terms with.

It took all of Sunday to recover. Neither surfaced from their rooms until five-thirty in the evening; time enough to catch the happy hour. They arranged to meet in the bar and plan the day ahead of them. Now, late-Monday, there persisted an air of added dread – the inevitable return trip.

During the day, they agreed to go their separate ways to

248

research. Lyneth, with her credentials as a lawyer, would take on the Peace River police department and Hu Su would revisit the local press archives, and follow his journalistic nose from there. Hu now had the briefest of descriptions of the stranger, from his parents. The visitor: a short, powerfully-built foreigner, of middle-age. His parents thought British, but they could not be sure as the man talked very quietly, and through an interpreter. Hu's mother added: *the man's eyes looked cold*; he wasn't quite sure what she meant, but at least, now, he had something to go on. They needed to connect the vague description of the visitor to events at the Tiger Oil site.

The site itself lay about forty kilometres North East of town; the plan being to meet up in the bar for dinner, to swap stories. They would both drive out to the site the next day, Tuesday, returning to London on Wednesday. That had been the plan.

The day did not produce the hoped-for results. Hu Su found the offices of the Record Gazette, across from a large fitness centre, further down One Hundred Street. He discovered nothing in any archived press reports to suggest witness descriptions, or names, let alone photographs. The accident did not rate highly in public interest at the time. The local press were more concerned over a forty-five thousand dollar drugs bust, and the long-term environmental effects of the oil boom in the run up to an election year. Shufang Su's accident merited a mere column inch as a *"tragic accident on oil site"*. Hu Su gained no more luck in either the town's library archive or its municipal museum.

The Peace River detachment of the Regional RCMP formed part of the Western Alberta Royal Canadian Mounted Police. The internet blurb Lyneth read before setting out on her quest, suggested the detachment provided "integrated services" to the Peace River township and the rural communities surrounding it, including Northern Sunrise County, and the Woodland Cree

First Nation.

'I'm sorry, Miss... err, Jones,' said the police-sergeant, checking the details on Lyneth's business card. His tone carried an air of genuine apology. '...but our policing contract only gives us nine regular RCMP members. We have asked for more, and we may get some later this year, but we have few resources at the moment.'

'Is the policeman...' began Lyneth.

'Corporal,' the sergeant corrected, '...you know, we still base our ranks on the British Army system.'

'Sorry, Sergeant... err? said Lyneth. She should at least know his name.

'Err... Sergeant Zimmerman,' said the kindly, not unattractive middle-aged, perhaps fifty-year old, policeman. He clearly wasn't accustomed to attractive female lawyers from London asking his name. He blushed slightly.

'Corporal...' she corrected. 'Thank you, Sergeant Zimmerman. Is the corporal who took the witness statements available to talk to, by any chance?' Lyneth had asked, hopefully.

'I'm sorry. Corporal Gauvreau was only here a short time. He supplemented our staff during the run up to last winter. He's based in Edmonton normally, if he's still there, that is.'

Lyneth had half anticipated the sergeant's honest, but unhelpful reply.

'We have the forensic team still here,' continued the sergeant, 'but I'm afraid they would not have been in contact with any of the witnesses directly. We don't work like the Las Vegas CSI here, and if they had seen anyone on site, they would not have made a connection with them. No. I'm afraid it would be the same with the General Investigation Services team also; Corporal Gauvreau spent his time attached to them. I doubt if any of the others would have been involved. It did seem to be a straight-forward case. Nothing untoward.'

That the officer who took the statement wasn't there,

frustrated Lyneth. The apologetic, almost embarrassed, sergeant had been as helpful as he could, and let her sit there, with a huge mug of coffee, going through the office archive on the case.

The official RCMP report named Scott Lindon as the person who found Shufang Su. It had been Lindon who made the 911 call. But she could find no description of him – either in any of the file notes or the report text.

Initially, she read, the RCMP questioned Scott Lindon on site, at the well-head. A follow-up interview then took place at the Sawridge Inn. Scott Lindon had been staying there with the other company representative, Jonathon Long. The RCMPs interviewed them both there, at around four o'clock in the afternoon, on the day of the accident. The file notes on Jonathon Long's brief interview held nothing either. She could find no corroboration at all. She could see nothing to tie the name of Scott Lindon with the description of the stranger visiting Hong Kong.

'So, that's the sum of it,' said Hu Su, frustration clearly etched into his voice. 'And I don't, for a minute, think we'll find much out on site. With all the standing snow on the ground, it's going to be pretty shut down this time of year.'

'I know,' said Lyneth. The enthusiasm with which they had both travelled out on a whim, had evaporated – it left them both jaded. She struggled to come up with something positive about the trip so far.

'Perhaps this trip ain't such a good idea,' said Hu Su, a little sardonically.

'No. I think we needed to try this. We just need a new angle for the morning.'

'Well, if y'all excuse me,' he said, 'I think I'll go shoot some pool. Terrible habit – I picked it up in the States. D'ya want to join me?'

'No, it's OK. You go ahead, I'm going to have another

drink and think some more.'

They left the table, Hu Su going off in the direction of the *Sharks* sports bar, Lyneth making her way to sit at one of the tall chairs arrayed against the empty bar opposite.

*

'What can I get you, lady?' the barman asked, as he stood polishing a tall glass he'd retrieved from a glass washer.

'Large vodka please – do you have any on ice?'

'Yes, especially for Russian guests.'

'You get many?'

'Not tonight.'

He brought the double measure over to her, then, stooping briefly below the level of the bar, he grabbed another glass to polish.

'You're not a hunter, or an oil-type, are you? So, what brings you way out here? I mean, we got snow and stuff, but I figure that's not your line either?' Tilting his head to one side, the barman looked at her. His face bore a quizzical but friendly expression.

'I'm a bitch of a lawyer,' she said, with a smile on her face.

'S'OK, I don't bite – well, not anyone who's serving me a drink.'

'I'm safe then,' he said, returning her smile.

'For now.'

'So… if I can be so bold – without getting bitten – what's a good looking bitch of a lawyer like you doing in a place like this. You know, it was a hot day today, we got to minus two C!'

'I'm investigating an accident,' she said. *It didn't hurt to talk, sometimes; you never know what might come out of a conversation.*

'What sort of accident?' The barman's curiosity grabbed

252

hold of him.'

'Careful, I might have to start biting.' She downed her drink. 'Can I have another?'

'Sure thing,' he said. He took her glass and went to wash it.

'Same glass is fine. Thanks. A young female engineer with an oil company, she was killed on a site near here, around October 2006.'

'Chinese?' the barman asked, as he brought the fresh drink and placed it in front of Lyneth, replacing the small, now damp, paper drink mat the previous glass stood on.

'How...'

'How did I know?'

'Yes,' she said.

'I'm a barman – been here three years, and I can tell you, there's only been one female engineer killed in that time. She was Chinese. She used to stay here. Pretty little thing; she liked vodka, too.'

'Wow,' exclaimed Lyneth. Her eyes lit up and her mind raced to form questions. 'You remember the accident?'

'Well, not the accident particularly. I was working here, obviously, mainly evenings. I remember the people around at the time. I'm a bit like that – good at remembering faces.'

'Do you want a drink?' she asked.

'I guess it won't hurt, thanks' he said, looking around the bar. 'There's no one else here at the moment. January is not a busy month here – too damn cold for many.

Lyneth downed her drink. 'And another for me, please.'

The barman brought two drinks over. 'JD for me ...OK?'

'Fine. I'm Lyneth,' she said, holding her hand out over the bar top.

'Jack... like the whisky,' he said, shaking her hand briefly, nodding at his glass. 'But I don't taste like fire.'

'Barman and raconteur,' she said, smiling.

'At your service, Lyneth.'

'So what can you tell me, Jack?'

'Well, it was kinda like there was two people, then there was four, then there was three, then two again.'

'How do you mean?' she quizzed, her curiosity pricked. There had been a word in there: "four" – it just didn't figure for her.

'The Chinese girl... I don't remember names... The Chinese girl... good-looking... I said that, right? ...She was. And quite young too... well, she came here with another guy; late-forties, fifty-ish, I guess. The two stayed here, together, at other times before then, but mostly I'd seen the Chinese girl before. She was kinda obvious in a place like this.' He rolled his eyes, casting his gaze around the room, as if to take in the unseen crowd of absent hunters and oilmen. 'I think they'd checked in around mid-week, before the accident. It was a Monday I think, the accident.'

'And others joined them?'

'Yeah,' said Jack, nodding. 'Could have been the weekend, but another two guys arrived...'

'Two?' Lyneth hoped Jack would notice the puzzled look on her face. She needn't have worried.

'Yeah. One was fairly tall, well built, and old, with grey hair. In his sixties, I guess, and well dressed. Oh yes,' he said, remembering something, '...and he wore a wide brimmed hat.'

'Grayson Barclay,' hissed Lyneth, with quiet passion.

'Pardon?'

'Nothing. Please, carry on – you're doing brilliantly,' she said, smiling encouragement. 'I'll only bite if you stop.'

'Err... right,' said Jack, apparently not quite knowing how to take the comment. 'The other guy was about mid-age, but he was just kinda... like, stocky, sort-of-thing. You know, muscles. Not sure on the brain front, but I wouldn't have liked to run up against him, despite his age. Didn't look the friendly sort, at all.'

Lyneth whistled. 'That's it... That's brilliant, Jack. Have another drink with me.

She grinned. Jack appeared to sense something. He stepped back, slightly.

'RRright,' he said. 'Err, thank you.' He turned to get the vodka for Lyneth's glass, poured another straight from bottle, without a measure, and then helped himself to another JD.

'Cheers, boyo,' she said; the touch of Welsh surprised even her, as she lifted her glass in salute to Jack. *I must be feeling good.*

'Cheers.' Jack took a quick gulp. 'I think I can do better,' he added, slightly nervously.

'What do you mean?' she asked.

'Wait a minute.' He put his glass down and went to the computer terminal on the bar top. He tapped away at the keys for a minute or two.

'I'm intrigued,' she said.

'I can access the hotel's archives from here. I'm just pulling up the register for the time. Late October 2006, wasn't it?'

'Yes. October twenty-third.'

'Ah. Here it is. I've got it for the whole of October.' He twisted the screen of the bar-top terminal round, so that Lyneth could see.

'Page down to the week before,' she said. 'That would make it around sixteenth onwards.'

'There you go,' said Jack, pointing. 'That's got to be them, the only Chinese girl's name I can see. Shufang Su and Jonathon Long checked in on eighteenth of October. Long for one week, Su for three weeks.'

'What does it give you later in the week?' she asked. The note of excitement rose in her voice.

'Saturday twenty-first – there are a few people there. Anyone you recognise?'

'Ssshhh,' she said, 'I'm looking.' Lyneth, leaning half over the bar top by now, scanned the entries. 'There! ...There they bloody well are. Grayson Barclay and bloody Scott Lindon.' The names shouted out to her. She dropped down onto her chair. Her grin broadened. 'I've got them! she said, more to herself than to Jack. Then: 'Jack, can you be a darling, and print those off for me?'

'It's the least I can do for the drinks, I guess.' He smiled, nervously. To Lyneth, he seemed unsure how he should read her: this passionate woman, who only bites occasionally. Jack pressed a couple of keys and a printer, unseen beneath the bar-top, churned out a few pages of text.

'There you are,' said Jack, retrieving the pages and passing them to Lyneth. 'Passport numbers and home addresses too.'

Lyneth took the papers. Suddenly, she got up from her seat. She reached over the bar and pulled Jack's totally surprised face towards her, kissing him full on. She held on for a few more seconds than decent. Then she let go, as fast as she had taken hold of him.

'Wow!' said Jack, dumbfounded.

'Good night,' she said, accompanied by one of her biggest smiles. She could feel his nervous, shocked gaze follow her, as she turned and walked away, towards her room.

Lying on her bed, she looked through the printout. Grayson Barclay arrived with Scott Lindon, but he checked out on his own, on the Monday, in the early hours of the morning. *Before the accident?* she mused. No wonder his name hadn't been on the report, or even mentioned before. He wasn't there when the police went round to interview the others. So, why the hell was he there? It just didn't make any sense. At least, now though, she had Scott Lindon pegged. Jack's description fitted the family's Hong Kong visitor; passport details and flight records would verify the connection. And she doubted Jack would mind adding his testimony, if it came to that.

She tried to call Hu Su's room, but no answer. Probably still out playing pool. No problem, it would wait until morning, and breakfast. She set the alarm on her mobile for five a.m., and the alarm on the room's television for the same. She needed to call Finn. He would be expecting her for lunch. She couldn't stop smiling to herself.

*

Finn arrived at Browns quite early for a Tuesday lunchtime. He never liked to be late, particularly if he planned to meet a woman. He always liked to watch a woman's approach; but he hadn't managed to beat Lyneth to a lunch venue yet – certainly not on her terms, at Gatti's.

He stood at the bar, toying with a large glass of the house pinot grigio, waiting for Lyneth to join him for lunch. He liked Browns. It wasn't a contemporary bar and brasserie. Despite its cavernous interior, the dark wood and restrained light from the relatively small frontage, leading from the narrow street outside, gave it an air of seclusion. The prices held reasonably too, compared with other places close by.

His head kept telling him not to get involved with Lyneth but, as he glanced at his watch for yet another time, he couldn't help but recognise his disappointment at her lateness. As he drank from the glass of cool wine, the noise of the regular lunchtime throng didn't help his mood. Many of the better tables now stood occupied. Despite his quip when they'd spoken last, he'd been hoping to get a table set against the rear wall, and explore just how much Lyneth might be prepared to flirt with him. Anticipation about seeing Lyneth for lunch had been building all morning, despite the problems he now faced. Christ, he had nothing else left to go for; he might as well have a little fun on the way down.

He'd tried to call Lyneth on Monday afternoon, when he

and Alexa returned to his house from their visit to the Lakes. But, he couldn't reach her. Her phone just kept ringing out, and not even going to voice mail. He'd texted as well, but with no luck. *Where the hell is she? Surely, she must have known what's happened.*

For the rest of Monday, he and Alexa just stayed low at the house. They travelled down to London that morning. He came straight to Browns to meet Lyneth, planning to seek her advice on how best to approach Abdulrahman Shah – how best to cover the loss. Alexa left him to go straight to her office, then on to the apartment. He would join her there later. He could do nothing now, no buying of shares. He checked on Monday morning, while sat with Alexa over breakfast on the edge of Ullswater. The Tiger Oil price opened at twelve pence. This morning, Tuesday, it opened a penny higher. No, they had taken it as far as they could. It was over, now – he could see that.

Finn barely heard the phone ring; the background chatter in Browns had lifted to a crescendo. He could not feel it either, buried as it was, in his overcoat pocket. He lifted the phone from his pocket.

'Hello? Lyneth?' He could not hear well. 'Just a minute…' He quickly downed what remained of his drink and walked to the door. He stepped out into the relative quiet of a cold Old Jewry street. '…Hi,' he said, finally.

'Hi you,' came the sound of the soft Welsh lilt of Lyneth's voice.

'Where are you?'

'I'm sorry, I can't make it for lunch; something came up.'

'Oh…'

'Don't sound too disappointed, Finn, it's good news for you.'

'Good news? What do you mean, good news? Haven't you heard?'

'Haven't I heard what?'

'It's all over, Lyneth. They've won. Grayson bloody Barclay pulled a frigging rabbit out of his damned hat. The price has risen; it's a rising market and we can't get the shares for a takeover. We've damn well lost.'

'Oh my God, Finn...' she sounded genuinely taken aback. 'No, I hadn't heard. I'm out of town at the moment.'

'What do you mean, out of town?'

'Peace River. . .' Lyneth's voice tailed off.

'Pardon?' he said, almost shouting into the phone. 'I thought you said Peace River... I can hardly hear you.'

'I *did* say Peace River, Finn.' She let the fact sink in. 'I think I've got them.'

'Got who?'

'Grayson bloody Barclay,' she said, mimicking him now. 'Barclay – that's who, you lovely fool,' she shouted, 'I've got him.'

'How... What... What's going on, Lyneth?'

'Look, I'm on my way back. I should get to Heathrow sometime tomorrow. I'll call you. We will need to plan the next steps carefully.'

'Christ, Lyneth,' he said – but he couldn't think straight. *She's telling me what...* Suddenly, the penny dropped. *She's been working the case herself!* 'What have you got, Lyneth?'

'Enough, Finn. Enough.'

'I could kiss you...' he shouted, attracting a few looks from passers-by.

'I have to go now, Finn, sorry. I'll call you soon. I'm on my way home!'

Sod it, he thought. This woman is helping him – and she wants him. Maybe he *should* reconsider his own rules. First, he needed to settle some accounts. Whatever Lyneth had found, with her help and Alexa's, they would do it.

TWENTY FOUR

THE DOORBELL RANG. Alexa put the rather formal looking letter she held down onto the table. She went from the lounge to open the door to her apartment.

'Hi, Finn,' she said, pleased to see him. He certainly looked happier than she felt.

'You sure about this, Alexa?' He referred to her invitation to stay with her a few days.

'Yes, of course. It will save you some money as well. The Tower can't be cheap. Anyway, I have some news about Aaron.'

'Yes?'

'He wants a divorce,' she said.

'Oh…' he replied. 'I'm sorry. I… I don't quite know what to say.'

'I s'pose it was inevitable after what's been going on recently. Why don't you go and put your bag in the spare room, and freshen up. We can sit and chat over some tea.'

'OK, thanks,' he said, turning to enter the bedroom Alexa indicated.

She was relieved Finn had arrived. When she left him at the Bank tube that morning, she went first to her office. She needed to check things out after her surprise Monday off. But, as anticipated, everything ran well there. She'd answered a few e-mails, and delegated a couple of actions to her team. After that, she'd hung around until about two before going home.

Homecoming proved something of a surprise. She did not expect to see Aaron there, in the middle of the day. She'd left returning home until two, to be sure he would be out; but there he was. His demeanour retained the hard edge of their last meeting. He was excessively brusque.

'I'll make this short,' he said. 'There's a letter for you, there,' he'd snarled, pointing to the envelope on the table. 'It's from my solicitor. I'm divorcing you on the grounds of your adultery.'

'BBBut...' she'd stammered in response, 'there's nothing between us; nothing between Finn and me, nothing!'

'Don't take me for a bloody fool, Alexa. I'm not talking about Finn, you bitch.'

'Aaron...' she began. Tears welled in her eyes.

'I'm talking about Ozzie Medwin. What were you thinking of? And the others, of course. You've been a busy little whore when I've been away, haven't you?' he'd said, spitting the words out like icicles shot from a bow. Each struck their intended target with effect. She hurt.

Despite the tears welling, she hadn't cried. She hadn't even replied – there really would have been no point in giving him the satisfaction. She just looked down at the envelope.

'Don't worry,' he'd said, sneering at her. 'You can keep the apartment... but, it's all you'll get. I'm not wasting any more time on you.'

Aaron had thrown down his apartment keys on the table, and left. They'd both returned to face the music all right, but she hadn't quite expected Aaron's letter, or his presence. She hadn't really known what to expect. She hadn't thought it through.

'Thanks for the weekend, Alexa,' said Finn, his voice breaking through her thoughts.

'Yes, it was good to get away, wasn't it?' she said.

The weekend did them both good. In truth, they'd done very little but walk around and take the occasional tea or coffee break. They drove out to Ullswater, spending time sitting by the lake, talking of this and that. They had driven on, and found an inconspicuous bed and breakfast with a couple of rooms vacant. On the return to York, she'd confirmed her invitation to Finn, to stay a while in London. She would feel safer, and Aaron should not have a problem with Finn. No, Aaron didn't seem to be an issue anymore.

'What about Aaron then?' asked Finn.

'Well, a divorce isn't such an issue really. I just hadn't expected it so soon. Being married has become a convenience. We've led separate lives for a while now. We're lucky if we see each other for more than a day in any week. It's all a bit of a sham. Don't get me wrong – I think we've always cared for each other, and we did get along fine; well, at least until recently.'

'I'm sorry,' said Finn.

She could see the concern writ large on his face. 'No, don't be,' she said. At least I know he's not going to be threatening violence. After last Friday morning, I really didn't know. I'll still change the locks, but I reckon it's not such a problem now.'

'What do you think has been going on?'

'Well, I think he's more involved in what happened to you than we've understood. But a lot of this is possibly me.'

'What do you mean, you?' he asked.

'Another time, Finn,' she said, smiling at him. 'Well, you look happier than you did this morning. How was lunch with the sexy Lyneth?' She winked at him.

'She stood me up,' said Finn, laughing.

His laugh triggered an involuntary, puzzled look on her face. Her question followed quickly. 'I don't get it,' she said, '…stood you up?"

'I was in Browns, waiting for her. She was around half an

hour late, when I got a call from her.'

'She's never struck me as the sort of person to let someone down like that.'

'Well, actually, she's not let me... sorry us... down at all.'

'What do you mean?' She was completely baffled, and Finn wasn't getting to the point quick enough; her impatience shone through.

'She went out to Peace River,' he said. 'I think she's been investigating Shufang's death on her own.'

'What do you mean, *you think*? Christ, Peace River... what on earth? ...Don't you know?'

'Well, it was a hurried call. She said she was on her way home with some info on Grayson Barclay. She said we could get them.'

'What?' she demanded.

'I don't know,' he said, 'I just know she sounded very sure of herself. I guess we'll find out tomorrow. I'm going to take the train out to Heathrow, to meet her.'

'My God, Finn, what the hell does this mean?'

'I don't know. I've held off calling Abdulrahman Shah, until we know.'

'You can't not call him, Finn. He has to realise something's wrong.'

'Not necessarily. He could be thinking the share price rise is due to our buying-up stock.'

'Come off it, Finn, there won't be any transactions recorded. You have to call him. He's got to know – you don't want to start making an enemy of him, do you?'

'I know,' Finn conceded. 'Could you give his PA a call for me? Play for time? Say I'm in talks – anything. Just buy me until we've spoken with Lyneth.'

'OK. I'll see what I can do,' she said. She checked her watch. Nearly four forty-five. Look, we've probably got away with it today. If he's in Geneva, then it's already nearly six. I'll go into the office early in the morning, and call from there. I'll have thought of something by then.'

She sat down on one of the two cream leather sofas. 'There's some of Aaron's claret in boxes, in the tall pull-out larder in the kitchen. Why don't you get a bottle, Finn? We can drink his health.' She smiled at the idea. 'Christ, I just hope Lyneth comes up with something good tomorrow. Otherwise, I just don't know what we're going to do.'

*

The return journey from Peace River was the reverse for Lyneth and Hu Su: another painful day, over twenty four hours of travelling. The uneventful nature did nothing to release their boredom. Even the adrenaline rush, triggered by discovering the evidence implicating Grayson Barclay, paled in the face of the journey's monotony. The only redeeming feature was the shorter stop-over in San Francisco. A tail wind reduced their overall journey by around three hours.

Landing though, Lyneth was again on a high. Hu Su's grin seemed even wider than the one he produced over breakfast on the Tuesday, after she told him of the Monday-night conversation with Jack, the barman. That was yesterday. And, to cap it all, as she approached the customs point from the baggage hall at Heathrow, she knew she'd returned with enough evidence to help Finn. There was also the promise of a long-wished-for first kiss.

Finn still knew nothing about Hu Su. She had texted her arrival time to Finn, from San Francisco, and he'd replied that he would be there to meet her at Terminal One. From seeing Finn standing in the Arrivals hall, the distance between them fell away, rapidly. She almost flung herself into his arms, wasting no time claiming her kiss. It was a deep, passionate kiss, with Finn's arms around her, drawing her body in close.

Finn broke away from the embrace first; he'd noticed the slightly-embarrassed look on the tall, slender Chinese man standing next to her.

'Finn, let me introduce you to Hu Su,' she said, leaving the puzzled look on Finn's face as she turned to face Hu Su. 'Hu, this is Finn Jackson.'

Hu Su dropped his bags as he stretched out two hands, placing them either side of Finn's right hand. With a slight bow, and grasping his hand, Hu Su shook it vigorously, greeting Finn like some revered, long-lost elder uncle. Hu's name clicked into place and Finn's puzzled expression dissolved as he caught the infection of Hu's wide, beaming grin.

'You...' said Finn, now also beaming like the proverbial Cheshire Cat.

'Yes, Shufang's brother,' said Hu Su. 'I am honoured to meet you, Mr Jackson.' He was still shaking Finn's hand.

'No. Finn... Please, call me Finn. This is great to meet you, Hu.'

They were in a taxi by two-fifteen, for the drive into London; they headed straight for Lyneth's apartment.

She was tired, but happy to be going home.

'Shufang held you in high esteem, Finn. She talked of you often, to our parents.' Hu Su had been chatting away, incessantly, ever since being introduced to Finn.

Amid tiredness, and the rapid recounting of the evidence she and Hu Su discovered, before and during the Peace River trip, she became aware of something else. She felt a little odd – as if she stood apart, detached, observing herself in conversation with the two men, sitting there in the rear of the taxi.

The kiss was not what she'd expected. More accurately, she supposed, it was exactly what she wanted – *it's just... it's just that the affect of the kiss wasn't expected.* Something was absent. Images of past relationships blurred her tired vision. Her eyes blinked hard as she fought to keep awake. *What?* She sat thinking. *What could it be about Finn?*

Abruptly, it became all so clear to her, like the final nod of the head that rocks you suddenly awake, as you are drifting asleep. It really was the chase, only the chase. Now she seemed to have found Finn, now she appeared to have caught him, signed by his passionate embrace, perversely, it seemed over.

She sat next to Finn on the bench seat. Hu Su sat on one of the flip-down rear-facing seats. Finn held her hand. He'd notice her closing eyes blink once more – he squeezed her hand, gently. Tiredness enveloped her. The battle had ended. She'd won – the chase now over. She needed the chase.

But there would be no loose ends, she promised herself. Through her tiredness she thought ... *tomorrow's another day.* Her eyes closed. She listened to the two of them talk. She would finish this for Finn. With no further emotional distraction for her, she could focus on the legal niceties. She would finish on good terms. She opened her eyes and smiled at Finn. She squeezed his hand, her eyes closed once more. She did like him – a lot.

*

By lunchtime on Thursday, the day after Lyneth and Hu Su had returned through Heathrow, Finn had his head around all of the information the others brought him. He sat in Alexa's apartment, running through the emotional upheaval of the past months. They had enough to get Tiger Oil back.

Tiger Oil's directors all needed to settle their account with him and his new-found team. He would not have done it without Alexa and Lyneth, and now Hu Su. The directors – Grayson Barclay, Aaron, Jonathon Long and David Kail – owed them all a pay-back.

The outer door of the apartment opened, closely followed by the sound of Alexa's keys jangling onto the console table. Finn got up from where he sat at the dining table and went over to the kitchen area.

'Hi, Alexa,' he called out, lifting the kettle to check it held sufficient water. 'You OK for tea?'

'Yes, fine thanks, Finn,' said Alexa, as she came through from the hallway. 'I've tried to put a call into Abdulrahman Shah, but he's still away. Heidi said she's expecting him in Geneva this afternoon. She suggested trying again, later.'

'OK. Thanks. At least we're making the effort to update him. It's bought us time to get the story from Lyneth.'

Alexa placed a Marks and Spencer's bag onto the kitchen island top. 'Lunch… M and S OK?' she said, laughing. 'You'll get to see I'm no chef!'

'Fine by me.'

'With the market as jittery as it is,' said Alexa, 'any hint of bad press will cause a nervous reaction. I think what Lyneth has returned with is enough to send the shares south again.'

'I reckon so. They've been holding at around thirteen pence today; they won't have to fall much, and we can bring the plan back on line. I really thought we'd lost.'

'Me too,' she said. 'A bit of a shock seeing Grayson on the News like that.'

'Just think,' he said, 'we have enough of a story, now, to suggest something really underhand took place to get Shufang's family to drop the case. Just think of the head-line: **Tiger Oil Employee Forces Family to Quit Action**. You wouldn't need much else. It would be enough to raise serious questions and that would rock confidence in the management again. In this market, it would work.'

267

'It wouldn't take much of a leak. I could use the US source again,' she said.

Alexa looked to be in the swing of it now.

'I can get onto those shareholders again,' he said. 'I'll say we have come across some concerns, which will become public soon... just to see if they're still interested in selling. But I'm not going to offer more than eleven and a half.'

'Whom do you think it was, sending Scott Lindon out to Hong Kong?' asked Alexa, '...Grayson or Aaron?'

'Probably Grayson, I think; he was the senior one there at the time... That gets me, that does. Why the heck did Grayson go out on site? He might be Chairman, but he's only a non-executive one. I know he put up some of the initial money, but it just doesn't add up.'

'Did Lyneth and Hu get out to the actual site?' asked Alexa.

'No. They wanted to return with what they'd found out, as quickly as possible. They also figured, with snow on the ground, they wouldn't have been able to see much anyway.'

'I suppose,' she said. 'It's all a bit underhand, isn't it? The fact Scott Lindon had got at the Su family. I guess he made some sort of threat – it can't have been a pay-off, surely. They could have done that out in the open...'

'Not if the money came from elsewhere,' he interrupted. 'It's what Lyneth and Hu Su reckoned too. Hu also said if they'd offered money, there would not have been any loss of face for his parents – well, not as much. It was his parents not wanting to discuss the matter at all, which set Hu onto trying to find out more. It was all a little too suspicious for him.'

'All we need, now, is a little spin,' she said. 'I'll get onto a *story* when I get into the office.' Alexa finished her cup of tea. 'Any proof we require should come out of disclosure, if it gets to that.'

'It's a shame though.'

'What's a shame?' asked Alexa.

'Well, it still just looks like it was a tragic lack of judgement on Shufang's part. She should have known going out to the site without safety cover was dangerous.'

'I know, but I don't think there is anything new we can find out about it. I'll go over the analysis again later, but first I need to get to the office. I still have my business to run! I can't have you monopolising my time,' she said, smiling warmly. 'I'm going to have to raise an invoice for all this.'

'What... the sandwiches?' he asked.

They both laughed.

It felt good. They were a world away from the weekend, when they'd pondered over tea leaves at cafés in Ullswater and Keswick.

'Right, Finn, you've got some calls to make. You need to see how many of the shareholders we can get. If we can get them all, we won't have to leak the story. If not...'

'If not... you'll be ready?'

'Yes, Finn, I'll be ready.' The light in her eyes, set against her deeply warm smile, said it all.

TWENTY FIVE

IT HAD JUST TURNED four. The light outside Alexa's office window faded fast. A print of Rothko's *Bathers* held her gaze, and her focus fell on the streaks of red and white skyline above the blue of the sea. The horizon, so prominent at the level of the bathers' heads, set her pondering about her own. *What is it I can't see out there?*

She had spent the afternoon repeatedly running her analysis of the Tiger Oil situation. Again and again, she ran it through in her head. She loved it: taking data – seemingly inconsequential facts, snippets of relative insignificance – and looking for a narrative angle to connect them all. She loved to discover, to reveal a hidden depth of meaning. Her analytic mind and proclivity for creative-thinking made her a natural for her PR role. She had not looked back since moving on from financial analysis. But she retained her love of detail.

Not for the first time, she was glad she could delegate. She had built a first-rate agency, with first-rate staff. It needed little help from her to keep it ticking over competently. She had always been like that – making sure she created space for herself, to do what she wanted. Her space provided a survival mechanism; it kept her sane. *But now?* Everything seemed to be changing. Along the way, she'd lost sight of the horizon or, more accurately, she thought, something propelled her towards it. That old horizon was now a reality – the new one unclear, even a threat. *Yes*, she mused, *the old horizon!* That horizon first came into view when her relationship, or at least the physical relationship with Aaron, dimmed. She'd kept the horizon at bay – the possibility of a breakup. She found her own solution, an island close by, an island of gratification, inhabited only by anonymous partners. Ozzie, the first; others followed. She preferred not to count; she'd found an equilibrium. But now? *Now is different,* she told herself. Events had lifted her from her island and thrown her at the horizon. Menacingly, a new world loomed before her – a new world she didn't welcome. But she had no option, not now.

She could see Tiger Oil's nobbling of Shufang's family could not be the whole story; there must be more.

Christ! It occurred to her, suddenly. *What about Ozzie?* The whereabouts of Ozzie remained a mystery. He was completely out of touch. Had they nobbled him, too? She hoped he was OK, somewhere, really – she still held a soft spot for his geeky nature and good looks. He was her first, after all. Fond memories, but…

In all their relief over finding sufficient evidence to mount a campaign against the company – a campaign they could use to leverage a takeover result – they continued to overlook something, someone. The presence of *three* men in Peace River; at the time of the accident there was another man. It hadn't been as they'd previously believed. Jonathon Long accompanied Shufang out on the routine visit, yes. But it wasn't that Scott Lindon had been some senior site worker, who had discovered her body, was it? It worried Lyneth too. Even she could not fathom why Grayson Barclay should have been there, or, for that matter, why he might have checked into the Sawridge hotel with Scott Lindon. It just didn't make any sense.

A puzzled frown erupted across her forehead. Her vision narrowed on the bathing, faceless forms of the figures in the painting. Faceless, yes! Exactly how the three men meeting in Peace River appeared to her now – three faceless, naked forms, bathers before a red-lit sky. What time? Morning? Did the red sky signal a harbinger of doom, the storm clouds gathering before her? Or could it be a peaceful evening, foretelling an enchantment to follow, her worrying conclusions a mere logical fallacy? Too many unanswered questions, still; far too many questions for her analytical mind to be comfortable with, and she couldn't find an angle, a thread to connect them.

She'd puzzled long and hard over exactly what position Scott Lindon held in the company. Even Finn had been unaware of him, until his name turned up in the accident report as the person who found Shufang's body. She just couldn't find the angle. It would be all too simple, she thought, just to take the line they'd agreed on at lunchtime. Why go to such extreme lengths – flying Scott Lindon out to Hong Kong to get Shufang's family to drop the case?

All the evidence pointed to a tragic accident; the only anomaly being nobody could point to why Shufang went to the site after dark. Lyneth had returned with a copy of the Mounties' police report. She confirmed, as best she could, there were no suspicious circumstances. Lyneth's previous defence work also turned up a report from the Canadian Ministry of Labour's investigation. Even they confirmed a cause of accidental death, with no evidence to suggest any safety apparatus or process failure. On the face of it, neither Tiger Oil nor its board of directors could stand as culpable. It came down to Shufang's error of judgement.

Grayson, too. For what reason did he travel out there? The hotel records Lyneth acquired, showed Grayson, accompanied by Scott Lindon, arriving three days after Jonathon Long. But Grayson left the morning of the accident, on his own, and clearly before news of the accident reached the hotel. She needed to talk it through with Finn, before he took any more action. She picked up her phone and dialled her home number. Finn answered.

'Finn, hi, how about we grab something to eat at the Café Rouge in the marina tonight?' She didn't wait for a reply. 'Shall we do early? Around six? I'll finish over here and walk over.' Finn was happy with the idea of an early dinner. 'OK, see you soon.' she said, and she put the phone down, ending the call.

*

Finn spent the majority of the afternoon sitting at the table in the lounge of Alexa's apartment. He found it a pleasant place to work. The impromptu work space came with a view down over the marina, its crowd of boats, large and small, bustled about at their warps, rocking to the whim of the strong breeze that blew and ricocheted off the surrounding buildings. It threw the movement of the boats into confusion – a dance of the avant-garde. He just loved the scene: the boats – all shapes and sizes, mostly expensive, but some not so. He had just risen from the table to take Alexa's call; he stood there, just looking out. *One day. ONE DAY!*

Curiously, he felt at home there.

Just before Alexa's call, he put a call through to Abdulrahman Shah's office, and spoke to Heidi. In her well-spoken German-Swiss-English, she informed him Abdulrahman was in the office, but presently occupied in a meeting. He would return Finn's call in around thirty minutes. Finn stood waiting.

He checked his watch. Just over thirty minutes had passed – any time now.

With predictable, Teutonic efficiency, Finn's mobile phone

vibrated on the table, erupting into the nondescript tone he'd found the least offensive amongst the phone's set of ring tones. He let it ring just twice.

'Finn Jackson,' he answered.

'I have Herr Shah for you now,' said Heidi.

'Thank you, Heidi.' He waited as Heidi put the connection through. 'Hello, Abdulrahman. I'm assuming you've seen the position with Tiger Oil.' He recalled Abdulrahman's maxim, *do business as strangers* – Finn cut out any pleasantries; they would not impress.

'Our plans, Finn?' said Abdulrahman.

'The announcement provided a minor setback, but we've been working on an issue which will throw the share price off again. We have just to gather some final evidence to support the issue. We will be on track for next week. I've been calling the potential sellers this afternoon.'

'Their response, Finn?' quizzed Abdulrahman, clearly not wasting his words.

'They are renewing their interest. I will be able to confirm the position with them by the end of this week.' Not strictly true, thought Finn, but it would buy him a few more days for the new story to spread.

'So, the issue of the Canadian accident will be resurrected. Is that so?'

'Yes,' he answered, both reassured and cautioned by the extent of Abdulrahman's interest – as well informed as ever; he'd assumed correctly.

'Good… though I am not happy with this turn of events, Finn… However, it seems you have the situation in hand…' Abdulrahman paused. 'I am content to let it unfold… for now.'

'There's a *but?*'

'Yes, Finn, there is, as you say, a *but.*' Finn could feel a cold chill in the low delivery of Abdulrahman's words. 'No more surprises, Finn. There must be no more surprises.'

'This time next week we will have our first thirty percent,' said Finn, expressing more confidence than he had a right to.'

'Good, Finn. I am counting on you. Please call me on Monday. I shall be in my office.'

'I will.'

'Until Monday, Finn, goodbye.'

The call ended and Finn slid his phone closed. *There must be no more surprises.* How the hell could he assure no more surprises? He'd felt apologetic in opening his call with Abdulrahman. Now he was just thankful Abdulrahman had taken the news so calmly. He had tried not to let any sign of weakness come through in his voice, but he wasn't sure. *There must be no more surprises, Finn.* Despite his work in the oil industry, this was his first time doing business, on a personal level, with an Arab. He knew it would be his last if he failed. Abdulrahman had given him a warning. He had just stepped out onto yet another tightrope.

*

Finn checked his watch. The time was five fifty-five. He grabbed his jacket from the back of the chair he'd been sitting at, and went through to the hallway. He picked up his overcoat and left the apartment for the short walk to the Café Rouge.

An afternoon sat making phone calls to the various friendly Tiger Oil investors, the ones he'd previously identified as potential sellers, and he was happy to get out and stretch his legs. Aside from his need to update Abdulrahman Shah on the present situation, Alexa had left him to reassess the potential allegiance of these friendly shareholders. If he could sound them out about the potential impact of a revitalised Shufang

Su story, then maybe he could manage to swing the deal without having to have the details leaked.

Unsurprisingly, he had to admit, he could not sway the investors by his hypothetical situation, and he wasn't prepared to corroborate a rumour with factual detail just yet. He understood. When Grayson Barclay's face appeared in the TV News report, the shareholders, all of them, focused more on their rising shares, than on the mere hypothesis of a disgruntled ex-director. He could see their logic; he would have reacted the same way.

Finn reached the Café Rouge and entered. He found Alexa already sitting at a table in front of the picture windows that overlooked the boats moored just feet away. The lights of the Tower hotel opposite cast a glow across the marina basin.

'It's a shame it's not summer,' he said, as he approached her table. The sound of his voice clearly interrupted her thoughts.

'Hi... Oh, sorry, Finn... I was miles away. I've been thinking all afternoon about this Tiger stuff.'

'Me too, when I've not been on the phone.'

'Did you get anywhere?' she asked, expectantly.

'Well, I think we have some days with Abdulrahman. He wasn't happy, but he'll let it unfold for now. I had to say we'd got a positive response from the shareholders.'

'Had to?'

'Yeah, a fib, I'm afraid. It's not going to be easy; we are going to have to go ahead with the leak. We aren't going to be able to carry out a bloodless coup.'

'I didn't think so, Finn.'

'No?' he said, quizzically raising his eyebrows. Then, dropping them, '...It was worth a try though,' he continued, smiling across at her.

'What did they say – the shareholders you spoke to?' asked Alexa.

'Well, they see their share price rising and, without any

corroboration, they couldn't really see it crashing in front of them. Grayson's upbeat message certainly seems to have won them all over – especially being so public.'

'Just like it was designed to,' she said. Then, changing tack, '…Have you any idea why Grayson was out in Canada with the others?'

'No. There'd been no talk at all; and no one had scheduled anything. He'd not even submitted any expenses. It came as a surprise to me, Lyneth unearthing his trip. A complete surprise!'

'Do you think they're trying to hide something?'

'Possibly, but I've no idea what? It just doesn't make any sense.'

'Well…' began Alexa, thoughtfully, 'I s'pose, short of an answer on his visit, we could always bluff.'

'What do you mean?'

'Well, rather than leak the story, you could face Grayson Barclay down.'

'I agree, leaking the story could get messy. If there *is* something behind it all, leaking the story could back-fire on us. It might stretch over in to our new management, once we get the takeover on the go. So, you think I just go to Barclay and confront him with what we have, and leave him to work out the consequences?'

'Yes, Finn. That's about it.'

'If they are hiding something,' he said, 'they've got to know it will come out if we leak the story. They might just decide to give up quietly. They would still make something on the deal.'

'It's a gamble.' Alexa thought for a moment. '…But at least the down-side is less risky than throwing the Shufang action into the ring again.'

'Yeah, but Grayson Barclay? I don't see him as particularly rational at the moment.' Another idea came to him. 'I could always face Aaron instead. He would be a rational go-between.

If anyone could persuade Barclay to give up quietly, perhaps Aaron could.'

Alexa considered this new angle a moment. 'I think you're right, Finn. I hadn't considered that.'

'Well, we have a plan then, of sorts... for tomorrow?'

'We can double check with Lyneth later, if you like; but I think it's the best course open to us for now,' said Alexa. 'Anyway, I'm starving, let's eat something.' She smiled warmly at him. 'Tomorrow will come soon enough.'

*

You can never enter the same river twice, Finn. Now r ... u... n... n... n... You have to.'

Shufang expected him to!

'Enter the river. You know you have to.' Shufang's ghostly voice reverberated throughout his head – pounding his skull, as if some large, unseen blunt object kept hitting him, repeatedly. The shiver, which had started in his soul, spread with the acceleration of a rampant bush-fire. His whole body racked with convulsions, the spasm forcing his lungs to struggle for breath. He knew what to do... what he had to do, to relieve the pain in his head... what he had to do, before the slowly advancing form of Shufang.

He fell, turning, twisting, rolling over and over, as he hit the grey foaming water, plunging into the dark depths of its embrace. The wetness of his tears now replaced by the pervading wetness of a watery grave. Panic erupted deep within, from where the shiver passed before, from the depth of his soul.

He tumbled with the rhythm of the turbulent depths. The force of the water's current whipped through the ground

278

rocks, forcing uncontrolled surges of flow. First this way, then that. He tried to control himself. He tried to manage the flailing of his limbs as the vengeful torrent of water forced itself past, buffeting them. The pounding of the water, as he spun round and round, had now replaced the pounding inside his head. He kicked out, again and again, struggling with the water's depths, until, at last, his head broke the surface.

He struggled to draw breath, to fill his aching, burning lungs. Through his stinging eyes, he could see the bank from which he had fallen. Shufang looked on, faceless. He turned to kick out for the refuge of the far side, where its mountainous rise stood as another obstacle to his safety. He kicked out, he needed to reach it, but he was tired... too tired. *Kick, Finn, kick.* He kicked out. '*You can never enter the same river twice, Finn, never.*'

Blackness descended on him.

Peace returned.

Everything was now strangely, darkly, menacingly quiet.

TWENTY SIX

THE RETURN KEY of the computer keyboard clicked as Alexa stabbed at it with the long, exquisitely manicured nail of her right index finger. It was the final flourish of a graceful, yet visceral movement. It commenced as a smile at the corner of her lips, traversing her body like the unwinding of a coiled spring, until the fingers of her hand moved in elegant harmony.

'There you are, Finn,' she said, smiling fully now; her eyes shone with mischief. The printer, on a table by the desk in Aaron's home-study, flashed into life, disgorging a single sheet of text. Aaron's study – Aaron's computer. The irony was not lost on her. *Poetic justice!*

Finn lifted the paper – an e-mail news bulletin from the *International Oil Economist*. He read the release, aloud:

> *Tiger Oil continues to baffle investors with news today that its shares were suspended from trading on London's AIM Market, late afternoon, after Dale-Eastgate, the firm's UK broker and nomad, resigned. International Oil Economist has been able to confirm Chinese press speculation claiming Tiger Oil's November announcement, "No Case to Answer", was misleading. A spokesman for the Su family stated they were now reconsidering the legal position over the death of their*

daughter, Shufang Su, the company's Chief Operations Officer. Shufang Su was killed in a tragic accident on the site of Tiger Oil's experimental extraction facility in Peace River, Canada, in October 2006.'

'The end of a good day,' said Finn.

Alexa nodded, a broad grin formed across her lips. *Yes, a good day*, she thought. 'But we are going to have to move quickly now. There are going to be a lot of phone calls this weekend. You all set, Finn?'

Finn looked thoughtful for a moment, before he too, sprouted a broad grin. 'Yes. I'm ready,' he said. 'Thank you, Alexa.'

'For what? We still have a long way to go.'

'I know, but your thinking has been key. I couldn't have got this far alone.'

'There's Lyneth as well, don't forget. You're new *girl*friend.' She laughed as she noticed Finn's face gain something of the colour of rouge. *No mere reflection off my lipstick.*

'Careful, I haven't actually seen her since Wednesday – she might be dating a Chinaman by now.'

'No champagne, but I think we might manage another of Aaron's clarets. You know where they are, Finn; why don't you get a bottle.' *It has been a good day.*

'Bathroom first,' said Finn, as he left to go to the guest room.

A very good day. It started well, at breakfast-time. While she waited for Finn's return, she recalled the episode.

'Morning, Finn. Did you sleep well?'

It had been about seven-forty when Finn put in an appearance. She had been up and dressed since seven. She sat on a stool at the breakfast bar, where she had set out freshly made coffee and orange juice.

'Do you fancy a croissant, too?' she'd asked.

'Lovely. Coffee smells good,' observed Finn. 'I think I slept, but the dream returned and I had a cold sweat again.'

'The river dream?'

'Yeah.' Finn sat down opposite her and poured himself a coffee. 'Just falling in the river. *Christ,* if that's what drowning is like, please, shoot me now!'

'I've read, somewhere, rivers in dreams are to do with flows of energy,' she said, '…a sort of journey through something – emotions and stuff. I suppose the raging river is something like a pretty tough situation.'

'It would figure, like, with what's going on. But I'm being chased, too,' he said, as he picked his coffee cup up to take a drink.

'I've been thinking, Finn…' she started. She had lain awake, restless, for most of the night. She worried. Things just did not add up.

'About rivers?' suggested Finn, clearly trying to keep the conversation light at such an early hour.

'No, silly,' she said, smiling. She got up, off her seat, to put a couple of croissants in the oven. She set the timer and returned to join Finn at the breakfast bar.

'And you told me you didn't cook?'

More humour. At least Finn seemed able to keep a perspective on things. 'You're on form, Finn,' she said.

They both laughed.

'No. I meant I've been thinking about today,' she continued. 'I think there's another way.'

'Like what?'

'I lay awake, last night, thinking about it all.'

'And?'

'Well, I think I know how we can achieve a takeover, without intentionally resurrecting the Shufang action, or hitting the headlines and inviting some other predatory strike from a competitor. It would be less of a risk than relying on Aaron accepting defeat and persuading Grayson Barclay too. But we would need to move quickly, Finn, very quickly.'

'So, what do you propose then, Alexa?' said Finn. His face wore a mask of seriousness, from behind which she could see a flash of doubt in his eyes.

'While I acted as Tiger Oil's PR advisor, I got to meet Marcus Green at Dale-Eastgate, their broker and nomad for the AIM market.' In fact, she fancied Marcus as another *potential friend*, but she could hardly describe Marcus as anonymous. Besides, it all seemed a bit academic now that Aaron was aware of her secret life – now that Aaron had thrown her from her island.

'Yeah, and...?' quizzed Finn, a little impatiently.

'Well, when a PR agent resigns, the company can take its time to find a new one. I still don't know if they've got anyone to replace me yet.'

It was a great idea; it came to her as she checked the clock for what seemed to be the hundredth time during her long night awake.

Finn's mind clearly raced ahead of her. His face had lit up, as she saw him recognise the potential in what she had been saying. Finn may have been naïve to some of the city's ways, but he was no fool.

'...But, when a nomad resigns, it forces the suspension of the company, until it can find a new one,' said Finn, mirroring what she was about to say.

'Right...' she confirmed. She had felt more than a little mischievous. And, so what if her eyes gave so much away to Finn. '...Despite what we'd said yesterday, yes! I just think bluffing Aaron or Grayson would be too risky; but I got on well with Marcus. If I slipped him a variation on the reason I'd resigned our agency from Tiger Oil, you know... throw in a little bit about what we know...'

'Something like the Hu Family action may be on again?' he said. 'And, if it is, it will show a representative of Tiger Oil got at the family, to stop them taking action.

'Exactly, Finn,' she said, smiling. 'Dale-Eastgate is a new brokerage; the AIM market has only just authorised them as nominated advisors. They've a small and growing oil and gas client-base – they just can't afford to attract any form of bad reputation. A continued association with Tiger Oil could be too much of a risk to their credibility in the market. If they knew the facts, I reckon they would resign with immediate effect.'

'Today?'

'If I call Marcus? In that case, yes, today. It would at least cause an immediate suspension of their shares from trading.'

'Chrisssst!' he said, the drawn-out "ssss" whistling through his teeth. 'I see what you mean; we *would* have to move fast.'

'And then some,' she added. 'We need to make sure Lyneth would be ready. She would need to tee up her partner, Hillary Keaton. We would need him to act as a go-between.'

'You've thought this through, haven't you, Alexa?'

'You could say that,' she said. Her smile, she remembered, had been particularly warm. The timer on the oven chimed twice. 'Breakfast,' she had said.

Finn returned from the guest room and busied himself finding a bottle of wine.

'Nice,' said Finn, his voice muffled somewhat, his head buried in the larder. 'He's got some good wines here. How about a *1996 Clerc Milon*?'

'Perfect,' she said.

Yes, breakfast had been a good start to the day. Moreover, the day panned out just as she hoped it would. After breakfast, she called Lyneth who, by then, already sat in her office, busy. Lyneth quickly agreed to the new plan, and to enlisting Hillary's help. She also suggested it wouldn't hurt to get Hu Su to add some "local" Chinese stories. Hu would be able to get the story out about the nobbling of his parents. Lyneth hadn't been as concerned about the repercussions as she and Finn had. Lyneth had even discussed the eventuality with Hu Su. He stood convinced his parents held no stomach for a fight; they just wanted to see the truth come out.

Alexa had then left for her office and, aside from making sure her other clients remained happy, she waited until the afternoon to speak with Marcus. She had met him for a coffee, at two.

Finn came over with the bottle of wine, now opened, and two glasses.

'I think we need some music,' she said, as she went over to the CD player. She tapped the on-button. 'It's going to get busy, these next few days.'

She returned to the sofa and took the glass Finn now held out to her. She smiled at him; Finn returned the gesture.

'Oh, I forgot to tell you,' she added, as the unmistakable strings of Vanessa Mae's electric violin, playing the *City Theme,* broke into the background. 'Marcus did say, if you manage to get the board out, they'd consider the company had resolved the issue and, in that case, they'd be happy to reconsider becoming your nomad.' She grinned at Finn across the top of her glass. 'Slainte mhath,' she said.

'Pardon?'

'It's Gaelic. ...Cheers!'

Oh, right... Cheers – to us,' he said. 'I like your choice of music; powerful.'

'Apposite,' she said, laughing.

*

Monday, ten a.m. and Finn entered the office of Keaton-Jones LLP. 'Hi, Lyneth,' he said, taking her outstretched hand; he drew her close, kissing her cheek.'

'Hi, you,' she said, as he stepped back from the kiss. 'You'd better hide that grin. There are some people in the boardroom who would love to see you dead right now.' She smiled at him and gave him an exaggerated wink. She lowered her voice to speak quietly. 'I think we have them on the run.'

'Think?'

'Hillary's been in with them all morning. Since seven, I gather.'

'Who's in there?'

'Full house. There's Aaron Philips, Grayson Barclay, David Kail and Jonathon Long. Come into my office,' she said, taking his arm and leading him down the corridor, towards the door at the far end of the office suite. Lyneth nodded to her right, as they walked past the boardroom with its closed door.

Finn looked at the door as he passed, and tried not to imagine the scene inside. He followed Lyneth into her office and closed the door behind them both.

'It's not good practice to talk in the open,' said Lyneth, smiling, as she went round to sit at her desk. She motioned to Finn to sit down.

Finn took a chair at the small circular meeting table in front of the desk.

'Hillary was on the phone to one or other of them, all weekend, or so he told me. The porters downstairs told me he came in this morning like a bear with a sore head. I just told him not to be stupid.' She laughed. 'I said we'd end up keeping the account – that pacified him a little. He's more interested in his fees than his clients.'

'I spent the weekend with Alexa.' Finn thought he saw Lyneth raise her eyebrows a little. '...She's given me the guest room until we get all this sorted,' he added. 'She took a number of calls from Aaron, who was evidently livid. He demanded to know what we'd said to their nomads. Alexa denied she'd anything to do with it. I don't think he bought it, but…'

'But, here we are,' finished Lyneth, smiling again.

'Yes,' he said. 'Here we are… What's on the agenda?'

'I went over it with Hillary, earlier,' she said. 'He's persuaded the board they need to consider your proposal. They want you in at ten-thirty. You ready, Finn?'

'Yeah… as I'll ever be. It's all quite straightforward, a sort-of "take it" or "leave it" Hobson's choice. I've called some of the investors this morning. I have verbal agreements from the fund managers of two institutions holding seventeen percent between them; they will sell at eleven and a half. I'm going to offer to buy Grayson Barclay's twenty percent at the same price. I want all the board members to step down. We'll put a new board in.'

'Who've you got?'

'Me, Alexa and you – that is, if you will join me. I could do with your counsel!'

'Mmmm, we'll see,' she said, wearing her inimitable smile.

Lyneth's reply seemed a little uncommitted. 'I still need to find an FD from somewhere,' he said, 'but I'm working on that with Alexa. We've a couple of options, and she's got her feelers out.'

'It's all happened quite fast, hasn't it,' said Lyneth. 'This time last week I stood freezing cold in Canada. And now… now it's heated the place up a bit, hasn't it?'

'Yeah. …How's Hu Su?' he asked.

'I put him on a flight to Hong Kong, on Saturday morning. He's going straight to see his parents. He was sorry he didn't get another chance to see you. Until you phoned on Saturday, I hadn't been thinking you would still be in town over the weekend.'

'Well, I didn't have much to return to, and Alexa and I agreed we might need to take some action over the weekend.'

'I guess so.'

They sat and talked a while longer, until they heard a knock at the door. It was ten-thirty.

'Come in.'

A young, petite and attractive girl entered. Finn noted her long blonde hair, gathered neatly in a ponytail behind her.

'Miss Jones, Mr Keaton is ready for you now.'

'Thank you, Claire. I'll be through in a moment.'

Claire turned and left, leaving the door slightly ajar as she did so; Finn noted her ponytail swing through a graceful arc.

'Now is as good a time as any,' he said, taking a deep breath.

They retraced their steps down the short corridor and entered the boardroom without knocking. Lyneth led the way as Finn's aide-de-camp. The atmosphere in the room reeked of palpable spite.

Gathered around the table, their backs to the window – trying to hold the advantage of having the daylight behind them – sat David, Grayson, Aaron and Jonathon. Hillary, whom Finn had not met in person before, sat between Grayson and Aaron. Another, younger man, in his late twenties, sat off to their right side, at the end of the table. He sat squarely, with a pad in hand, busy writing up some notes. Presumably a junior, Finn reasoned – he'd be catching up on whatever they had said prior to his and Lyneth's entrance.

'I think we know why we are gathered here this morning,' said the man sat between Grayson and Aaron. 'I don't think we need introductions.' He turned his face to address Finn directly. 'We haven't met before, but we have spoken on the phone a few times, Finn. I'm Hillary Keaton.' He did not offer his hand across the table.

Finn nodded his acknowledgment.

'I would like to say, in clarification…' Keaton continued. 'We all accept that it is not the normal course of events, for two sides to be represented by the same practice. But, I have agreed with my clients that this is not strictly a legal matter, as yet. We are therefore acting only as a mediator in what we would prefer to call a management dispute. Is this accepted?'

All eyes looked to Finn. He glanced towards Lyneth, who had taken a seat on his right. She nodded her agreement. 'Yes,' said Finn, in a sardonic voice. 'I am happy to consider this a continuation of our previous management meetings, where Mr Barclay was kind enough to suggest I step down from the board.' Finn looked Grayson Barclay straight in the eyes and took pleasure in noting Barclay sitting there, quietly apoplectic. Under his mop of grey-white hair, Barclay's face reddened, noticeably. To Finn, it appeared as if his shirt collar inexplicably, and without warning, reduced by two sizes, squeezing on his throat, choking him.

Keaton spoke again. 'I have advised the board that, as a consequence of... shall we say... certain events and information coming to light, they are faced with a particularly urgent need to come up with a management solution.'

Finn noticed Keaton glance to both sides – as if anticipating some reaction from his clients, but seemingly warning them with his steely gaze to keep silent.

'The suspension of Tiger Oil,' continued Keaton, '... under such circumstances, has created a major problem which could, consequentially, require the board to answer charges of misrepresenting the company during its AIM admission.'

Finn stifled his surprise. He'd not considered that particular angle.

Keaton carried on with his opening. 'There has been an attempt to find another nomad, who would help remove the company's AIM suspension. So far, given the nature of the issues now becoming known, no nomad has been willing to come forward.

Finn wished Keaton would get to the point. But he'd sat through this sort of legal mumbo-jumbo before. It stretched the fee-time out. *All part of the game,* he mused, cynically.

'Miss Jones has advised me that you have a proposition to put to the board. Is that correct, Mr Jackson?'

Finally! 'Yes,' he said.

'If I may…' interjected Lyneth, 'Mr Jackson believes the only option for Tiger Oil is to successfully, and quickly, regain its AIM status, before suspension turns to de-listing. This would require a management change, a change of the full board of directors.

'For Christ's sake…' spluttered the shouting, seething form of Grayson Barclay. 'You can't…'

'Mr Barclay,' interrupted Hillary Keaton. 'I do not think you are helping.'

'Go on,' said Aaron, leaning forward to look past Keaton at Grayson. Aaron's gaze shot another silent warning, berating the Chairman.

Both David Kail and Jonathon Long sat impassively, their unmoving, unfriendly gaze set on Finn.

'Thank you, Hillary… Mr Philips,' resumed Lyneth, nodding her appreciation to each, in turn. 'As I was saying, we believe only a full management change, at board level, will restore the necessary confidence in the Tiger Oil business. The history, which now seems to be in danger of unfolding before the market's eyes, will not tar a new management team. If unchecked, it would appear this same history could create untold damage to the company's reputation and leave it open to charges we, as yet, cannot determine, but which could impact investor wealth and leave the present directors open to fiduciary liability.'

'Thank you, Lyneth. I believe we understand the matter at hand,' said Hillary Keaton, fingering the inside of his shirt collar. He was clearly unused to being on the opposite side of the table to his junior partner. 'And Mr Jackson's proposal?' he asked.

'On the resignation of all current board members,' said

Lyneth, '...Mr Jackson will retake his position as CEO, and Ms Stuart...'

This time Aaron found difficulty holding his anger. He let rip. 'Bitch,' he hissed. His expression held impassive, but his face turned as red as Barclay's.'

'Ms Alexa Stuart,' repeated Lyneth, '...will join the board as a director; two other directors will be nominated shortly thereafter.'

'And?' asked Hillary Keaton of his partner, knowing her well enough to anticipate some conditionality.

'And this offer is conditional on the departing board members relinquishing a minimum of twenty percent of their combined shareholdings, at a price of eleven and a half pence per ordinary share,' concluded Lyneth.

'Shit... Damn you, Jackson. I'll sue the arse of you for this,' shouted Grayson Barclay, his temper finally getting the better of him.

'Quiet, Grayson,' hissed Aaron, across the face of Hillary Keaton.

'Mr Barclay, I do not think your attitude is helping clarity here,' censured Lyneth. 'We need a quick resolution with no in-fighting,' she continued. 'If this proposal is to work, it has to be seen that it is the company which has reached the decision for change, and that the incoming board has the support of the outgoing board.'

'Over my fucking dead body,' raged Grayson, still clearly apoplectic.

'It might come to that if you don't shut up, Grayson,' spat Aaron, now on the verge of apoplexy himself. His struggle to retain a measure of control, long since absent from Grayson's demeanour, was clear for all to see.

Christ, she's good; she's playing them nicely.

'I've read your statement of facts in this matter, Finn,' said Keaton, breaking the momentary silence.

291

Finn and Alexa had put together the brief statement over the weekend; they'd taken Lyneth's advice through e-mails and phone calls.

Hillary continued, tapping his fingers against a copy of the statement lying on the desk in front of him. 'Some of what you have said in here, leaves you open to accusations of defamatory conduct against both the business and its directors. I am sure I do not need to remind you, Mr Jackson, a condition of the compromise agreement, when you resigned…'

'Was forced,' interrupted Finn.

'Resigned,' corrected Lyneth, with a look that told Finn to watch his tongue. They held the moral high ground still.

'I do not need to remind you,' repeated Hillary, '…a condition of *your* compromise agreement is that you cannot say anything to bring the directors or the company into disrepute. I am sure my clients, here, would like to reflect on the seriousness of your conduct, and decide whether or not they would seek their own recompense against you.'

The last act of the dying. Lyneth forewarned him of the possibility Hillary would try a final, feeble attempt at turning the proceedings onto him. Right again! Feeble! The last act of the dying proved to be nothing more than an empty threat – far too personal, given the circumstances, and greatly lacking in imagination. Keaton did not appear as sharp a lawyer as Lyneth. His tone came across as more conciliatory. Lyneth had mentioned that Hillary mainly practised commercial law, not litigation. Finn could now see the marked difference between the two styles. Again, he congratulated himself on his new-found friendships.

Hillary spoke, interrupting the short silence. 'I think, Lyneth… perhaps you and Mr Jackson should retire, and consider his position carefully. I will talk the proposition over with my clients.'

Lyneth nodded her approval to Finn. He knew he did not

need to consider his position; Lyneth had briefed him on that ploy, too. Hillary Keaton needed the face-saving time-out. He needed to brief the board that their position had now become untenable. The resignation of the nomad had done the damage – it had been the *coup de grâce*. Clearly, Aaron and the board had tried, and failed, to get a new nomad to take them on. However, to gain success, they would have needed to submit to some additional due diligence. Aaron would know the company could not afford for the suspension to turn into an automatic de-listing from AIM. The board needed to consider the proposition put to them, and quickly. No other option lay open to them.

Everyone could see clearly – only a full change of management would get rid of the Shufang story and encourage a new nomad to take up Tiger Oil. But Finn already had that angle covered.

*

'Lyneth, they want to know what Finn is playing at. He's asked for only twenty percent.' Hillary and Lyneth sat in Hillary's office, the door pushed closed to the corridor outside. 'I've just about got them there,' he added.

'Finn has agreement on another fifteen or so percent,' said Lyneth, hiding the exact figure in case they tried to work out who the selling shareholders were.

'How the hell…' Hillary began to quiz her.

'It's not important how. You just need to know Finn's pulled it together. Effectively, it's a takeover,' she said.

'Shit!' said Hillary. 'They're not going to like that.'

'Your problem, not mine, partner,' she said. Her smile would have made a hyena proud.

'Remind me not to go against you again.'

'It's why you took me on as a full partner, I recall. ...So, you'll need the board to call an extraordinary meeting to pass a resolution; they will recommend the shareholders accept the offer put forward by Finn.'

'Jesus, they've no option, have they?'

'Not if they want to get out with a small profit and no more problems. It would be best if they all sold all of their shares.'

'You've got the funds?' asked Hillary.

Lyneth smiled at her partner. 'What do *you* think, Hillary?'

'OK, I'll go tell them,' he said.

Hillary turned and left for the boardroom, leaving her in his office. She grew conscious that Finn sat alone, in her own office, waiting for the board to reach its decision.

Finn had offered the incumbent directors a perfect way out. She imagined them all sitting there, as livid as rabid dogs at the moment. But Finn's proposal meant they would all make a healthy profit if they sold their shares at his offer price. If they left the company to crash and burn, they would have nothing. It was, as Hillary agreed with her earlier that morning, the board's only way out. Hillary knew it; he would advise the board accordingly. They would call a short-notice EM, and recommend acceptance of Finn's offer of eleven-and-a-half pence a share.

She was in her element. She smiled, for no one but herself. She would see through her "no loose ends" promise to finish this matter for Finn; she would have a draft heads of agreement by lunchtime. And, as for a member of the board? *Join me. I could do with your counsel!* No, Finn, I don't think so, she mused. The chase had been fun, real fun; the kiss nice. Finn could kiss a girl all right... no great consolation, but... *maybe not, Finn.* 'Maybe not,' she repeated aloud, to the empty office, to no one but herself. 'I guess I'd better rejoin Finn.'

She sensed victory in the air.

TWENTY SEVEN

An anti-climax par excellence! Finn sat in his office, mulling over the day's main event. He kicked his foot against the desk and his chair swivelled, turning him around to look out of the office window. He could clearly see the Gherkin, lit up in its evening splendour. *Probably still fried, at least on the inside,* he mused, recalling his thoughts, way-back, during the previous August.

The position for the outgoing board of directors had been untenable. They understood: they'd covered up something, something that clearly would not remain covered. Finn was certain of that. Under those circumstances, the offer of a profit to walk away with no more questions had been an offer they could not refuse. *Yes!* He'd forced them all, Grayson, Aaron, David and Jonathon, to harvest their fallen, now rotten fruit, to take what they could escape with.

It hadn't been a problem, three weeks ago, for Hillary to get the board's agreement. After their vitriolic outburst faded to a dull, chronic pain, they all saw it for the best. They all saw they should go quietly and, of course, quickly. Lyneth prepared the heads of agreement for the deal; she'd already partially drafted them in anticipation. The board signed up that lunchtime. They, he Lyneth and Alexa, had their deal – all bar the short-notice Extraordinary Meeting passing the necessary resolution. But, with the board's recommendation, and half the institutional investors on side, they had not anticipated any problems.

It took a full three weeks to progress the EM and share sales. Because of Keaton-Jones' closeness to the deal, new lawyers were brought in for both parties. The shareholders met for the EM on February fourteenth – a fitting date he thought. They passed the resolution agreeing the sale of shares to Finn's new company without a single vote of dissent. Lyneth, not unexpectedly, made the St Valentine's Day massacre connection when the two of them met for dinner together, later on the evening of the fourteenth. He found no roses on the table; disappointing, a little, but in retrospect he reasoned she might not be that type of girl. Still, they passed a great evening together, and he'd returned to Alexa's apartment in good spirits. He let himself in with his own key. At Alexa's insistence, he'd made himself quite at home in her guest room.

He'd arrived at the Tiger Oil office suite at eleven a.m. that morning, with his new lawyer in tow, and Alexa. By eleven thirty, they concluded all the Tiger Oil share transfers to Finn's new company. The lawyer authorised the wiring of payment transfers. Abdulrahman Shah's finance, in effect, took Tiger Oil private again. They received a full response from all the shareholders – they all wanted out. None of the original board wanted to keep in, and all the external investors decided to get out with their minimal profits.

The share transfer meeting was another cold, clinical meeting, reminiscent of Finn's exit the previous August. There was no love lost between him and either Aaron or David Kail, the only two who actually bothered to attend the meeting. Aaron, noticeably, kept his distance from Alexa, as they all signed-off on the various documents. He had to admit it to himself; he'd taken great pleasure in signing the directors' resignation forms for the four outgoing incumbents. He'd seen enough of the names of Philips, Barclay, Kail and Long.

He stood, again, before the small door at his feet, now ajar, now seemingly of a size to accept his passage. The enchantment of the garden – the richness of the city – lay before him, beyond the threshold on which he now stood. He had regained control of Tiger Oil, his creation; he now had executive control of a well-backed private company. He had Abdulrahman Shah to thank for making it possible – without his money… Well, it could not have happened at all.

Now a private company, AIM would de-list Tiger Oil – *no matter*. Importantly, they would be unfettered and no longer required to comply with the strict reporting rules of public markets. He would no longer need to keep one eye out for the share price. There would be time again for that, but not yet.

Hu Su came up trumps. He took a call from him the week before. As a result, he and Hu came together to arrange talks, through some of Hu's contacts, with CNPC. It turned out Grayson Barclay had not been in detailed negotiations with anyone at the Chinese oil giant. Apparently, Barclay spoke to some lowly manager about possible talks, yes, but nothing could have been progressed formally at such a low level. Clearly, Grayson Barclay fabricated the story to manipulate the share price. *What the hell did Grayson think he could do …nothing more than plain stupid!* Now though, with the promise of real talks, the market gossip told of a company to watch – he'd read the chatter on the bulletin boards.

In her position as media relations director of the new Tiger Oil, Alexa put out a story announcing a possible re-admission to AIM. Indeed, there had been substantial interest from Dale-Eastgate to return Tiger Oil to the stock market. But other, more notable nomads, also made unofficial approaches to them. Tiger Oil was hot again.

As he sat looking out of the office window, through at the

Gherkin, he did not doubt they could expect a major success in any future fund-raising they might attempt. That would give Abdulrahman Shah a good exit plan, if he wanted it. They would certainly need further funds to move from the pilot project to large scale production.

He had a lot to do, still, before he and the others could reap their rewards. And that was, he thought, the cause of the anticlimatic feeling. Yes, they regained control of the company, but this was only the beginning. They all knew there remained a great deal of work to do, not least the work required to get the project back on track. It would be spring soon – that great hope! But, he knew hope was no strategy. They could not afford to waste time. They needed to get the well into operation and complete the pilot extraction phase. Only when they'd completed the full testing of the technology and its process, could they really begin to envisage a return on the huge investment they'd all now made.

Finn spun round to look down onto his desk. The printed e-mail confirmed details of his flight bookings for his forthcoming trip to Peace River. He would fly out on Sunday, the twenty-fourth. He was also due to meet up with Len Nash, on the Monday, at the Sawridge Hotel. He knew Len from old, having worked with him at Petróleos de Venezuela.

Finn held Len Nash, a Canadian-American, in great respect as an engineer, and, importantly, as someone he could share a few drinks with. A drinking partner counted for a lot in Finn's book – unlike family and clients, you could chose whom to drink with. He'd been surprised by Len's unexpected call.

'I hear you've taken the reins at Tiger again,' said Len.

'Yeah, Len, it's been a while,' he'd replied.

'About time, if you ask me. I hear you might need a new number two. That right, buddy?'

'You telling me you're free, Len? I haven't advertised… but, yes.'

'I've just come to the end of a contract in Saudi and, to be honest, I can't be bothered with the Middle East anymore. It's no fun these days.'

'You should try the City of London!'

'Yeah, heard you had some fun,' said Len.

'Well, I do need someone to take over ops in Canada. Fancy the job?'

'Let's talk. Are you coming out? I'm in Houston at the moment, but I can join you there.'

'Next week as it happens,' he'd said, warming to the possibility of having an honest friend working the other side of the Atlantic; he would need such support. Alexa and Lyneth were great, but they did not do oil.

'Tuesday good for you?' asked Len.

'How about we grab some beers Monday night, if you can get out there for then. We can go out to the site Tuesday. Get a feel for what we have to do there.'

'Sounds a plan, Finn. You staying at the Sawridge?'

'Yeah.'

'OK. I'll see you then, Finn.'

Peace River. It had been a while since he had last been there, with Shufang. It would trigger memories – he was sure. He folded the e-mail and put it into his jacket pocket. He grabbed his briefcase and overcoat and headed for the door. The cleaner would get all the lights. He looked forward to the dinner with Alexa and Lyneth that evening, and he looked forward to a few drinks from the store of Aaron's remaining claret. *To you, Aaron*, he mouthed the toast in anticipation.

What was it Shufang told him about Peace River? Yeah, he remembered – a saying of the Beaver First Nation people: *drink the waters of the Peace River and you will return*. Finn pulled the door of the office suite closed behind him. He turned and locked it. He was going to return.

TWENTY EIGHT

'OK. LET'S SEE what we've got,' said Finn.

It had reached around ten, Mountain Time – a late Tuesday morning – by the time they pulled up to the site. Although it had been fully light now for a couple hours, the temperature at the Tiger Oil experimental site still stood around minus four. A good carpet of snow lay thickly on the ground, as if, unseen, some giant hand had rolled out an oversized insulation blanket of cotton wool. The weather bureau recorded a steady thirty-six centimetre covering; out at the site though, it looked far deeper. There had been some slight snow flurries overnight, and the snow lying all around them possessed the clean look of an un-trodden wilderness.

Finn braced himself, checked the fastenings on his thick Parka, and opened the front passenger door of the rented Ranger pickup. To his left side, Len followed suit. Finn tugged at the collar of his jacket, lifting it up around his neck; the fur-edged trim provided a measure of comfort. The wind did not blow too hard, but it was steady, icy and penetrating.

'Looks deserted,' shouted Len, from over the other side of the pickup.

They both looked forward, toward the site office – a single, light-grey painted, low-slung prefabricated accommodation unit. A sort of oversized Portacabin, but with upgraded insulation providing just a little protection against the icy cold of the Canadian winters. It lay quiet, undisturbed; it lay just as he remembered it. He shivered. *A ghost?*

They'd arrived not quite knowing what to expect. He had been before, of course, but not since Shufang's accident. In fact, the last time he saw Shufang alive had been in Peace River, the month before her death. The two of them came out for a week to supervise the assembly of the first rig.

'I know you said you'd put this all on care and maintenance over the winter, but Finn…' said Len. The slow-soft tone of his southern drawl, now raised to outside volume, drew stark contrast to the sharpness of the biting breeze flowing around Finn's neck.

'I know,' he said. 'This all kind of seems a bit Marie Celeste-ville to me. You know? The deserted boat found bobbing around on the ocean.'

'Yeah, yeah. I'm just gonna wander round while you get your bearings,' offered Len. 'We're going to need to clear a few paths.' Len went to the rear of the pick-up and lifted a large snow shovel.

'Right O,' said Finn.

Finn had met up with Len as arranged, in the Sawridge the previous evening. Since Len flew up from Texas, his body clock did not register the same distortion as Finn's. But, having arrived in the early hours of Monday, Finn at least got some sleep. They'd both managed a good few beers the night before, catching up on things and, consequently, breakfast proved a later-than-expected affair. However, they were not on a schedule and, after he'd quickly arranged the rental, Len offered to drive the Ranger the forty kilometres to the deserted site.

Over the years, there had been a lot of development in the area. Shell's Peace River operations became the major visible sign of the oil industry thereabouts. The two of them drove through the centre of the Shell facility, in order to reach their own. The Tiger Oil site lay on the outer-edge of what Shell called its Carmon Creek development. There, growth continued with Shell in the process of extending their bitumen production with a new, one-hundred-thousand-barrel-per-day expansion project.

In the Peace River area, Shell produced its bitumen through both steam and cold recovery methods, with a drilling program designed to help them maintain existing production. To increase their understanding of the Peace River oil sands reservoir, Shell also drilled a number of delineation and appraisal wells throughout their leases. While their delineation wells were generally non-producing, they drilled the appraisal wells for production in areas they believed extraction might be viable. Originally, the Tiger Oil site had been just such an appraisal well, on one of four adjacent leases on the edge of the expansion project. But it proved to be unviable. With Shufang's help, Finn happened upon Shell's operation at just the right time. He acquired the four sub-leases, for a total annual rental of ten thousand Canadian dollars. If he could make the wells pay, the value of the sub-leases would rocket.

When Finn regained control of Tiger Oil, he discovered the site, and its equipment, had been put on care and maintenance. Clearly, Aaron had sought to minimise operational costs over the winter. With the company upheaval, and the winter climate, it did not surprise Finn that Tiger Oil put a delay on the pilot schedule, until they could get a new operations director in post. Finn reached his decision before travelling out: if Len wanted the job, it was his.

'Christ, it's ball-breaking work, clearing paths!' said Len, his voice breaking the silence as he reappeared from around the end of the site office. 'I've tried to work my way down to the well head, but I think we might need to get some local labour in to clear it all, if we need a closer look. It looks OK at first glance though. I can't see anything out of the ordinary – just a shit load of snow. How'ya doing here, Finn?'

Finn had been busy clearing snow to make a path up to the doorway of the office. It was uncomfortable, sweaty work; vapour rose, like steam, from inside his jacket. It did not make his back feel too good either. 'Nearly done,' he said. 'There's coffee in a flask, in my bag; why don't you grab some. It's in the cab.'

'Great,' said Len, and he made his way over to the Ranger.

Finally, Finn's cleared pathway reached up to the door of the site office. He placed his snow shovel aside, then he removed a glove to feel for the key he'd been keeping warm in an inner pocket.

Unlocking the door, he opened it and jumped back, quickly. A cascade of snow slid from the low-pitched roof and fell before him. *No. No one has been this way for a while.* He heard the sound of Len approaching behind him; *with the coffee,* he hoped. He stepped forward through the door into a small passage. The closed internal door lay before him. He put his hand on it.

'The suspense is killing me,' joked Len, from behind.

The internal door opened easily. Ample light streamed in through the windows in the cabin – daylight, reflected by the snowy whiteness of the exterior, light up what lay before them.

Finn stopped, jarred – as if he'd run up against an invisible wall of steel. 'Christ... NO! There's something wrong,' he said, letting out a long, slow groaning noise. He stood shaking his head, vigorously, repeatedly swinging it left and right. 'No... No... No... No...' he kept saying. He stepped forward into the main office.

'Shit, Finn,' exclaimed Len, the sound of his voice coming from over Finn's shoulder. 'This don't look too good, pal.' Len side-stepped, and drew level with Finn.

They both stood there, jaws agape.

Len spoke first, breaking the shock that held Finn and set him motionless. 'I've heard of a clean desk policy when you leave an office, but this…?'

'This can't be… No. NO! *The fucking bastards!*' shouted Finn.

'Steady, Finn,' said Len, '…there's the other rooms off – we need to check those.'

'There's nothing here. NOTHING!' said Finn.

The space before them, the main office area, stood empty, devoid of anything. There were none of the tables and chairs, cupboards and file cabinets, which Finn remembered – things that he'd even paid for, bought there in an office supplies store, in Peace River. GONE! Someone had stripped the cabin bare. Len moved off to the left, to the smaller office at the rear of the main room. He entered.

'Same thing here,' Len shouted out. 'Stripped. It's all gone, Finn. It's all been well and truly cleaned out.'

'What… what about the rest area? The other side,' said Finn. He dropped to his knees as a wave of nausea overcame him.

The feeling of sickness subsided and Finn regained his composure. He got to his feet again, and went to join Len at the door to the rest area.

'Christ, Finn. What the hell's going on?' A distinct frown accompanied Len's question. 'There's nothing here. It doesn't make sense. Not if you have a *real* operation going on here. Even if you had maintenance staff coming and going, this place would still show something inside – some evidence of activity. There'd be plenty of stuff… computers too.'

'I know,' said Finn, his reply sounding subdued and listless – dejected.

'It's been cleaned for a reason, buddy – someone wanted to make sure *nothing* was damn well left behind. Finn, you getting this?' Len's voice sounded matter-of-fact. 'Someone's covering up what's been going on here, Finn. I think you've got a real problem, buddy.'

Finn's head turned as he cast his gaze around the room. Slowly, his body turned, following the movement of his head. There was nothing there. The whole place seemed to have been... well, almost clinically emptied. An ultimate attempt at stopping any forensic examination. Why, for Christ sake? WHY?

'We can't stop here. There's nothing we can do here,' said Len.

Finn watched, dumbstruck, as the dismayed Len turned and left the cabin. 'You fucking bastards,' he mouthed to the unseen Barclay and his cronies. The truth started to creep up on Finn with all the inevitability of death's final embrace. 'The bloody project had failed, hadn't it, Aaron? Grayson? You fucking bastards, the lot of you,' he shouted, venting his spleen at the absent criminals.

Finn walked from the cabin. He closed the door behind him and locked it. Turning, he saw Len already re-seated in the Ranger. The engine ran; smoke from the exhaust kicked up from behind the truck, the wind whipping it to a frenzy of white cotton-candy, as it dissipated against the backdrop of un-trodden snow still blanketing the eerie, desolate landscape. Suddenly, Finn felt colder than he'd ever felt before – the shiver that ran his spine was as intense as the one in his dream. He spun around, suddenly, almost dropping to his knees again. But he saw no apparition. No vision of Shufang chasing him. All he saw were the thickets of Aspen clouded around the site, the whiteness of the snow and the greyness of the gathering clouds. A snow flurry began to fall.

'C'mon, Finn,' shouted Len, through the now open passenger window. 'Let's get the shit outa here.'

Slowly, Finn moved to the Ranger and flung his snow shovel

305

in the rear. He climbed into the cab, shut the door and stabbed his finger at the window-up button.

'Jeez, fella,' said Len, as he reversed the pick-up away from the cabin, '…I'm sorry, but there ain't anything here for me.'

They sat in silence on the return drive to Peace River. Gradually, the intermittent buildings, well machinery and pipe-work of the sprawling Shell facility gave way to clearer aspects of Aspen and snow covered parkland. They sped their way down Highway 986.

Is this what Grayson Barclay was doing over here with Jonathon Long? he thought. The penny dropped. The pilot project must have been failing… no, IT HAD failed. Shufang must have realised it when she visited the site the week before her accident. Jonathon had been out there, specifically to report on the trial's progress. Barclay must have travelled out on Jonathon's request. The two of them, Barclay and Long, were particularly close. They both worked together in a number of companies – two hard-and-fast oil men, together. Grayson even nominated Jonathon to the board. Clearly now, he could see it, Jonathon Long had been looking after Grayson's interests; the man nursed a potential half-million loss if the business went down. *People have killed for less.* Lyneth's prophetic words rang in his mind.

TWENTY NINE

The sudden realisation that Tiger Oil possessed nothing had shaken Finn to the very core of his being. Even the intellectual property in the patents had been rendered worthless. He had failed. He was a failure.

He sat in the reception area of the hotel. Its internal climate had replaced the cold February wind that continued to blow outside – a cold February wind that blew no promise of spring's great hope. Despite the interior warmth, the deep cold he continued to feel came from an altogether different source. He was stiff. He ached. His blood ran, chilled, through his veins and arteries. Unseen ice crystals formed throughout his body – a million sharp edges tore at his very being.

Len reappeared. 'Hey, Finn, I'm sorry I'm leaving you like this,' he said. He held his bag, now packed, in his hand. 'I've managed to get an earlier flight to Houston. I can return the Ranger if you like?'

'No. It's OK,' said Finn. 'I'll use it to get to the airport. You go. I'm sorry I dragged you out. . .' Finn's voice trailed off.

'Look, buddy, I'm real sorry...' said Len, apologising again.

Finn looked up at Len and their gaze locked. 'I think they killed her, Len. They killed her...' he said.

'Killed? What…? Shufang?' Len sounded incredulous. 'Hey, I'm real sorry… I just can't get mixed up in all this shit. Look, call me when you can, Finn. Hey?'

'Yeah,' said Finn, his tone lacklustre, even dead. He watched Len turn and leave. Through the doors, he could see a cab waiting outside, its engine running. He watched Len get into the rear of car, and it drove off. Finn just sat there.

Snap out of it, Finn! his thoughts screamed at him.

He left the reception area and returned to his room. He undressed and climbed into a hot-running shower, trying to return some warmth to his system. He needed to think. *Snap out of it, Finn!*

He checked his watch. It was nearing six. He'd had enough of the thoughts swirling, chaotically around his head. He'd had enough of the invasion of conversation snippets, seemingly hanging, unspoken, unseen, unyielding – running in rivulets, bouncing off each other, a chaos of networked connections, more complex than a spider's web, more disturbed than iron filings trapped in a randomly varying magnetic field. He needed a drink. He needed some focus. He dressed and made his way down to the *Sternwheeler* bar.

'Whisky, please,' Finn requested of the barman. 'Make it a single-malt; what do you keep?'

The barman stood, idly polishing glasses, trying his best to look gainfully employed. He turned to look behind him. 'Usual stuff… Glen Morangie, Livet, Macallan, Glenfarclas…'

Finn interrupted, 'that the 105?'

'Sure. Glenfarclas 105.'

'I'll take a large one.'

'You got it, Sir.' The barman put his cloth, and the now polished glass, down on the bar top. He poured Finn's drink. 'Water?' he asked.

'No thanks, no ice either.'

'But that's…'

308

'Yeah, I know, cask strength, sixty proof,' said Finn.

'There you go, Sir,' said the barman, in a tone that inferred respect for Finn's knowledge of the whisky.

Finn put his key card on the bar. 'Can you put it on my room, please?'

'Sure thing.'

The barman seemed friendly. Any other time he would have stayed at the bar to chat. Not tonight. He picked up his key card and glass and found himself a table, away from the gaming end of the bar. With little custom, a sense of quiet pervaded everywhere – he just didn't like gaming machines, with their incessant flashing lights and strange, erratic noises emanating at seemingly random intervals, trying their best to attract what little passing trade they could at this time of year.

Grayson and Jonathon must have decided to keep the failing project quiet. They must have decided to develop some story or other to get the company listed and to maintain the share price until they could arrange their own exit. And he? Yes, he! *Finn Jackson*! He had handed them just the right opportunity – handed it to them on a plate. The realisation of one who finally finds out he has been set up to take a fall, hit him. He picked up his glass to draw on the fiery liquid. He swayed, as the nausea of a premonition flashed before him. He lost his grip on the river bank and fell again into the raging water. *Christ...* his eyes closed, trying to clear the vision. He drew, instinctively, on the glass in his hand, halving the level of whisky it contained.

He was crestfallen. It was all pointless, all hopeless. He couldn't even think to call either Lyneth or Alexa. What would he say? What *could* he say? *It's too late now; I just need to get home.*

The realisation that Tiger Oil had nothing left, put him well and truly out on his own. The music had stopped; the bloody door slammed shut in his face, a final time. The company he had fought long and hard for, the company he had got

309

Lyneth and Alexa involved in, helping him to take it over – that company was now worthless. *Twenty-six-million pounds, lost!*

He saw it clearly now. The technology he'd designed and patented, simply did not work. He... they... had nothing. Never mind his own credibility, how the hell was he going to get round Abdulrahman Shah. *Twenty-six-million pounds, lost! Christ...!* He shuddered violently. *There must be no more surprises...* Abdulrahman Shah's words tolled a dangerous bell. He felt even colder.

The barman glanced over at Finn. A concerned looked flashed across his young face, settling as Finn regained his composure.

Abdulrahman Shah. He had succeeded in persuading a wealthy Arab businessman to spend over twenty six million on shares, taking the company private – he just could not afford to make an enemy of a Persian dynasty. *There must be no more surprises, Finn.* Quickly, he downed the rest of his glass. He caught the eye of the barman and mouthed a repeat order – another large one.

The fiery whisky seemed to help his focus, so he told himself. He needed to think fast, before the focus lost itself; before it morphed into a glowing, growing alcoholic stupor, brought about by even greater quantities of the gloriously rich-tasting Spey-side malt he now desired. He knew it merely dulled the pain; but shit, he needed the drink. The illusion of focus would do for now. He set his gaze on the solid, now empty glass in his hand. Yes! It would do for now.

People have killed for less. The words he'd recalled on the drive from the site, as he'd sat in a state of shock, Len driving, the two of them in silence – those words came to him again. *People have killed for less.* They haunted him.

All the loose ends from Lyneth and Alexa's research, and from his experiences, drew themselves together, slowly, inexorably, in his over-active mind. Shufang's death could not have been an accident. *People have killed for less.* The possibility stared at him in the face. It had been in front of them all the time, ever since Lyneth read the accident report, and then, when she'd found the other files in Hillary's archive. *Scott Lindon!*

The barman walked over to Finn and placed a fresh drink before him. 'On your room?'

'Thanks.'

The barman had sense enough not to engage him in small talk. Clearly, the guy had seen a man troubled by hidden demons many times in the past.

Lindon! Lindon was the common denominator at a number of site accidents. He took another drink, the fire spread deep inside him; the oak finish lingered on his throat, keeping his senses on edge, keeping him alive. He had blinkered them all with his drive to regain control of the company. Alexa had sensed it, but she couldn't see it. They'd sought just enough evidence to prove a wrong doing – they completely missed the wrong. They looked for information to support *his* goal. They'd misinterpreted the facts. They'd denied themselves the knowledge of what actually happened. They – his friends – fixated on *him*. They rode to his rescue, and he had welcomed them selfishly. How the hell could he have been so blind?

The phrase *don't get mad, get even* assaulted him. It clashed with his thinking, entangling itself with the other strands of thought – the loose threads that now, gradually, sought to form a cloudy, obscured picture. Get even for what? For his loss? What about Shufang's family? What consideration had he given them? In reality, little. Shame washed his senses. He felt sick. He could not remember feeling for them, with them, for their loss, his loss also; a dear, innocent, friend. His passion, his business; his passion for his business – his passion clouded his judgement. The whole damn thing was *his* error of judgement, not Shufang's.

Damn it! Who really recruited Scott Lindon? *Not me, for sure.* Jonathon Long? But he could no longer be certain. Grayson Barclay, then? Barclay made up the connection between Scott, Peace River and Shufang. OK, so Barclay was an oil-man, like this Scott was supposed to be. But Barclay was not the sort of person to travel around with the hired help. No. NO! Someone else orchestrated this sham. Some clever thinking lay behind it – clever, but stupid. Such a plan did not bear the hallmark of a bully such as Barclay. Think, Finn, THINK! He downed more of the second glass. The cumulative effect of the high strength whisky fanned the flames now dancing in his soul – they burned deep inside him. THINK, damn you!

Suddenly, it hit him. The hammer fell against the cartridge. A simple fact he'd been denying himself… since when… since whenever – it didn't matter. He'd denied it. The cartridge exploded, shooting the name between his eyes. AARON! A burning, spiralling bullet of a name released from its case. It rifled deep into his forehead. AARON! He had not wanted to see it, then; but Aaron Philips' name now rose high above him, pummelling down onto his head, pounding the thoughts now streaming together, as if a beam of light, focused from a lens, fell onto the retina of his mind, burning its image there. Aaron must have been behind the whole thing. Aaron's name appeared with Lindon in the old files Lyneth found, not Barclay's. She told him. He'd pushed the fact aside, then. He'd concentrated on the Lindon-Peace River connection. It had fitted his need, then. It must have been Aaron sending Grayson and Scott Lindon out to Peace River, together. No, Aaron was far too clever – he would never have gone himself. Oh no! Not smiling, charming Aaron; Aaron, his friend since the MBA at Lancaster five years ago.

The phone conversation, between Jonathon and David, the one Lyneth picked up on – could it have been a distraction? *Entirely possible.* Lyneth's concentration on the call may even have played into their hands. Sure, there most probably was a conversation, and when they said it happened, but there must have been other conversations, too – before the accident. Conversations when Jonathon would have called Aaron, to tell him about the problems. Christ, they probably even held a conference call, to agree on what to do about Shufang – she would have known too much, she would be a risk to their plans. *They knew! They knew the first thing she would have done, would be to confirm with me.* He held the thought, taking another long drink. Yes, there must be records somewhere – records linking them all together, records of calls before the accident.

Rapidly, the separate strands of his thinking fell into place, one after the other, deftly. His reasoning rolled. Perhaps Aaron's phone call, the one Alexa overheard, had been an oblique reference to their actions. No wonder she found it strange. It would not have made any sense – there would have been no context for her. *No, it must have been murder.* It could not have been anything else. The departure of Barclay, on the morning Shufang died, most probably pointed to Scott Lindon staging her "accidental" death. From the files they'd seen, Lindon had obviously seen a few accidents before. Christ! For all they knew, he probably "did" accidents to order – Aaron's order. The thought trajectories blew his mind. How far did Aaron's activities extend?

Suddenly, Finn stiffened. Another partial thought came to him. It wasn't clear. He fought to get it out, but it held off. He relaxed, his thought train back on its track. Yes. Scott Lindon, the mysterious common denominator – the man who, mysteriously, had appeared at other notable accidents. The man who…?

The held-back thought now reared its head. *Christ, my own accident?* he realised. *No, it's too much, too much to contemplate.* He'd never given the accident any consideration before – it was an accident, surely? But, now…? *No! It's all too much.* He needed to get to his room and write down as much of this as he could. He could do nothing else. He needed to return to London, to let the authorities take over. He could see no solution. Any action, now, lay beyond all their capabilities – his, Lyneth's, Alexa's; even, he supposed, Abdulrahman Shah's. There would be no recompense. They had lost everything. But he would damn well make sure the others – the scheming Aaron, David, John, bloody Grayson frigging Barclay and the mysterious Lindon – they would pay for their scheming. He would honour Shufang, finally.

Finn downed the last of his whisky. He realised he'd only drunk the two. He also realised, acutely, and for the first time clearly, he needed to get even. He had not done it yet. He'd made a series of judgements in trying to fight Barclay – poor judgements. He'd been reacting to the situation, not taking control. Why did they axe him? He would work that one out later. He knew he needed to make notes while this thinking lay fresh in his mind. Another thought occurred to him – *good God! Some trick of Aaron's, that!* Aaron had even got him to pay for the company's legal costs in drafting the compromise agreement, by suggesting *he* seek legal advice. No wonder the agreement seemed to protect the company more than himself. *'The sly fucking bastard!'* said Finn, slowly, hissing the words out under his breath. *'Well, Aaron fucking Philips, watch this frigging space.'*

THIRTY

Within the week, by Thursday lunchtime, sixth of March, it was all over bar the detail. Finn had returned to London, travelling overnight on the previous Wednesday. Alexa went out to meet him at Heathrow, and they talked over the basics in the cab ride to her apartment. She let him sleep a few hours, and got Lyneth to meet them both for supper.

They stayed close to the apartment, resigned to the fate awaiting them – waiting for it all to close in on them. They had ended up at the centre of what appeared to be a twenty six million pound fraud.

Alexa's lack of cooking skills, and the desire not to get stuck in the kitchen discussing things, led them all to the Indian restaurant in the marina. Given the early evening, the restaurant stood quite empty of customers. They chose a table set against the rear wall, away from the popular window seats and prying ears. He had recounted the story more fully to them both.

'We have no options left, said Lyneth, reaching the obvious conclusion – though she clearly felt the need to say it anyway.

'They've been idiots. How could they have expected to get away with it?' asked Alexa.

'It's a sad truth, Alexa,' said Lyneth, 'but most city-type

315

financial crimes go unpunished.'

'I don't think they'd considered the consequences of their actions, far enough ahead,' he had added. 'Their greed carried them too far. It must have been greed. They'd seen my business plan, and realised how much they would stand to make out of it, once the company listed on the stock market. Just look at their ages. They're all wealthy, yes, but not multi-millionaires. They would have seen this as their last shot at making some big money. They probably reasoned that if the project had failed, they'd lost. Maybe they panicked, thinking that they couldn't afford not to keep going through with it.'

Both Alexa and Lyneth had agreed – his reasoning was plausible.

'But I don't think the worsening financial situation helped,' added Alexa. 'The difficulty raising funds must have got them thinking it would all come out sooner or later – particularly with you responsible for the AIM drafting process, Finn.'

He'd considered that. 'Yeah, I guess that's why they wanted me out of the way – probably why Aaron got Grayson to give me the push... You know something? I remember David Kail looked real uncomfortable at the signing of my compromise agreement. I could have pushed on him, if I'd thought hard about it. Maybe he would have cracked then?'

'Maybe, Finn,' said Lyneth. Then she voiced the connection, which, up to the moment, had remained unspoken. 'The accident, Finn...' she said, hesitantly.

'Mine?' he asked. The clarification had been redundant.

'Yes. It wasn't an accident, was it?'

'I don't know for sure; but they can't have expected me to put up a fight – maybe it was more panic,' he said, acknowledging his own thinking at last.

'It explains the call I overheard Aaron make, too,' added Alexa, '...*we can't do that again*. I heard him say it.'

'We've been idiots, too,' said Lyneth, towards the end of

supper. 'We sat on such a lot of information – we passed over what really mattered, right there, in front of us.'

They all agreed.

And they all agreed on the only course of action left open to them. Finn would report the whole matter to the police. He did so, late on the Friday morning. Firstly, though, they all took the step of going to their offices, and gathering what papers they could, to get them ready. The police would want everything.

Finn did not quite know where to start, or to whom he should report the matter. But the Tiger Oil affair started as a financial fraud – he could be sure of the city-type involvement. Aaron, Grayson, David and Jonathon all played in the city space. He called the Economic Crime Division of the City of London Police.

The ECD sent Detective Constable Bob Lewis over to the apartment, for an initial interview. The notes Finn had prepared impressed DC Lewis, who interviewed him for almost two hours. He received a call, later in the afternoon, from the City of London Police again. After liaison with the Serious Fraud Office, they both wanted to interview him, this time at the CLP office in the square mile. The second interview, under caution, late on the Friday afternoon, lasted over three hours. Despite the formal caution, the same DC Bob Lewis led the interview, remaining courteous. At no time did anyone infer Finn's implication in the crime – the caution being a formality, so he was informed. An SFO man attended the interview, but he kept in the background. Despite the SFO man naming himself, for the benefit of the tape recorder, Finn could not even remember his name.

He received a few calls during the Monday and Tuesday, mostly from DC Bob Lewis seeking clarification on matters of detail. On the Wednesday afternoon, Finn heard that the SFO and CLP had carried out dawn raids on the homes of David

Kail, Jonathon Long, and Grayson Barclay. Wednesday's *Evening Standard* carried a report of the arrest of the three, and their release on police bail pending completion of enquiries. They also arrested Scott Lindon, picking him up at Heathrow Airport. The *Standard* reported Lindon's detention for questioning, in connection with the suspected murder of Shufang Su. He could not find the name of Aaron Philips anywhere in the press reports.

DC Bob Lewis called, late Wednesday, to confirm they had drawn up an international warrant for Aaron's arrest. They interviewed Alexa, as the SFO tried to piece together her husband's movements. She could confirm Aaron's frequent overseas trips; but she really did have no idea where he might have gone – overseas she imagined. He had not returned to the apartment since serving her with the divorce papers.

Not for the first time, Finn thanked God that Tiger Oil had de-listed as an AIM company. He needed to make no formal announcements to the city. He would not have known what to say.

That morning, Thursday, DC Lewis called again, having been in touch with the Canadian authorities. He informed Finn that an opposite number in the RCMP's Peace River division confirmed they would be seeking extradition proceedings against the whole lot, for murder and conspiracy to murder. DC Lewis also confirmed the SFO's parallel investigation into the matter as a serious fraud. They concluded the original fraud, against the city – against public shareholders – had been diverted only with the innocent intervention of Finn's team, leaving Abdulrahman Shah as the major injured party.

Abdulrahman Shah! Yes, against all odds… To the day he died, he would never understand how the enigmatic man could take such events so philosophically. Abdulrahman Shah did not call for his blood, as he and the girls thought would happen; instead, he remained quiet as he listened to the details.

'Finn…' Abdulrahman began, during their phone call on the Monday morning. Finn felt another proverb coming on – he proved to be right. 'A chameleon does not leave one tree until he is sure of another. I have seen no other trees before me. I have backed you in business, not your business. We shall see where we end up. I would be grateful if you would arrange to visit and debrief my legal team more fully. This week, I suggest. I shall need to ensure the appropriate liaisons are in place, in order to ensure my influence is brought to bear on the perpetrators.'

Jesus, I'd rather experience jail than the influence of someone like Abdulrahman Shah. Still…

But, in truth, whether Abdulrahman Shah supported him or not, he knew Tiger Oil had crashed. He'd lost. It would take some time to get anything going again. His route to the enchantment he sought lay ahead of him, un-trodden, beyond the door still so firmly closed.

He heard the key in the lock; the outer door opened to the sound of Alexa's return, breaking his train of thought.

'Finn,' she shouted through to the lounge where he sat. She sounded upbeat. 'Hey, guess who I've brought for tea…'

He heard more than two voices in the corridor, two female, the other…

'Hi, Finn,' shouted Hu Su, as he burst through the doorway into Finn's presence; his great beaming smile still, seemingly, etched deeply across his face, tying ear to ear. His unruly mop of thick black hair gave him the appearance of someone who had just blown in on a gale.

'Hi,' he replied, smiling, despite the weight of recent events pressing heavily on his conscience. Hu's infectious grin had caught everyone. Finn saw it in the faces of Lyneth and Alexa, as they came into view behind Hu. Lyneth carried two bottles of champagne.

'You'd better listen to what this mad Chinaman has to say,

Finn,' said Lyneth. 'Alexa, glasses please.'

Hu Su could not stop grinning. He put his hand into his canvas shoulder bag and brought out something small and rectangular, made from clear plastic.

Finn recognised the object immediately. 'Jeez,' he said, 'I've not seen one of those in years, Hu. I thought you Chinese snapped up all the latest gadgets. Didn't you lot know they got rid of tape Dictaphones a few years ago – they're all digital now.'

'Ah! We're an inscrutable lot, we Chinese; we can often do what you least expect,' said Hu Su; his grin did not fade. 'It was Shufang's,' he added, explaining the object. For a second, a glimpse of sadness flashed into Hu's eyes at the mention of his sister's name. 'She's got the last laugh,' he said.

'Tell me,' Finn said, puzzled by Hu's remark.

'No!' Hu's riposte was as quick as his hand, as he delved into the bag again, this time pulling out a hand-held Dictaphone. 'Shufang can.' Hu clipped the tape inside the little black machine and pressed play. He carefully placed the Dictaphone on the table-top, as the tape started winding its path across the playback-head. 'Listen,' he said, quietly.

As Shufang's voice came through, against the clutter of a windy background, they all fell quiet. Lyneth placed the bottles, soundlessly, down onto the polished granite of breakfast-bar. Alexa did the same with the glasses she'd taken from an overhead cupboard. All eyes turned to Finn, as he stood there, mesmerised. Shufang was dictating what had clearly proved to be her last site report. It sounded as if she was walking around the site, noting her observations.

They listened in silence for nearly fifteen minutes.

'Where did you find this, Hu?' asked Finn, finally – breaking the eerie silence that followed the end of the report. No message, just a factual report. Shufang had not been expecting the consequences arising from the unseen acts of others.

'It came over with her personal stuff, sent to our parents in Hong Kong. They received it shortly after the Canadian Ministry of Labour investigation concluded. It was just the tape,' he said. 'She must have placed it somewhere where it wasn't seen.'

'Or they didn't even know it existed,' said Lyneth.

'This changes things, doesn't it, Finn?' he said, his grin even wider now.

'Yes it does,' said Finn, '…and I know an Arab gentleman who would probably like to call you Brother.'

'Steady on, Finn,' laughed Hu. 'I'm not sure I'm ready for that.'

'Well, as soon as Hu played it for us. I reckoned we'd better let you hear it, too,' said Lyneth, smiling. 'He dropped by specially.'

'Dropped by?' quizzed Finn, raising his eyebrows.

'Yes,' said Hu, '…I'm going out to see if I can help the investigation in Peace River. I reckoned I'd pass through and let you have a copy. I guess I might see you out there soon, too.' Hu winked.

'It's all there, isn't it?' asked Alexa. 'Everything you need to know to correct the pilot project.'

'Y…Yes,' said Finn. He could hardly speak. His mind raced ahead at the sudden possibilities. The project failed in its initial configuration, yes; but the brilliant geologist she was, Shufang had understood what they needed to do to fix it. She'd taped her findings on her trusty Dictaphone. She'd described the design changes and process steps required to overcome the problems she'd seen.

'She must have finished this tape in her hotel room and left it there. It can't have been on her at the time she died,' said Finn. 'I don't think Jonathon Long had any idea about Shufang's recommendations. He must have called Aaron or Grayson, whoever, and reported the failure. I'm sure, if they'd

321

known the problem could be fixed, none of this would have happened.'

'I'm sure, too,' said Hu. There was sadness in his voice.

A cork popped under the control of Alexa's hand. 'A drink,' she said, '…a toast to Shufang, I'd say.' She poured four glasses and they each took one.

'To Shufang,' they chorused.

THIRTY ONE

IT WAS A BRIGHT, sunny, but chilly Saturday afternoon. Finn and Alexa sat at a table inside the Café Rouge, in St Katherine's Dock. Copies of the *Saturday Financial Times* and *The Times on Saturday* lay spread on the table in front of them; two large cappuccinos rested on the open pages.

The Tiger Oil story had made it into both papers. They had also seen the International Oil Economist's version, on an e-mail bulletin the night before.

'I could get used to this,' said Finn.

'What? A life as a commercial fraud detective?' quipped Alexa.

'No, silly. This,' he said, waiving his hand briefly, casting an arc that took in the vista of the marina that lay just the other side of the plate-glass windows. He cast his gaze around, following the movement of his hand, inviting her to follow. 'This,' he said, '...the café society – it's a bit different to Yorkshire's hills.'

'I like it,' she said, smiling at him.

'I ought to find my own place down here.'

'What do you think about Lyneth,' giggled Alexa. 'Abdulrahman Shah! Who would have thought...?'

'I think you would have,' he said '...you're not one to miss

323

something like that.

'I don't know what you mean, Finn Jackson,' she said, attempting to feign indignance, but her smile belied her.

On the Thursday evening, after they'd seen Hu Su safely into a taxi, and on his way to Heathrow, they sat around with Lyneth, finishing the other bottle of champagne. Then a bottle of Aaron's claret appeared.

Finn had mentioned Abdulrahman Shah's request for a debrief, and Lyneth offered to fly out the next day. She'd fancied a weekend out in Geneva. She knew all the details, and was probably the best person they could all think of to brief Abdulrahman Shah's legal team, so they'd agreed. Early Friday, Finn called Heidi and cleared it for Lyneth to go out. Heidi fixed an appointment for a dinner meeting the Friday evening, and there would be a full legal debrief on the Monday. Sorted!

'What did she say, exactly?' asked Alexa, '…when she called you this morning? She wasn't on long, was she?'

'No, nosey,' he chided her, playfully. 'You women… she just said last night's meeting with Abdulrahman went extremely well. He'd asked her if she wanted to join his team out there, with a seat on our board – just to keep an eye on us.'

'And she's staying over there?'

'Well, I guess she'll return first – she'll need to sort things out her with her practice, but yes. I think she'll move out,' he said.

'I think our Abdulrahman has taken a bit of a shine to our Lyneth,' said Alexa, giving an exaggerated wink. 'He does like pretty women around him.'

'Pretty women with brains and a bite, I'd say.'

'You're not disappointed then, Finn?'

'No. In the end, I figured it was just the fun of the chase for her.'

'She's got a new chase there all right.'

'I received another call this morning, while you were out,'

he said.

'Oh?'

'Yeah, Abdulrahman Shah himself.'

'Wow. A Saturday morning. Was Lyneth there?'

'Stop it,' he said, laughing. 'Be serious now… he's signing ten percent of the company over to me…'

'That's brilliant, Finn! I'm so pleased for you.'

'But, that's not all. He's also giving five percent to you.' He smiled at her, as he saw her jaw drop. 'Don't be so shocked. You've done a great deal of work on this deal. And we still have a lot to do.'

'I know, but…'

'No buts, Alexa. You deserve it. He wishes us both well and he said we will continue to earn it!'

'Business as strangers, eh?' She winked.

'Yeah. We need to keep friendship and brotherly love out of this.'

They both turned their heads to look out of the picture windows – out over the marina. The sun had brought out many people; they walked about, wrapped up warm against the chilly outside temperature.

'What's going to happen to them all?' asked Alexa.

'I'm not sure. Prison for certain. After that, who knows. One thing though, if they ever get out they will be finished in the city, or anywhere else I reckon. Abdulrahman Shah is of the fourth paradigm school of management.' He saw the puzzled look on her face. 'You only ever screw someone over once. Abdulrahman will take what they did very personally; he will not forget them.'

'What do you think happened to Ozzie? she asked, suddenly concerned. 'You don't think he met the same fate as…'

'Shufang? No, I don't.' He saw the relief wash into her bright eyes. 'I do think Aaron got hold of him though, but with what Ozzie stood to gain, Aaron probably told him to disappear for a while. I don't think I can hold Ozzie responsible – he was stuck in the middle of all this.'

'I'm glad,' she said, with genuine relief.

They fell silent again.

Outside, it could have been the French Riviera, Antibes perhaps, or the harbour-side in Vieux Nice, but without the heat.

'I've been thinking, Finn…'

'Let's get the bill, and you can tell me as we walk home.'

Finn rose, to go over to the counter. He'd learnt a while ago that table service could be unpredictably slow at times; not that it bothered him, he rather enjoyed the *laissez-faire* quality it evoked – very Mediterranean. He paid the bill and returned. Alexa gathered the papers together.

'Why don't you stay with me for now?' she suggested. 'You can get your house on the market and sort things out with Aisling before you need to look for somewhere. I've got plenty of room, and God knows I could do with the company.'

They put their coats on and headed for the door.

'If you really think so, Alexa. I can pay my keep now, you know – I don't want to be a kept man.'

'Can you cook?' she asked, looking hopefully at him.

'A little.'

'That's perfect. I can't!' she said, laughing. Then, more seriously, she added: 'I need to say something about Aaron and me.'

They stood at the railings, overlooking the boats and the water below.

'You don't need to say anything. It's not my business, Alexa.'

'I want to,' she said. 'I've had affairs… quite a few really… well, not affairs exactly… don't misunderstand, I'm not ashamed. Aaron and I didn't have much physical contact – almost none over the last four years. I just needed to do my own thing…' She looked at him, and a frown appeared on her face. 'You're not taking me seriously, Finn. You're smiling...'

'It's not that... you don't know...' he said.

'Don't know what?' Alexa looked puzzled by his reaction.

'We've been living similar lives.'

'What do you mean... similar?'

'I guessed about you and Ozzie. I didn't think of others, but... well, I've been seeing someone... rather, I *was* seeing someone... 'till around the time Aisling left me. I called it off, then. It would have become too messy. I would have been a risk for her and her family. I didn't want to become a problem for her; we had rules.'

'Finn... I... I just didn't know.' Her frown, and the puzzled look, both now faded, replaced by her warm, soft smile.

'Why? You weren't supposed to know. What does anyone really know of anyone else, eh? He smiled. 'All we can try and do is trust one another. We have to take so much for granted. Without trust we have nothing.'

'I know what you mean,' she said, as she turned to look at the water again. 'Can I ask...'

'How we met?'

'Yes,' she said.

'It's the anonymity of the web – nobody knows you there in cyberspace. You can be anywhere or anything. That kind of anonymity gives you confidence to explore, and it's quite amazing, really, how many other explorers there are out there with similar ideas to your own.'

'I know,' she said. She turned to look at him. She was looking at him in a new light. 'Was it purely sex, or did love figure in it too?'

'Just sex, I guess; but sex within a meaningful relationship, nonetheless. The closeness of a woman's body, the intimacy, the touching; all things I missed. Respect, too. And, perversely, honesty. But mostly just sex.'

'Yes,' she said, simply. 'I suppose the mistake I made was

carrying on with Ozzie in the same building. We should have walked away from each other the moment we realised we lived in the same apartment block.'

'He was your first?' he asked, looking at Alexa, as she looked, again, down towards the water below her. It wasn't the first time he'd noticed her attractiveness.

'Yes. He got too close... he wanted more from the relationship; I didn't. It's a problem, dating a single guy.'

'But you finished as friends?'

'Yes,' she said.

'That's important,' he said. 'How long do you think Aaron had known?'

'Maybe all the time; I don't know. Anyway, it's over now.'

'He'd kept quiet until it suited him to use it against you.'

'I think so.'

They stood in silence for a few minutes, enjoying the peace of the sunny afternoon. The coolness of the breeze dancing between the boats was no hardship.

Alexa broke their trance. She giggled, girlishly, as she turned to look Finn straight in the eyes. 'I suppose...' she said. 'I suppose we *could* take the second bedroom and turn it into a proper office for you.'

Alexa lifted her hand and took hold of Finn's. He did not resist.

*

The water buffeted his head as he spun round and round. He kicked out, again and again, struggling with the water's depths until, finally, his head broke the surface. He struggled to draw breath, to fill his aching, burning lungs. Through his stinging eyes, he could see the bank from which he had fallen. Shufang smiled, no longer a faceless apparition. He turned to kick out for the safety of the far side. He kicked out, he needed to reach it, but he was tired. *Kick, Finn, kick.* He kicked out, again and again. Slowly, he reached the water's edge, the eddy calmer under the drop of the river bank. 'You *can never enter the same river twice, Finn, never.*'

He thrust out his arm, flailing to reach something, to grab something on the bank that he could pull against. A hand reached down to meet him. The hand found his and the two locked together. Gradually, the water fell away from his body as his unseen helper pulled him up onto the side of the river bank. The cool dampness of grass lay against his cheek as he struggled to steady his breathing.

He glanced down, below him, across the river to where Shufang stood, waving.

'She's going, Finn,' said the voice of his saviour – a voice he somehow knew. 'She's seen you across. You're safe now.'

Finn looked up, from the hand that still held his, to the face of the voice.

Blackness. Peace. No longer the sound of rushing water. Finn's eyes opened and, for a moment, he sensed the strangeness of his surroundings. It disorientated him. Then, slowly, in the dark, he relaxed – more than he had relaxed for months. All tension left his body. His hand reached up and took hold of the hand that lay across his chest. A feeling of incredible warmth crept over him, like the wash of a gentle, sun-kissed wave, rolling over a tropical beach.

He sensed his delicious state of semi-conscious, but satisfied, half-sleep. He knew he'd been pulled from the water – but he could not have reached the river bank without help. Now he had the garden stretched out before him to explore. Enchantment! *One step at a time, Finn.* He drifted into sleep.

~

www.davidsartof.com